JUST THE FACTS . . .

"You're asking me to execute a million-dollar bond. As a businessman, would you risk a million bucks without checking on the financial and personal integrity of the person you're doing business with?" Ruby asked.

"You can't be serious! I'm one of the richest men in the state. Everyone knows that," Gibson insisted.

"It never pays to rely on what everyone knows."

Ruby moved on to the names, addresses, and phone numbers of friends, relatives, girlfriends, business colleagues, shareholders, key employees.

"What's all this for?" Gibson prostested meekly. "Why do you need to know the names of my friends and relatives? They don't have anything to do with this or with my personal financial stability."

"In case I have to track you down."

"But I told you, I'm not going to run."

Ruby leaned forward slightly to emphasize her point. "You better not. Understand, honey, if I post bond for you I own you. You skip on me, I want to know where I can find your ass. And believe me, if you skip, I will find you!"

Dear Mystery Lover,

DEAD LETTER has started the careers of a number of writers by publishing their first mysteries in the paperback original format. I'm pleased to say that DEAD LETTER'S core of paperback original authors—Donna Huston Murray, David Leitz, and Lou Jane Temple—have made fabulous debuts and are continuing to build their readerships.

So, it is with no small amount of excitement that I introduce our fourth paperback original series author, Bruce W. Most, and his terrific first mystery *Bonded for Murder.* Set in scenic Denver, Colorado, *Bonded for Murder* brings mystery readers a fresh and sassy lead protagonist who takes no guff from anyone. Ruby Dark is a feisty fifty-year-old bail bondswoman who is a Denver institution. If you're a fan of Janet Evanovich's Stephanie Plum mysteries (*One for the Money, Two for the Dough*), you'll definitely want to get to know Ruby Dark.

Be on the lookout for the next Ruby Dark mystery, *Missing Bonds*, coming from DEAD LETTER in August 1997.

Keep your eye out for DEAD LETTER, and build yourself a library of paperback mysteries to die for.

Yours in crime,

Shawn Coyne
Senior Editor
St. Martin's DEAD LETTER Paperback Mysteries

Other titles from St. Martin's Dead Letter Mysteries

Bonded for Murder

Bruce W. Most

NOTE: If you purchased this book without a cover you should be aware that this book is stolen property. It was reported as "unsold and destroyed" to the publisher, and neither the author nor the publisher has received any payment for this "stripped book."

BONDED FOR MURDER

ISBN: 0-312-96051-4

Printed in the United States of America

St. Martin's Paperbacks edition/December 1996

10 9 8 7 6 5 4 3 2 1

This book is dedicated to:

Ruth, for her love and patience.

Philip Spitzer, for his unwavering faith in my writing.

The CAL critique group, for their insightful comments.

My parents, for their wise upbringing.

1

"Ruby's Bail Bonds."

David Piszek attempted to suppress a yawn as he answered the phone but failed miserably. How long he'd been asleep he wasn't sure. Not long enough, he knew. In his brief tenure as a licensed bail bondsman he'd wearily come to realize that success in the bail bonding business was less a matter of business acumen than a test of sleep deprivation. Friday nights were the worst—every lost soul in Denver got arrested on Friday nights.

"I want to speak to Ruby Dark."

The voice was male and as smooth as polished chrome—not the typical voice of a hooker or DUI or junkie calling from the city jail. He'd heard the chrome voices before: the wealthy, the politicians, the corporate pinstripes, the judges, the society types, calling to quietly bail out sons driving drunk or daughters caught selling coke. They called Ruby Dark because she was known for her discretion and honesty—characteristics that generally didn't weigh down the bail bonding business.

"She's not available right now," David said, straightening in his chair and attempting to sound semi-alert. "May I help?" He picked up his watch lying next to the open pages of his *Black's Law Dictionary*. Vaguely, he recalled that he was looking up a term for his contracts class when he'd fallen asleep, but now he couldn't remember the term. He held the watch under a green-shaded banker's lamp. He tapped the crystal. The digital numbers said 2:23 and the hands said 2:24. He reset the hands.

"I prefer to speak directly with *Mzzzz* Dark."

Mzzzz Dark? Nobody called Ruby Dark *Ms.* Dark. Certainly not her clients. To them, she was simply Ruby, or sometimes, Angel. Angel of the Outlaws. That's what the hookers and drug dealers and killers and assorted lowlife had christened her. And the newspapers had picked up on it, too. Angel of the Outlaws. Savior. Mother Teresa of the imprisoned. Well, Mother Teresa in expensive clothes and a 1982 red Lamborghini, anyway. A few called her Mrs. Dark—those who'd been bailed out years ago by her husband Al, before she'd found him one night lying face down in the parking lot behind the office with a bullet in the back of his head. Some of her competitors had other names for her, none of them fit for public exposure.

To David, she was Aunt Ruby. Half-aunt, actually, on his father's side.

"I can pass along a message," said David. He pushed aside stacks of business papers and mail looking for a pen. How the hell does the woman ever find anything in this black lagoon! He pulled open a desk drawer and burrowed through drifts of business cards, half a dozen ticket stubs from Denver Nuggets games, a worn unlabeled photo of a young boy, and empty key rings before he found a pen.

"It's urgent that I speak to *Mzzzz* Dark directly and immediately."

"It's late," David said, rubbing sleep out of his eyes with the heel of his hand. "I won't be able to reach her until morning."

"My client won't wait that long! He needs to be released now."

So what else is new? They all want out immediately. But no way in hell was he going to disturb his aunt at this hour. Whoever it was could stew in jail a few more hours. It'd probably do the guy some good.

"You his attorney?" asked David.

"I'm his *business* attorney. Another attorney—someone more . . . familiar . . . than myself with these matters—referred *Mzzzz* Dark to me. He indicated that she is unusually . . . reputable."

It must have been only through superhuman effort that the lawyer managed to keep the word "sleazy" from creeping into his language. While part of David chafed at the man's arrogant tone, part of him secretly concurred with the unspoken assessment. Bonding out criminals for money *was* a sleazy business. That was why he wanted to be a prosecuting attorney, why he was studying law at night school. He wanted to put people *in* jail, not bail them *out*.

"Perhaps I can help if you told me exactly what your client needs. I'm an associate of Ruby Dark. The name is David Piszek. I'm legally licensed in the state of Colorado to arrange bond, Mr.—?"

The lawyer hesitated, as if the utterance of his name in the presence of a bondsman would forever taint it. "Lamprey," he finally managed. "E. Ezzard Lamprey."

The lawyer's tone suggested that David should instantly recognize the name, but he'd been in Denver less than a year and there were only a few zillion lawyers in town. He said aloud, "Okay, Mr. Lamprey, if you tell me who your client is and what he's in for and what bail is set at, I can expedite matters. You can speak to Ms. Dark tomorrow, if that becomes necessary."

He didn't really want to expedite matters. He just wanted to climb to his loft above the office and go to sleep. But it was his aunt's business, and every bond he wrote helped pay for law school.

While the lawyer pondered the idea of working with the second string, David cracked the blinds and peered out the window of the office, which sat on the second floor above a spay-neuter clinic. The rain must have stopped while he'd dozed, but it still looked threatening. The large, featureless exterior of Denver Police Headquarters, the city jail behind it, loomed larger than usual in the wet heavy air. Directly to the west of police headquarters, on Delaware Street, kitty-corner from Ruby's Bail Bonds, the neon signs of the half-dozen bonding offices along Bondsman Row threw a gaudy stain of blues, greens, and reds across the dark wet pavement. The sign at Liberty Bonds, the biggest of all the bonding agencies along the Row, and owned by Ruby's arch-rival, the infamous Cadillac Johnson, caught David's eye. One of the red neon tubes in the American flag had burned out.

"Yes, perhaps that is the best course," Lamprey said grudgingly. The arrogance in his voice was fading. Now he merely sounded weary and uneasy.

David prepared to write on a yellow pad. "Let's get some details, first. Your client's name is—?"

"Bayne C. Gibson, Jr. He's been arrested for first-degree murder."

The pen started to move, then stopped. *Bayne C. Gib—!* Everybody in the city who wasn't dead knew that name, ever since the police and building security had found Royce Kray, a loudmouthed, left-wing talk show host, floating naked in a fish pond on Gibson's thirty-first floor downtown penthouse with two bullet holes in his chest and the media mogul standing nearby. Kray had worked on a local radio station, KPOL, owned, along with several other radio stations and medium-sized newspapers, by Gibson Media. Gibson had been arrested yesterday afternoon, four days after Kray's murder, amid rampant speculation about why it had taken the DA so long to charge him.

David fumbled with the cordless phone. "What's bail set at?"

"One million dollars," said Lamprey, as if he were reading off the stock market ticker tape on a slow day.

David whistled uncontrollably into the phone. "Who set bond?"

"Judge Andrew Slater."

That explained it. "King Andy," as courthouse wags referred to the judge, was one tough sonofabitch most bondsmen dreaded doing business with, though his aunt generally had stayed on his good side.

"Prima facie, it's an unreasonable and oppressive bond," Lamprey said with sudden anger. "The DA asked for bond to be set at half a million and the judge *raised* it. *Raised it!* In light of Bayne's unequivocal innocence and his exemplary record in this community, a personal recognizance bond would have been quite adequate. The size of the bond is legally indefensible."

David's mouth went dry. He grabbed a half-empty cup of coffee with a lipstick print on its rim. He didn't drink coffee, only mineral water, but it was the only liquid within reach. He took a sip, and the moment he saw the bright red chile pepper design on the cup he knew he'd made a mistake.

His tongue went numb and his eyes began to water. Shit! He knew better than to eat or drink anything his aunt left around. God knows what she'd spiced the coffee with. The woman was an unapologetic chilehead.

He tried to say something to Lamprey but it was like trying to talk with lips shot full of Novocain.

"Is there a problem?" said Lamprey.

"No," David finally managed. The fire in his mouth began to subside. His lips tingled. "It's just that writing a bond that size might take a little longer than usual."

"How much longer?" A desperate edge crept into the lawyer's voice.

Good question. David had heard of $1 million bonds, of course. Even larger. But he'd personally never written one for anywhere near that size, and the largest one his aunt had written was $400,000 on a man who'd murdered his twin daughters. David wasn't even sure Ruby could execute a bond that large. There were statutes about the bonding agent having sufficient financial resources to cover the face value of a bond. Usually bondsmen backed by insurance companies, not cash bondsmen like his aunt, wrote the really big ones. Still, it didn't take an accountant to calculate on his toes that the standard fifteen percent premium for posting a $1 million bond was $150,000.

"Three or four days, minimum," said David, knowing that even that was unrealistic.

"Bayne won't wait that long!" yelled Lamprey. "He's at city jail right now in a holding cell full of perverts throwing up all over him. He wants out—tonight!"

The infamous "fish tank." The place must be one helluva shock for a rich bastard like Bayne Gibson.

"He's not going to get out tonight, Mr. Lamprey. We're talking about a major bond here. We'd need to draw up a list of personal assets as collateral to secure the bond, examine his corporate records, obtain bank account numbers, talk to relatives and friends and business associates, draw up an indemnity agreement—and it's Friday night. It'll be Monday at the soonest before we can start moving on much of this.''

The phone was silent on the other end. The man may be a crackerjack business attorney, thought David, but he was out of his league when it came to murder one.

''All right, how do we proceed?'' the attorney said heavily.

David scribbled down a few vital pieces of information and assured the lawyer he would get right on it, though he wasn't sure where one started with a bond this big.

''You *will* be bringing *Mzzzz* Dark in on this, won't you?'' said Lamprey. ''It's imperative that she be involved.''

''There's no doubt about it, Mr. Lamprey. She'll be in touch.''

David hung up. The soft patter of the rain had started up again, but it wasn't loud enough to drown out the snoring of Collateral. David looked over in the dim light at the lazy, overweight Old English mastiff, sprawled on the parquet floor, his body twitching now and then in dog dreams. Collateral *always* was asleep. Like any bondsman's dog, he had learned to sleep through ringing telephones and human conversations.

Although Collateral was Ruby's dog, his aunt couldn't care less about canines in general, or Collateral in particular. She didn't like things that slobbered. Her tastes ran more to cats, like Alabaster, her black Persian who'd mysteriously appeared at the office one early spring morning and had made herself at home ever since.

The only reason Ruby had kept the dog was because he was, as his name implied, collateral for a bond. A forty-year-old man—at least as his aunt had told the story—had been arrested for stealing a new Porsche, but he didn't have any assets to back up his $2,500 bond. Ruby noticed that he appeared overly attached to his Old English mastiff, so she took in the dog as collateral. Over the years, she'd taken in cars, jewelry, guns, rare books, paintings, computers, and even a new washing machine, so why not a dog? Her rationale was that a man might skip out on his premium, his wife and kids, his home or business, even on a home put up by his own parents—but never, never would a man skip out on his dog.

Where his aunt had developed this blind, quaint faith in canines and their loyal owners, David had no idea, but it proved a faith betrayed. The dog's owner lit out two days before trial, never to be seen again.

Ruby went after him, of course. She went after every skip, even if it was only on a $100 bond. In the bail bonding business, you either build a reputation that you'll chase, or you're history.

That was two years ago. The last she'd heard, the skip was sticking up convenience stores in Arkansas. After a year of appeals and delaying tactics, his aunt had been finally forced to make good on the bond. She'd catch the man someday, or the cops would do it for her. When that happened, maybe the judge would rescind the forfeiture. The judge wasn't required to by law, but some did now and then, especially if good faith was shown by the bondsman. Until then, Collateral had a home.

David looked just above the dog, on the brick wall near the file cabinets. A framed copy of his aunt's personal motto hung there. He couldn't see it well in the shadowed light, but he knew what was inscribed in Latin: *Illigitium non carborundum.*

Don't let the bastards grind you down.

He called Ruby Dark.

2

The lobby of the Pre-Arraignment Detention Facility of the City and County of Denver, more commonly referred to as city jail, had the weary look of a building doomed for urban renewal. Graffiti scarred the walls, cigarette burns blackened the chairs and floors, and none of the pay phones worked. An odor of depression permeated the stale air.

At peak hours, the small lobby was standing room only, the overflow of relatives, friends, pimps, gang brothers, lovers, and attorneys spilling out onto the concrete plaza between the jail and police headquarters. But at this hour—nearly four in the morning—only three people besides David waited in the lobby. A pale teenage girl with stringy brown hair chain-smoked and stared morosely at the linoleum floor. Two seats away, in an expensive business suit, a Hispanic man languidly flipped through a worn copy of *Time*. Two chairs away from David dozed a middle-aged man with military cropped hair.

A few minutes earlier the man had been awake, complaining loudly to the sheriff's deputy behind the glass-topped booth that he'd already waited eleven hours to bail out his son on a traffic charge and that in all his years in the navy he'd never had that kind of runaround. "It's Friday night," snapped the deputy. "We process a lot of people on Friday night." When the Navy man protested again, the deputy threatened to kick him out of the lobby, and when the man's voice grew louder the deputy said that if he didn't shut the fuck up he'd see to it that the man joined his son in the second-floor lockup. "Motherfuckers," muttered the navy man under his breath as he sat down.

David had seen the navy man and the teenage girl earlier in the evening, first when he'd come over to bond out a thirty-year-old female lush arrested for redesigning her boyfriend's car with her pickup, and later when he'd posted bond for a nineteen-year-old male albino charged with sexually assaulting a seventy-three-year-old grandmother. Seventeen grand in bonds, $14,000 riding on the albino.

He hoped he'd made the right call on the albino. "Bondsmen are gamblers," his aunt had told him more than once. On paper, a defendant, or a defendant's cosigner, might have sufficient collateral to back up a bond, but that's no guarantee the defendant will appear in court at the appointed hour. And seizing a defendant's assets to satisfy a failed bond usually was costly, time consuming, and sometimes, in the end, futile. No, warned his aunt, it's far more important to read their souls than their financial statements. What are the emotional ties that will bind them like a ball and chain, however guilty or innocent they may be? Do they have family, who are their friends, how long have they lived in the city, do they have a job? "In this business," said Ruby, "you make decisions with your gut, not your head."

Well, he wasn't a gambler, and he didn't trust his gut.

David tapped his watch, then glanced at the lobby clock: 3:47. The lobby clock was slow by two minutes.

He had barely dozed off in the hard lobby chair when the Hispanic man jostled him awake and said the deputy wanted to talk to him. He yawned on his way over to the booth. Sheriff's Deputy Erickson had worked at the jail only a few weeks, but already he carried the fleshy, dyspeptic look of a man condemned there for longer than the jailees. He would not last long, wagered David, who'd seen a lot of turnover in the jail staff during his five-month tenure as a bondsman.

"Your aunt just called," the deputy said through a six-inch hole in the glass. "From her *car* phone. Said she was late getting away but that she'll be here inside ten minutes."

"Thanks." David turned back toward his chair but the deputy's voice summoned him again.

"Them car phones must be kinda handy."

David blinked. "Yeah, I suppose they are."

"What kinda car your aunt drive?"

David tried to ignore the hostile tone in the deputy's voice. Unlike the others waiting in the lobby, he and his aunt came to city jail nearly every day. If the deputies wanted to make life miserable for a bondsman and his clients, they could. So he said civilly, "It's just an old car."

The deputy cocked his head. "How old?"

"I don't know . . . an eighty-two, I think."

"I heard it's a *nice* old car. What kind of old car is it, exactly?"

David paused, but finally said, "A Lamborghini."

"A Lambo?" The deputy rolled the name around in his mouth like a piece of mint candy. "A Lambo with a fucking car phone in it. Shit! Must be nice you people can afford to own *old* cars like that."

David decided not to mention that he owned a twenty-year-old pea green Duster with 215,000 miles on the original engine and a heater that didn't work and doors that didn't lock. It would only sound like whining.

"It's a living," mumbled David.

"Fuck, we all should make your kind of living."

His father wouldn't think so. His father wouldn't think so at all. Especially if he knew his son was making it working for Ruby Dark.

David again tried to return to his chair, but Deputy Erickson called after him. "Angel really your aunt?"

David nodded almost imperceptibly. No point getting into the half-aunt business or the black sheep business. Her maiden name was the same as his, but she'd retained her husband's name after his murder. Whether out of deep love of his memory or a hatred of her parents, David didn't know.

The deputy leaned conspiratorially toward the hole in the glass. His watery eyes flicked toward the others in the lobby and then toward David. "The stories I hear about her—they true?"

"What stories?" David said, trying to play dumb.

The deputy raised his hands as if the stories were ghosts buried in the lobby walls. "You know . . . stories."

Stories. Yeah, he knew the stories. They were different

each time he heard them, with as many variations as storytellers. But the themes were basically the same: Ruby Dark had a mysterious—and perhaps illegal—past. There was the story that she'd run a high-class prostitution ring in Houston, that she'd served a year in Chino for fencing stolen credit cards, that she and Al Dark had run a multimillion-dollar insurance scam in Atlanta, that she'd been an undercover vice cop in Baltimore and an operative for the CIA.

Speculative stories about his aunt weren't new. He'd heard them since he was a child, mostly from his father, Jack, whose own father had abandoned the family when Jack was only two to marry a rummy on the other side of the tracks in St. Jo, Missouri. It was understood that no one in the Piszek family would speak, openly or privately, of this outsider or of her "problem." It was as though her alcoholism had corrupted everyone, even those in the Piszek clan who had never met the woman.

The stormy relationship spawned three children, including Ruby (out of wedlock, went the rumors). David's father crossed paths with his notorious half-sister only a handful of times before she fled St. Jo at sixteen. No one heard from her for the next twenty-four years. Yet they all seemed to know something about her. She'd married into San Francisco high society, she'd died in Peru fighting with the guerrillas, she'd taken up with a lesbian lover in Seattle, she'd had an abortion at age seventeen, she'd died of a drug overdose in St. Louis, she'd joined an all-women rock band in Boston. When her alchie mother died and Ruby didn't show up for the funeral, no one knew if it was by choice, if she just didn't know that her mother's liver had finally given out, or whether, for that matter, Ruby was even alive.

The only sure thing about his aunt's past was, in the words of Mark Twain, that her many deaths had been greatly exaggerated. She'd surfaced ten years ago in Denver married to Al Dark, who himself, so the stories went, had moved from New Orleans under shady circumstances. Her appearance in Denver did nothing to throw clear light on her missing years, but the fact that she'd married a bondsman only reinforced speculations about a lawless past. David's own father even speculated that Ruby and Al had met because he'd bailed her out of a New Orleans jail.

Whatever the truth about the past of Ruby Dark, it wasn't going to come from her lips. David had probed gently around the edges, like a dental hygienist probing a questionable tooth, looking for the patient to wince in response. His aunt had not winced. Even at his most direct questions, she neither refuted nor acknowledged the veracity of the many stories about her. Indeed, she seemed almost to relish them. Perhaps she saw her mysterious past as a useful public relations gimmick—clients identified with someone who themselves may have strayed over the line. Ruby Dark. Angel of the Outlaws. Perhaps she merely enjoyed the mystique. Or perhaps, just perhaps, among all those stories, lay one that was—

David cut off his own thoughts. "They're just stories, that's all," he said aloud to the deputy. "Rumors. Nothing more. No truth to them."

Deputy Erickson, however, was just warming up to the subject. "I heard her husband was murdered a coupla years ago."

David nodded.

"I heard they ain't arrested nobody for it."

"That's what I understand."

"Don't they got no suspects?"

David stood uncomfortably. "I really don't know much about it. He was killed before I moved here."

"Who does your aunt think murdered him?"

"She doesn't talk about it."

"Maybe he stiffed one of his clients. Some of these bondsman rip off their—"

"I'm told that Al Dark was a very honest bondsman."

The deputy had the look of someone didn't believe any bondsman could be honest.

"Coulda been another bondsman," speculated the deputy. "It wouldn't be the first time. Some of these guys are ex-cons themselves."

David shrugged. It wasn't a bad theory. Although his aunt never spoke about it, he knew there'd been bad blood between Cadillac Johnson and her husband, though he didn't know exactly what the bad blood was about.

The deputy looked around the lobby and then whispered,

"I heard her husband drank too much. That he beat her. I heard she may have hired a hit man to take care of the problem."

It was preposterous, of course, the Ruby Dark-as-killer theory. Only the people who didn't know her put any credence into it. Still, the theory had persisted, like a communicable disease. A cop—someone who was deeply attracted to Ruby—had once strongly hinted to him that Cadillac Johnson had been the main carrier of the disease. If so, no wonder his aunt hated the bondsman.

The deputy stared, waiting for a reply. To hell with civility, thought David. "That's bullshit!" he said, and returned to his chair.

3

Ruby Dark made her grand entrance a few minutes later. All of his aunt's entrances, David had discovered soon after he had met her, were grand. She was a tall, striking woman, with mounds of thick red hair that fell to her shoulders like that of a country-western singer. She was around fifty, he'd calculated from what he knew of her past. He'd asked her once, as off-handily and diplomatically as he could, just to confirm his math. Her reply had been brief: "Don't ask. I'll just lie."

Despite the hour, her large, jade green eyes looked as fresh and alert as if it were midmorning. Like any veteran in the bail bonding business, Ruby Dark had learned to survive for days on only snatches of sleep, to answer the telephone in the middle of the night halfway through the first ring.

Ruby strode across the lobby in a mid-calf burgundy dress slashed diagonally by a bold swatch of white, her quilted maroon high-heeled pumps clicking on the concrete floor. The silver of her pierced earrings, shaped like stylized chile peppers, caught the dim lobby light. She carried a black leather briefcase in one hand and a brown paper bag in the other. Even the navy man stirred from his dozing to stare.

David secretly enjoyed watching people beguiled by his aunt's brass and thunder. Few of them got beyond the stylish clothes and confident walk and bold features. Few noticed the mouth that was too large and the lips that were a little too thick for her high, smooth cheekbones and oval face, or that she walked taller than she stood, that her body possessed a certain thickness, a fullness inevitable in maturity. Few, if any, were alert enough or fortuitous enough or sly enough to catch Ruby in one of her rare, unguarded moments, as he had, that they might glimpse the scar, a thin, shiny, jagged line that ran for an inch along the back of her left jawline, artfully hidden under makeup.

David, dressed in a frayed blue oxford shirt and jeans and jogging shoes, rose as his aunt approached. A whiff of an undefinable but intense perfume hit him as she gave him a cheerful hello. She set the briefcase on the floor and dangled the brown paper bag in front of him. He could see the McDonald's logo on it. "Here, I figured you'd be starved at this hour," she said in her raspy voice.

The nauseating smell of burnt meat assaulted him. He fended off the sack with a hand. "You know I don't eat that stuff, Aunt Ruby."

"I couldn't find goat cheese and bottled wheatgrass at this hour."

"There's nothing wrong with wheatgrass."

"It's not fit for human consumption."

"What's not fit is the contents of that bag."

Ruby raised her free gloved hand and said, "I agree. Dying from fast-food arteriosclerosis is a sin against God. Better that you gum up your arteries with *real* food. I plan to die happily over foie gras and almond-chocolate mousse at Christopher's—or at least over a plate of pork carnitas from Mama Rosita's." She raised a finger at him. "And I want no extraordinary lifesaving measures on your part."

"The way you eat, you'll succeed."

She sighed exaggeratedly. "Have a little fun in life, David." Ruby looked over at the navy man, who was staring wide-eyed her. "Let me ask you, sir. If food was sex—which sometimes I think we'd all be better off if it was—wouldn't you rather have sex with foie gras than oat bran?"

The navy man's mouth moved but any words he may have had apparently had drifted out to sea.

"I haven't gotten the visitation slip yet, Aunt Ruby," David said, standing up.

Ruby ignored him and walked over to the chain-smoking teenager with the stringy brown hair. She thrust the hamburger bag into the girl's face. "Here, honey, eat this. You look as skinny as a jail cell bar."

The girl shook her head but Ruby persisted. "Who you waiting for?"

The girl looked at her, annoyed. David could read the girl's thoughts from across the room. Who was this nosy bitch dressed up as if she'd just spent the night out on the town?

"My boyfriend," the girl mumbled.

"How long you been waiting?"

"Several hours."

"Is he bonded out?"

"Yes. I'm waiting for 'em to finish the paperwork and release him."

"Hon, you could wait here all night for these yo-yos to finish masturbating with their paperwork. You don't eat something soon your boyfriend's gonna find you shriveled up and blown away. There's a Dr Pepper in here, too." Ruby pushed the bag in the girl's face, and the girl took it without saying thanks, probably figuring it was the easiest way to get rid of the bitch. But Ruby wasn't halfway back to David before the girl tore into the bag and began wolfing down the hamburger.

Ruby picked up her briefcase. "Let's go see our million dollar prize."

Deputy Erickson gave her an obsequious good morning and handed her a visitation slip. They rode the elevator to the third floor, where a deputy behind another glass cage took the slip. "Window Two," he said curtly, less impressed with Ruby than Deputy Erickson.

As they walked along the narrow egg-white cinderblock hallway to the visitation room, David peppered his aunt with whispered questions. Was she going to post the bond? What kind of collateral would they need? Would the judge go for a cash bondsman posting such a large bond, or would they have to split it with an insurance company?

But Ruby seemed more interested in needling him with a lawyer joke.

"You know why the post office recalled its lawyer stamp?"

"I'm sure I can't guess," David said glumly.

"'Cause people didn't know which side to spit on."

"What is it you have against lawyers, Aunt Ruby?"

"I was a lawyer in a past life. I'm still trying to live it down."

The visitation room was small, flanked by opposite rows of windowed cubicles for the prisoners. Visitors sat between the two rows, back-to-back, on black metal stools built to encourage short stays. Ruby set the briefcase on the stool in front of Window Two and paced until Bayne C. Gibson, Jr., arrived, escorted to the cubicle by a deputy.

The multimillionaire stood six four, was in his mid-thirties and blond-haired, with a handsome boyish face. But his skin had already taken on the gray pallor of prison life, deadened still more by the sickly fluorescent jail lights, and his gray eyes betrayed the soul of a man shell-shocked by an experience he had yet to fully comprehend.

He'd been stripped of all personal effects, though he still had on his civvies—a $200 white sweatsuit that now looked as though he could barter it for a mere five bucks worth of cigarettes. When they moved him to the county jail they would issue the dark green jumpsuit for defendants up on felony charges.

Ruby moved her briefcase and sat on the stool. Gibson stood for several moments, staring slack-jawed at her. Finally, he sank onto his stool. He said something but his words were muffled by the thick glass.

Ruby pointed to the black telephone lying on the steel counter in front of him. He picked it up, staring at it as if he'd never seen a telephone before.

"*You're* Ruby Dark?" he said into the phone, his eyes returning to her. She held her phone away from her ear slightly so David, who stood directly behind her, could overhear.

"You were expecting Tugboat Annie with tattoos?"

"No, of course not. But I . . . I wasn't quite expecting . . ."

Ruby smiled gently and said, "This is my associate, David Piszek."

Gibson's eyes barely flicked an acknowledgement in David's direction. Then he looked at Ruby with the sudden wild-eyed look of a cornered animal. "I'm innocent! Please believe me. I'm innocent! I had nothing to do with killing Royce Kray. I swear to god, Ms. Dark. The man was my bread and butter, for God's sake! We had our differences, to be sure. Everyone did with Royce. But I would never have killed him! He was already dead when I . . ."

A rich whiner. A rich *guilty* whiner. A good lawyer, David knew, entered situations with an open mind, prepared to explore all avenues. But there was no doubt in his mind, despite Gibson's passionate outburst, that the man was guilty as hell. Gibson had been police suspect Numero Uno from the moment the police and the building's security guard had entered his penthouse and found him standing only a few feet from Kray's body. The murder weapon, a small automatic, was found hidden under the cushions of a nearby couch, along with a glove stained with traces of gunpowder. The companion glove was found in a closet, inside one of Gibson's coats. The gun, though clean of fingerprints, was registered to Gibson. Equally damaging, according to press reports, was the fact the two men had argued publicly several times recently, including a nasty exchange at Gibson's penthouse the night before the murder, on the occasion of a fifth anniversary party for Kray's radio show. Finally, there was the small matter of the $1.2 million life insurance policy Gibson had taken out on Kray only two months before he was killed.

Not that there weren't other suspects. As the hottest, most insulting radio personality in town, Royce Kray had as many enemies as he had listeners—and he had a lot of listeners, a fair number of whom had made death threats. But if one of them had killed Kray, it seemed more likely they would have shot him in the radio station parking lot or outside his own home—not in the high-security confines of Bayne Gibson's penthouse. No, the police had their man.

But while part of David burned with prosecutorial conviction, another part of him had begun to think like his aunt. Gibson may be a guilty whiner, but he was a rich guilty whiner and that made him the perfect client. Guys like him don't jump bail, even if they're guilty as hell—not with their kind of money. Not when they can buy the best lawyers in town. Even if a jury were to convict him, he wouldn't do serious time. The rich never did serious time. No, Gibson wouldn't run. Gibson was money in the bank. One hundred fifty grand. It didn't get any easier.

Gibson was still pleading his case for innocence when Ruby raised a hand to silence him.

"I don't care whether you're innocent or not, honey."

"But I—"

"I'm not your lawyer, judge, or jury. I'm a businesswoman. My decision whether to post your bond is strictly a business decision, Mr. Gibson. You're a businessman. You can appreciate that."

Gibson looked at her with the pleading eyes of a drowning man. "But I didn't kill him, I tell you! I'm innocent! I swear! You must understand . . ."

Ruby let him go on. People had a way of wanting to talk to his aunt. She would start out as their bondswoman, but end up as their father-confessor, their confidant, their friend.

When Gibson momentarily ran out of emotional gas, Ruby cut in. "The issue here, hon, is whether you're the kind of guy who's going to show up for your court dates . . . and if you don't show up, whether you're good for one million bucks."

Gibson looked hurt. "Of course I'll make the court dates. Why wouldn't I make the court dates? I'm innocent, for God's sake!"

"If I bonded out people only on the basis of innocence, I'd been broke years ago."

His shoulders sagged. "Okay, okay. What do you need to know?"

"How soon can you put your hands on a hundred and fifty thousand dollars? Cash or a certified check is fine."

He said numbly, "One hundred fifty thousand . . . that much?"

"Fifteen percent. Standard rate. That's the maximum a bondsman is legally entitled to in the State of Colorado for posting bond. That's our premium for doing business. It's nonrefundable, unless I revoke your bond within the first thirty days. After thirty days, you give me cause to suspect—

to even *think*—you're going to skip, I'll revoke your bond and stick your ass right back in jail. And I keep the premium."

"Jesus!"

Ruby shrugged. "You can always post the entire bond yourself. You'll get it all back from the court after the trial's over. You're wealthy enough to do that, aren't you?"

Wealthy to the tune of $15 million, David had read.

Gibson lowered his haggard eyes. "Most of my money's tied up. I don't have a million dollars in liquid assets I can afford to relinquish at the moment."

"Then you can stay in jail, honey. It won't cost you a dime, though I wouldn't recommend eating the food, especially at county. And some of the guys over there are a little . . . different."

Gibson sunk his face deep into the wells of his hands and his shoulders trembled. After a long time he raised his grizzled face and said, "I'll talk to Ezzard about our cash position. I'm sure he can take care of it. Just tell me what I have to do to get out of here. I can't take this place another day!"

"I can't bond you out today, hon. Nobody's going to get you outa here before Tuesday or Wednesday at the earliest, maybe longer."

"Tuesday! That's four days from now!"

"You're asking me to execute a million dollar bond. As a businessman, would you risk a million bucks without checking on the financial and personal integrity of the person you're doing business with?"

"You can't be serious! I'm one of the richest men in the state. Everyone knows that."

"It never pays to rely on what everyone knows."

Gibson's jaw moved but no words came out of the telephone. Ruby pulled an application and indemnity form out of her briefcase and pressed them with both hands against the two-inch thick cubicle glass. Gibson read the fine print slowly, his lips moving ever so slightly. "Maybe I should have Ezzard read this before I sign it," he said. "Especially this part about holding you harmless for incurring any liabilities—"

"That's standard. It's to cover any expenses if we have to track you down and bring you back to court. But by all means, take your time."

"No! No, let's move on."

Ruby went through the questions: addresses of all residences and businesses, favorite hangouts, physical characteristics, previous arrests, attorney of record, bank accounts, corporate and personal assets, liabilities. . . .

"You better talk to Ezzard about some of this stuff," Gibson said at one point, "especially the numbers. He keeps track of all of that." Gibson was rubbing his fingertips together furiously, trying to remove the last traces of fingerprint ink from them.

Ruby moved on to the names, addresses, and phone numbers of friends, relatives, girlfriends, business colleagues, shareholders, key employees.

"What's all this for?" Gibson protested meekly. "Why do you need to know the names of my friends and relatives? They don't have anything to do with this or with my personal financial stability."

"In case I have to track you down."

"But I told you, I'm not going to run."

Ruby leaned forward slightly to emphasize her point. "You better not. Understand, honey, if I post bond for you I *own* you. You skip on me, I want to know where I can find your ass. And believe me, if you skip, I *will* find you!"

4

David returned from Monday evening law classes to find Ruby where he'd left her hours earlier, heels clicking sharply on the floor, the cordless phone attached to her ear. One of her scratchy jazz records played in the background. "Real jazz," she called it, "not this elevator music today they call jazz." Personally, he found most of her "real jazz" too discordant for his taste. He much preferred the ordered view of classical music. Besides, who played *records* these days!

But the scene wasn't quite as he had left it. Morgan Reed had come a callin' on his aunt.

Reed was ensconced in a high-backed black leather chair in front of Ruby's desk, a large knuckled fist wrapped loosely around one of her infamous chile pepper mugs. Collateral, who worshipped Reed, was sprawled contentedly at his feet, his head propped against Reed's crossed ankles.

"Ah, the young law student returns from the F. Lee Bailey School of Ambulance Chasing," cracked Reed over Ruby's hushed phone voice.

"Detective." David nodded curtly.

Detective Morgan Reed of the famous Caldwell murder case, the Martinez kidnapping, the Levy bombing conspiracy, and a long list of other headline makers. A Denver Police Department legend. Once a rising star. A cinch to make captain, Ruby had said. Maybe a division chief. Hell, maybe chief of the whole damn place—which would have been a touch of irony considering Reed had a streak of Sioux blood. But that was history, Reed would bluntly say today. That was before he tried to end run his superiors during an internal graft investigation they didn't want investigated. That was before they exiled him to auto theft.

David went into the back room for a bottle of mineral water from the small refrigerator. When he returned, his aunt was off the phone and sitting behind her desk coveting a plate of chile peppers sent over from her favorite Mexican restaurant, Mama Rosita's.

Reed was on his feet, leaning on the desk, his face inches from her. He was a big man with the rough-hewn look of a tree with the bark still on. He always wore sport coats that were too small and ties that were hopelessly out of date. Although he was a few years younger than Ruby, he looked older. Maybe it was his silver-blue hair—the color of his .38—or maybe it was because his wife had died of lupus four years ago and he was raising two teenage daughters by himself. Or maybe it was the boredom of being exiled to auto theft.

"I'm telling you, Ruby, you're nuts if you bail out this Gibson guy," he said, his neck muscles bulging. "Let the surety boys put their asses on the line."

Ruby poked at the thumb-sized chile peppers. They'd been roasted until their skins had turned black and blistered, and then slit open. "Why?" she asked.

"He's guilty as hell, that's why, and guilty guys run."

"Morgan, most of the people I bail out are guilty. You know that. It's my job."

"Yeah, but it's not your job to risk a million bucks doing it! You've never taken one this big. You could get hurt real bad if it sours. You could lose your business—everything!"

David, who'd settled onto the edge of a chair at the periphery of Reed's vision, bristled at the detective's lobbying efforts. It was not the first time the detective had butted into their business, but this time it was particularly irritating. Guilty or not, Gibson was a sure thing. Open and shut. Found money. What the hell was the detective so damned worried about?

"That's not a reason, Morgan," said Ruby. "This business is inherently risky. The bigger the risk, the bigger the reward."

"Dammit, Ruby, I just worry about you, that's all."

She smiled affectionately. "I know you do, Morgan. I appreciate it."

She selected one of the peppers, doused it with lime juice and salt, and bit off half of it. Almost immediately her eyes brimmed with tears and she blew out her breath. Sweat beaded on her forehead and under her eyes. Tears came to David's eyes just watching her.

"Why do you punish yourself like that?" said Reed. "It's masochistic."

"Most things worth enjoying usually are." She grabbed a tortilla from a side dish, ripped off a large chunk, and ate it. "Go ahead, try one."

Reed warily eyed the plate. "How hot are they?"

"They'll take the rust off your car."

The man's a damn fool if he even *thinks* about trying one, thought David. Chile peppers weren't food to his aunt . . . they were an addiction, a religious experience. The more thermonuclear the better. Blast-furnace hot. Bullets from hell.

"Too much for you to handle, hon?" she taunted, her voice raspier than normal.

Reed stiffened in mock offense. "What kind are they?"

"Habañeros. From the Yucatán. Hottest peppers in the world. They call them 'scotch bonnets' in the Caribbean. Mama Rosita's the only one in town who knows how to fix them right."

"Never heard of 'em."

"They don't leave many survivors."

Reed sat down, but made no move toward the plate.

Ruby bit off the rest of the pepper, and quickly ate more tortilla.

"Look, Ruby, I got two tickets to the Rockies tomorrow," Reed offered. "An afternoon game. We'll have a coupla beers and talk over Gibson."

"I sleep through baseball."

"It's their new stadium. You haven't even gone to a game yet. You gotta see the Blake Street Bombers. I'll grant you, the pitching staff's ERA is bigger than my waist line, but—"

"That's why I hate baseball, Morgan. It's an accountant's

game. They can tell you what the guy's batting average is hitting left handed against one-armed right handers pitching on Friday nights with runners on first and third and one out and the team behind three runs. Who the hell cares?''

''I don't know anybody in this town who hasn't been to at least one Rockies game. It's . . . un-American.''

''Thanks for the invitation, Morgan. Really. But I can't. I've got too much work to do.''

''Dammit, Ruby, you work too hard! You never take any time off.'' He scowled at David, as if to blame *him* for the fact that Ruby was a workaholic.

Collateral, disturbed by Reed's outburst, stirred in a rare demonstration of life. Reed bent over to scratch his neck. He ought to take the dog home with him, thought David, a consolation prize for not getting anywhere with the dog's owner. He could use a good home—the dog, that is.

Ruby worked on another pepper. ''So what do your homicide buddies have to say about Gibson?'' she prodded. The brass across the street may have thought they had exiled Morgan Reed, but he still maintained a tight web of connections all over the Department, especially to homicide.

The detective quit scratching the dog and leaned back in the chair. ''Oh, he seems clean enough—'cept they've got him dead to rights on Murder One. No priors other than a coupla speeding tickets. He wasn't under any previous investigations that I know of. Belongs to the Chamber, sits on the Denver Athletic Club board, gives to charities, all that shit. Of course, with fifteen mil to his name, I suppose he could afford to give some of it away.''

''So what's bothering you, Morgan? The man sounds like a Boy Scout. You know something I don't know?''

Reed shrugged. ''He's got money stashed away in one of those offshore banks in the Grand Caymans. I never trust guys who hide their money. I know a few drug dealers who-'ve laundered shit through there.''

''How much money?''

''Coupla of mil, maybe.''

''The rich always have money stashed away for a rainy day. Anything else?''

''I just got a bad feeling about the whole case, that's all.''

"You sound like me, Morgan."

"Good cops have a sixth sense, too. It's what keeps us alive."

"I know. That's why I take your feelings seriously."

Jesus, thought David, these two and their gut feelings. It was worse than a third-rate cop show.

"So what's your sixth sense telling you?" Ruby asked.

"I don't know. Maybe it's not Gibson himself. Maybe it's this Kray guy who's bothering me."

"I'm not bailing Kray out, Morgan. *Nobody* is bailing him out, unless God's planning a return engagement sooner than we expect."

"It's just that . . . the guy was an asshole."

"Probably explains why he was killed."

"Did you ever hear about Kray's son?"

"I didn't know he had a son."

"He did, once. Kid killed himself at fourteen. Coupla years ago. Kray used his media connections to keep it pretty well buried when it happened. But get this. A few months after the kid dies, Kray's ranting on the air one day about how suicidal people are cowards, and suddenly he tells everyone in fifteen states about his son cutting his wrists and how his wife found the kid's bloody body in the bathtub. He goes on and on about his kid being such a wimp he couldn't even kill himself like a man."

"Jesus!" interjected David.

"Guess he woulda thought better of his kid if he'd just shot himself," said Reed.

"They know why the kid killed himself?" Ruby asked.

David saw the gleam his aunt always got in her eyes when she latched on to something. The psychodynamics of the Kray family had nothing to do, of course, with the issue of whether to post bond for the man accused of killing Royce Kray. But his aunt was by nature intensely curious—or was it just nosy?—about other people. It was a characteristic that had made her not only a survivor in this business, but a very successful survivor.

"No. But it runs in the family. Kray's wife tried to kill herself about three months ago. Cut her wrists . . . just like her son. She woulda made it 'cept one of her daughters found her in time."

"I hadn't heard any of this," said Ruby.

"Hell, the way his wife and daughter talk about him in the press, you'd think Kray'd been God's gift to man."

Ruby nodded her head. "Families have a way of protecting their own. Even bad families."

"It's a bad family, all right. And I've got a bad feeling about this whole nasty case. Leave it alone!"

"We're still checking things out, Morgan. Gibson's business attorney is taking us through the penthouse tomorrow. Maybe I'll get a better feel for things there."

Reed leaned over the desk. "You sure you won't go to the game with me? I promise I won't talk about my girls."

David felt almost embarrassed watching the detective grovel.

"It's not your girls, Morgan. I enjoy hearing about your girls. It's my work." She set a hand on a stack of papers like a court witness laying a hand on the Bible.

"You're a stubborn woman, Ruby Dark."

"Good night, Morgan," she said, her voice warmly but firmly ushering him toward the door.

The detective rose, snatched a pepper from the plate, and offered it to David. "Try one, David?"

"No thanks. I'm not into culinary suicide."

Reed bit off the pepper almost to the stem, tossed the stem in a wastebasket, and headed for the back stairs that led to the dark parking lot below. It was the way Reed always entered and left. Fraternizing with bondsmen was frowned on by the brass, and they would really frown if they knew that Reed was Ruby's main pipeline into the Department.

Suddenly the detective stopped and grasped at his mouth. "Holy shit!" he croaked. "Water!"

Ruby hurried to his side, shaking salt over a tortilla. "No water, Morgan, it only spreads the heat around. Eat this."

Reed crammed the tortilla into his mouth.

"You okay?" she asked, gently putting a hand on the back of his hunched, broad shoulders. Reed couldn't see the grin on her face.

He nodded a violent yes. His eyes overflowed with tears.

He mumbled through the tortilla. "My fucking lips feel like they're gonna fall off!"

"That's what I love about habañeros," said Ruby. "They make grown men cry."

5

"Is that where Kray was murdered?" asked David, pointing through French doors at a stone-lined pond sunk into a faded cedar deck. Only moments before, he and his aunt and Bayne Gibson's business attorney, E. Ezzard Lamprey, had stepped out of a private elevator into the cool, airless interior of Gibson's penthouse on the thirty-first floor of The Polo Club.

Lamprey grudgingly admitted it was. He turned toward the interior of the penthouse, but Ruby opened the French doors and stepped out into the sunlight. The two men followed. She walked to the east side of a waist-high brick wall that ringed the deck. Below her sprawled the glass and steel heart of downtown Denver, the muted sounds of street traffic drifting up. Beyond lay prairie land, the soil broken and sown in townhomes, condos, split-levels, strip centers, shopping malls, and freeway. But Ruby seemed uninterested in the panoramic view. Instead, she stroked the shiny smoothness of the brass railing that ran along the top of the wall, as if assessing its resale value.

David wandered toward the pond, which had been built on the northwest corner of the deck with a commanding view of the Front Range peaks still blanketed under leftover late spring snows. Directly on the north and south sides of the deck office towers rose another ten stories. From one of them a woman had called the police that night to say she'd just seen a man shot on the top of The Polo Club.

The pond was oval shaped, ten feet long and seven feet wide and quite deep, edged with grasses and sprinkled with water lilies. A tiny waterfall trickled over buff-colored rocks. Several white wire chairs sat along one side, turned in unison toward the mountains. David didn't see Gibson as the pond type. A swimming pool, maybe, but not a pond that looked like something out of *House and Garden.*

As he circled the water, he felt his heart race. This was where the police and the security guard had found Kray's body, floating naked on his back, two bullets in his chest. (*Naked! Why on earth was he naked?*) And Gibson standing only a few feet away. David had never seen where a human being had been murdered. He searched the gray weathered deck for telltale dark stains. He peered into the waters, but the reflection of the high overhead sun and the ruffling of the surface by the waterfall obscured any view into the depths. He cupped a hand over his eyes, tipped his head, and squinted. The reflections disappeared, and suddenly, between the lilies, just beneath the surface, the water came alive with huge, darting, rainbow-colored fish.

"Wow! What kind of fish are these? They look like goldfish on steroids."

"They're colored carp," corrected the attorney.

David turned toward Lamprey. The chrome voice he remembered so distinctly from that first late-night call didn't match the man who stood impatiently in the doorway. Instead of a young man in a dark Armani suit, a man as gaunt and fit as his client, Lamprey was a man well into his fifties, with blotched skin and a short, overweight body that had never stepped onto a stairclimber or jogged so much as around the block. He wore the ugliest brown suit David had ever seen, along with black unpolished shoes. He looked more like a low-volume insurance salesman than a high-priced, big-city lawyer.

"Colored carp?" said David.

"They're called koi," said Lamprey, as if he were addressing a kindergarten class.

"Oh, yeah, I've heard of them. They're real popular to collect these days. Gibson actually collects carp?"

"Koi are a passion of his. Second only to running."

David didn't see Gibson as a fish freak any more than he saw him as a pond man. He looked into the waters. "People pay a lot of money for koi, don't they?"

"There's a matched pair of males in there worth one hundred and thirty thousand dollars each."

"A hundred thirty thousand!"

"They're competition level koi. He purchased them from the Konishi Koi Farm in Hiroshima and had them flown over."

"Jesus. I remember reading in the paper that Kray was wading around in this pond at that party—the one the night before he was killed. Real drunk, I guess. He was threatening to urinate in the pond and kill the fish. That was an expensive threat."

Lamprey looked impatient. "I pay little credence to what appears in the media."

"Witnesses claimed that Gibson got real angry at Kray and Kray dared him to get his gun and do something about it. Is that right?"

Lamprey frowned. "That is a police matter involving my client, not something I'm privy to discuss here with you."

"Weren't you at the party?"

"My presence or nonpresence is not germane to the issue. The issue is the question of posting bond for my—"

"Is anyone taking care of them while he's in jail?" interjected Ruby.

Lamprey stared at Ruby. "Taking care of who?"

"The koi. Is someone taking care of the koi? If they're so expensive . . ."

Lamprey looked irritated. "I wouldn't know. Are you considering them for collateral, *Mzzzz* Dark?"

Ruby adjusted her white straw hat against the harsh sun. "Two-hundred sixty thousand bucks is a lot of collateral, honey. I could rent a fish tank and keep 'em in my office."

The interior of Bayne Gibson's penthouse was so large David wondered if Gibson issued road maps to visitors. Some of the rooms could have been homesteaded, and the walk-in closets were spacious enough to park Gibson's Jeep Grand Cherokee—larger, in fact, than the cramped attic room David lived in above Ruby's office.

Despite its impressive size, however, the penthouse had a

spare, industrial age feel that David found unappealing, furniture designed more for art than function and comfort, rooms neat and unused. An office, whose floor-to-ceiling windows offered an expansive view of south Denver, had the requisite computer, fax machine, copier, black leather executive chair, and an oak desk someone must have cut half an acre of timber for. Yet David saw no papers, no clutter, no signs that significant business was conducted here.

Lamprey played official tour guide, but Ruby often pushed her way ahead of him, opening doors, barraging him with questions, touching everything with her hands, as if a psychic attempting to make a telepathic connection with the occupant.

It was the red room that stopped her cold.

The dark, windowless room was located somewhere in the southeast interior of the penthouse, if David had accurately triangulated his bearings. Lamprey had to unlock the room. A red light, like that in a photographic darkroom, cast a murky glow, dimly revealing a wall of high-tech electronic equipment and video tapes, womb-like chairs, a futon, and in one corner, a large, black, coffin-shaped box.

"Good god, what's this place?" she said, holding back in the doorway.

"It's his refuge," said Lamprey, not quite able to repress the scorn in his voice. "It's where he comes to get away from things."

"Looks more like Count Dracula's bedroom."

"No, it's a brain gym!" David said excitedly, sidling past his aunt into the room.

"A what?"

"Kind of a health club for the head."

"It's this New Age stuff," muttered Lamprey.

"Most of the commercial operations are on the coasts, but there's one in Boulder," David went on. "They hook you up to gadgets that shoot electric currents and lights and music through your head. Suppose to relieve stress. But I've never seen a private gym—certainly not equipped like this."

"I'll take my masseuse any day," said Ruby.

David slipped on a set of headphones and ski-like goggles. He felt like an escapee from a science-fiction movie.

"What's that do?" Ruby asked.

"You stare into flashing lights for thirty minutes a day and it changes your beta brain waves—the kind that make you anxious and jumpy—into more relaxing theta waves. Puts you into an alpha state."

"It'd put me into cardiac arrest. Is this what you and your friends do between courses of tofu?"

"I know a law student who's into this stuff," he said, taking off the headphones and goggles. He fingered several crystals scattered on a nearby table, their true colors indeterminate in the hazy red light.

"That isn't what it looks like, is it?" said Ruby, dubiously pointing to the black, coffin-shaped box.

David went over and opened the lid. "It's a flotation tank. You climb inside, close the lid, and float in saltwater while you listen to soft music, birds chirping, environmental sounds, that sort of stuff. You're completely sealed off from the world. I've tried it a couple of times. It's very relaxing."

"I can see where the dead would enjoy it," she shuddered.

They finished the tour of the penthouse and returned to the living room looking out onto the deck and the koi pond. The usual summer afternoon storm clouds were starting to boil over the foothills.

"This place is all very nice, honey," Ruby said to Lamprey, "but it makes for very illiquid collateral."

"I'm sure Bayne's assets are quite sufficient to cover any of your requirements."

"Not if I can't put my hands on them quickly. Most of them are tied up in real estate and his company."

From Gibson's financials, they knew his penthouse condo was worth $1.4 million and his villa in Ixtapa $400,000. Another $1 million was tied up in investment real estate. The rest of his wealth was in his company's stock.

Ruby had preached that illiquid assets were impossible to go after for quick cash if the client skipped and one needed the money in a hurry to pay the court the face value of the bond. Eventually—sometimes years later—one might be able to foreclose on real estate and business assets, but a bondsman could be out on the street before then if the bond was large enough. Benevolent judges sometimes delayed the day of reckoning with the court, but King Andy was not a benevolent judge.

Said Lamprey, "There will be no need to obtain any of Bayne's assets. We are confident that these preposterous charges will be dropped."

"If you're so confident, hon, why don't you co-sign for him." When that drew only a cold glare from the attorney, Ruby said, "Tell you what. Transfer a million bucks out of that offshore trust fund you neglected to tell us about and deposit it into a money market account here in town where I can get my hands on it if I need to. Put that up for collateral and we'd have no problem."

"That's another piece of misinformation created by the press," Lamprey said angrily. "There is no such trust."

"Okay, play it that way. If your client wants to sit in jail, that's his choice. What about this million-two life insurance policy he had on Kray?"

"It's a key person policy. The *company* owns the policy and is sole beneficiary—not Bayne. That fact has not been made clear by the press, nor is it clear, I believe, to the police."

"Still a helluva lot of life insurance to take out on someone such a short time before they're murdered."

Lamprey glared at her. "Arbitron ratings for the last quarter jumped an eleven-point-four share for his time slot. That made it not only the highest rated show for the time slot, but the highest rated show in the market for all time slots. In light of his increased value to the station, I personally recommended the drawing up of a new policy. It would not have been in Bayne's best financial interests to murder his station's number one source of revenue for an insurance policy on which he could not personally collect."

"People kill for many reasons besides money," said Ruby.

"You would know more about that than I," said Lamprey.

"You and Gibson seem like an odd couple. How'd you get hooked up with him?"

"I started with his father—Sam Gibson. In fact, our firm has represented Gibson Media for nearly twenty-five years. Sam was an announcer in the forties. He worked on the Lux

Radio Hour and several other national programs. He bought his first station in Butte, Montana, in nineteen fifty-one and built his company from there. *He* loved radio."

"At the jail, Gibson said his father was dead and he didn't seem sure where his mother was."

"Sam died while Bayne was in college. His mother left when he was a child. The last I heard she was married to a plastic surgeon in Georgia."

"So junior took the company over after his dad died?"

"Basically, my firm ran the company for several years after Sam died, until Bayne graduated and learned the fundamentals of the business."

"From all the marathons he does, it sounds like you still run the place."

The attorney looked at his watch. "I have a call to—"

"How well did you know Royce Kray?" asked Ruby.

Lamprey stiffened. "Not well." His tone hinted that he was glad he hadn't known him better.

"I caught his show now and then," she said. "He seemed to enjoy pissing off his listeners more than talking about the issues."

"Misanthropy sells well these days."

"It was all an act?"

"Royce understood that people listened and called in because they found a kind of self-gratification in his contempt of them. People expect to be victimized these days. In fact, they enjoy being abused. It reinforces their fundamental lack of self-worth. Royce played to that. He was a smart showman, after all. But deep down it was no act. Royce Kray genuinely hated everyone."

"Including you?"

"As I said, he was very egalitarian in that regard."

Lamprey excused himself to make his phone call.

"What do you think?" David asked his aunt the moment Lamprey was out of earshot.

She looked dubious. "Something doesn't feel right about this place . . . Gibson . . . the whole thing."

He could hear Morgan Reed in her words. "Like what?"

"I don't know. It's just a feeling."

"It's too easy, Aunt Ruby, that's the problem. You've

been around too many lowlifes. You never had to bail out a Chamber of Commerce member worth fifteen million.''

"Remember what I told you—judge the man, not his assets.''

"Aren't they the same thing with guys like Gibson?''

"Normally, yes. But I'm not sure with him. His passions seem to run in different directions.''

"Yeah, like fish. So what does that mean?''

"I'd feel better if I knew Gibson was enslaved to his money. Then I'd have him by the balls, if you'll pardon the expression. I mean, look at this place.'' She swept her hand across the room.

"What about it?''

"There's no life here. Half the rooms are shut off. The place looks unlived in, except for that weird room with the coffin. He musta hired a Benedictine monk to decorate. Where's all the money? Rich people blow their money on things—art, antiques, gold faucets in the bathrooms, something ostentatious.''

"I'd call the fish pretty damn ostentatious.''

"But they aren't worth a million dollars.''

"At least they're a liquid asset,'' cracked David.

Ruby laughed. "When you bond people out, David, you gotta have a hold on them. Maybe it's family, a girlfriend, roots in the community, money—something you know is going to keep 'em around. I can't figure out a hold on Gibson. It's like trying to grab one of those fish.''

Lamprey returned, looking pale and edgy. He said to Ruby, "Are you prepared to bond my client out?''

"I told you this would take several days. We still have some details to go over and—''

"Bayne is very anxious to get out *now*, *Mzzzz* Dark.''

"He'll have to remain anxious a while longer.''

"Perhaps another bonding agency could expedite the matter more quickly.'' His smooth assured voice reclaimed itself. Here was something the lawyer could sink his teeth into—arm twisting. But Lamprey hadn't learned yet that the harder you push Ruby Dark, the harder she pushes back.

"Call any of them you want,'' she said. "The phone book's full of 'em. But nobody's going to write your client a bond in the next few hours, honey—not for that kind of money. At least nobody you can trust.''

''That remains unsatisfactory,'' Lamprey said stiffly. ''You have twenty-four hours to post bond, or we take our business elsewhere.''

6

Big Jim Brodie watched the northwest Denver home through a pair of military field glasses. "Just twenty-four hours, eh?"

David looked at his watch. "Actually only three hours and twenty minutes now."

"She gonna bond him out?"

"I was hoping you would know. She never tells me what she's thinking."

"Don't take it personally, kid. She keeps things to herself. Has as long as I've known her. She usually doesn't call me unless there's a fire."

They were on one such fire, a skip named Reuben Alvarez who'd failed on a ten grander three months before. A tip from one of Ruby's many street sources had put Alvarez inside the brick home of one of his girlfriends, a fourteen-year-old jailbait named Lisa, and Ruby had dispatched Brodie to bring him in.

Although the bounty hunter usually worked alone, Ruby had sent David along this time. She'd done that a couple of times before, so he could learn a few things about the business of tracking down and bringing in skips. And there was no doubt he'd learned more about skip-tracing in five months from the ox than he would learn in a lifetime on his own—not that he had any intention of doing this business for a lifetime. Big Jim was the best bounty hunter in the state, if not the entire West. Put him on a skip's trail and the skip was as good as caught. Brodie had been a deep recon man in Vietnam, one of those crazies who operated alone in enemy territory where nobody else dared go. He'd infiltrate Viet Cong positions, read their love letters and marching orders in Vietnamese, and steal away unheard and unseen.

But this trip around, David was convinced his aunt had sent him with Brodie for reasons other than education. Lamprey's twenty-four-hour deadline was drawing near and she didn't want him hanging around lobbying her anymore to bail out Bayne Gibson.

So he and Brodie waited, baking in the early afternoon sun, parked half a block from the house on the opposite side of the street, Brodie's two-year-old maroon Ford LTD pointed away from the target house so it would be less noticeable. Brodie kept vigilance through his field glasses and sang off-key to a Waylon Jennings tape, while David tried to chew on chunks of obtuse legal prose.

David checked his watch. "We've been here two hours, Jim. Maybe the tip was bad." Actually, he was beginning to suspect Alvarez was a ruse, that his aunt had received no such tip and had intentionally sent them on a goose chase.

"Ruby ain't wrong often," Brodie said in his Oklahoma panhandle drawl. He set down his binoculars and bulldozed a chunk out of a cold cheeseburger, the last of three he'd consumed since they'd arrived. The front seat between them was cluttered with handcuffs, shackles, a restraining belt, a heavy duty nightstick-flashlight, empty soft drink cups, and hamburger wrappers. "Where'd she get the tip?" Brodie asked.

"Another girlfriend."

Brodie nodded his massive head. "Then it's probably a good lead. Girlfriends make great snitches. Especially *ex*-girlfriends. Half the time they're scared of 'em, pissed at 'em, or both. Twenty to one she's pissed off he's with another broad."

"It just doesn't make sense the guy would show up here. Wouldn't he figure we'd check the place?"

"People are funny that way, David. They feel safest where it's the least safe. Creatures of habit, I suppose. Especially if there's poontang involved. You'd be surprised how many guys I catch 'cause their popsicles are bigger than their brains."

David looked at his watch again and rubbed the back of his sweaty neck. "Whew, it's hot. How much longer are we going to wait? The guy could be in there the rest of the day."

"We'll see."

"Do you think we should go in after him?"

The thought of actually busting into the house for the guy made David queasy, but it would have been easy for Brodie. Standing six four and 265 pounds—even at age forty-seven, with a salt-and-pepper beard and thinning hair and high blood pressure and a stomach that was beginning to concede to the gravity of time—the bounty hunter could have kicked in the front door and yanked the jumper out by the scruff of the neck. Hell, he could have kicked in the entire front wall.

"Not if I don't have to," said Brodie, eating the last of the cheeseburger.

Despite his size and strength, violence wasn't Big Jim's style. Why risk being hurt or hurting someone else when stealth, cunning, deception, tactical surprise, and speed worked better, he'd told David. Too many bounty hunters—Brodie despised the term; he preferred to say he was in fugitive management—used their brawn instead of their brains. They liked being physical. They enjoyed terrorizing.

But David knew there was another reason Brodie wouldn't kick in the door if Alvarez really was in there, a reason unspoken but no less powerful than his philosophical approach to capturing skips. A young girl was allegedly in the house, and Brodie was always uneasy when females were involved. Ruby complained that he was like a mindless teddy bear around women, and the few occasions she needed a female jumper tracked down she gave the job to bounty hunters who were less gentlemanly.

Brodie leaned back over the seat and peered through his field glasses and began singing to "A Good-Hearted Woman." David returned to his law book but after a few minutes of staring uncomprehendingly at the small print he looked over at Brodie. "You've known my aunt a lot longer than I have, Jim. What do you think she'll do about Gibson?"

Brodie shrugged his block shoulders. "You never know with her. She follows her own sixth sense."

"Yeah. She keeps talking about how Gibson doesn't *feel* right."

"Don't knock it, David. She's got good instincts. I don't mean 'a woman's intuition,' either. Her instincts have a lot of experience behind them."

"I know, I know. 'Go with your gut.' 'Play it by ear.' 'Listen to your heart.' Plays too damn much of that scratchy jazz, is what she does. I'll take logic and common sense any day."

Brodie put down his binoculars and looked hard at David. "I've worked for a lot of bondsmen over the years, David, and Ruby's the best—the best. The guys I end up working for the most are the ones who don't have the good instincts."

David motioned toward the house. "Well, even my aunt's instincts aren't always right."

But it was her instincts that had made her reputation. David still vividly remembered the first day he'd met his aunt. He'd had been in Denver only two months, and was sharing a crowded apartment with three other law students. A morning headline in *The Denver Post* feature section had caught his eye: "Angel of the Outlaws: Bondswoman Follows in Murdered Husband's Footsteps." An odd, slimy business for a woman, he'd thought. He'd read on and quickly came to realize that the successful bondswoman being profiled was the black sheep of his own family, the infamous Ruby Dark who'd left St. Jo so many years ago.

With a rare sense of impulsiveness, he'd gone to see her that very afternoon. A McCoy paying a secret call on a Hatfield. He hadn't been sure what to expect. The two column photo in the article, with Collateral dozing in the background, had portrayed a well-dressed woman of indeterminate age (it wasn't mentioned in the article) in a neat-looking office. But he knew photos could be deceptive. He'd been prepared to find a sleazy, rundown building in some godforsaken part of town. It turned out that while her office wasn't exactly in the high rent district, and that it did sit atop a spay-neuter clinic as the article had wryly noted, it wasn't a dump either. The sanded hardwood floors, clean brick walls, framed posters of jazz festivals, and a brightness in the office had surprised him.

She'd surprised him, too. He, like Bayne Gibson, had expected a Tugboat Annie with tattoos. She was rough around the edges to be sure, but she wasn't the woman painted in black tones by his family over the years. They had hit it off right away. He still wasn't sure why. Like everyone else, he'd been taken with her flamboyance and independence and toughness and spirit. And she'd seemed genuinely moved by his unannounced appearance on her doorstep—even if he was half-kin from the side of the family she knew detested her. But they saw eye-to-eye on little, from politics and food to music and the criminal justice system. Her sloppiness drove him nuts. Opposites attract, he supposed.

She'd shocked him by offering him a job and free board an hour after they'd met. Only later would he come to realize that making quick judgments of people was her *modus operandi.* Not that her judgments were always right. A few days before he introduced himself, she'd fired a bondsman she'd caught ripping off her clients. She needed somebody to help her part time to run the office. Who better than her own half-nephew? She'd even post a $50,000 guarantee bond with the State Insurance Commission for him to become a licensed bondsman.

He'd balked at the idea initially. Good God, he was studying law so that someday he could put away the very people she was bailing out! But she'd been damned persuasive. What better way to learn about the criminal justice system, to see criminals up close? He'd found himself sucked into the logic of it. Besides, he needed the money and a place of his own. After three days of wavering, he'd accepted—with two conditions.

First, his law studies were priority. He'd answer the phones and handle the clerical chores, but if he didn't want to take the time to bond out someone and earn a share of the premium, that was his option. Of course, law school wasn't cheap. Financial aid was tight and his parents were in no financial shape to offer any support but their blessings. He'd found himself scrounging for every dime he could, and he'd ended up bailing out more scumbags than he'd care to remember.

The second condition was that his parents—especially his

father—must never learn that he was working for Ruby. She'd agreed to both terms without hesitation.

To this day, he remained unsure why his aunt had offered him a job and free room . . . Family blood? Guilt? Loneliness? Charity? Whatever her motives, he'd developed a strong sense of loyalty and attachment toward her. That was why he was sitting in the front seat of Big Jim Brodie's car in ninety degree heat.

Suddenly the bounty hunter snapped the binoculars to his eyes. "Target at twelve o'clock high."

David squinted out the rear window to see a tall, thin Hispanic in his mid-twenties stagger out of the house with a young *señorita* who walked with a slight limp.

"That's him!" said Brodie, holding up the mug shot Ruby had given them.

The couple, kissing and laughing hysterically over something known only to them, stumbled to a dark, raggedy Monte Carlo parked on the quiet street and got in. Brodie put his hand on the ignition key, ready to turn on the LTD's powerful engine the moment Alvarez started his car. Instead, the couple sat in the front seat exploring each other's faces. The young girl's head soon disappeared from view and Alvarez laid his head back on the seat.

"Don't hog the binoculars, Jim," David chided.

After a while, she sat up, then both of them slid from view onto the front seat. A small bare foot hooked up over the front seat. Alvarez's head and shoulders suddenly appeared, then disappeared, then appeared again, rhythmically.

"Christ, it's broad daylight!" said David.

Brodie chuckled. "Told you a lotta guys think with their dicks. Come on, let's nail this asshole."

They approached the Monte Carlo on cat's feet. Not that the couple would have heard a tank approaching. The closer Brodie and David got, the louder the heavy breathing and the moans and the grinding of seat springs got. Brodie edged up on the driver's side, motioning to David to circle around on the passenger side. The bounty hunter reached in through the open car window and whacked the man's hairy ass in mid stroke with a heavy flashlight. Alvarez bolted upright so fast he slammed his head into the ceiling and fell back on top of the girl, who began screaming. Brodie yanked open the door just as Alvarez struggled to get up again, his dropped pants hobbling his efforts like ankle chains.

"*¡Quedar poner, amigo!*" Brodie whacked his butt again with the flashlight. Seconds later Alvarez lay atop the sobbing girl, his wrists cuffed behind him.

"Who the fuck are you, man?" Alvarez demanded in clear English, twisting his head toward Brodie.

"The Pope's sex squad. Now lie still." Brodie searched under the car seat and rifled the Hispanic's pants pockets for a weapon.

Alvarez noticed David for the first time, leaning over the passenger window. He craned his neck in his direction. "What the fuck you staring at? You guys cops?"

"Ruby's Bail Bonds," said David.

Alvarez mumbled something in Spanish. The girl was still pinned below him, but her sobbing had turned to whimpering. Her wet brown eyes, as big as dinner plates, looked up imploringly at David.

Brodie pocketed the car keys and a pocket knife, and told Alvarez to slide out of the car.

"My pants, man."

"Your pants are fine."

"I ain't gettin' out without my goddamn pants on."

"You don't have a choice, *amigo*. Slide the fuck out!"

Alvarez sidled his way backwards out of the front seat until he stood in the street facing the car, his pants shackling his ankles. Several neighborhood kids had gathered to watch, giggling but keeping a safe distance. Two men watched from separate doorways, sour-faced and silent.

"Fuck, man, this is shit! This ain't no way to treat me!"

"Don't jump bail next time." Brodie tossed his car keys to David. "Bring the car down. I'll babysit studhammer here."

David pulled the LTD up beside the Monte Carlo. The girl had sat up in the front seat and pulled her underwear and shorts back on. Tears streamed down her face, taking makeup with it, and her entire body trembled. Brodie leaned in the driver's window and said softly, "Go back in the house. Vamoose." Hesitantly, the girl climbed out.

Alvarez yelled at her in Spanish, two or three sentences worth, though David didn't know what he said. When she stood there, frozen, Alvarez yelled louder, in words unmistakable in any language. She turned and fled toward the house.

Brodie shoved Alvarez into the back seat, his pants still bunched around his ankles. He looked across the hot shimmering roof of the LTD at David. "We taking him to city or county?"

"The office. Ruby wants to see him first."

Brodie started to get into the car when David asked, "What would you do, Jim?"

The bounty hunter stood back up. "What would I do about what?"

"About Gibson? Wouldn't you bail him out? I mean, the guy's money in the bank, right? It doesn't take a lot of touchy-feely intuition to figure that out. The guy's not going to skip. Not with all that money and his high-priced lawyers. You should have seen his penthouse, Jim. The place is so damn big you need a golf cart to get around in it."

"Nothing in this business is money in the bank, David. Nothing."

"It's Reed. That guy muddles her thinking. He's convinced her it's too risky."

It wasn't like his aunt to shy away from risk or a good challenge. Maybe her affections for the cop ran deeper than he realized.

They drove off, leaving the driver's door of the Monte Carlo wide open.

"Hey, man, you can't just leave my car like that," yelled Alvarez. "Somebody'll steal it, man."

"Don't sweat it," said Brodie. "It'll probably be somebody you know."

7

Brodie called ahead from his car phone and Ruby met them in the rear parking lot her office shared with the spay-neuter clinic. She leaned through the open driver's window and peered into the back seat where Alvarez sat semi-naked, hunched over in an effort to cover himself up.

"New security procedures, Jim?" she said lightly.

"Yeah, think I'll use it more often."

Alvarez looked up, his face full of rage. "Tell this motherfucker to put my fucking pants back on."

"I see you're as eloquent as ever," said Ruby.

"This sonofabitch is worse 'n a cop. I ain't never had no cop do this to me."

"Why'd you jump, Reuben?"

"I didn't jump, Angel," he said, suddenly contrite. "I just forgot, that's all."

"A ten-grander on a cocaine bust and you just *forgot?* For three months?"

"I been busy." Eyes downcast. "People forget."

"I was good to you, honey. I didn't even charge you a premium—as a favor to your father and a favor to you, for all those tips over the years. I treated you more than fair. Yet you pay me back by skipping on me!"

"You gonna revoke my bond?"

"Damn right I am!"

"Can't I talk to you straight up, Angel?"

"Too late for that, hon. You shoulda called me three

months ago. We coulda worked something out. Not now. Now you're going to jail."

"Fuck you!"

Ruby straightened up and said disgustedly, "Get him outta there."

Brodie yanked Alvarez out of the car with one hand and stood him up, hands cuffed behind him, his privates hanging in the summer breeze.

"Hitch up his pants, Jim," said Ruby. "As much as he deserves it, we can't parade him to jail like that."

A tear-streaked woman sniffling over a Pekinese cradled in her arms walked past them toward the clinic, never so much as glancing toward the half-naked man.

Ruby asked David the time and he told her it was 3:47. "Let's skip the jail for now and take him straight to Judge Lambert's chambers," she said.

"Why?"

"Because the judge gave me ninety days to track down this bastard and I want to make sure he knows I did my job. Then the next time I need to ask him for more time, he'll remember that Ruby Dark keeps her word."

They jaywalked across 13th, through early rush hour traffic. Drivers gawked and honked at the Pied Piper processional as Ruby, in a green dress, high heels, and a black bolero-style hat, led the way. Brodie walked a few feet behind her, his huge hand pushing Alvarez along every few steps. David brought up the rear.

The shortest route to the City and County Building would have been to cut kitty-corner through the Police Administration plaza to 14th and Cherokee. But Ruby chose a more circuitous route, down 13th to Delaware Street and then along Bondsmen Row—in order to let her competition know she got her man, conjectured David.

"I'm gonna come see you when I get out, Angel!" yelled Alvarez, puffing to stay up with Ruby, whose angry strides, even in heels, had put her twenty feet ahead of the rest of them.

"I'll look forward to that, honey," she yelled back over her shoulder. "You know where I am. You come see me any time."

From Delaware they swung up 14th behind the Denver Mint. As they neared the City and County Building, its clock tower rising into a clear blue sky, a Sheriff's bus pulled away, headed to county jail, its load of prisoners gawking out the screened windows at Ruby and her entourage. This was better than paid advertising, David knew: DON'T SKIP ON RUBY DARK.

Inside the City and County Building, David and Brodie and their prisoner waited in the echoey granite hallway while Ruby went into the judge's fourth-floor chambers to do her good deed for the day. She'd barely left when a familiar middle-aged man, who looked as though he'd hijacked a few too many Hostess Twinkie trucks in his youth, lumbered toward them.

"Shit!" David muttered under his breath. Of all the people in the city, why did he have to run into the one man his aunt detested more than anyone—and in her circle of acquaintances anyone included a fair number of murderers, rapists, child molesters, and general all-around assholes.

"Jumper?" asked Cadillac Johnson, nodding his large squat head toward Alvarez.

"Was," said David firmly.

"Big Jim doesn't miss often, does he?" said Cadillac. "Best in the business, no question about it."

He offered this praise without actually looking at Brodie, keeping his shiny damp face turned toward David. It was false praise, too, David knew, for Brodie refused to work for Cadillac because of some conflict the two had had well before David had arrived on the scene.

Johnson's sausage-fingered right hand, surprisingly strong, gripped David's arm and steered him out of earshot of Brodie and Alvarez. His breath came in violent heaves, as if he'd just finished running up all four flights of worn granite steps. David worried that Cadillac would have a stroke right there. They'd need a bulldozer to push him out of the hallway. "Hey, Piper, I hear you got a million dollar fish on the line. You gonna reel him in?"

The two other unfortunate times they'd crossed paths Cadillac had gotten his name wrong too. Which was just as well.

At least Cadillac couldn't slander his real name as he'd done with Ruby.

"Who are you talking about?" said David, trying to put puzzlement into his voice.

Cadillac grinned like a Cheshire cat and squeezed David's arm. "Come on, son, don't blow smoke at C.J. Every bondsman in town knows Ruby's got Bayne Gibson by his gold balls. It may be a big city, but it's a small town. How's he checking out?"

"You'll have to talk to Ruby about that."

Cadillac laughed, then his thick lips suddenly turned grim. "Look, son, just between you and me, I'd warn your aunt to drop golden boy like a rabid dog."

David hesitated for a moment. He knew you didn't talk clients with other bondsmen, especially with a competitor like Cadillac Johnson, and especially about a case involving a million dollars. His aunt was skeptical enough about Gibson, and talking about it with Cadillac would only increase the chances that the bond would slip through their fingers. Still, curiosity twisted his better judgment and he heard himself asking, "Why?"

Cadillac lowered his head still closer. His hot sour breath burned David's neck. "Straight talk, Piper—the guy's too high a risk. Me and my insurance company wouldn't touch him with a ten-foot pole. No way in hell."

"Why's he too high a risk?" David asked against his will, as though the man had drawn the question out of him like a magnet. Why was Cadillac so leery of Gibson? Did he have a "hunch," too, like his aunt?

"Well, son, the fact is the man's got too much money," whispered Cadillac, as if no one else knew Gibson was stinking rich.

"*Too* much money?"

"Hell, yes. Take that fancy villa down in Mexico. Around four, five hundred grand, right? Employs a full-time staff of five, including a gardener just to tend the fucking bougainvillea. A guy could live damn comfortably in a villa like that the rest of his life, drinking tequila shots and fucking *señoritas*. And I hear he's got a coupla mil stashed in one of them offshore banks. Grand Cayman, ain't it? You do know about that, don't you? You ever try to pry bail money outta one of them banks? No, siree, the way I see it, the guy's guilty as sin, and there ain't nothing to keep him from skipping town and cooling his heels down south. Beats a six-by-ten in Cañon City. You ever try to bring a guy back from down south?''

Instinctively, David shook his head, then regretted it. Responding to Cadillac only encouraged the man, like responding, even negatively, to a persistent salesman on the phone. As long as they can keep you on the line . . .

But the truth of the matter was he'd never even been to Mexico and he had no desire to go. He'd heard the war stories from the bounty hunters who'd gone behind the Tortilla Curtain. It was a dangerous place. Fugitive warrants issued in the United States were as worthless in Mexico as pesos on a New York subway. Bounty hunters stopped by Mexican authorities were as likely to be jailed on kidnapping charges as they were to be helped.

He remembered a story Ruby had told him about Big Jim bringing back a Mexican national, a big-time drug dealer who'd skipped on a $150,000 federal bond her husband had posted. It took Brodie a week to find the guy, somewhere near Veracruz, and another week to snatch him out from under the noses of his bodyguards. Word was the dealer had high connections, not only with the federales but with the U.S. Border Patrol. So Brodie smuggled the skip out on one of the wetback routes, carrying the man bound and gagged across the shallow Rio Grande in the dead of night.

''And I heard his business really ain't as healthy as it looks,'' insisted Cadillac in a voice that, like gum on the bottom of a shoe, wouldn't go away. ''Radio stations ain't the money machines they once were. He's running a paper empire, is what I hear. Word is, this dickhead's gonna jump the first chance he gets.''

David pulled himself away from the bondsman's grip and his sour breath, ashamed that he was fraternizing with the enemy. He caught Brodie watching them intently. ''Why are you telling me this?''

''Outta professional courtesy.''

David cocked his head skeptically at the bondsman.

Professional courtesy! Cadillac was about as professional as a cockroach. He was the epitome of the slimy bondsman David had seen portrayed in movies and books over the years. If his aunt had her way, Cadillac would be posting his own bond. The litany of abuses she claimed he'd committed, some of them outright illegal, included paying kickbacks to cops and court officers and attorneys for referrals, selling drugs and fencing stolen goods given to him as collateral, falsifying surety documents, bribing witnesses and court officials for clients, and hiring bounty hunters who were just this side of Mafia thugs.

None of this had ever been proved in a court of law or sufficiently documented in order for the State Insurance Commissioner to revoke Cadillac's license. Indeed, Cadillac had never been arrested for these or any other offenses as far as David was aware. But Ruby swore that Cadillac had committed them and God knows what other abominations. David, knowing his aunt, and having been around Cadillac on more than one occasion, believed her.

"Hey, I know me and your aunt ain't too chummy," said Cadillac, "but I respect her, I really do—despite the malicious lies she spreads about me. I'd really hate to see her go under on this one. I really would. The bonding business would be as dull as hell without Angel around."

Suddenly Cadillac stepped back, his bulbous eyes alert. David turned to see his aunt emerge from Judge Lambert's chambers.

"What the hell do you want?" she snapped at Cadillac.

"Just passing by, Angel, just passing by."

"Then keep on passing."

Cadillac threw up his hands in mock imploration. "As feisty as ever, Angel, as feisty as ever. Just talkin' to the kid about the big fish you caught."

"Go peddle your diseases somewhere else."

The fat bondsman gave a sharp little bow and scurried off.

"What was he saying about Gibson?" she asked David.

He shrugged. "Nothing much."

"Cadillac never wants just nothing much."

"He was just nosing around." Then he hastily added, "I didn't tell him anything."

Ruby humphed. "He and Majestic Insurance would *love* to get their grubby little paws on Gibson."

She turned toward Alvarez and motioned her head toward the judge's chambers. "The judge wants to see your ass." Brodie marched Alvarez into the room. Ruby looked down the hall just as Cadillac disappeared into an elevator. "What exactly did he say to you?"

"He'd heard we might bail Gibson out. He wanted to know how reliable a bond he was."

"That's it?"

"He seemed to know exactly how many people work at Gibson's villa. And he knew about the two million in the offshore bank."

David didn't mention Cadillac's misgivings about Gibson as a client risk. Why bother her with more doubts?

"He's up to something," she said, visibly agitated.

"I didn't tell him anything, Aunt Ruby," he reiterated.

"You don't need to tell him anything. He finds out. He has his ways. That's one credit I'll give the prick. He's a resourceful sonofabitch. He's been poking around, David. He smells the bond and he wants it."

Maybe she was right. Maybe that really was Cadillac's motive, and he was doing a little number on him. Still, he thought she was being a little too paranoid about the whole thing. Granted, the man was a jerk, but . . .

"He can't just steal Gibson from you, can he?" said David. "He can't—"

"No, he can't," she said. A fierce look of determination flared on her face, her eyes still riveted in the direction Cadillac had disappeared. "He can't because we're going to post it."

8

David and Ruby settled into the back row of arraignment and advisements Courtroom 12T located directly below city jail. The cops had been busy the night before, and the wooden pews were jammed with anxious friends and relatives of those awaiting their appearance before the Honorable Judge Andrew T. Slater. Waiting with them was a phalanx of reporters, photographers, and TV cameramen. Bayne Gibson, Jr., was still hot news.

David nervously combed the large holding cell off to the left of the judge's bench. Twenty-five to thirty men were crowded into the cell. Some talked among themselves, or laughed. They'd been through the routine before. Others sat silent with heads bowed or stared vacant-eyed through the huge plate glass window onto the courtroom. Three women defendants sat in a pew just outside the holding cell.

David finally spotted Gibson. He was huddled in conference with a man in a western-yoked gray suit who had shoulder-length, prematurely gray hair and a salt-and-pepper beard. David recognized him instantly as Randall Taylor, Gibson's defense attorney. He'd seen Taylor several times prowling the gloomy halls of the City and County Building with his mountain man face, exotic-skin cowboy boots, intense black eyes, and a body that could bench press small foreign cars. While he may have looked like he belonged in a previous century, "Rasputin," as Taylor's cohorts called him behind his back, was already a legend for taking on high-profile "loser" cases no one else would touch—and winning.

Despite Gibson's and Taylor's reputations—or perhaps because of them—Judge Slater bestowed no preferential treatment on them. Both men waited as a string of defendants, many of them looking malnourished and sullen, some dressed in street clothes, others in jail-issued green or orange jumpsuits, paraded one by one from the holding cell to a podium in front of the judge. They were separated from the spectators by a waist-high wooden railing. They answered meekly to charges ranging from drunk driving to possessing a controlled substance. Most pled "no contest," and, after the judge inquired if there were any extenuating circumstances surrounding the commission of the crime, which typically drew transparently lame excuses, he imposed a fine or jail time, or both. For those who pled "not guilty," he set bail and a trial date, and authorized appointment of a public defender if necessary.

The majority of the defendants stood alone before the judge, but a few consulted with private attorneys. Several were represented by an attorney from the public defender's office, a harried-looking thin man who didn't appear old enough to vote, and who, under the withering gaze and impatient tongue of King Andy, struggled to read the notes his fellow PDs had scribbled on the jackets of the case files. David sympathized with the PD. He wondered how well he would hold up some day as a prosecuting attorney under the whip cracking of the King Andys.

As the string of accused went on forever, David grew restless. He scanned the crowded courtroom, half expecting to see a dejected Cadillac Johnson standing in the wings, but Blimpie was nowhere in sight. Finally Judge Slater read from his docket beneath a small brass lamp, in the same emotionless tone he'd used all morning, "People of the State of Colorado versus Bayne C. Gibson, Jr."

Escorted by an armed, brown-shirted sheriff's deputy, a visibly shaken Gibson shuffled from the holding cell to the podium, his pale face downcast to avoid the rape of the clicking cameras. Taylor, who had left the holding cell earlier, came forward through a gate in the railing obligingly swung open by a deputy, and met his client at the podium in an arrival as perfectly timed as a well-executed pass pattern.

Moments later, with far less fanfare, a short, dark-suited man walked through the gate and stood to one side. "Who's the guy?" David asked his aunt. "Lew Cady," came her whispered reply. Cady was a senior district attorney, and one of their biggest and best guns.

The courtroom had grown noisy after Gibson was called forward, and Judge Slater gaveled for silence. He was a judge who tolerated no breach of courtroom etiquette. He'd already banished a chatty teenager and a mother with a squalling baby.

King Andy leaned forward on the bench, his large body evident even below the black robes, and directed his heavy-lidded gaze towards Taylor and Gibson. "All right, counselor, I'll entertain your motion for bail reduction. But it better be good—and brief."

Taylor, in a baritone voice, argued eloquently and forcefully, though anything but briefly, that his client had lived in Denver for over fifteen years, that he had deep personal as well as financial roots in the community, that he was a respected CEO of a major corporation, that he was well recognized for his numerous philanthropic contributions to local civic and charitable organizations, that his police record was spotless except for two minor traffic tickets, that he had cooperated fully with investigating authorities, and as this was Mr. Gibson's first arrest, leniency seemed the appropriate approach to—

"This is a capital offense, Mr. Taylor," interrupted King Andy, "not a simple traffic violation. Leniency has no bearing on a charge of murder." He looked in the direction of the DA and said, "Mr. Cady, I'll hear the State on bail."

Lew Cady, resting both hands on the podium like a preacher leaning over his Sunday flock, argued that the defendant had substantial assets deposited in various financial institutions outside of the United State, that he could flee to a comfortable lifestyle in Mexico, and that in light of the severity of the charges the risk of the defendant fleeing was overwhelming.

"Your Honor!" interjected Taylor, leaning across the DA

to speak into the microphone. Taylor began reciting chapter and verse the state laws regarding oppressive bonds, but the judge cut him short again.

"Enough, counselor. I'm well versed on state statutes regarding the setting of bail! The issue before us is how does the court best ensure that Mr. Gibson remain in this jurisdiction in order to fully comply with all court appearances and judicial procedures."

"Your Honor, I—"

King Andy visibly flared. "You already hold the record for the most contempt citations of any attorney in the state, Mr. Taylor. Let's not add to the record today. Motion for reduction of bail is hereby denied."

Taylor patted a gloomy Gibson reassuringly on his hunched shoulders as a deputy led him back to the holding cell.

The request for court approval of a bonding agency went more smoothly, but Taylor was not involved this time. Ruby's own attorney, Cyndee Valone, a tall black-haired woman David found as feisty as his aunt, argued her case before King Andy. The judge initially expressed surprise that the defendant wasn't posting his own bond and then his misgivings that a cash bondsman, not a bondsman underwritten by an insurance company, was being asked to post a bond so large. His misgivings clearly were tempered, however, by the fact that the bondsman was Ruby Dark. In fact, when Valone began to sing the praises of Ruby's Bail Bonds the judge silenced her with a raised hand. "Can the speech, counselor. The court knows well the reputation of Mrs. Dark. I'm sure she can speak quite well for herself. Is she in the courtroom?"

King Andy searched the courtroom as heads in the pews began to twist and turn for signs of the legendary Ruby Dark. Ruby didn't wave or stand, but merely waited until the judge spotted her. With one of her trademark hats on, it didn't take long. He wiggled a finger at her. "Please approach the bench, Mrs. Dark."

David felt his stomach tighten as he watched his aunt join Valone at the podium. Valone whispered something in her ear before King Andy said, "I consider request by counsel for you to serve as bondsman in this matter to be highly irregular, Mrs. Dark.''

Despite the gravity in his voice, King Andy couldn't restrain the quiver of a smile in his face, the first smile David had seen all morning.

Ruby said, ''There is no state statute preventing a cash bondsman from posting any size bond, Your Honor. Approval or disapproval is at the court's discretion.''

''That's correct, Mrs. Dark. But the court has set a substantial bail. I have some concerns that in the event the defendant should choose to flee the court's jurisdiction and remain at large, that your agency would be capable of making prompt and full restitution of the face amount of the bond to the court. Frankly, some of my colleagues on the bench are lax in their enforcement of this area of the law. They allow too many bondsmen to drag out the restitution process. I, however, am much more inclined to operate in the fashion of the federal courts, which is to expect prompt and full restitution upon failure to appear.''

''Your Honor, I can pledge adequate personal assets to the court.'' Ruby held up a thick white envelope in her hand. ''I also will provide the court with documentation showing that the defendant, Mr. Gibson, has legally obligated his substantial personal and corporate assets to our firm in the event that he fails to appear.''

Did his aunt really have enough personal assets to pledge to the court for a $1 million bond? Had she made that much money since her husband had been murdered? Had he been that wealthy? Or had the money come from somewhere deep in her past, as those many rumors had hinted at?

But it wasn't just the money that surprised David. It was the fact that she'd apparently kept her assets in her name. Many bondsmen play three-card monte with their personal assets by putting them in somebody else's name. That way, if a big bond goes sour, it's more difficult for the courts or the insurance companies to pick the assets clean to satisfy restitution.

King Andy summoned Ruby before the bench, and she approached. She wore a dark, well-tailored suit, the kind that didn't always sit well with clients who didn't like seeing their premiums going toward expensive clothes, but which played well before a judge who needed convincing that she was financially secure enough to back a $1 million bond.

Ruby handed an envelope of documentation to the judge and stood resolutely in front of the bench while he perused the papers. Twice he asked her questions. After several minutes, King Andy covered the microphone with his hand and leaned forward to whisper something to Ruby, who leaned forward to reply. Spectators cocked ears in vain hope of catching the private conversation. Ruby nodded at something King Andy said and the judge broke into a large smile and a small chuckle.

Ruby returned to the podium beside Cyndee Valone. Judge Slater said, "The court grants permission to Ruby's Bail Bonds to be the bonding agency of record for Bayne C. Gibson."

I hope the hell we're right, thought David.

A few minutes later, Lamprey and Taylor caught up with Ruby, David, and Valone just outside the bonding office in the jail lobby. Taylor ignored Ruby and David for the moment, staring instead at Valone. It was the closest that David had ever stood to Rasputin, and his eyes were indeed penetrating.

"I didn't know you did work for Ruby, Miss Valone," he said.

"We're old friends."

"I hadn't heard your name in a while. I understood that after that . . . unfortunate . . . Lefavi case you'd given up the practice of law. I guess my sources were incorrect."

Valone looked him unblinkingly and said, "I'm still around. If you need better sources, though, feel free to call me any time."

Taylor turned his icy smile on Ruby. "You acquitted yourself well in there, Ruby. What exactly did Judge Slater say to you off the record?"

"Privileged information, counselor."

Taylor laughed but his eyes didn't. Lamprey, looking impatient with this banter, withdrew an envelope from his inside coat pocket and held it in front of Ruby. "Here is your premium, *Mzzzz* Dark. A certified check for one hundred and fifty thousand dollars." He held the check a moment longer before thrusting it at her and adding sarcastically, "Not bad for a couple of days' work."

Ruby put the check in her purse without examination or comment. She looked at Lamprey, then at Taylor. This time David had no trouble discerning the intent of the expression on his aunt's face. "Your client is free and in your hands now, gentlemen. If he gets out of your hands, I won't be a very pleasant person to deal with."

"Everything will be fine, Ruby," Taylor assured her.

"I've heard that one before, honey."

9

With Gibson out on bail and back in his penthouse with his fish, David tried once again to concentrate on his law studies and re-establish some semblance of order and balance in his life. It was a futile effort. The reading load had grown onerous, the professors more surly, and the material increasingly impenetrable. Did he really need to study archaic property rules created in the Middle Ages?

And the office was inundated with business calls, particularly the small potatoes his aunt allowed him to bail out on his own. Maybe they figured they deserved to be bailed out by the agency that had bailed out a multimillionaire. Or maybe the rash of calls was due to the fact that the moon had turned full.

Whatever the reason, his studies grew increasingly problematic. An exam in Civil Procedure—an essay analyzing some of the prominent ideas on jurisdiction raised in the case of *Pennoyer v. Neff*—proved a disaster. It should have been a snap. The class had analyzed the case ad nauseam. Yet when he'd opened his Blue Book he'd become disoriented, his skull turned to mush. Halfway through the exam he'd torn up the crap he'd written and started over. By then, it was too late.

While it was tempting to blame the publicity surrounding the Gibson case, or the full moon, David knew that the real reason for his academic failures was his growing anxiety about Bayne Gibson's approaching preliminary hearing. It had been *he* who had persuaded his aunt to post Gibson's bond. He'd overcome her "bad vibes" at the penthouse and Morgan Reed's misgivings. Sure, she'd made the final decision. Their chance encounter with Cadillac Johnson at the courthouse had no doubt sparked her decision. Her rivalry with the fat man was too compelling for her to ignore. But David had laid the groundwork with impeccable lawyerly logic. Now, the closer the prelim the less certain he was that Gibson was a sure bet. It was one thing to post $17,000 for an albino rapist, it was another to risk a bond that could drive his aunt into bankruptcy—and himself out of law school. If Gibson were to skip . . .

His anxiety was heightened when Big Jim Brodie called Ruby just two days before the millionaire's scheduled prelim.

By chance, David was at his aunt's loft apartment when the call came in. She'd spent most of that morning there, which was unusual, and shortly before noon she'd called him to bring over some papers on another case.

He'd parked in the Union Station lot directly across the street from her loft. The large red brick building had been constructed in 1896 as a factory for manufacturing mining equipment. Later, it had been used for making sugar beet refining machinery. The faded lettering on the water tower on the roof read DOBSON MANUFACTURING, INC. Ninety years after its construction, including two decades of drawing transients and the homeless for sleepovers, the building had been converted into pricy residential lofts. Coffee bars and restaurants and jazz joints and art galleries had sprung up in the area, part of a revitalization of Denver's historic lower downtown, or LoDo as its pioneer denizens called it.

Amid the almost nauseating aroma of a nearby microbrewery, he made his way up to the fifth floor in an elevator lined with acid-washed metal plates. He walked down the hushed carpeted hallway. The doorways were few.

"Come on in," she said as she whisked the papers out of his hand and headed toward a dark green leather couch in the middle of the loft. "I may need you to deliver these for me in a few minutes."

He shut the door and wandered into the huge, cluttered, yet airy room. It was only the second time he'd been to her loft, and he was still taken by the fourteen-foot-high timbered ceiling, red brick walls, and the massive hardwood floor stripped from a western Colorado high school gym that still bore splotches of color from the foul lines. The room was crammed with contemporary furniture, stands of large leafy plants, and bookcases filled mostly with biographies and jazz histories. A white baby grand piano stood against the north wall below a large abstract painting of vivid reds and greens done in bold brush strokes by a local female artist. A similar, smaller painting by the same artist hung on the opposite wall. According to his aunt, the two paintings made her the artist's biggest collector. A kitchen work station and a dining table formed another part of the large room, though he suspected they were rarely used. Both the table and counter surfaces were littered with stacks of books, magazines, and old newspapers. Not a dirty dish in sight.

Only her bedroom and bathroom were physically sealed off, the bathroom behind a long curved glass-brick wall. He'd used it the last time he was here. Everything was black marble, with a jacuzzi tub and a gas fireplace.

The phone rang.

"Answer it for me, will you, David."

"Sure," he said, surprised the phone wasn't at her side.

It rang again. Now if he could just find it. The phone was on the fifth ring before he located a red cordless lying behind a plant on a table near the piano. It was Brodie.

"She's pretty busy, Jim," he said.

"Tell her it's about Gibson."

David tried to read the bounty hunter's voice. "A problem?"

"Not really. But I need to talk to her about him."

A chill shot down David's back.

Not really? That was the kind of equivocal answer people give just before they tell you that you're fired or you've contracted AIDS or the stock market just fell into the basement. Sometimes Brodie could be as maddeningly laconic as Ruby.

Big Jim had kept loose tabs on Gibson since the millionaire had been released on bond. It was an unusual assignment for a bounty hunter, but then $1 million was an unusual bond.

According to Brodie, Gibson had gone about his business as usual, or at least as usual as one might expect for a man charged with first-degree murder. He'd met nearly every day with his defense team, spent time at his corporate headquarters located at the radio station where Kray had broadcast his vitriolic brand of talk radio, and worked out for hours on end at the Denver Athletic Club. There'd been no obvious signs of a man preparing to skip.

David cupped the mouthpiece and told Ruby what Brodie wanted. She took the phone immediately and began pacing the floor, sipping a glass of iced tea.

David tinkled on the piano keys, but kept his ears cocked. Sheet music full of thick notes lay open. He flipped to the cover. *On Green Dolphin Street.* He'd noticed a lot of sheet music strewn around the house. Did she play?

"What'd he do then?" he suddenly heard her say. After a pause, she said something else but he couldn't catch her words. She stopped in front of one of the narrow, arched windows that looked onto the rooftop of another building and into an alley below. She looked down as she listened. Looked at what, he didn't know, and didn't care. He remembered what she'd told him the first time he'd visited the loft, after she'd given him the grand tour and he'd commented on the rather depressing view and didn't she wish the loft was on the other side of the building looking onto the mountain peaks of the Front Range? No, she had intentionally chosen this side. Not because all the mountain-side lofts were already taken, which they weren't, or that the alley-side was cheaper, which it was, but because postcard views of the mountains bored her. She liked the humanity of the alley, the changing scenes. He presumed that meant drunks throwing up and hookers giving guys $30 blow jobs.

"Any talk on the street?" Ruby said.

David tried to read the expression on her face, looking anxiously for some sign of alarm. But she remained enigmatic.

"Okay, stick with him. I'll get David to help you."

When she hung up, David said, "He sounded worried about Gibson."

"He wasn't. But I want you guys to stick to Gibson like a horny dog on a pant leg. Tuck him into bed the next two nights and make sure he shows up for his prelim."

Her last sentence faded as she walked into her bedroom. David followed a few steps and then stopped. The door and its frame once belonged to the manufacturing company's walk-in safe. The renovator had built the bedroom wall around the six-inch-thick frame.

Ruby reappeared and handed him a business card and the paperwork he'd brought her earlier. "Drop this off at this lawyer's office. His secretary's expecting you."

David didn't care right now about a lousy two-bit arsonist. "Jim's been watching Gibson, Aunt Ruby. Why suddenly the full-time babysitting?"

"'Cause this is when defendants get real skittish. Especially virgins like Gibson. Hell, the judge could even decide to revoke bail. Taylor will have told Gibson that."

David felt his stomach roll. "Should we be worried?"

"No. But I'm not going to gamble a million bucks to find out I'm wrong. Call it insurance. Al always told me, 'Make bail with your guts . . . but keep it with your head.' "

Yeah, but Al's dead, David thought nervously as he rode the elevator down.

10

The call came in from Brodie at 9:08 A.M. according to David's watch.

The bounty hunter had not seen Gibson leave The Polo Club for his nine o'clock preliminary hearing. No early morning run, no Grand Cherokee exiting the parking garage, nothing. The doorman hadn't seen him either.

Within minutes Ruby confirmed from the court bailiff that Gibson had not yet shown up. The millionaire didn't answer the phone at his penthouse or his office, and he'd not been seen at the athletic club.

Fifteen minutes later Ruby and David were on the fourth floor hallway of the City and County Building. On the way over, David had prayed that by some miracle Gibson had slipped by Brodie and the doorman and would be at the courthouse when they arrived. But the moment he spotted the clutch of reporters and photographers and TV cameramen surrounding Randall Taylor, David knew that today would not be a day for miracles.

"Where the hell's Gibson?" demanded Ruby, wading into the press corps to face Taylor.

The attorney, one arm occupied with a bulging black briefcase, threw up his free hand to still her voice. "As I was just telling these gentlemen, Ruby, I'm sure Bayne will be here momentarily."

"You know that for a fact, honey?"

Taylor glanced at his wristwatch. "It's only nine-twenty."

"What's he doing, jogging over in his three-piece suit and wing tips?"

Several reporters laughed and furiously scribbled notes.

Taylor steered Ruby out of the press feeding area. "Let's try to keep this discussion *in camera*, Ruby," he said, struggling to keep his massive voice subdued.

She shrugged off his hand. "The hell I will, Taylor. You may be out a fat fee if your client doesn't show up, but I could be out of business and my home."

Taylor said, "I sympathize with your concerns, Ruby, but I'm sure there's a logical explanation for his tardiness."

"Like what? Like he suddenly decided to run a goddamn marathon this morning, that he just *forgot* that he's facing murder one and he's out on a million dollar bond and that the judge would like to speak to his ass about this matter?"

"I'm not trying to tell you anything but the facts as I know them."

"Which doesn't amount to a puddle of mouse piss!"

The hallway had begun to fill with potential jurors waiting to be ushered into the various neighboring courtrooms. Most stood chatting in small knots, balancing Styrofoam cups of coffee and looking bored or slightly apprehensive about the solemn duty they were about to perform. A few sprawled on the floor, open newspapers draped across their laps. Ruby's angry voice had turned several heads toward them. Taylor's diamond-hard eyes scanned the hallway, then said softly, "I need to go back in to ask the judge for a brief continuance. We'll speak in a few minutes, Ruby."

The attorney disappeared behind the tall frosted glass doors of Court Room 17. "William O. Benson, Judge" was etched in thick black letters. Benson was a fair judge, David knew, but a tough one. He would not tolerate Gibson's absence for long.

A few minutes later, a worried-looking E. Ezzard Lamprey arrived at the courtroom, about the time Taylor emerged from behind the doors. The two men spoke in hushed conversation, fended off reporters, and came over to Ruby, who stood in a shaft of light that spilled through a grungy window overlooking an air shaft.

"The judge gave us a continuance until ten-thirty," Taylor

said triumphantly, as if he'd won a major legal battle.

"Swell. Your legal skills truly astound me, hon. That gives us another whole hour to watch our ship sink."

Taylor smiled tightly. "I'm sure Bayne will be here by—"

"You aren't sure of shit!" She raked both men with a cold stare. "Either of you talk to Gibson this morning?"

Neither had.

"Anybody check his penthouse?"

Lamprey said he'd just arrived from there. He'd gone through every room and found no sign of him, though the four-wheel drive was still parked in the garage.

"When did'ya last talk to Gibson?"

"I really don't appreciate this cross-examination," snapped Lamprey.

"Get used to it, honey. I'm just getting started. I'll cross-examine the damn mayor if it'll help me find the sonofabitch. Did you talk to Gibson last night?"

David knew she knew the answer, or at least the truth, since they'd kept Gibson under tight surveillance for the last thirty-six hours. He'd personally watched Gibson and Lamprey eat dinner together at Strings on Seventeenth, and Gibson return alone to his penthouse about 7:45. That had been the last time anyone had seen him.

"We had dinner together," said the attorney. "Around six o'clock."

Chalk up a rare one for truth.

"You talk about the prelim?"

Lamprey's raised eyebrows threw the warning that she was treading very close to client confidentiality. "Only in the broadest of terms."

"Did you advise him to skip?"

"That's an outrageous question!"

"So humor me."

"I advised him of no such thing."

"Was he thinking of skipping? He drop any hints?"

"Definitely not! Bayne was quite confident about the outcome of the preliminary hearing."

"What about his voice, his demeanor?"

Lamprey was momentarily distracted as two men in green

jumpsuits shackled together shuffled down the hallway behind a sheriff's deputy. His eyes were still riveted on them when he finally replied. "He was nervous—as anyone would be in that situation. But as I said, he was quite confident about the outcome. He is, after all, completely and unequivocally innocent."

"What about suicide?"

Lamprey looked appalled. "Kill himself? Bayne? No, no, most certainly not."

"He struck me as a weak, frightened man," said Ruby. "The fear of facing the judge and the press, and the possibility of a lengthy jail stretch could have been too much. People—even innocent people—snap. I've seen it happen before."

Lamprey shook his head. "No, no, I'm quite confident that Bayne did not kill himself."

"Then how do you explain his disappearance?"

The attorney bristled. "I have no explanation. Nor do I have any obligation to supply one to you. I would have thought you would have made certain he was here!"

"I run a bail bonding business, honey, not a baby-sitting service." She motioned her head toward Taylor. "Ask God's gift to law here who's supposed to make sure his client shows up for all court appearances."

David knew his aunt was not about to let on that they'd put Gibson under surveillance. Lawyers hear that, they start expecting bondsmen to baby-sit all the time. Too many attorneys took advantage of bondsmen as it was.

"When did you last talk to your client?" she asked Taylor.

"Last night on the phone."

"What time was that?"

"Nine-fifteen."

"You *sure* about the time?" asked Ruby.

"Quite sure. I have a very accurate timepiece."

A $5,000 watch if the gossip was accurate.

"Oh, yes, I forgot," said Ruby. "For billing purposes. All successful lawyers live life in fifteen-minute increments. Tell me, do you guys have sex by the quarter-hour?"

Neither man responded

"What'd you talk about?" Ruby asked Taylor.

"We reviewed the different scenarios that might occur this morning. I reiterated what courtroom and what time and who the presiding judge would be."

"Describe his mood."

"Upbeat. In fact, he seemed surprisingly calm on the phone. Very confident."

"You call him or he call you?"

"He called me."

"Where from?"

"His penthouse."

"You know that for a fact?"

"Yes. He said he'd just finished feeding his fish. He went on quite some time about them, as a matter of fact. He was concerned about who would take care of them if he went back to jail."

"But he could have called from his office at the radio station. Or from anywhere else for that matter."

Taylor suddenly looked wary and alert, as if suspecting Ruby to spring some sort of trap. "I'm not sure I . . ."

"You can't say with certainty that Gibson called you from his penthouse."

Taylor was temporarily at a rare loss for words. "I can't . . . no . . . I suppose I can't. Obviously I wasn't at his place to confirm that he was making the phone call to me from where he said he was."

What was his aunt thinking? wondered David. Had Gibson entered The Polo Club at 7:45 that night only to slip out the back less than an hour and a half later? And if so, why call Taylor at all?

"Do you think he was suicidal?"

"Absolutely not."

Ruby glowered at both lawyers. "When I find his ass, he'll wish he *had* committed suicide."

At 10:33 A.M., the patience of Judge William O. Benson officially expired. He revoked bond, automatically bound the case over to District Court for trial, and issued a bench warrant for Bayne C. Gibson, Jr., for failure to appear on charges of murder in the first degree. He also entered a judgment against Ruby's Bail Bonds to pay the forfeited bond, and gave the company thirty days in which to locate and return the defendant or show cause why it should not make full restitution to the court in the amount of $1 million.

11

David could count on both hands the number of hours he slept during the next three days. Classes were skipped, case studies went unread, briefs went unwritten. But he knew where his loyalty—and his guilt—lay. As painful as it would be, if he fell too far behind in his studies he could drop out for the semester and start again. But his aunt had no such option. They had to find Bayne C. Gibson, Jr., and find him soon, or she would be out of business.

They had one element in their favor. Gibson had been gone at most twelve to fourteen hours. That was far better notice than usual. Bondsmen often didn't learn of a skip until the mail carrier dropped off a registered letter from court notifying them of a defendant's failure to appear and that they were to show cause within thirty days of why they should not make full restitution of the bond. Often the scheduled court appearance was days before—even weeks or months if the court bureaucracy really screwed up. Even when court notification was prompt, the defendant might have skipped long before the appearance date. Sometimes a skip's attorney would alert the bondsman to an FTA, but defense attorneys were notoriously slow in their notification—if they bothered at all.

Despite the quick jump on Gibson, tracking down anyone who wanted to disappear, especially someone with substantial financial resources, was not easy. Gibson could already be soaking up rays at his Mexican villa. Det. Jason Zechman, the lead detective of the major case squad that had been assembled originally to investigate Royce Kray's murder, wasn't very cooperative with Ruby. But he did tell her they had canvased the airport and car rental agencies, alerted the airlines, put out an APB to the surrounding Western states, and notified Mexican authorities.

Christ, thought David, if all those damn cops couldn't find Gibson, how the hell would he and Ruby and Brodie track him down?

They tried anyway. They made dozens of phone calls and chased leads all over the city. They talked to Gibson's friends and business acquaintances, checked out places he frequented, such as athletic clubs and favorite restaurants, and tracked down tips from informants. None of the leads panned out. At one point, working on a tip, David and Brodie raided a third-floor room in a crummy lower downtown hotel, but all they caught was an executive having a nooner with his secretary. By Day Three, David was so exhausted he fell asleep in the front seat of his car while eating a tuna sandwich outside a deli. A meter maid woke him up to make sure he was okay.

When Ruby wasn't out on the street herself, she was tapping into her sources in the judicial system. She scoured the minute reports—the court records accumulated since Gibson's arrest—for clues to his whereabouts, but found little she didn't already know. Morgan Reed filched a copy of Gibson's case file and threw in a mug shot for good measure. A high-ranking executive at the telephone company, whose son Ruby had once bailed out on charges of vehicular manslaughter, ran a computer check of Gibson's phone records. No phone calls had been made from his penthouse the night before the prelim. If Randall Taylor was telling the truth about having talked to Gibson that night, Gibson had called him from somewhere else. But where?

The white-haired man sitting behind the shiny cherry wood desk polishing a pair of frameless glasses with a handkerchief looked as if he'd been watching over the lobby of The Polo Club since the last world war.

"Yes, sir?" he said, rising, with alert eyes and an ingratiating smile as David came through the revolving entrance door. He seemed genuinely surprised and pleased that someone actually needed his services. His bent frame straightened automatically from years of practice. He wore a dark blue frock coat and starched white shirt, both frayed but clean. Crossed gold keys on each lapel winked in the light of a small lamp on the desk. He wrapped the wire glasses on his face.

"You were here the other day, with Mr. Lamprey and that wonderful woman," the doorman said.

"You have a good memory for faces, Mr.—?"

"Gérard Damonte."

David introduced himself and then asked the doorman if he'd been on duty around the same time a couple of evenings ago.

"Oh, yes. I'm here from seven in the morning until ten o'clock at night six days a week, sir," the man said proudly.

"Long hours," David said sympathetically. The man must have a social life about as exciting as mine, he thought.

"My residents have many needs—flowers, limousines, theater tickets. My duty is to their welfare."

The doorman spoke the last line in a slow, sad tone, as if the residents of The Polo Club were his children, yet children he seldom saw and who didn't appreciate him when they were around.

"Then you must have seen Bayne Gibson come in that night? About this time?"

The doorman's smile faded. "Are you with the police, sir?" He frowned when David told him he was with a bail bonding agency. He obviously did not want the stench of murder and bondsmen spoiling his fiefdom. "I'm not at liberty to discuss the activities of my residents. I will not betray their heartfelt trust in me."

David flipped open his wallet to the glassine envelope that held his blue, state-issued bondsman identification card, License Number 612, with a photograph that made him look like he was carrying some kind of contagious disease. "Look, Gérard, your loyalty to your residents is admirable, but I'm licensed as a bondsman by the State of Colorado, and I'm empowered by Statute Twelve-Seven-One-Oh-Two to call the police here to legally compel you to assist me in locating this fugitive. You don't want cop cars outside your entrance again, do you?''

Of course, David had no more legal authority to compel the doorman to cooperate than did Mickey Mouse. But he'd heard Ruby pull the same line a few times, and most people didn't know the law or were too intimidated to call her on it.

Yes, the doorman conceded after much hesitation, he'd seen Mr. Gibson come in early that evening. No, he did not see him leave again, nor had the night concierge who relieved him at ten. He had not seen Mr. Gibson the next morning either, which he thought was odd since the man ran early every morning. So odd, in fact, that Damonte had called Gibson's penthouse around 7:45 to make sure he was okay, but no one had answered.

''Could he have left the building without you seeing him?''

The doorman said it wasn't likely, since everyone entered and exited through the lobby. Security was extremely tight. David spotted a TV camera mounted high on the wall behind the desk. Not tight enough to prevent the murder of Royce Kray.

''Surely there are other exits besides this lobby entrance and the garage?''

Three service doors. But the residents rarely used them except to jog.

''Jog?''

Damonte discouraged residents from trekking through the lobby and out the front door in sweaty exercise clothes. It detracted from the ambiance. The importance of ambiance he'd learned many years before while serving as the night concierge at the Hotel Meridien Montparnasse in Paris. Hence, most of the building's joggers either used the stairs or the service elevator and then exited through one of the service doors. Mr. Gibson, of course, used the private elevator that went only to the penthouse. David remembered riding the elevator the day they'd toured the penthouse. It was around the corner from the two main mahogany and brass trimmed lobby elevators, out of sight of the concierge's desk.

"So if Gibson had wanted to leave the building without being seen—including by whoever was on duty here—he could have taken the penthouse elevator and slipped out one of the service doors?"

The doorman conceded that it was possible, since the doors were not locked from the inside due to fire regulations. But he noticed Gibson most mornings, and of course Gibson always had to ring the service bell to be let back in.

"Did anyone come to visit Gibson that night?" David asked.

No.

"Could anyone have been waiting for him at his penthouse *before* he arrived that night?"

Impossible. Anyone entering The Polo Club had to come through the lobby, or ring the service bell, since the service doors automatically locked to the outside. The garage afforded no easy way in or out either. Anyone coming from or going to the garage had to pass through the lobby.

David thought about asking the doorman if he dozed off now and then, but he already knew the answer to the question. "Did anyone come to visit Gibson the next morning?"

Mr. Lamprey had shown up around 8:15 and the doorman had immediately expressed his concerns to the lawyer about not having seen Mr. Gibson yet. The lawyer appeared too preoccupied to answer. When he came down half an hour later he seemed even more preoccupied and had not replied when the doorman asked him if Mr. Gibson was okay. It was not until later, said the doorman, that he learned from a resident that Mr. Gibson had failed to appear at his court hearing.

"I'm curious," said David. "Do you think Gibson killed Kray?"

The doorman looked shocked at the question. No kiss and tell man was he. No *Confessions of a Concierge* with the inside scoop on the tawdry high life of the residents of The Polo Club. No selling his story to the inquiring minds of the *National Enquirer*. This was a man who would guard his residents' darkest secrets with aplomb and discretion.

"Did you hear the shots that night?"

The doorman shook his head.

"Hey, get away from there!" the doorman suddenly yelled in the direction of the revolving entrance door. He moved toward the door and made awkward shooing motions with his arms, as if he were trying to scare away birds from a garden patch. The faces of three boys disappeared.

"Damn kids! They stop to stare every day, like this was the Tower of London or some other ghoulish tourist trap. Even this long after . . ." He looked gloomily at David and let his words die.

12

"Dead air!" yelled the young man with the urgency of someone yelling "fire" in a smoke-filled building. "God, I hate dead air! Isn't anybody calling in? I haven't seen a goddamn light on that control board for the last ten minutes. Anybody check to see if the phone lines are working? What about the phone company? Did we pay the phone company? Call and make sure we've paid our damn phone bill. Christ, the staff's gonna have to start calling in again. I *hate* playing the eco-nut."

The man fired his stream of questions and commands at a middle-aged woman who clutched a clipboard to her chest and frantically nodded yes or no as they stood outside the broadcast booth. A car dealership ad whined through overhead speakers.

"Did you see the latest Arbitrons, Martha?" Martha tried to reply but the young man was already on to the next sentence. "Listeners and advertisers dropping off in droves. In *droves!* Numbers look like a fucking stock market crash. Did Murray Prince call yet from Seattle?" The woman shook her head. "He's the guy I want. He's got the same shtick Royce had. He'd pick things up. Course, I don't know why the hell he'd want to work in this hick market."

He glared into the booth, his intense yet boyish features reflected in the thick glass. He banged on the glass and yelled, "Wake up in there, Allan."

A man in his fifties, languidly sitting at a console in front of a microphone, looked up. He cupped a hand to his ear to indicate he couldn't hear. The young man motioned with his hands, one of them holding a cigarette, to pick up the pace. "This is a talk show, Allan," he yelled at the glass, "not a goddamn requiem mass."

The young man turned away from the booth and caught sight of David watching from ten feet away.

"Who the hell are you?" he said, tensing. "How'd you get back here? No unauthorized people are allowed back here."

David identified himself and said he was looking for KPOL's program director, Peter Deveraux.

"Oh, yeah, you're the guy who called earlier . . . about Bayne. The front desk is supposed to call me first before they send anyone back. Security regs. Can't just let anyone walk in. Especially after Royce. Too many loonies out there." He rapped his knuckles against the glass. The show host glanced up, this time annoyed. "This shit's thick but it isn't bulletproof. There's a new person on the desk. She obviously doesn't know what the hell she's doing." He turned to Martha. "Get that rectified." She looked relieved as she scurried by David, past a long poster on the wall with huge green letters that said, KPOL—Life's Electric Connection.

Deveraux approached David. He was in his mid-twenties, much too young to be the program director of a major radio station, but with eyes that looked ten years older. He was in shirtsleeves, with his tie yanked loose around his neck—a tie with garish swatches of reds and blues and greens, as if an artist had wiped her brushes on it. He dragged hard on his cigarette, smoke drifting up in front of his unblemished skin and blue eyes and sandy hair. "I can give you two minutes."

The voice of the talk show host filtered out into the hallway through overhead speakers. It did drone, like a priest chanting in Latin.

"Has Gibson contacted you or left any messages since he skipped his preliminary hearing?"

"No. Why would he?"

"He listed you as a reference," said David. "I understand that he personally hired you, that you two were buddies in college."

"Buddies? No, we weren't buddies. We both took broadcast journalism at Columbia, but we're eight years apart in age. Bayne's old man sent him to school to learn the business. I started at sixteen. One of those Los Alamos whiz kids. My dad's a physicist there, nosing around in sub*sub*atomic particles. Not my thing. Bayne and I took a few classes together, but we didn't spend much time together other than that. I wouldn't characterize us as buddies—then or now. Frankly, I'm not sure why Bayne hired me."

"When was the last time you talked to him?"

"Two . . . three days before the preliminary hearing."

Deveraux's clothes reeked of smoke and David repressed an urge to gag. "Did he give any hints that he was thinking about skipping—you know, talked about taking a trip or vacationing in Mexico or seeing someone?"

"No, nothing like that. But I didn't see him for very long that last time. In fact, I didn't see him much at all after his arrest. He was pretty busy with his lawyers and pretty bummed out. I'd be too if I were in his position. Actually, he never spent much time here even before his arrest."

"Any ideas where he might have gone?"

"Zippo. I wasn't privy to Bayne's private life."

David tried to read Deveraux—read him the way Aunt Ruby read everyone she saw. Was the man lying? Hiding something? Did he really know where Gibson was? David wasn't sure. He distrusted his own senses. They led him astray more often than not. Law professors didn't teach the nuances of lying, despite public perception. You played with words, concepts, principles, not body language. That was his aunt's expertise. She could spot a liar at fifty paces.

"What about his villa in Mexico?" prodded David. "Think he went there?"

Deveraux shrugged. "Maybe, but I never had the impression it was the love of his life. Course, if I were running from a murder charge I guess it wouldn't be a bad place to make the love of my life."

"What was the love of his life?"

"Punishing his body."

"Got any names of people he punished his body with?"

The program director shook his head. "I'm not into that

stuff. It's a waste of human evolution. But I think he had a girlfriend he worked out a lot with. Christina somebody." Deveraux glanced at a clock in the booth. "Your two minutes are up. Sorry I couldn't help you more."

David was glad to leave. He was tired, the reek of cigarette smoke nauseated him, and his head throbbed from the droning bodiless voice of the announcer. It was as though the building itself was talking.

He was several steps down the hallway when Deveraux called after him. "Hey, I don't want to leave the wrong impression about Bayne. I like the man. I like him for hiring me. I've never believed for a minute that he murdered Royce. Even as bad as the evidence looks against him."

David came back toward Deveraux. "If he's innocent, why did he skip?"

Deveraux looked stumped. "Scared, maybe. He's not a strong man. I know he didn't like Royce, but I don't think he killed him. Nobody *liked* Royce. Of course, liking Royce had nothing to do with business. He was the best. The best!" Deveraux nodded toward the man in the booth. "You know what the problem is with Allan?"

"I don't know anything about the radio business."

"People *like* him, that's what. He's a nice guy. Sends flowers to his sister on her birthday. He was our head newsman until Royce was killed. He's in there temporarily, until we can find a permanent replacement. That's if we have any listeners left by then."

"Tough going these days, huh?"

"See, the problem is nobody hates Allan. At least, nobody except me. That was a plus once in radio, but not today. Now Royce—everybody hated Royce. He used to cut off callers in mid-sentence. Even callers he agreed with! He'd bludgeon people with his mike. But they loved it. The more insulting, rude, obnoxious, and offensive he became, the higher the ratings climbed. He was the last of the angry men."

"What was he angry about?"

"Nothing . . . everything. Himself, mostly. He didn't like himself anymore than anybody else did. He was always convinced he'd be fired and never work again. He didn't trust Bayne . . . me . . . anybody."

"A lot of people must be happy he's dead."

"Yeah, he was a bastard. But in there . . ." Deveraux nodded toward the studio with a suddenly affectionate, nostalgic look. ". . . in there he was a genius. He'd roll his chair around on the floor and chain-smoke Camels and flail his arms and talk faster than anybody I knew. The words poured out of him. He loved words. They were his life breath. I think they were the only thing that kept the voices in his head from getting to him."

"Did he believe in what he said on the radio?"

"Who knew? Who cared? He knew how to light people's fuses. Man, there was never dead air on 'Back Talk.' We had callers stacked up like airplanes in a snowstorm, waiting to take their best shot at him." Deveraux suddenly seemed conscious of his own words. "No pun intended."

"You think one of his callers could have killed him instead of Gibson?"

Deveraux humphed. "Sure as hell's possible, though I don't know how they could have gotten into his penthouse. Royce received death threats all the time. It's the nature of the business if you're doing it right. You shoulda seen the hate mail he'd get. You didn't have to burn it. Just stack it up in a corner and the shit would ignite by itself."

"Wasn't there an attempt on his life recently?"

"We had a car bombed in the parking lot several months ago. Fortunately nobody was in it. Belonged to one of the engineers, but the police suspect it was intended for Royce."

"Any suspects?"

"No one specific. But I could run out a computer list a mile long of people with motives to kill Royce."

"Who would you put at the top of the list?"

"The Brotherhood of the Transcendental Light."

"I've heard of them," said David. "Call themselves New Age survivalists, or something like that."

"Whatever the hell that means. Got a big ranch an hour southwest of town, near Pine Junction. They act real friendly and open—not like some of these neo-Nazi groups—but the word is they've got bomb shelters and guns and God knows what other shit hidden up there. Royce called them a 'spiritual version of AIDS.' Any show about them really drew the calls.''

''Did they make threats against Kray?''

''Their leader did once, in so many words. Tanner's his name. We'd been trying to get him on the show for some time. Royce finally goaded him into it, just a couple of weeks before Royce was murdered. Wow, it was an hour of mud wrestling. Royce called him a religious Svengali and he called Royce an atheistic Nazi. The whole thing was great. Blew the ratings right through the roof.''

''You said this Tanner guy made a threat against Kray?''

''Royce accused him of being a fraud. Said he wasn't a messiah, but a con man. That's when the shit really hit the fan. Tanner predicted that one of these days somebody would permanently silence Royce's loud mouth. So Royce taunts him, tells him he doesn't have the guts to do it, and Tanner says he wouldn't need to, that there were plenty of people out there willing to, and then Royce brings up the fact that Tanner had been arrested a couple of months before on firearms possession charges. It was nasty.''

''Was Kray afraid of Tanner?''

''Damn right. First time I ever saw him truly scared, despite almost daily threats from people. He got a gun permit right after that show. Even made me help him pick out a gun, and I don't know shit about guns. He carried it around with him in a side holster.''

Deveraux patted his rib cage.

''You think Tanner killed him, or had him killed?''

''Who knows. Sometimes the people with the biggest mouths are the ones you have to worry about the least. It's the quiet ones that scare me.''

''Anybody else high on your list?''

''The local skinheads. Royce went after them pretty hard too. His daughter—his youngest one, Darcy, I think her name is—runs around with a skinhead. I think she did it to piss off her old man—and it did. Burned Royce's ass plenty. Threatened to kill the kid if he ever caught up with him. Vowed to run every skinhead out of town if it was the last thing he ever did. . . . Maybe it was.''

"The police are convinced they have the right man."

"If you want my opinion, I think it was one of the loonies. The Mark David Chapman types—you know, the guy who shot Lennon. On one of the anniversaries of Lennon's death, Royce said the Beatles were vastly overrated. He hated rock. He was into classical music. The Beatles remark really pissed off some of his listeners. God, he knew how to touch raw nerves. I think he really got into the American psyche and poked around in it like a dentist working without Novocain—made people feel uncomfortable about things they should feel uncomfortable about."

"Too uncomfortable?"

"Maybe. If you ask me, I think Royce Kray died for our sins."

The seventy-two hours following Bayne Gibson's failure to appear came and went, and they still had no clue to his whereabouts. It rained hard twice in those seventy-two hours, the first rains since the night they'd met Gibson in jail. But the rain didn't break their own dry spell. The day before, a two-time loser who'd skipped on a twenty-grander six months before turned up in a New Mexico jail. Turned out he'd been sitting there for the past four months on an auto theft charge and the local authorities had neglected to inform Colorado authorities. Only by a fluke phone call had Ruby learned he was there. At that point, many judges would have released Ruby from the bond, particularly in light of the foul-up by the law enforcement agencies and by Ruby's demonstration of good faith ($763 in expenses) in trying to track the man down. But the district judge in Golden—the foothills community that was home to Coors beer and a large gravel pit—would hear none of it. Ruby hadn't turned the man in within ninety days and that was her tough luck, bureaucratic fuckup notwithstanding.

It was also during that same seventy-two hours that David and his aunt realized that Big Jim Brodie had disappeared.

13

The law book David was reading fell onto his face.

He jerked awake, pushed the book to the floor, rolled off the mattress, and stood up. Well, sort of stood up. His bedroom was squeezed into the garret above the office and the spay-neuter clinic, two-and-a-half stories up. The room was ten feet long and six feet wide—about as large as a maximum-security prison cell—with walls that slanted to a peak so low he had to hunch his shoulders like an old man. The room was crammed with a mattress, a desk fashioned out of an interior door set on cinder blocks, a lamp, a peeling chest of drawers he'd fished out of a dumpster, and an extension of the office telephone. Interior decorating consisted of a green carpet remnant and posters of Kathleen Turner from *Body Heat* and an Arctic wolf leaping onto an ice floe. He kept his shaving equipment and toiletries in the office bathroom and hanging clothes in the office coat closet. Any miscellaneous items that wouldn't fit into those locations he tossed into the trunk of his Duster. Fortunately, having lived only seven months in Denver and plowing what funds he earned into law school, the trunk wasn't full—yet. Whenever claustrophobia struck, he looked out the small window, which provided a commanding view of Bondsman Row, police headquarters, and city jail.

According to Ruby, a moderately wealthy mining engineer with six daughters had built the Victorian house in the 1920s. By the 1940s, it had become a home for orphans, and later still, office space for hookers. Eventually the house was bought by the Planned Pethood Spay-Neuter Clinic. The clinic had ambitious designs for becoming the McDonald's of spay-neuter clinics, franchising its eugenics programs for out of control dog and cat populations across America, and maybe—who knew·the possibilities of the free enterprise system—across the world. The dream hadn't quite cut it. Three years after his aunt and her husband Al had arrived in Denver from parts unknown, the clinic leased them the second floor, though it still retained the lower floor. They threw in the garret for free.

David picked the law book up off the floor, set it on a stack of other books, and carefully aligned them by running his finger along the edges before he cautiously climbed down a steep narrow flight of stairs to the bathroom. It was seventeen minutes after midnight, but a light still glowed in his aunt's office. She'd come in around eight, and had spent most of the evening on the telephone before he'd gone upstairs around nine-thirty to study.

He found her asleep in her high-backed leather chair. Her head lolled over her right shoulder, and her breathing was shallow and unsettled. A ballpoint pen lay clutched between the red fingertips of her left hand. Over in a corner, Collateral was zonked as only Collateral could be. But Alabaster, the coal black Persian perched in Ruby's lap, watched him intently with her aloof copper eyes as he stood in the doorway.

No one knew where Alabaster had come from. She'd simply materialized one winter morning on a second-floor window ledge, demanding to be let in. Collateral had wandered over to investigate, but one hiss from Alabaster and the dog ceded all previously established territorial rights. Ruby speculated that the cat had miraculously escaped the chamber of horrors on the floor below them—a "survivor," she called her. Though Ruby never made any inquiries to see if the clinic was missing a black Persian, nor had any distraught owner ever climbed the stairs in search of such a feline.

If Ruby's speculation was right, perhaps that explained the cat's general unsociability. From the first day, Alabaster had taken to Ruby, and only Ruby. Which was okay with David, since he was not overly fond of cats, especially purebreds. Perhaps Alabaster's mysterious past also explained why she never purred. David had never heard of a cat that didn't purr. Yet Alabaster, even when Ruby scratched behind her ears, stubbornly remained silent. He'd asked Ruby about it one day, and she'd replied, cryptically, "She purrs only when she thinks no one is listening."

David noticed the stereo's power light was still on and he tiptoed over to turn it off. Suddenly Alabaster leaped pantherlike to the floor and scurried off to parts unknown. Ruby's eyes snapped open.

"Sorry, didn't mean to bother you, Aunt Ruby. I saw the office light still on. I thought you'd left."

She yawned, stared at the pen still in her hand, and set it down on the cluttered desk. Her makeup had faded and her hair was flat on one side from sleeping. She looked tired under the glare of the small banker's light. He rarely saw her look tired.

He walked to the windows and peered out through the slats of the oak blinds. "Hear anything from Jim?" he asked.

"No." Her voice sounded dispirited. "I called Marian again tonight. She still hadn't heard from him."

Brodie's wife hadn't seen him in two days and she didn't know where he was. That wasn't unusual. Big Jim was gone frequently, and to protect her and their eleven-year-old daughter from his dangerous line of work he rarely told them where he was going or who he was going after. But Ruby usually knew where he was if he was tracking a skip for her. In the first forty-eight hours after Gibson jumped, she'd talked to him several times, supplying him with leads, names, addresses, phone numbers, places Gibson hung out. Then, suddenly, calls to his answering machine and his pager went unreturned. They had heard nothing the past two days—nothing since he and David had found the executive and his secretary in the cheap downtown hotel room.

"I'm sure he's on some hot lead," David said as he traced a finger along one of the wooden slats of the blind. He examined the dust on his fingertip.

"Don't humor me like some old woman," snapped Ruby.

David looked at her, startled at the anger in her voice. "Sorry," he said quickly. He took a white handkerchief out of his hip pocket and began dusting the slats, one at a time. "Maybe he went to Mexico."

"He would have told me."

"Maybe he didn't have time to call, or maybe he can't call."

Ruby started to say something, then stopped. "What the hell are you doing?"

"Dusting the blinds."

"Is compulsiveness a required course in law school, or is it on the entrance exam?"

"The slats are filthy."

"We have a cleaning service for that."

"They miss a lot. See?" Triumphantly, he held up his dust-streaked handkerchief.

"That's great if you plan to eat off the blinds."

"Well, no, but—" He refolded his handkerchief, trapping the dust securely inside.

Ruby shook her head. "God, we gotta find you something to do with your life." She bolted to her feet, and snatched a wide-brimmed straw hat from the antique oak hat rack. "Come on, let's go for a drive."

"A drive? Where?"

"To look for Big Jim."

"It's after midnight."

"That's the best time to look for Jim."

The rush of cool air through the open windows of the Lamborghini slapped him awake. The tape deck played a lush, moody sax whose notes drifted lazily into the air like cigarette smoke. Lester Young, Ruby told him, though he hadn't asked. Died of acute alcoholism in fifty-nine, she added, though he still hadn't said a word. She often provided instant mini bios on musicians she was playing, as if the personal note would somehow convert his "dull" musical tastes to jazz. Judging from the histories she spun, most of the musicians his aunt listened to were long dead, and had usually died at an early age, and in some tragic way.

They drove to the west side of town, to Lakewood, down an alley behind a row of modest, well-kept ranch-style homes. Ruby turned down the stereo and slowed behind a house with an old swing set in the backyard, a scraggly Russian olive tree, and a hedge of lilacs in full bloom that scratched against a detached garage.

"What's this place?" he asked.

"Jim's house."

"You think he's home?"

"I was hoping he'd come in late. But I don't see his LTD."

"Maybe it's in the garage."

"No. You couldn't find room to park a skateboard in there. Marian's a pack rat. If he was back, his LTD'd be parked in the driveway."

They stared silently into the darkness.

"I shouldn't have called her tonight, David," said Ruby, her voice subdued. "Now she's scared to death."

They canvased several beer-and-shot bars and all night diners in the area, but no one had seen a man fitting Big Jim's description in the last few days, though several male patrons weren't shy about conveying their interest in seeing more of Ruby.

As they drove, the air turned colder. David shivered. Summer nights were always warm in Missouri, he remembered. The air hung like a wet, heavy blanket. Here it hung dry and electric.

They zigzagged across the north side of Denver, stopping in haunts Ruby knew Big Jim frequented. No luck. No one had seen him recently. David dozed fitfully between stops. The street lights blurred into globs of sodium yellow. The Great Dead Ones of jazz played on.

"It's 2:06, Aunt Ruby," he finally said after they'd made yet another stop. "Let's go home."

"I got a coupla more stops."

"We don't have a clue where Big Jim is. We could drive around all night. I'm exhausted. I have a test tomorrow night . . . No, it's tonight."

"To hell with your sleep."

"My studies come first, Aunt Ruby! That was our agreement when I started working for you."

She dramatically swung a hand toward the black streets. "*This* is your study, David. You'll learn more about the law out here than you will in all your damn textbooks."

"We'd have less problems out on the street if we'd put more criminals away."

They went through this argument at least once every other week, like a stubborn married couple who's fought the same damn battle for thirty years, but who can't resist reenacting it one more time.

David tried to sleep again but his aunt was wired.

"Why *do* you want to be a lawyer, David? And a prosecutor to boot."

"For truth, justice, and the American way," he mumbled through sleep-numb lips.

"I thought that was your father's dream."

His jaw clenched at the mention of his father. True, his lawyerly ambitions had started out as his father's dream. A great liberal of a man, his father had himself wanted to be the Clarence Darrow of his day. But that was before his father's father had abandoned the family for the drunken bitch on the other side of the St. Jo tracks. Jack's mother, who clerked at a local drugstore and was too proud to hook up again with any old Joe just to pay the bills, couldn't afford to send his father to law school. His father had tried to work his way through, but he got married along the way and David was born and eventually he'd passed his unfulfilled dream on to his son. After that, he had held an endless string of crummy jobs, from night watchman to owner of a bankrupt tire store. He was a man heavy of heart and bitter of soul. Yes, it had been his father's dream, once, but now it was his, an inheritance not to be squandered.

"I think my father would applaud whatever I choose to do," said David.

"Is that why you haven't told him about working for me?" she taunted.

"He wouldn't understand. You know that."

His parents believed he drove a cab and lived with various school friends, which was why the only way they could get in touch with him was through a post office box or the school.

"He'll find out, David . . . if he doesn't already know."

David sat up in the car. "You didn't tell him, did you? You promised you'd—"

"David, I haven't talked to your father in thirty-five years. And I haven't talked to anyone who knows him. But word's gonna get back someday. Or Jack's gonna suddenly show up in Denver looking for you. One way or another he's going to find out."

David slumped back into his seat. His raw eyes stung.

"One more stop tonight," said Ruby. "I promise."

"Fine."

She dialed a number on her car phone. "J.T., how are you?. . . . Yeah, I know, it's been a while. You gonna be around in the next fifteen? I need to talk to you. . . . Good. See you soon."

"Who's J.T.?" David asked when she hung up.

"J.T. Cale."

"That name sounds familiar."

"A repo man in Commerce City. Actually prefers to call himself a 'recovery specialist.' "

"He knows Jim?"

"They knew each other in Vietnam. Jim worked for him before he went into skip tracing. They're real good friends. I don't know why I didn't think of him sooner. I must be getting smarter in my old age. If Jim told anyone about what he was up to, it was J.T."

14

Gas flares from oil refineries shot into the darkness. Ruby and David drove past a dog track and an endless stretch of low industrial buildings, and along streets where you wouldn't want your car to break down. Finally, they pulled into the driveway of a large, nameless, brightly lit corrugated metal building that looked like an auto repair garage. The huge entrance door was open, and David could see half a dozen vehicles parked haphazardly inside, most of them newer models.

He didn't know much about the repossession business, other than that creditors hired repo men to legally steal cars, trucks, boats, or nearly anything else people got behind on in payments. That, and the fact that the reputation of repos was even sleazier than that of bail bondsmen.

They entered the garage and followed the sound of country music into a small, spare office where two men stood before a large wall map of the metro area that was flecked with red and blue pins. One of the men removed a red pin and added two blue pins. David guessed the man moving the pins was J.T. Cale. A big, white-bearded man, he wore a black cowboy hat with an expensive silver hatband, a black leather vest over a dark shirt, cowboy boots, and a silver belt buckle the size of a dinner plate. The guy next to him faded into the surroundings with a nondescript face, mousy brown hair, and dull clothes.

"Angel!" said the man in the cowboy hat, giving her a hug. More of a bear hug, considering he was nearly as large as Brodie. It was the first time David had ever seen his aunt hug anyone, even Morgan Reed.

"Looks like a busy night, J.T.," she said, nodding toward the cars in the garage, one of which was a big white limo. A wall behind the cars was covered with hundreds of license plates—trophies from the vehicles Cale had repossessed, speculated David, like the black silhouette kills painted on the fuselages of old fighter planes.

"Business is always great when the economy's in the tank," said Cale in a voice surprisingly high-pitched for his size. "Steve's on his way back with another one, and Billy and I were just plotting our next run. A county judge with a BMW five months in arrears. Got one of them damn magnetic keys."

Ruby introduced David, and Cale's dirty but firm hand crunched his. Billy nodded grimly but offered no hand.

"Your aunt's told me about you," said Cale. "Studying economics or something like that, right?"

"Law."

"Right."

David pointed in friendly curiosity toward a white limo in the garage. "Whose pimpmobile?"

"Mine, son," Cale said, laughing. "It's what I meet my clients in. Gets their attention."

"Oh . . . sorry."

Cale laughed again. "Actually a candy man did own the car before I took it back. I thought drug dealers *always* made money, but this schmuck didn't. I was the only repo man in town with the guts to boost it from him. I liked it so much I bought it from the bank for what he had left on the payments."

"You talk to Jim lately?" asked Ruby, mercifully diverting attention from David's embarrassment.

"Mmmm . . . coupla of nights ago. Stopped by to say hello. Brought his usual burgers and shake. Offered him a beer but he said he was on the job. Now me, I can always use a shot or two before I go out to boost a car. Just to loosen things up."

"He say what job he was on?"

"Yeah, that... that skip who killed that talk show guy, uh..."

"Gibson," interjected the grim-faced Billy.

"Yeah, that's him. I heard about him on the news. It was a big bond, wasn't it, Angel?"

"A million bucks."

Cale whistled. "No wonder Jim was excited. What would be his take on that if he found him—a hundred grand?"

"Why was he excited?"

"Said he had a real good lead. He looked pumped up."

"What kinda lead, J.T.?" Ruby asked impatiently.

Cale turned down the music on a beat-up orange plastic radio, leaned against a ratty gun-metal gray table, and crossed his arms. Behind him were laid out a big ring of keys, a right-angled screwdriver, a crowbar, and various tools David couldn't identify but figured were for breaking into and starting cars.

"He was headed someplace up in the foothills, I think. I don't remember the details. You remember, Billy?"

"It was around Evergreen. The guy supposedly was hiding in one of them fancy mountain retreats around there."

"He didn't get any more specific than that?"

"No, ma'am."

"How did he find out about this place?"

"Somebody told him," said Cale. "He was gonna meet somebody who was gonna show him where Gibson was hiding."

"Jim say who he was going to meet?"

Cale shook his head, then looked at Billy for confirmation. Billy said, "He didn't say who. But he mentioned that the radio fella's wife was mixed up in it somehow."

"Yeah, that's right," cut in Cale. "I remember that. Never listened to that Kray fella's show. I'm asleep at that hour. Didn't much like his politics anyway. You ask me, I'd—"

"Wait a minute! Wait a minute! Jim said Kray's *wife* was mixed up in Gibson's skip?"

"That's what he said, didn't he, Billy?"

"I don't know if he meant the skip or the killing or what. He just said the dead guy's wife was mixed up in it."

"Did the person Big Jim was going to meet in Evergreen

tell him about Mrs. Kray?'' Ruby looked at Billy first this time.

''He said some ex-girlfriend of Gibson told him. I don't know if she was the same person he was meeting in Evergreen.''

''He mention a name, or anything about her?''

''No, ma'am.''

''Hell, I wouldn't believe an ex-girlfriend, anyway,'' offered Cale. ''I got a bunch of 'em and they'd say anything about me if it'd make me look like shit.''

Ruby was pacing now. ''He say anything else?''

The two men shook their heads, and Cale said, ''He didn't tell us any details. Got on to a new reel he'd bought. We're goin' fishin' next Saturday.''

''What time was he here that night?''

''Eight . . . eight-thirty, maybe. We were just laying out the evening. Hadn't even sent out a crew. Why, all the questions, Angel?'' Cale's voice grew worried.

Ruby's voice was even. ''I haven't talked to him for a coupla days. I need to get hold of him. Thought you might know where he is.''

''You know Jim. He's a loner.''

''Yeah, I'm sure that's what it is.''

A tow truck barreled into the garage dragging a big blue van. Large white letters on the side of the van said Mountain View Baptist Church. Everyone followed Cale into the garage. The driver piled out and let out a war whoop.

''Man, was that guy pissed! He come out in his skivvies wavin' a fuckin' two-by-four. I wasn't sure if I was gonna get away. I didn't think a sky pilot could get so damn mad.''

''Sometimes they're the worst,'' said Cale. ''Go call it into the cops. Billy and I got a BMW to snatch.'' He turned to Ruby and David. ''Gotta run. Nice meeting you, son.''

''You hear anything from Jim, let me know immediately, J.T.''

''Sure will, Angel.''

15

Bayne Gibson, it turned out, had quite a few ex-girlfriends himself. Two of them admitted talking with a big sonofabitch named Brodie, but neither knew anything about Gibson's whereabouts, or a place in Evergreen where he might have gone into hiding, or any possible involvement by Kray's wife in Gibson's skip or Kray's murder. But the name of one former girlfriend began to consistently crop up among the ex-girlfriends and other Gibson acquaintances: Christina Nilsson. By most accounts, Gibson and Nilsson, who ran her own computer consulting company, had been a hot item for better than a year until they abruptly broke off a month before Kray's murder. Rumor was the breakup was due to another woman—none of them knew whom—and that Nilsson had taken the breakup bitterly.

Nilsson, it also turned out, was a fitness freak like Gibson. That's where Ruby and David would find her every afternoon, said their sources, working out at the Denver Athletic Club.

It was mid-afternoon and only four people were in the DAC's well-equipped weight room. Three of them looked like they belonged there. The fourth was a middle-aged man whose body sagged in places that all the state-of-the-art exercise equipment in the world would never put back together again.

Ruby and David found Christina Nilsson entangled amid the chains, pulleys, stainless steel bars, and pads of an elaborate exercise machine that looked like a mechanical monster in some Stephen King horror novel. Not that Nilsson couldn't give the monster a good match, David quickly noted. She'd *done* her reps. Her short, tanned body, a healthy portion of it exposed by a sweat-stained braless gray cutoff T-shirt and short gray shorts, was more muscular than most men, though not obscenely rippled like the oiled amazons he'd caught on late-night cable television.

The woman's arms, held shoulder high, folded and unfolded padded bars across impressive breasts. Black weights rose and fell behind her with a *clink*. Her eyes were focused on a mirrored wall.

"Christina Nilsson?" asked Ruby, stepping between the woman and the mirror.

"Move!" The woman spit the word out as she strained against the machine, each repetition coming more painfully. The veins in her neck corded and her face contorted at the peak of each repetition.

"You're Nilsson?"

"You're blocking my view!"

Ruby stepped to one side. Five torturous reps later, Nilsson stopped. She breathed heavily as she wiped her face with a small white towel decorated with the club seal. Relaxing, her face turned smooth and attractive, even without makeup. Late twenties, tops, he estimated. Blond hair in a tight ponytail that snaked down the middle of her back, and large, expressive blue eyes. He was a sucker for blue eyes.

"Yes, I'm Christina Nilsson," said the woman. "The mirror isn't there for vanity, much as most people think it is. It helps us see that we're doing our reps properly." She extracted herself from the torture rack, went around to the back, pulled a silver pin that connected the chain to the weights, and slipped it into the next notch down, adding weight.

"I have a few questions about Bayne Gibson," said Ruby.

The woman straightened up and rolled her eyes. "Christ, not again. Are you cops? You don't look like cops."

"No, we're not the police. Have they talked to you?"

Not since he disappeared, said Nilsson. They had talked to her briefly before his arrest. David caught the look of relief in his aunt's face. She wanted to find Gibson first, before the police did. It was a matter of pride—and money.

"Not unless the big galoot in the cowboy hat who was here the other day was a cop," Nilsson added. "He was asking about Gibby, but he claimed he wasn't a cop. He gave me some nonsense about being in *fugitive management*. Whatever that means."

"He said his name was Brodie?"

"I don't remember his name."

"He was my man. A bounty hunter." Ruby flashed a business card in her fingers, like a magician producing a brightly colored scarf from up a sleeve. Nilsson glanced at the card, then ran her eyes up and down Ruby, whose jade dress and matching hat looked wildly out of place in the room. "Gibby was *your* client?"

"No, honey, not *was—is!* Any client who skips on Ruby Dark remains my client until I find him."

Nilsson sat down again. Hands protected by fingerless white gloves grabbed a bar above her head. She pulled the bar down behind her head to her shoulders, then let the weight retract it. "I can't help you," she said as she exhaled and repeated the pull. "Like I told the other guy, I don't know where Gibby is."

"Did you talk to him after his arrest?"

Her words came grudgingly between pulls. "I haven't talked to him . . . since before . . . Kray was murdered."

With each return and extension of her arms above her head, her cutoff T-shirt rode high, exposing a taut midriff between her shirt and a brown leather kidney belt, and coming tantalizingly close to exposing the underside of her breasts. The smooth tanned skin beaded with sweat as each rep became tougher,

"Where do you think we might find him?"

"I wouldn't . . . have . . . a clue."

"What about his hangouts, friends he might try to hide with, where he might go, what his habits are?"

"He didn't . . . have . . . friends."

"What about people he ran marathons with or worked out here with? Would they hide him?"

"They weren't . . . friends. They were . . . the . . . competition."

"Christ, honey, you went with the guy over a year. You must know something about the man."

When Nilsson didn't reply, Ruby again stepped in front of the mirror.

Nilsson glared but said nothing.

"It's important!" said Ruby.

"So's . . . my . . . workout," grunted Nilsson. She finished her reps without the mirror.

Ruby pressed again as Nilsson toweled her face. "You know anything about a place in Evergreen that Gibson owns or might go to hide? Some kind of fancy mountain retreat. Maybe a place a friend has."

The movement of the towel slowed. "No. Gibby had a villa in Mexico. That and his penthouse are all I know about."

"You didn't arrange to meet Brodie a coupla nights ago and take him to this retreat?"

"I told you, lady, I don't know anything about any place in Evergreen where Gibby might be hiding. I didn't meet your bounty hunter any place but here. Ask one of Gibby's other ex-girlfriends. He's got a stable of them."

Nilsson went over to a water cooler. Ruby and David tagged along. Walking behind her, David stared—he tried not to stare but he stared anyway—at the shapely, powerful curve of her thigh muscles. He wondered what they would feel like, wrapped around . . .

"Why did you and Gibson break up?" Ruby asked as Nilsson filled a Styrofoam cup with water.

"What difference does it make to you *why* we broke up? I had nothing to do with his arrest *or* his disappearance."

"People jump bail for many different reasons, hon. Sometimes that reason can be a clue to where they've run. Your breakup came shortly before Kray was murdered. Maybe it was still on Gibson's mind. Maybe it had something to do with why he skipped."

She downed the water as though it were a shot of bitter whiskey. "Frankly, lady, why he and I broke up is none of your business. But I'm sure it had nothing to do with why he skipped."

Nilsson walked over to a low weight machine. She adjusted the amount of weights and stretched her body out on a long padded bench with a bar over her chest.

Ruby looked down on her. "Do you think he ran because he killed Kray?"

Nilsson's eyes turned soft. "No. I don't think Gibby could hurt anyone."

"Then why did he skip?"

Nilsson averted her eyes. "I have no idea. Ask him."

"What about people at work or business connections? Did he ever talk about them, somebody he had a special relationship with?"

"I told you, he didn't have friends." Nilsson wrapped her hands on the bar and began doing bench presses.

"Will you stop your damn workout for a minute and talk!" demanded Ruby.

"I can't let my . . . body . . . cool down."

Suddenly, Ruby strode around the back of the machine and stepped on the weights, forcing Nilsson to stop. Ruby yanked out the pin.

Nilsson swung wildly out of the bench and squared off against Ruby, her sweaty face scowling, her chest heaving. Ruby tapped the pin against the palm of her hand. David coiled his body, ready to jump between them, though the thought of tangling with Nilsson no longer appealed to him. He didn't think his aunt would have a chance if it came to blows, but then again his aunt perpetually surprised him.

"What's with you, lady?" Nilsson yelled in her face.

Ruby kept tapping the key in her hand. "I don't like bastards who skip on me and I don't like people who won't help me find them."

"I can't help you."

One of the other jocks, doing overhead presses with free weights, grunted loudly and dropped the weights to the floor with a loud *clank*. He looked their way, slightly embarrassed, then bent over to change weights.

"What about Kray's wife? What did she have to do with Gibson skipping? Or the murder of her husband?"

Nilsson's coiled body went slack. "I don't know anything about Kray's wife."

"You told Brodie she was mixed up in it."

"I was angry at Gibby. I said things I shouldn't have."

"You're saying you lied?"

"Yeah, I lied."

"I don't believe you, honey. I don't believe you'd just pull Mrs. Kray's name out of thin air. I think you told Brodie the truth."

"I don't care if you believe me or not."

"Was Gibson seeing Mrs. Kray? Is that why you two broke up?"

David caught the momentary flash of fear and pain in Christina Nilsson's beautiful blue eyes before the woman shut it down.

"I told you, it's none of your business." She went over to a rack of dumbbells, picked out one, and began feverishly doing arm curls.

Ruby pursued her. "That's a powerful motive for murder, honey. Lover shoots lover's husband after lover's husband learns of affair with lover."

"I wouldn't know."

"It's a helluva more powerful motive than the lame money motive the police arrested him on. It would explain why Gibson and Kray were arguing at the party the night before the murder."

"Go away."

"When Brodie left here did he say where he was going?"

"No."

Suddenly several women, most of them dressed in brightly colored designer leotards, tights, and expensive white pump jogging shoes, invaded the weight room. They looked breathless and lightly sweating, as if they'd just come from an aerobics class. They swarmed over a row of empty stairclimbers and exercise cycles, and two of them went to the weight machines. Nilsson eyed them contemptuously while she did her curls.

Ruby stepped in close to Nilsson and spoke softly, almost pleadingly. "That bounty hunter you talked to is missing. I'm worried about him. His wife and daughter are worried about him. If you know *anything* about his whereabouts or about Gibson or Mrs. Kray or Evergreen, tell me now."

Nilsson kept her head turned away, her voice subdued. "I can't help you."

"Now what?" David asked gloomily as they stood under the DAC's sidewalk canopy. It was bad enough he blamed himself for the whole damn business because he'd tried to push his aunt into bonding out Bayne Gibson. But his aunt's expressed concerns about Big Jim had cast a suffocating pall over him. If Ruby was worried . . .

"We're going to pay a visit to Anna Lee Kray," said Ruby.

"Are you nuts!"

"No more than usual."

Ruby had called the Kray home from the DAC. The daughter who'd answered the phone said no one named Brodie had talked to her mother, or any of them, and would Ruby please leave their family alone.

"If we show up on their doorstep Mrs. Kray could legally scream harassment to the cops," warned David.

"She could."

Ruby bolted through traffic to the lot they'd parked in next to the Denver Press Club, David scurrying to catch her.

"Or the press," he went on. "Have you thought about that? You know how the press treats the bail bonding business. They make us all look like slimeballs. God knows what they'd do if they find out we're accusing the wife of a dead man of cheating with her husband's killer."

"You gotta take risks, David," said Ruby as she unlocked the car. "We're running out of leads."

"Us"? Had he really said "Us"?

"Okay, what if Mrs. Kray really is Gibson's lover?" David leaned against the hood of the car as he spoke and immediately yanked his hands off the hot metal. "We show up on her doorstep she might warn Gibson. What if she knows where he is? What if she gets in touch with him?"

"That's exactly what I want her to do."

16

The Royce Kray family lived in a three-story Victorian home that backed onto Cheesman Park. Dead vines strangled a wrought iron fence. Iron bars, bolted deep into the native stone, covered the windows, even those on the upper floors. Chimes rang muffled behind a thick front door.

"I still don't like this, Aunt Ruby," protested David as he surveyed the house from the front steps.

"You worry too much, David."

"With you I need to worry."

"It just shortens life." Ruby punched the doorbell again, twice close together.

"Maybe nobody's home," David said hopefully.

But moments later the door cracked open a few inches. Half of a young woman's face appeared.

"What do you want?" she said. A slate gray eye strip searched them.

"You must be one of the Kray daughters," Ruby said pleasantly.

The crack didn't widen. "Who are you?"

Ruby introduced themselves. "We're looking for Bayne Gibson."

The young woman's face darkened. "He sure as hell isn't hiding *here*! Go away!"

"We're also looking for a man named Jim Brodie."

"I told you on the phone, he never came here. We never saw him. We never talked to him. We can't help you. Go away!"

"Is your mother here?"

"She's resting."

"I need to talk to her. Just for a few minutes."

"She can't see anyone right now."

"It's urgent."

"I'll call the police if you don't leave us alone."

"Call 'em," invited Ruby. "They want to find Gibson as badly as I do."

The young woman hesitated. "I told you, we can't help you. I don't know anything about this bounty hunter, and we certainly don't know where Gibson is."

"Your mother may."

The lone eye widened. "That's ridiculous! Go away!" The woman started to shut the door but Ruby slammed her hand against it. She was stronger than she looked. The door stopped.

"Look, honey, the man wanted for killing your father is roaming the streets. And my friend who was looking for him is missing. I intend to find both of them."

"I hope you do, but I don't know why you think we can—"

"If I have to make life difficult for you and your family, I will."

The young woman hesitated a moment longer before opening the door.

"Thank you," said Ruby. They stepped into a cool hardwood entryway. Half a dozen plants lined the room, looking undernourished in the poor light. Dry, curled leaves lay in the soil of the pots and on the floor where they crinkled underfoot.

"Your name is . . . ?" Ruby asked, her voice soft again.

"Sarah."

Sarah Kray appeared to be in her late teens. She wore a starched white blouse with the collar turned up and white shorts and big clunker sandals. Her brown hair was of indeterminate length, having been severely drawn back and pinned up. She stood five five, flat-chested and wide-hipped, but there was a tough guy quality about her stance, her back foot planted as though she were braced to throw a roundhouse swing if she felt the need.

"You live here, Sarah?"

"I have my own apartment. But I'm here a lot to take care of my mom."

"That's very generous of you. A lot of young women today wouldn't do that."

"Somebody has to."

She abruptly spun on her heels and led them into a large formal sitting room that looked out small windows onto the thick afternoon light. Heavy drapes, rich, polished mahogany furniture with large flower designs in the fabric, heavy-framed oil paintings of flowers and hunting scenes, an ornate area rug, and leather-bound books gave the room a cluttered, stiff, Old World feel. Not the kind of taste David would have pegged for Royce Kray.

Ruby stopped cold in the middle of the room. "Jesus!"

David caught the direction of her stunned gaze and sucked in his breath. In a corner of the room a man sat on the floor, leaning against a polished chairside chest. He looked in his twenties. He was unshaven, and wore dirty pants, filthy jogging shoes, and an unbuttoned denim shirt that exposed a tattered T-shirt and thick black chest hair. The man didn't move at their appearance, and didn't even open his shuttered eyes to look their way. In his right hand he gripped a hypodermic needle. An elastic band pinched his left arm, just above the elbow, making the veins of his forearm and wrist pop out like those of a weightlifter. On the floor between his splayed legs lay a spoon, a pack of matches, and a small packet of aluminum foil.

A heroin addict! thought David. A fucking heroin addict shooting up in Royce Kray's sitting room. Who the hell is this guy? One of the daughter's boyfriends? A son he hadn't heard about? Some wayward soul Kray had taken in from his talk show?

His aunt stepped toward the young man. David warned her to stay back, but she bent down and touched the man's arm. He didn't flinch. She recoiled her hand as if she'd touched a hot stove.

Swell! The man's dead! OD'd right in their goddamned sitting room! A lovely scene. Stick that in your Ethan Allen catalog.

"An *incredible* likeness," said Ruby, turning toward Sarah Kray, who was watching with detachment.

"A miracle of modern chemistry," the girl said tonelessly. "Polyester resin and fiberglass. My father bought it. He had the artist on his show once."

David stared again at the man. He felt foolish, angry, conned. Was that how Kray's listeners felt?

"Your father had a strange sense of taste," said Ruby.

"A *sick* sense. It was one of his many political statements. He insisted that all guests sit in here. I've seen people leave the house physically ill."

"Why keep it now? Give it away to a museum. He'd make a great poster child for the 'Just Say No' folks."

"I'd love to. I hate the thing. But the rest of the family is afraid to get rid of it."

"Afraid?"

Sarah Kray looked surprised that Ruby didn't understand. "It's my father's," she said, as if that explained everything. She contemplated the figure. "Maybe I'll call 911 and have the paramedics take him away."

She vanished, returning a few minutes later accompanied by a middle-aged woman with stylishly short blond hair, a sallow complexion, and tired blue eyes. The woman moved in slow, thick-legged steps, as if walking through waist-high water.

As David rose from the floral chair he'd been sitting in, his first thought was that his aunt was wrong. Christina Nilsson had told them the truth. No way was this woman Bayne Gibson's lover. She was at least fifteen years his senior and far from a specimen of athletic prowess. Her delicate features carried their own attractiveness—personally, he liked thin women—but they were hardly a match for the raw, fit looks of Nilsson that an athlete like Gibson would go for. No . . . no, this woman harbored no secret liaison with Bayne Gibson nor was she involved in any love-triangle murder of her husband.

Introductions made, Anna Lee Kray sat down on the front edge of a loveseat, her hands crossed in her wide lap over a pair of burgundy slacks. Heavy bracelets jangled from each wrist. Sarah sat next to her, but farther back in the seat.

Neither of them looked in the direction of the junkie.

"It would be best if we talked alone," Ruby said to Mrs. Kray.

"Oh, no, I want Sarah beside me," she said in a voice as delicate as her skin. She patted her daughter's arm. "She's been my strength through this entire ordeal."

"Suit yourself." Ruby leaned forward in her chair, her eyes barely visible beneath the brim of her hat. "Did a man named Jim Brodie visit you recently? A large man with a black and white beard? He was looking for Gibson."

"Yes . . . yes, he did. I'd forgotten his name, but he said he was some kind of detective. Does he work for you?"

"Sometimes. He's a bounty hunter. When was he here?"

"Two days ago, I think. In the afternoon. I'm not sure. Everything's been a blur since . . . since . . ." No tears surfaced, but she bowed her head.

"Your daughter told me he was never here, that you'd never spoken to him."

Mrs. Kray smiled apologetically in the direction of her daughter. "Please understand that Sarah tries to protect me. Sometimes she tries too hard."

"Protect you from what?"

"From outsiders, reporters, curiosity seekers, people pestering us about Royce."

"How long was he here?"

"Not very long. He was . . . well, he was a little rude. Sarah asked him to leave."

"Rude? How was he rude?"

There was a moment of silence. David heard the sounds of a loud stereo off somewhere else in the house. Sarah's? Another daughter's?

"He implied that I might know where Bayne—Mr. Gibson—might be hiding."

"Do you?"

"No!" Sarah Kray's shrill voice startled everyone. "That's outrageous. How can you accuse my mom of having anything to do with that awful man?"

"Sarah . . . Sarah," said her mother softly, squeezing her arm.

"I'm not going to let anyone say such garbage like that

about you. My God, he killed Father! Why would anyone even *think* you would know anything?''

"I'm sure no one thinks—''

"How well did you know Bayne Gibson?'' interjected Ruby.

"We met a few times at business functions and we exchanged pleasantries on the telephone . . . but that's all. He never came to our house, and I rarely went to the radio station. Never, actually. I just listened to Royce.''

"Do you know anything about a mountain retreat in or near Evergreen that Gibson may have owned or may have gone to after he skipped?''

"No, I don't.''

Mrs. Kray fidgeted with her bracelets. David glimpsed tiny white scars on her wrists. A suicide attempt, Reed had told them, three months before her husband was murdered. Not as successful as her son. One of her daughters had saved her life. Which one? Sarah?

"What about you, Sarah?'' asked Ruby. "Did you ever hear your father say anything about a retreat Gibson owned?''

"No, I never did,'' she said coldly.

"You have two other daughters, don't you, Mrs. Kray?''

She looked up from her wrists and nodded.

"Would they know something about the retreat?''

"No . . . no, I'm sure they wouldn't. Aspen—she's our oldest—came home from college just a few days before Royce was . . . was killed. She's up in her room right now but I don't want to disturb her. She's taken this all very hard. She and my husband had a . . . a—''

"—very special relationship,'' finished Sarah in a mocking tone.

"Sarah, please—''

"And your other daughter is . . . ?''

"Darcy . . . our youngest. She's not here right now.'' From her tone, David surmised that Darcy rarely was here. "She wouldn't know anything about this retreat, anyway. I don't think she ever met . . . Mr. Gibson.''

"You never secretly met with him at this retreat?''

Anna Lee Kray's face filled with alarm.

"There you go again!" snapped Sarah.

"Sarah, please." Mrs. Kray looked at Ruby. "I'll repeat what I told your bounty hunter. I was not having an affair with Bayne. I rarely even spoke to him except at parties. We weren't lovers."

"That's not what I've been told."

"That's a damn lie!" shouted Sarah, bolting to her feet. "Who told you that? Whoever told you that is lying. Is it that girlfriend of his? It's her, isn't it? She's the one telling these damn lies!"

"Sarah, please," said Mrs. Kray, reaching up toward her daughter. "They're only trying to—" Suddenly her face drained of color and she sagged against the back of the loveseat.

Sarah pressed over her mother, holding her hand. "Mom . . . are you okay, Mom?"

"I'm fine," she said weakly. "A little water would be nice. I'd like a little water."

Sarah whirled on Ruby and David. "Get out! Get the hell out! I should never have let you in here. I should never have let you talk to her. Get out or I *will* call the police!"

As they walked toward the Lamborghini under a canopy of trees, David asked his aunt, "What do you make of all that? She really faint?"

"Pretty good acting if she didn't."

"Was she lying?"

"Mrs. Kray?"

"Yes. Was she lying about her and Gibson? About the place in Evergreen?"

"The closest thing to the truth in that house was the dead junkie."

17

David was reading everything he didn't want to know about tort law when Aspen Kray walked into the office.

He knew she was a Kray the moment he saw her. The resemblance to her mother was striking: the same delicate facial features, the porcelain skin, the fashionably short blond hair, the hips that were too wide. She looked slightly older than Sarah Kray, so he assumed she was Royce Kray's eldest daughter, the one who had returned from college only days before he was murdered. From Wellesley, if the red T-shirt she wore accurately reflected where she was enrolled. Bet she wasn't working her way through college as a bondsman.

Her eyes took in the office in one sweep and dismissed it.

"Is Ms. Dark here?" she asked, her eyes ignoring him. She didn't choke on the salutation as Lamprey did. Probably all the women at those pricey Eastern schools addressed each other that way—even in the can.

David rose to his feet. "No. May I help you?"

"You expect her back soon?"

"I'm not sure when she'll be back. May I help?"

"I'll come back later." She turned on her heels.

"You're Aspen Kray, aren't you?"

She stopped and turned back. Her eyes took him in, appraised him directly this time. They were large blue eyes, like remote alpine lakes, so clear and deep and still he wanted to dive in and swim around even though he suspected the waters were icy.

"You look like your mother," he said, answering the question on her face.

The surface of the lakes froze over. "You must be the dweeb who was with this bondswoman when she harassed my mother."

"We didn't harass—"

She stepped close to the desk. "What's your name?"

"David Piszek."

"Piszek. What kind of name is that?"

"Polish."

"Well, Piszek the Pole, I want you to pass along a message to your boss. Quit raggin' my mother. She's not a well woman, she is not Gibson's lover, and she has no idea where he is. Accusing her of protecting the man who murdered my father is—"

"They were fair questions."

"Why, because some intellectually challenged bimbo claimed my mother was sleeping with him? Do you buy into everything people tell you?"

"Actually, in this business, you don't believe most of what people tell you. But I had the impression there was a grain of truth in what she said."

"I hope you're not a man who trusts his impressions often."

He didn't want to play twenty questions with Aspen Kray. Not that there weren't twenty to ask. But interrogation was his aunt's job. He just wanted to take in her eyes and yammer on about the weather and school and other inconsequential social chit chat. Yet he found himself caught up in the heat of her bitchy responses, in his own anger and guilt over Gibson's and now Big Jim's disappearance.

"A bounty hunter named Jim Brodie talked to your mother a couple of days before we did. Did you talk to him?"

"No. I heard about him. Sarah told me he was as insulting as you two."

"He's missing."

"Good. That's one less scuz in the world."

David banked his rising anger. What the hell did they teach these girls in those Eastern schools, anyway? "You ever hear anything about a mountain retreat in Evergreen that Gibson had—maybe your father mentioned it?''

''You don't get with the program very quickly, do you?''

''You didn't answer my question.''

''I don't have to answer your questions.''

''Look Ms. Kray, we're trying to track down the man who killed your father. You *do* want your father's murderer caught and brought to trial, don't you?''

Pain cut into her face. She said in a tired voice, ''I've never heard anything about any retreat Gibson had in the mountains—from my father or mother or anyone else. I don't keep up on that stuff.''

David motioned toward the chair in front of the desk. ''Please, let's start over. I don't mean to push so hard, but we're very worried about Jim. He's got a wife and a daughter, and they're worried too. Maybe he was too blunt with your mother, but he is on your side. He wants to catch Gibson too.''

Her body relaxed slightly, but she remained standing, silent.

David sat down. ''I understand your hostility. I'm sure your father's death has been very hard on you. Your sister said you had a very special relationship with him.''

Aspen stiffened again. ''My sister?''

''Sarah.''

''She said I had a special relationship with him?''

''Yes. You were his oldest child, right? Don't fathers often have a special relationship with their first born?''

He'd been his father's first born, and they'd had a special relationship. It had not been an easy one.

''I wouldn't call it special . . . but . . . he was my father.''

Not a trace of tears in her cool blue eyes. His aunt was right: even bad families protect their own. Royce Kray may have been the All-American asshole, but it must have been tough for a daughter, even one who may have hated him, to admit to herself, let alone anyone else, that her own father was such an asshole that someone would deliberately murder him. It must feel as if they had shot her too.

He motioned again to the red leather chair on the other side of the desk, and this time she accepted his invitation.

She plopped her black handbag atop stone-washed jeans, dug out cigarettes, and lit one with a small enamel lighter. Her eyes appraised him steadily through the smoke.

"How does one get into the bail bonding business, Piszek the Pole? It's not exactly a career most people grow up aspiring to. It sounds like the kind of thing they advertise on late-night television."

"It's just temporary," he said hastily. "Ruby Dark's my aunt. I'm paying my way through law school."

"A lawyer! God, how nineteen sixties!"

"Did you learn to be this warm and friendly at Wellesley or from your father?"

"Leave my father out of it."

She blew smoke out hard and looked around the desk for an ashtray. David pulled open a desk drawer, took out a cheap glass ashtray with a motel name etched on it, and reluctantly set it in front of her. His aunt didn't smoke, though he suspected she once did. But she'd kept an ashtray on top of the desk for clients who did, and there were many. He'd argued that leaving out an ashtray was as bad as leaving a liquor bottle out in front of an alcoholic. The drawer was their compromise.

Aspen Kray exaggeratedly tapped the ashes onto the glass tray with her forefinger. "You're one of those fascist health police, aren't you?" She took another hard, defiant drag.

"No, I'm not. Really."

"Then why are you looking at me as though I'm a serial killer?"

He tried to change the subject. "What are you studying at Wellesley?"

"Biz ad . . . this year, anyway. Last year it was French lit. My freshman year it was poli sci—my father's choice, as was the school. Next year, who knows. It doesn't make any difference."

She seemed to take singular pride in her lack of direction.

"Why doesn't it make any difference?" he asked.

"Because there's nothing but McJobs out there. Haven't you noticed—or are you brain dead too?"

"It's tough, I know, but—"

"Tough? A friend of mine graduated last year with an

MBA. She's now an office temp. I know a bio grad who's installing auto glass. Who needs a BA in cellular biology to install auto glass? Look at you. Talk about a McJob."

"It's temporary. When I graduate, I—"

"Yeah, yeah, like the world needs another fucking lawyer. Fact is, Piszek, our generation is the lowest on the economic food chain and it's going to stay that way. Our parents blew our future."

David had heard a lot of the same carping among his fellow law students. Generation X, the 13th generation to be born since the American Revolution: raised on *The Brady Bunch* and junk food, boooooooored with Vietnam, and angry at the politically, morally, and economically bankrupt society their parents had left them with. A part of him understood their anger and anxiousness. Yet a part of him was tired of the whining. The world didn't need more victims.

"Are you at home for the summer?" he asked, hoping to change the subject.

"Yeah."

"Sisters around much?"

"What does that have to do with anything?"

His aunt had raised the possible but improbable scenario that Bayne Gibson was hiding out in the Kray home. It'd be a perfect hiding place, as long as the police never learned Gibson and Mrs. Kray were lovers. But the three daughters presented a problem for the scenario. It would be impossible for Gibson to hide there without their complicity.

David said, "I was curious . . . about your younger sister—Darcy, isn't that her name? Is she around much? Would she know anything about Jim or this Evergreen place?"

Aspen let out an explosive laugh. "Darcy? She's sixteen. She wears a ring in her nose and hangs out with friends that I can only politely describe as fascists. She's rarely home. She wouldn't know a thing about anything. None of us do."

"You don't exactly sound like the Three Musketeers."

She rose and crushed out her cigarette. "Sisters fight, Piszek. It's part of the DNA. But when it comes to the important things, we stick together. Our mother is important. You and your aunt leave her alone. Leave us alone."

* * *

Ruby splashed Buckshot Salsa over a plate of nachos she'd zapped in the microwave while David gave her a blow-by-blow description of Aspen Kray's visit. Except for the eyes. He didn't tell her about the deep blue eyes. That he'd kept to himself.

"Sounds like we pushed a button when we visited the Kray home," she said between mouthfuls.

"I think she was genuinely angry," said David. "Maybe her mother really doesn't know where Gibson is and Aspen simply wants to protect her."

Ruby shook her head. Anna Lee Kray knows, she said. She knows something. Ruby couldn't say what it was she knew or why she didn't believe Mrs. Kray. She just *sensed* she was lying. Angel's legendary intuition, figured David. Like the carnival man who uncannily guesses to the ounce the weight of all takers.

But David wasn't convinced. Why, he reasoned aloud to his aunt, would Bayne Gibson risk an affair with the older, sickly-looking, suicidal wife of his prize radio personality when there were younger, more energetic, healthy, and attractive alternatives like Christina Nilsson? Did she seriously believe that Anna Lee Kray was someone Bayne Gibson would murder for? Money, yes, but love? And if he did kill for love, wouldn't Mrs. Kray have some serious reservations about contacting a lover who'd murdered her husband—unless she was directly involved in the murder?

His observation brought a cold eye from his aunt, and a verbal rebuke. Why *couldn't* a younger man be emotionally attracted to an older woman? she argued. Why should he assume that physical lust was the sole determining factor in a man's love for a woman—though God knows that often was the case. Maybe something in Gibson's own personality attracted him to a woman with more vulnerable qualities.

Bayne Gibson did not strike him as a man given to emotional generosity, countered David. Hadn't Ruby herself noted the man's shallowness, his self-absorption in his running?

His aunt gave him a "when you grow up and know what I know" look.

The phone rang. Ruby picked it up.

"Oh, hi, Marian . . . What? . . . Damn! . . . The LTD? . . . Where'd they find it? . . . How long ago? . . . Any signs of— Any prints? . . . He still hasn't called? . . . I know you're scared, Marian. But I'm sure he's okay. Jim's a tough guy . . . Yeah, we'll do everything we can to find him, hon. . . ."

"What's the matter?" he asked before the phone hit the cradle.

"Marian said the police found Big Jim's car."

"But no Jim?"

"Nothing. No sign of him."

"Shit! Where'd they find it?"

"Downtown on top of the DCPA parking garage. Nobody probably woulda noticed it for days except some geezer backed into it and was actually honest enough to report it to the lot management. When nobody came for the car, they called the cops, they traced the plates, got hold of Marian. Car was wiped clean of prints. No ticket in it, so they don't know when the car came in."

The awful knot returned to the pit of his stomach, the feeling that everything had gone terribly wrong and that it was all his fault. He bowed his head. "Marian's pretty worried?"

"Yeah."

He looked up at her. "What do we do? We've been looking everywhere for him."

Ruby stared at the nachos but didn't touch them. "We're gonna push the Kray family a lot harder."

18

"Sarah just left. Mrs. Kray's alone." Ruby had staked out the Kray home from her car since late afternoon.

David shook his head at the other end of the phone line. "I still don't think this is a good idea."

"You never do, David."

"It's illegal."

"It's a gray area."

"*Gray?* There's nothing gray about impersonating a police officer. It's against the law!"

"She won't be able to prove a thing."

"That's beside the point."

"You're the only one I can trust to do it, David. They know something about Jim and we've got to find out what real soon."

"There must be another way," he said with no fight in his voice. He was thinking of Brodie.

"I'm open to ideas."

He didn't have any.

"Remember to use a pay phone," she said. "Call me when you're done."

He called from a pay phone on Colfax, one of those half-shelled jobs with no privacy and no way to muffle the street noise. Which was probably to the good. The last thing he wanted was for Mrs. Kray to recognize his voice, though he'd barely spoken to her during their visit.

She answered on the fifth ring in her pale voice.

"Mrs. Kray? This is Detective Greene of the Denver Police Department,'' he said, hoping she wouldn't notice the shakiness in his voice. ''I'm one of the officers assigned to the Major Case squad investigating the murder of your husband.'' There was a real Detective Greene and he was assigned to the Kray case. That was about the only piece of truth David would tell her. ''Pardon my call from a noisy pay phone, but we've just received a tip that Bayne Gibson has made threats against your family.''

Anna Lee Kray choked a cry in her throat.

Jesus, this is beyond the bounds of common decency—even if she does know something about Jim's or Gibson's whereabouts, David thought.

''I—I don't understand,'' she said. ''I really can't believe he would . . .'' Her voice trailed off.

David looked at the notes he and his aunt had sketched out. ''The tip is from a reliable source, ma'am, and we're taking the threat very seriously. There's evidence he may also be involved in the recent disappearance of a bounty hunter who was looking for him.''

''A bounty hunter?'' Her voice was distant.

''Yes, ma'am. Name of Brodie.''

''Brodie?''

''Ma'am?'' He could barely hear her.

She asked, more strongly this time, what he wanted her to do.

''The best thing is for you and your daughters to remain at your home. Keep the doors and windows locked. We'll beef up street patrols around your house. I don't want to alarm you, but we felt it was best that you knew of the threat.''

''I still can't believe . . .'' Suddenly the tone of her voice turned cool. ''You said you received a tip.''

''Yes, ma'am.

''Does that mean someone knows where he is?''

''Confidentially, ma'am—you swear you won't divulge to anyone, including your daughters, what I'm about to tell you?''

''No. Yes. I mean, I won't say anything.''

''We believe Gibson is hiding in a house somewhere in the Evergreen area, and we anticipate apprehending him within the next twenty-four hours."

"That's . . . that's good news, Officer . . . ?

"Detective Greene, ma'am."

"Detective Greene, yes. Yes. Thank you, detective."

He immediately called Ruby on her car phone. "I hope we're doing the right thing, Aunt Ruby. I think I scared the hell out of her."

"Good. At worse, we scared her for nothing. But if she does know something, then maybe it'll panic her into action."

"What if she doesn't do anything? What if she calls Greene?"

"He's not at his desk, and won't be until tomorrow."

"And what about the next day? At some point, Aunt Ruby, the shit's going to hit the fan."

"Then let's hope we're not in the way when it does."

The young woman in the hot pink and black Lycra shorts and expensive in-line skates cruised hard down the middle of the street, artfully dodging moving cars and startled pedestrians. With each long stride, the muscles in her buttocks and firm thighs contracted in poetic motion, powered her into her next stride, propelled her into faster and more dangerous maneuvers between obstacles. Her arms swept back and forth in perfect symmetry with each stride, like those of an Olympic speed skater. Her short blond hair bobbed in the wind as—

Somewhere a distant ringing intruded. The image of the young woman began to break up, like a signal from outer space disturbed by the intrusion of distance and cosmic forces. David stirred drowsily in the front seat of his car and tried to hang on to her image, tried to shut out the irritating noise. He hadn't gotten her name yet and she was skating so fast and he—

"Damn!" he said when he realized the ringing was coming from the cell phone laying beside him. He wasn't sure how many times it had rung. He fumbled for the phone and punched the receive key.

"Asleep, David?" said Ruby.

"Just resting."

He squinted at his watch in the weak yellow light of a street lamp: 1:17 A.M. When had he last looked at the watch? It hadn't been more than ten or fifteen minutes, had it?

"Need me to relieve you?" she asked.

Don't they shoot soldiers for sleeping on guard duty in the middle of a war? he thought.

"No, no, I'm fine," he said, rubbing his neck.

"You sure?"

"Yeah, I'm sure."

The hell he was fine. He'd relieved his aunt shortly after it had turned dark, switching parking places with her a third of a block down and across from the Kray home. Now his whole body was stiff and sore, and his butt had gone to sleep. Since his arrival, Ruby had called every thirty minutes.

"Still just Aspen and her mother in the house?" she asked.

Nothing had changed, he told her. Forty-five minutes after Ruby had left, Aspen Kray had showed up driving a sporty green Mazda. She'd parked on the street, picking a space only three cars from where David sat. He'd slumped in his seat until she'd entered the house.

It was nearly midnight when the third daughter of the Kray family, Darcy, stopped by. At least, he assumed it was Darcy Kray. She'd arrived in an old black and white hearse with a Dixie flag on the side and a stereo system cranked up so loud the entire car throbbed. Behind the wheel sat a young male whose hair was shaved to his scalp. She climbed out through the passenger window. He couldn't see her clearly through the binoculars under the street lights, but he could make out a head of hair that was wild and black and shaved along the sides. She wore all black, and white-laced black combat boots. An army surplus gas mask bag hung from her shoulder. She drank from what looked like a can of beer. And once, when the street light hit her face just right, something bright winked from her nose. She must have irritated the hell out of her father.

The car sat double parked while she went inside the house, which was dark except for security lights. A light went on somewhere in the interior. A few minutes later she stomped out of the house. From the hearse she gave the finger in the general direction of the house, but he couldn't tell if anyone was watching at the receiving end. The hearse squealed its tires as it raced off down the street.

Ruby hung up. David was awake now. The interior of the Duster was sweltering. He took a drink of mineral water and rolled down his window. Or tried. The window crank stuck part way down. He got out of the car and pissed on the trunk of a huge silver maple. A dog barked nearby. He got back in and tried to sleep again, tried to find the young blond woman in the hot pink shorts. It was Aspen Kray, he realized now. Pale skin and lake blue eyes. Or did those muscular thighs belong to Christina Nilsson?

But he couldn't find her again. He couldn't recapture the dream.

He was in the middle of a stupid dream about a naked weatherman when the slamming of a car door woke him. He fumbled for his binoculars and looked over the back seat in the direction of the Kray home. An engine rumbled to life. A white Honda parked directly in front of the house pulled swiftly out into the street and away from him. He glimpsed short blond hair and the profile of Mrs. Kray.

He turned on his engine and pulled out without his lights on. As was Big Jim Brodie's habit, he'd parked facing away from his quarry, to lessen suspicion, and he had to awkwardly turn around in the street. The power steering was gone in the Duster and by the time he was headed in the right direction, the Honda had turned west onto Eighth.

Frantically, he tried to speed dial his aunt. It took a block and a half to find the right key combination.

She answered before the first ring was finished.

"Mrs. Kray just pulled away," he said. He glanced at his watch. 1:59. Where the hell was she going at this hour?

"Where's she headed?"

"West on Eighth."

"Stay with her! I'm headed for my car." At least there wasn't an I-told-you-so in her voice.

He trailed the Honda past the Governor's Mansion and across Speer Avenue. About the time she swung onto 6th Avenue going west, Ruby checked in from her car phone.

Mrs. Kray passed Sheridan, Wadsworth, and Kipling.

"She's headed to Evergreen!" Ruby said.

My god, thought David, maybe she really is going for Bayne Gibson.

"Don't lose her, David. Don't lose her! I'm not far behind you."

Following the white Honda in light traffic under a nearly full moon was easy. What worried him was if they reached the foothills and began to do some serious climbing. The aging Duster would be no match for the newer Honda. She was already ten miles above the speed limit. If she decided to push it—

The phone rang. "I'm right behind you, David," Ruby said. In his rearview mirror, a dozen car lengths behind, prowled a big dark Buick, the car his aunt drove when she thought the Lamborghini would look too conspicuous. It was also her skip-hauling car. The rear doors had special locks that couldn't be opened from the inside, and skips could be handcuffed to iron rings chained to the floor.

Mrs. Kray swung onto I-70 and headed into the foothills, past Genesee Park, past the turnoff to Buffalo Bill's Grave, past the herd of buffalo standing shadowy somewhere in the meadow off the side of the freeway. At the El Rancho exit, she abruptly exited and cut south on the two lane road to Evergreen.

David and Ruby exited with her, but, following his aunt's advice, David turned off onto a frontage road in case Mrs. Kray was watching her rearview mirror. Ruby passed the frontage road a few moments later. Both she and Mrs. Kray were quickly out of sight on the curvy, hilly road.

David caught up with them on the outskirts of Evergreen, and hung behind his aunt an eighth of a mile. When Mrs. Kray turned onto Upper Bear Creek Road by Evergreen Lake, Ruby drove on by, letting David take the turn. He followed the Honda west through a shallow canyon, running alongside a stream that sliced through the front yards of huge, expensive homes. The road was narrow and winding, and Mrs. Kray was driving very fast. The Duster struggled to keep her in sight. His window was still partially rolled down and he could hear the bald tires squeal on the tight curves. The phone connection started breaking up in the rugged foothills, but after a while Ruby's headlights loomed reassuringly behind him.

Several miles later Mrs. Kray turned left onto a gravel road that disappeared into thick pine trees in a place called Elk Meadow Estates. David drove by the entrance, knowing his aunt would make the turn into the Estates. Once over the next hill, he turned around and came back to the entrance.

He eased into Elk Meadow Estates, his lights doused. Nothing but blackness lay ahead. No headlights, no flicker of lights bouncing off the trees. He drove slowly, his head cantered toward the open window, alert for sounds above the noise of the Duster's own engine. Nothing. Not even the familiar night sounds of a summer's evening. The lonely stillness of the West in the summertime was strange to him, almost oppressive and frightening in its silence. Missouri nights were so alive with sounds, with the chatter and chirp of insects. Here, he could only hear the faint moaning of the pine trees in the breeze.

In the moon's broken light he could make out widely separated driveways leading to large houses set back from the roadway, half hidden in the trees, or longer, rutted driveways disappearing into the timber, no house in sight. Virtually all the homes were dark, except for security lights and low accent lights demarcating driveways.

At one point, a huge dog of undetermined breed lunged out of the darkness at him, barking madly and scaring the shit out of him. Then as suddenly as the dog had appeared, it retreated, its duty complete as David passed beyond the boundaries of its master's yard.

Around a curve the reflection of red taillights of a car flashed in front of him, and his heart jumped again. He hit the brakes.

It was Ruby's Buick. She'd doused the lights and stood beside the car, waiting for him. She walked up to his window. She was hatless, her long hair a dark red mass. She wore slacks and a blouse, and, for once, sensible shoes.

"She's down the road somewhere," said Ruby. "I don't know exactly where. I couldn't risk following her too close."

"How are we going to find her?"

"I've been here before, maybe a year ago. The place isn't

very large and there's only the one entrance. If we don't spot her, we'll wait for her to come out. Gibson's somewhere around here, David, I can smell him. The sonofabitch isn't getting away again.''

She got back in her car and began to slowly drive down the road, David following, their lights off. An eighth of a mile later Ruby suddenly stopped at the entrance to a long gravel driveway. A white Honda was parked at the far end, two hundred feet from the road. David couldn't see the house through the dark stand of pines, but from the ball of light splayed in the tree tops it looked as if a party was in progress—every light must have been thrown on, though he could hear no music, no voices, no loud drunken laughter.

He stepped out of his car. Stirred dust tickled his nose. Through binoculars, he confirmed it was the same Honda they'd followed from the Kray home. They blocked the driveway with their cars. The only way out for Gibson was by tank or on foot.

''What do we do?'' he whispered, his heart pounding. He wished Big Jim was with them.

''We walk right up the driveway. But keep to the edge.''

He tried to sense if his aunt was scared, if *he* should be scared, but her rough voice, as usual, disguised her innermost feelings. He tried to discern some sign in her face, but the shadowy light from the moon and the house made her look edgy one moment and stone confident the next.

Ruby reached into her purse in the front seat of the car and pulled out a handgun. He knew she owned a gun, but he'd never seen it, and he had never seen her hold it or clean or take it to a firing range. He wasn't even sure what make or model it was. An automatic of some sort, he thought.

He stared at the gun in her hand. His experience with guns was limited to occasionally tramping through frozen December cornfields hunting pheasant or stray rabbits. His father had never owned a gun, so the few hunting trips he'd made he had borrowed a .410 shotgun from one of his buddies.

''Are you sure that's necessary?'' he said.

''I'm not sure it's not.''

Even when he'd helped Big Jim bring in a couple of rough characters, the bounty hunter had never pulled a gun. But while Ruby certainly had Big Jim's stealth and cunning, she didn't have his intimidating size and strength. A gun was a great equalizer, he supposed without much comfort. His aunt looked at ease with it in her hand. Probably a card-carrying member of the NRA. Still, it made him nervous. Guns meant that someone could get shot. Not a pheasant or stray rabbit, but a live breathing human being . . .

They walked briskly along the gravel driveway toward the bright lights. Ruby stayed ahead of him ten feet, crouched slightly as she moved. Occasionally he caught glimpses of the outline of the gun in her hand in the scattered light. He armed himself with a large stick he found along the way. It would be useless against a gun, but its solidness gave him a sense, if only a false one, of safety.

Halfway down the driveway, they began to make out the ghostly shape of the home. It was huge, with a high pitched wood shingle roof, thick log walls, and a massive stone fireplace. Tall slender pines pushed to within a few feet of its sides. The driveway looped in front of it. Lights exploded out of every window.

There was no sign of movement and still no sounds except for the slight breeze in the treetops and the soft crunch of gravel beneath their feet. They were thirty yards from the house when a scream shattered the stillness of the clear mountain air.

19

The scream came from inside the house. A long, high-pitched scream, barely muffled even by the thick log walls.

Ruby bolted down the driveway, her gun raised. David, momentarily frozen, raced after her, his body hunched forward, braced for gunshots.

Oh, to cradle that friend's shotgun again.

As they neared the house, a second scream came, closer and clearer, less haunting than before, more of a guttural moan than a piercing sound.

Suddenly Mrs. Kray burst out of the front door and ran toward her car, horror etched on her face.

Only it wasn't Mrs. Kray. The woman was blond and had Mrs. Kray's features, but the face was much younger.

"Jesus!" yelled David.

Aspen.

She collapsed against the driver's side of the car, fumbled with the door, and tumbled into the front seat.

"She's hurt!" he yelled at his aunt, who was closing in on the woman.

Stabbed, shot, beaten—he couldn't tell in the shadowy light, but he was sure she was hurt.

The Honda's motor turned over and the car began to spin around in the circular driveway, tires spraying gravel, the headlights flashing on.

Ruby covered the last ten yards to the car with surprising speed, and leapt into the glare of the headlights, gun raised, just as the car skidded around to face the way out.

Aspen Kray, who had shown no awareness of either of them, screamed at the sight of Ruby and her gun in the headlights, and threw her hands up in front of her face. The car careened off to the left, cutting diagonally across the driveway in what seemed slow motion before plowing to a stop in a thick Ponderosa pine.

Ruby pulled the door open and yanked the keys out of the ignition. Aspen's hands covered her face. She was shaking violently, moaning, "Don't kill me! Don't kill me! Please don't kill me!"

"Nobody's going to kill you," Ruby said, putting her hand on her shoulder. Aspen jerked. "I'm Ruby Dark. From the bail bonding company. You must be Aspen."

Still shaking, Aspen stared into Ruby's face. Her breath fell in heavy gasps. Her gaze jumped to David as he arrived at his aunt's side. Recognition seeped into her expression.

"Are you okay?" he said.

Her white blouse and short white shorts were slightly dirty and disheveled, but he saw no visible signs of blood or injuries or physical pain, just the drained look of someone going into emotional shock.

A low moan escaped her pale lips. "He's dead! He's dead!"

"Who's dead?" said Ruby.

"He's dead," she whimpered, hugging herself and rocking back and forth. "I can't believe . . . he's dead."

"Who?" Ruby's voice turned impatient. "Gibson?"

Aspen seemed to gather herself for a moment. "I . . . I don't know who the man is."

David looked toward the house. *Brodie?* Not Jim! Shit no, God, not Jim!

"There's a dead man in the house, honey?" Ruby asked.

Aspen began to cry.

"Is anyone in there who's alive and armed?"

Aspen sobbed uncontrollably now, unable to speak.

"Stay with her," commanded Ruby.

"What the hell are you going to do, storm the place alone?" David yelled. "The killer could still be in there!"

"She didn't say anyone was murdered. Just that someone's dead."

"I'm still going in with you."

"You're not armed."

David waved his stick. "The hell I'm not."

"Someone needs to stay here with her."

"Someone needs to look after *you.*"

Ruby moved off toward the house before he could argue further. She kept out of direct line of the front door. David scanned the front of the house for signs of movement, for shadows sliding against the interior lights, for a gun. But the house merely stared, aloof and silent and overlit.

Moments later Ruby slipped through the front door. Twice David saw her outline move past a window, then nothing. He strained to listen for a signal, a sign that she'd found the dead man or that she was yelling for someone to give himself up or that she was in trouble. But he could hear nothing but the damn wind in the trees and Aspen's hysterical sobbing.

He started toward the house, stopped, and then came back to Aspen. "Are you going to be okay?"

She was too hysterical to protest, or to even notice him. "I need to go inside, Aspen," he said softly.

She still didn't speak or acknowledge him. Her eyes looked glazed. Hell, she wasn't going anywhere.

He moved toward the house, stick clenched in his right fist.

Like his aunt, he kept out of direct line of the front door. He flattened his back against the rough logs and peered through the storm door into the interior. Seeing no one, he eased open the door and slipped into the house.

He found himself in the living room. Everything looked neat and in place: polished oak furniture, hardwood floors, white-stained logs, Indian throw rugs and pottery, a stone fireplace that soared twenty-five feet to the vaulted ceiling. Like Gibson's penthouse, it had a sterile, unlived-in feel, as though a cleaning lady was on duty twenty-four hours a day.

The only difference was the odor.

It was faint but noticeable. An odor, a mild stench, something that didn't quite sit right with him.

He tried to ignore it and look around. Three doorways spoked off the living room: an open entry on his left led to a kitchen, another to a dining room. Both were empty. The third led to a hallway.

He tiptoed several feet down the hallway. Lights flared from three rooms.

The odor grew stronger. He gulped, trying to quell the uneasiness in his stomach. The only time he'd smelled anything remotely like it was when he had traveled through Europe. He'd been in a backwater town in Spain, at an open market, where meat sat in unrefrigerated trays. Meat that had sat too long.

"Aunt Ruby!"

A muffled reply came from one of the bedrooms. He slid along a wall, peering into each room, his stick raised high in his hand. The first two were empty guest rooms, the third the master bedroom, which was twice as large as the others. In the middle of the room, at the foot of a king-sized bed, a rug had been flung back and a trap door in the middle of the hardwood floor was open.

"Aunt Ruby? You down there?"

"Just a minute, David. I'm coming up." Her voice filtered up with the light from the hole.

He approached the hole warily. Someone could be holding her against her will—a trap could be waiting. He sucked in his breath and gripped his club. What the hell would he do if Gibson suddenly appeared with a gun? Throw the stick at him?

"You okay?" he yelled. He peered over the edge of the hole. A short stairway led to a room below. He couldn't see her.

But the odor was strong now, almost overpowering. He swallowed hard. Jesus!

Suddenly Ruby appeared at the foot of the stairs and looked up at him. Her face was pale and drawn, and her eyes moist.

"Call the police, David."

He had never heard her so shaken and so somber. "Is it Jim?" He could barely get the name out.

"Just call the police."

"Dammit, Aunt Ruby, is it Jim?"

"Yes."

Fuck! He squeezed his eyes closed to shut out the pain and the smell.

"I'm coming down," he said.

"Don't. There's nothing you can do."

He went down anyway. The windowless room was roughly the size of the master bedroom above it, and was harshly lit by two rows of fluorescent lights. At first, he saw nothing. The room was empty. No furniture, no signs of occupancy. The beige carpet was worn in spots, but freshly vacuumed. The air was hot and damp and cloying.

He gagged and nearly threw up, but somehow managed not to. The room reeked . . . reeked of the most dreadful stench he had ever smelled in his life. How had his aunt stood it down here?

Then he looked into a corner behind the stairs. "God!" he said.

Big Jim sat slumped against a wall. His head lolled to one side. His facial features were nearly unrecognizable. The skin was swollen and greenish red. His arms dangled at his sides, palms up and empty. Two small red patches of blood, one chest high and the other on his stomach, stained his cowboy shirt.

"There's so little blood," said Ruby, her voice far away. "Such a big man and so little blood."

It was hard to believe someone had killed him, that he had *let* somebody kill him. He'd always been so damn smart, so careful, so invincible. Anger flared in David. Anger at Big Jim for failing, for letting him down, as if all Brodie's advice and tips had suddenly turned to lies. But most of all, anger at himself. Ruby had been right about her qualms about Gibson, and he'd been wrong. Dead wrong.

"Damn it!" he screamed. "God *damn* it!"

He turned away from Big Jim's body and began pacing around and around the room, like a carousel out of control. Walls of oppressive dark paneling and beige carpeting blurred by him. Maybe if he kept moving, maybe if he didn't look back, maybe if he circled the room enough times, Big Jim's body would be gone, maybe—

Suddenly he stopped. A wall curiously lined with half a dozen phone jacks two feet above the floor caught his attention. Shoulder high above the jacks a scrap of smooth blue paper, the size of his fingernail, lay trapped under a thumbtack. He pried the paper loose and examined it. A corner of a poster, judging from the numerous pinholes and thumbtacks left in the wall.

Ruby's hand touched his arm. He jumped.

"Where's the girl?" she asked.

"What?"

"Aspen? Where is she?"

"Oh . . . I left her in her car."

Ruby moved quickly toward the stairway. "I don't want her running."

"You have the keys. She's not going anywhere. She's in shock."

He was in shock. When he'd stood over the spot on Gibson's penthouse deck where Royce Kray had been shot, there'd been a certain vicarious thrill, a rush that he'd seen what everyone in town had read about but few had glimpsed. But his speculative images of Kray's body floating in the pond had been movie images, distilled from reality. There had been no stench, no grotesque body, no pall of real, ugly death.

Not like this.

"Let's go," said Ruby. "We have to call the police."

"Goddamn Gibson!" he said.

Ruby shook her head. "I don't think so."

She disappeared up the stairs. David followed. Halfway up, he glanced back at Brodie, secretly hoping he would see a faint sign that Big Jim had moved, that by some miracle a pulse still coursed through his massive body. But all he saw that he hadn't seen before was that Big Jim had worn a hole in the bottom of one of his cowboy boots.

Aspen Kray was where he had left her, sitting in the front seat of the car, the door still wide open. She had stopped sobbing. Now she stared catatonically out the windshield into the dark trees. She didn't look up when they approached.

Ruby leaned over her and said angrily, "Who killed Brodie?"

Aspen said nothing.

"The dead man in there. Who killed him?"

Aspen's body shook. "I don't know. I don't even know who he is. I never saw him before."

"His name is Brodie. Jim Brodie. He talked to your mother three days ago at your house. He was looking for Gibson."

Aspen nodded in vague acknowledgement.

"He'd been told that your mother was having an affair with Gibson. But now I'm wondering if it was you who was seeing Gibson."

Ruby's speculation stirred the young woman from her stupor. She looked up, bewildered, then back out the windshield of the car. She didn't say anything.

David found the notion of Aspen Kray and Gibson as lovers even more ludicrous than the notion of her mother being his lover. Aspen wasn't Gibson's type. Yet what explained her presence here only hours after his phone call as "Detective Greene"? Had she come in her mother's place, to warn Gibson for her mother? Would a daughter, even for the sake of her own mother, warn the man who had murdered her own father? Or was his aunt's speculations correct?

"How did you know about this place, honey?" Ruby asked.

Aspen kept her silence.

"Why did you come here? What were you looking for? Did you come to warn Gibson?"

David wasn't sure she was even hearing Ruby's questions.

"Look, we know you didn't kill Jim. He's been dead for at least two days. You obviously didn't know he was here. Just tell us why you came."

No response.

"Do you know where Gibson is now? Does your mother know where he's hiding?"

Aspen's hands gripped the dead steering wheel and twisted back and forth.

Ruby straightened up in exasperation. "You'll have to talk about it sometime, honey. If not to us, then to the police."

Ruby might as well have talked to the trees.

* * *

David called the Clear Creek County Sheriff's office from his aunt's car phone.

When he returned, Aspen had swung her legs out through the open car door and was smoking a cigarette. The smoke broke apart in the glare of the house lights. Ruby silently watched her from the front steps. David sat beside her.

"The sheriff'll be here in a few minutes. She say anything?"

"No."

"You don't *really* think she was seeing Gibson?"

"I don't know, David. I really don't know."

"Why not? Don't your damn gut feelings tell you anything?"

Ruby glanced sharply at him.

He looked away. "Sorry. I . . . I blame myself for this, for Jim's death."

"Why? You didn't kill Jim. Somebody else did. Don't blame yourself for what somebody else did."

"But if I hadn't pushed for the bond, Jim would be—"

"To hell with the 'but ifs,' David. For most people, that's all life is, one 'but if' after another."

"But you were right about him, Aunt Ruby. You didn't feel right about him, and you were right."

"There's no right or wrong about it, David. You make the best decisions you can at the time. Sometimes the results turn out the way we want them, sometimes not. That doesn't make our decisions right or wrong, it just means the results are different than we wanted. You accept the consequences and move on and quit bitchin'."

"I was so damn sure there was no way the man was going to skip."

"*I* made the final decision to bail him out, David. I went against my own instincts."

A sudden gust of wind rippled through the treetops, and brought with it the distant wail of a police siren.

20

Det. Morgan Reed rocked impatiently on the balls of his feet in front of the second-story window of Ruby's Bail Bonds, staring toward the buff-colored police headquarters.

"That was real timely, the way you two just happened to show up right after the Kray girl finds Brodie . . . in the middle of the fucking night." He spoke with his back to them, as if his remark was directed more at the brass across the street than to them.

"Is that an observation, Morgan, or a question?" Ruby said.

Reed half turned on his heels, his arms akimbo. He was dressed in another one of his ill-fitting Salvation Army sport coats and a tie that was so hopelessly out of date David wondered if it had been given to him as a gag gift—and he'd missed the gag. Reed sighed. "It's a question, Ruby."

"Official or unofficial?"

He turned all the way around toward her. "Will it make a difference in what story you tell me?"

"No. I just want to know whether I should call my lawyer."

Reed looked offended. "Jesus, Ruby, it's a friendly, unofficial question. Just between us." He glared at David to let him know he was an intruder. "Nothing gets passed on to the Department. I'm not wired, either. You want to pat me down me for a wire?"

He lifted his arms straight out from his side. His coat rode up uneasily over his broad shoulders.

Ruby smiled. "You'd like me to pat you down, wouldn't you?" He didn't look amused. "Okay, I'll give you a friendly, unofficial answer. We got a tip."

"From who?"

"Come on, Morgan. We have our confidential sources, just like cops. A very good string of them, I might add."

"This source told you Gibson was hiding there?"

"More or less."

"I see," said Reed, not seeing. "I'm asking, Ruby, because it seems Mrs. Kray was called last night by someone claiming to be Detective Greene—he's one of the investigators on Gibson's case, if you don't already know that. And this person claiming to be Greene told Mrs. Kray that Gibson had made threats against the Kray family and that the cops were about to close in on him. Only problem is, the real Detective Greene never called Mrs. Kray last night. Neither he, nor anyone else in the Department, know a thing about any threat from Gibson or about this house. You wouldn't know anything about that call, would you, Ruby?"

The expression on his face conceded that he knew that if Ruby knew she wouldn't tell him anyway.

Ruby struck an exaggerated vamp pose. "Do I look like a Detective Greene?"

Reed rolled his eyes and looked at David, who gave him an edgy "don't look at me" expression.

"So what does this alleged call to Mrs. Kray have to do with Aspen showing up at Gibson's?" Ruby asked.

"We don't know. The girl's clammed up. Won't say anything to anyone about why she went there or how she even knew the place existed."

"Think she was fooling around with Gibson?" asked Ruby.

"Maybe. The sheriff found a key to the house on her."

"Did Mrs. Kray have any explanation for her daughter's behavior?"

"She isn't saying much either. Mentioned the phone call and nothing else. She's pretty unstable. Guess they've got her doped up pretty good."

David saw a flash of relief in his aunt's face. Apparently, neither Mrs. Kray nor her daughters had said anything about their earlier visit, about Big Jim's visit, about the claim that Mrs. Kray and Gibson were having an affair. But that raised a question: why not?

"How did Brodie find out about the place?" asked Reed.

"We were told he was going to meet someone who knew where Gibson might be hiding. It was the last time anybody saw him alive."

"This same source told you about the house?"

"More or less."

"Jesus, Ruby, you could be a little more helpful than that. Your own bounty hunter's dead and you still got a million dollar-skip loose."

"County sheriff tell you guys what they've learned so far?"

"What is this, a one way street? I answer you but you don't answer me?"

"I'll find out another way if I have to."

Reed sighed. "Actually, the county's been extremely cooperative. Guess they recognized the connection to Kray and the hot potato this whole damn case is. Our own boys have been up there investigating alongside them."

"What've they found?"

"He'd been dead three days. Which would match about the time you said he disappeared."

David's stomach turned over at the flashback of the stench, of the horrible sight of Brodie's decomposing body. The floor moved under his feet and he leaned against the doorway to steady himself, hoping neither of them would notice his weakness.

Reed went on. "County coroner says he took the first shot in the stomach and the second one in the pump. Don't ask me how the hell the coroner knows which shot came first, but he claims he knows. Bullets came from a twenty-two, probably a handgun, distance of eight to ten feet. Even a guy like Brodie can't take a twenty-two in the pump at that range."

Ruby turned her back at Reed's blunt description and knelt in front of a sleeping Collateral. She scratched the dog behind his ears, something David had never seen her do before.

The dog jerked his head up in surprise and blinked at her with wet mournful eyes.

"Then he was shot by someone facing him and at close range?" she asked Reed, her back still turned to him.

"Yeah."

"Big Jim would never allow himself to be surprised like that by Gibson," she said. Her voice almost cracked.

"Well, he obviously did. Otherwise he'd be alive today."

Ruby stood and whirled on Reed.

"Christ, Morgan, do you think Big Jim just walked up to the front door and knocked? There's no way on God's green earth that he'd let a twerp like Gibson shoot him point blank head on. No way!"

"Maybe if he'd been carrying a gun . . ."

"Jim never used guns because he never needed one . . . because he thought the things were more dangerous than they were worth." The color in her face matched the color of her hair. "Guns attract guns, and then somebody gets hurt. Jim used his brains and his size. He was a bounty hunter for thirteen years, and I knew him for ten of those years. He brought back skips that would curl you hair . . . and he never used a gun."

Reed raised his hands to calm her down. "Maybe he just made a mistake, Ruby. Even the best of us do. He isn't the first bounty hunter to get killed. Damn good cops get killed too."

"Not by twerps like Gibson."

"They're the most dangerous kind. Guys let down their guard."

"I don't believe Gibson shot him. I don't believe he was capable of shooting Jim."

"Why not?"

"He's too weak."

"Weak men kill people every day," said an exasperated Reed. "I suppose you don't think he killed Kray, either?"

Ruby began pacing the floor. "Frankly, I hadn't thought much about it much until Jim died. But no, I don't think he did."

"It's a simple case, Ruby. Gibson and Kray didn't get along. They had their business differences. That's well documented. Now there's the added possibility that one of Kray's own daughters was having an affair with Gibson. Maybe Kray finds out. Maybe that's what he and Gibson were arguing about at the party the night before he was shot. The next day, Kray goes to the penthouse, waits for Gibson to arrive, and then confronts him again. Only this time Gibson says 'Fuck you,' and blows him away. It's a story as old as man. Two guys get in an argument and one of 'em grabs a gun. Bang! Bang! Fall down dead."

"Were Gibson's prints on the gun that killed Kray?"

"The prints on the weapon were smudged by his gloves."

"People don't take the time to put on gloves so they can shoot someone in self-defense, Morgan."

"So that just makes it premeditated."

"Why wear gloves for a gun he owns? His prints would naturally be on it."

"He wore 'em to keep any traces of gun metal or nitrates off his hand. That way homicide couldn't prove he actually fired the weapon. They ran an NAA and found traces of nitrates and barium on the glove but not on his hands."

"What's an NAA?" interjected David.

"A neutron activation analysis. The gun Gibson used was well constructed, and guns like that often don't leave much evidence of gunpowder. A standard chemical analysis might not turn up nitrates or barium or antimony, but an NAA will."

Ruby cut in. "None of this makes any sense, Morgan. If Gibson went to the trouble to wear gloves to hide powder burns, why shoot someone in his own penthouse with his own gun? Why hide the gun and the gloves in a place a rookie investigator would find in ten minutes and then hang around until the cops show up?"

"Nobody said murder makes sense, Ruby. A murderer's mind doesn't work like yours or mine. You know that."

"I know this whole thing smells."

"You want my best take on it? Gibson comes home and finds Kray standing piss-ass naked in his fish pond and they end up arguing. Gibson stomps off for his gun but puts just enough forethought into it to put on gloves."

"If he had that much presence of mind, he wouldn't have

shot Kray in the pond and let him just float there bleeding all over his prize fish.''

''Nobody else could have done it!'' said Reed testily. ''Nobody else could have snuck into the building and reached the penthouse without being seen. You can't even take the damn elevator up unless you have a key or are buzzed up.''

''Kray bought a gun two weeks before he was killed,'' Ruby said. ''Supposedly he carried it with him all the time for protection. But they didn't find the gun on his body or in the penthouse, did they?''

''No. It hasn't turned up anywhere.''

''If Gibson took it that night, where did he hide it? And why hide it in the first place? He could have argued self-defense if the gun had been left.''

Reed didn't have an answer.

''What kind of gun did Kray own?'' Ruby asked.

''A twenty-two, I think.''

''Same caliber that killed Jim.''

''Which makes the case that much stronger against Gibson. Brodie catches Gibson at the house. Gibson panics and shoots him with Kray's gun.''

''No, you're wrong, Morgan. You're wrong.''

''That's what I've always admired about you, Ruby, your open-mindedness.''

''What do they know about the place in Evergreen? Gibson own it?''

''It's under the name of a small property management company owned by Gibson Media. They're not yet sure if he used it for a retreat for his business clients or rented it out or what.''

So his aunt had been right, thought David. Lamprey had lied about there being no such place. The financial records Lamprey had given them had neglected to list the property as an asset.

He asked Reed, ''Do they know what was in that room where we found Jim? Somebody stripped that place clean.''

''Cleaned is right. The whole house was wiped down of prints. Only ones they found were the ones you two and the Kray girl left. They found her prints all over the place.''

"What about all those phone jacks?"

"Phone company says the place has a WATS line, in the name of the realty company."

"Selling hot mountain property?" Ruby asked.

"Could be. Sheriff found hair fibers in the carpet that belonged to several different individuals, identities unknown. There were also impressions in the carpet that would match a couple of long tables and several folding chairs, though they didn't find any in the house."

"Sounds like a boiler room scam," suggested Ruby.

"If that's the case, why run a scam out of an expensive house in Evergreen? Why not just rent cheap space in town?"

"Good question. Neighbors see anything?"

"There were reports of van traffic around the place in the mornings and evenings, and they found some tire tracks that don't belong to Brodie's car or Gibson's Cherokee or the girl's car. But that's about it. Oh, one other piece of evidence I forgot to mention. Homicide believes Brodie was shot in the living room, by the fireplace, not down in the room where you found him. They found blood in the cracks of the living room floor. There were no signs of a struggle—no broken glass or knocked-over lamps or broken furniture. He was shot and died without doing much about it. The coroner says the body was moved from there to the basement room twenty-four hours after he was killed."

Ruby stopped her pacing. "Was Jim dragged or carried downstairs?"

Reed looked perplexed. "Hell, I don't know. Does it make a difference?"

"It could prove my feeling that Gibson's been framed for both murders."

"How?"

"If he shot Jim, he woulda had to drag him downstairs by himself. No way could he have carried Jim. But if somebody else killed him—somebody with help—they could have carried him down."

"That sounds pretty thin to me."

"Then consider this. If Gibson did shoot him, that means he left Jim's body in the living room for twenty-four hours while he cleaned the place, hauled away tables and chairs from the basement room, and then hauled Jim's body downstairs. Then he coolly drives Jim's car back into Denver, where his mug is all over town, and parks it in a public lot. This doesn't fit the description of the owner of a fifteen million dollar media empire."

"Killing gets easier the second time around."

"Wait a minute," interjected David. "If somebody framed Gibson for Jim's murder, why hide Jim's body? Wouldn't they want it easily found?"

"I don't know, David. But I intend to find out."

Ruby picked a black bolero hat off the oak hat rack.

"Where are you going?" asked Reed.

She adjusted her hat. "I'm going to find who killed Jim and Royce Kray."

"Leave the damn detective work to someone else and stick to finding Gibson."

"Oh, I'm gonna find Gibson. I got a million bucks riding on his ass. But if I can't find him, maybe I can find the real killer. Find the real killer and maybe I find out where Gibson is. Find the real killer and the charges against Gibson go away—along with the bond."

Reed look toward David for help, but David raised his arms, palms up. Her quest was news to him.

Reed looked back at Ruby. "That's crazy, Ruby!"

"It's not crazy, Morgan, it's personal. Big Jim was a friend. He was a good man. He had a wife and a daughter. And he died looking for someone I sent him after. I owe him."

21

David dropped a sheaf of photocopied articles from the public library onto the middle of the clutter of Ruby's desk. A large photo of a sober-faced, bespectacled man stared up at her.

"This Tanner?" she said.

"Lincoln William Tanner, age forty-one, former barber, carpenter, truck driver, real estate broker, stockbroker, and now esteemed leader of the Brotherhood of the Transcendental Light. That's not counting occupations from previous lives."

Ruby looked up. "He believes in reincarnation?"

"Claims to have been everything from an Egyptian Pharaoh to a nineteenth-century London beggar. You'll notice a downward arc of karma there."

"We all carry our karma, David. Some of us just carry it longer than others."

Great, thought David. She and Tanner are soul mates.

Ruby slipped on her reading glasses and studied the photo. "He looks like an R.V. salesman."

"The guy may not look like Charles Manson, but I can assure you his elevator does not go all the way to the top."

"A lotta elevators don't," Ruby said. "The question is, did his stop enough floors shy for him to have killed Kray and Big Jim?"

"That could depend on whether he or this dead Mayan warrior-king he talks to was in charge at the time."

"He channels?"

"Daily. Mayan's named Chac."

Ruby mulled that over for a minute. "What else?"

"The rest is Horatio Alger stuff. He claims to have gone through million dollar fortunes twice before he started the Brotherhood. Actually, he claims a lot of things. The details vary substantially depending on which article you read. A couple of investigative reporters say most of what he claims about his personal life is fabricated."

Ruby shrugged. "Nothing unusual about that. Lots of people make up their lives as they go along. Sorta like buying new clothes." She put down the photo. "When did he start channeling?"

David snapped up the photocopies before they sank below the surface of clutter.

"About eight years ago." He thumbed through them until he found what he was looking for. "He said he'd grown 'weary of society's financial greed and moral corruptness.' Feeling guilty about all his money, I guess. That's when this Mayan priest called up. During an office Christmas party at the Chicago brokerage where Tanner was the top broker, he finds himself channeling for this Mayan character."

"Who is this Mayan?"

"Guy's only been dead since around eight hundred A.D. Murdered in some political intrigue. But what's a few years between friends. So here's Tanner, babbling away in the middle of this party. He'd never channeled before—I don't know about the Mayan. Anyway, Tanner's out of a job before the party's over, so this Chac character commands him to sell off all his possessions and move to Colorado to found the Brotherhood of the Transcendental Light. The mission of the Brotherhood is to lead the country out of its moral decay. Why Chac picked Colorado, I don't know."

Ruby laughed. "This state attracts more spiritual flakes than anywhere but northern California. Astrologers, tarot readers, Eastern mystics, UFO freaks, survivalists—you name it, we got it."

"Why?"

"I don't know. Don't mystics and mountains go together? I suppose it's tough getting in touch with yourself in the middle of downtown Chicago."

"Well, Tanner did as Chac instructed him. Sold off his possessions, moved out here, and bought two acres of land out beyond Conifer. He starts preaching—guided by his daily bull sessions with Chac. A regular Mr. Ed of Cosmic Consciousness." David paused, then said, "You know, when I was reading this stuff I got to wondering: if you put a group of channelers in a single room, could the dead hold a conference call?"

Ruby laughed again. "What exactly is this Chac's message?"

"Kinda of a mishmash of Edgar Cayce, Nostradamus, astrology, Buddhism, survivalism, and theosophy. Good thoughts and good deeds produce good karma, and negative thoughts and negative deeds produce bad karma. Each of us creates our own reality. Your truth is not necessarily my truth. Sort of a spiritual Velveeta cheese."

"A lotta people like Velveeta cheese," Ruby said. "It's safe."

"I guess so, because after a couple of 'years in the wilderness,' as Tanner likes to put it, the money started to pour in. He now owns over eighteen *thousand* acres. Calls it Tikal Ranch. That's the name of the Mayan city where this Chac guy lived. The ranch is pretty self sufficient. They raise organic crops for their macrobiotic vegetarian diet. Also cut timber for internal construction and outside sale. More impressive, though, is they have a state of the art media center on the grounds for taping Tanner's weekly radio broadcasts. Syndicates to about seventy-five stations. Also produces video and audio tapes based on his chitchats with the Mayan. And get this: they have a nine hundred number for people to call in to listen to taped messages from Chac. Can you believe that shit?"

"How many people live on the ranch?"

"About six hundred. They call themselves 'Light Keepers.' Most of them have sold off their possessions for the *privilege* of paying to live at the ranch. Tanner handpicks a few of them to be 'Chosen' ones. Basically his most trusted. He claims another seventy thousand followers world wide. They're called 'Seekers.' I can't believe he could find *seventy* people to swallow this shit."

"People are always looking for someone else to save them. It's easier than trying to save yourself. What about the firearms charge against Tanner?"

David fished out a newspaper clipping and scanned it. "State Patrol stopped Tanner and a couple of his cohorts for speeding about two . . . three months ago. They found twenty-five thousand dollars worth of assault rifles and ammunition in the car. They charged them in federal court on several counts of possession of illegal firearms, but two counts have already been dropped, and a couple of newspaper columnists suggest he's got enough influence that he may get the rest dropped."

"Sounds like someone we should visit," Ruby said. "I made a few calls while you were at the library. Tanner's at the ranch right now."

David tensed. "The place is an armed camp, Aunt Ruby. They're not going to let us in."

"We'll improvise."

"Okay, what if we do get in? What if we see Tanner? What are you going to ask him?" David lowered his voice an octave and took on a prosecutorial tone. "'Did you or one of your wacko followers kill Royce Kray and Jim Brodie? Or was it Chac who did the dirty deed?' " His voice returned to normal. "What the hell do you think he's going to tell us?"

"Probably nothing. Maybe he won't even talk to us. But sometimes, David—if you're alert—you can learn more by what people *don't* say than what they do. Maybe just seeing the place will tell us a few things."

Swell. Aunt Ruby the psychic.

The Brotherhood of the Transcendental Light occupied a remote, wide mountain valley an hour southwest of Denver. It was not, as David had nervously envisioned, an armed compound hidden among the cliffs and pine trees behind a chain link fence, gated roads, and Uzi-toting guards. Instead, a well-marked entrance road flowed invitingly onto a ranch sprawling with planted fields, neatly constructed homes, dormitories, and dozens of support buildings. People smiled and waved as Ruby and David drove in. They looked contented, well-fed, well-groomed, and friendly enough. The place resembled a small Midwestern town more than the center of a worldwide cult.

Ruby parked the Lambo next to several cars in front of a huge white domed building with a sign out front that said:

Meditation and Visitors Center
Tours Available

Inside, they found a well-stocked gift shop where half a dozen people rummaged through T-shirts, caps, books, video tapes, posters, tarot cards, pyramids, crystals, and other New Age trinkets.

"Hello," said a smiling young woman behind a glass counter. "Can I help you?"

"We want to speak with Chac," confided Ruby, reverence lacing her voice. "We've heard so much about him."

The woman smiled harder. "Father is extremely busy. If you would call to arrange—"

"Tanner is your father?" Ruby said incredulously.

The woman blushed. "Oh, no. All of us here address Mr. Tanner as Father."

She extended a brightly colored brochure and said it would explain all about the Brotherhood.

Ruby pushed aside the brochure and leaned across the counter. "Look, honey, it's really urgent that we speak with him today. I'm only in Denver for one day on business."

"I'm sorry, but I'm afraid that's not possible," she said with the patience of a woman who'd heard hundreds of similar pleas. "Are you aware of our nine hundred number?"

"Yeah. But we need to speak to him personally. You see—" Ruby leaned closer "—we're from California. I've spoken with Ramtha—you do know who Ramtha is, don't you?"

The woman's eyes widened. "Of course. I—"

"And Mafu. I've spoken with Mafu, too."

The woman's eyes grew bigger.

"I asked them—Ramtha and Mafu—about what to do with my money. You see, I recently came into a very *large* inheritance, and both of them told me to speak to Chac. They said Chac is the one who speaks with true wisdom.''

David should have been surprised that his aunt had heard of two of the most famous deadies around, but he wasn't.

The clerk was momentarily befuddled, but finally managed to regain enough composure to say, ''Let me make a phone call. What's your name?''

''Thelma O'Neill,'' Ruby said.

While the clerk spoke quietly on a phone on a counter behind her, her back to them, David's attention turned to a poster pinned to the wall above the clerk. Unlike the other posters on display, this one did not have Tanner's puss plastered on it. Instead, a glowing, stylized green crystal that shot out rays of light was set against a solid dark blue background. Bold white letters above the crystal said CRYSTAL AGE RADIO NETWORK.

He looked closer at the blue background. If that color matched what he . . .

Suddenly the clerk hung up and said, ''Mr. Stahl will be over in a few minutes to talk to you.''

''But we really need to talk to Chac.''

''Mr. Stahl is a Chosen one. I'm sure he can answer all your questions. Perhaps he can even take you on a personal tour.''

''But can we meet Chac?''

''I really can't say,'' she said, but her expression said it didn't look promising.

''We'll wait outside,'' said Ruby, turning to leave.

''About that poster—'' David said to the clerk, pointing above her head.

''Come on,'' prodded Ruby, heading for the door.

''I'll be right out.''

He caught up with his aunt a couple of minutes later, a rolled up poster in his hands.

''You into souvenirs?'' she said impatiently.

''No, but this poster may match—''

''Tell me about it later,'' she said, bolting down a gravel footpath, one of several that radiated from the Visitors Center like spokes on a wheel. ''We're getting the bureaucratic shuffle. Let's take our own little tour before this Stahl guy arrives.''

David scurried after her. "I don't think this is a good idea, Aunt Ruby," he said, expecting armed guards to surround them at any moment.

"We'll find out, won't we?"

"What exactly are we looking for?"

"A cosmic phone booth."

The footpath was wide and well-maintained, and cut through sunlit aspen groves, across an empty gravel road, and past dormitories, modular homes, a school, a clinic, and a maintenance shop. Several times they passed residents, who smiled and said hello in childlike voices and asked if they could help. None were visibly armed. But when Ruby said they were looking for Tanner, each person suddenly couldn't help.

Two blocks from the Visitors Center they stopped at a huge sheet metal structure with a sign outside that said:

FULFILLMENT CENTER

"Looks like a cosmic phone booth to me," said Ruby. "Let's check it out."

"Aunt Ruby, I—"

Suddenly in the distance the motors of two vehicles echoed in the valley. Ruby and David stood silent and listened, and when the sound of the vehicles drew closer, Ruby opened a door and they hastily entered the building.

When their eyes had adjusted to the semi-darkness, they could make out several people working in front of a bank of TV monitors splattered with various images of Lincoln William Tanner, aka Chac. A yellow sign pinned to the wall above a stack of videotapes said "Larry King Live—$14." Tanner's appearance on "Phil Donahue" went for $10 a tape and videos of channeling sessions with Chac went for $25 to $30 a pop.

Everyone was so involved in their work that for a few moments no one seemed to notice Ruby and David's presence, until suddenly a middle-aged woman in stone-washed jeans approached.

"Only authorized people are allowed in here," she said almost apologetically.

"We got separated from our tour," Ruby said. "I feel really embarrassed. I don't know where they are right now. Maybe we could wait here until they show up. They do stop here, don't they? What's your name?"

"Shirley," the woman said hesitantly.

"Glad to meet you, Shirley." Ruby pumped the woman's hand. "My name's Thelma O'Neill, and this here's my son, Lincoln. Just like Mr. Tanner's—Father's—name. We're Seekers from California, but we're interested in living here. My, that's a beautiful necklace."

Ruby fondled an Apache teardrop obsidian crystal necklace hanging on Shirley.

"It's a crystal for transforming worry, fear, and anxiety," said Shirley, looking down at the stone. "They sell them in the gift shop."

"I must get one. Have you lived here long, honey?"

"Two wonderful years," said Shirley, who, they quickly learned, had been a Pittsburgh ad executive before she'd grown disgusted with the rapaciousness of the business and the sordidness of city life and sold off her home and most of her possessions for the privilege of living at the ranch.

"You must be one of the Chosen," Ruby said.

"Oh, no," Shirley said modestly. "I'm a Light Keeper."

"But I bet you've heard Chac speak!"

"Oh, yes . . . many times. He speaks through Father regularly, usually in our Meditation Center. But he speaks at other times, too. One of my favorite places is a meadow not far from here. It's a transforming experience, especially under a full moon."

"I hope we can hear him speak someday," Ruby said breathlessly.

"He speaks to anyone who is open to listening," said Shirley. "You vibrate well. I'm sure you will hear."

"Do you know Father personally?"

"Oh, yes."

"What's he like? . . . In person? . . . When he isn't channeling for Chac?"

"He's a strong, compassionate leader," said Shirley. "And deeply misunderstood by outsiders."

"Is he here? Could we meet him?"

"He's not in this building right now. Though he does tape his shows here."

"What is this place, exactly?"

"It's our Fulfillment Center. It's where we process all the requests for the wisdom of Chac."

She explained about the radio show and the videotapes, and took them into a room where people were shipping out hundreds of posters, pamphlets, and books. When David saw a duplicate of the poster in his hand, he asked Shirley about the Crystal Age Radio Network.

"Father wants to build a network of radio stations across the country so we can spread Chac's good message. We're establishing partnerships of investors to help us obtain the licenses and buy or build stations. All of us here have invested. Perhaps you'd like to help spread Chac's message."

"I don't have the money," said David. "But my au—my mom does."

The woman looked expectedly at Ruby. "It's a small sacrifice for the salvation of earth."

"I'm always interested in salvation," Ruby said.

Just then a young man with neatly trimmed hair and a neatly trimmed suit and tie approached them. The two men he'd entered with—burly men not so neatly trimmed—hung back by the door.

"I'm Jerry Stahl, one of Father's assistants. Can I help you in some way, Mrs. Dark?"

"Call me Ruby," she said, nonplussed that he knew her real name.

"What is it you want here, Mrs. Dark?"

"I want to speak to your boss. I know he's here."

The man smiled a tightly trimmed smile. "I'm afraid he isn't available."

"When's a good time to catch him?"

"I can't think of any time in the immediate future."

Ruby flashed a business card in Stahl's face. "You obviously know who I am, hon, but why don't you give him my card next time you see him and have him call me. It's important."

The man ignored the card and looked at Shirley. "What have they been asking you?" His voice was cold.

Shirley the Light Keeper looked alarmed and apologetic and totally confused. "Uhh—just the usual tour questions, Mr. Stahl. They said they'd gotten lost from their tour. I was—I was just showing them around."

"One must learn to divine the true nature of all those around you," he said. "Observe their energy fields. We must be alert to our enemies."

Shirley's eyes grew wide. "I'm sorry, Mr. Stahl. I'll try harder to learn Chac's ways."

"You didn't divine shit, honey," Ruby snapped.

"I beg your pardon?" said Stahl.

"You didn't divine shit. You checked the car when we drove in and traced the license plate through DMV."

Or he just read the damn vanity plate, thought David. A red Lamborghini with a license plate that screams BONDED tells it all.

"I don't know what you're talking about, Mrs. Dark," said Stahl.

"You have impressive connections."

"These men can show you the way to your car." Stahl nodded toward the two burly men in the doorway.

Ruby and David had nearly reached the door when Ruby turned back toward Stahl and said loudly, "You tell Tanner to talk to me real soon about Kray and the dead bounty hunter. Soon, or I'll see to it his cosmic telephone gets disconnected."

22

"You planning to talk to Chac?" needled Ruby as David unrolled the poster he'd brought from the Brotherhood out onto the floor next to Collateral. He pinned down the four corners with three law books and a coffee cup. The dog opened one eye, considered the activity for a moment, and closed it.

"If my hunch is right, Chac's going to call us." Ruby looked at him, puzzled. For once, he got to play it as coy as his aunt always did.

He sat on his knees, dug a small scrap of paper out of his shirt pocket—blue with a thin green line cutting across it—and slid the scrap around all four corners of the poster until, on the fourth corner, the blue edges and the green line fit like the lost piece of a puzzle.

"They match," he said, leaning back on his heels triumphantly.

Ruby picked up the scrap lying on the poster. "Where did you get this piece?"

"From the room where we found Jim's body. It was stuck to the wall under a thumbtack."

Ruby slipped on her reading glasses, bent down on one knee, and moved the scrap of paper around on the slick surface of the poster until it came to rest in the same spot David had placed it.

"Could be a coincidence," she said.

"Could be," he conceded without conceding. He had her on this one. Yeah, he had her for once.

"There must be hundreds of different posters that use these colors."

"I'm sure there are. But not *exactly* like this one."

Ruby stood up and took off her reading glasses. She tapped them against the palm of her hand.

"Someone else could have put that poster down in that room. It doesn't prove a connection between Gibson and Tanner."

"True. In fact, I would have sworn that the only church Gibson would be involved in would be the Church of the Risen Mercedes. But that's not what you feel in your gut, is it?" He tried to keep himself from gloating.

His aunt put on a teal hat. "I've got some errands to run."

David rolled up the poster. "Shall I check out this Crystal Age Radio Network?"

"No. I'll look into it. I want you to check out that skinhead boyfriend of Darcy's. See where he was the night Kray was murdered. See if he or anyone in the skinhead community is claiming to have murdered Kray. Some of these pinheads like to brag."

"The kid you want is named Jimmy Marten," said Detective Barrett, a member of the police department's intelligence unit. Barrett had instantly recognized David's description of the black and silver Cadillac hearse with the Dixie flag on the side that he'd seen in front of the Kray home, and the fact that the skinhead ran around with one of Kray's daughters.

"Pimple-faced kid, late teens. Split from his parent's half-mil home about a year ago. Crashes in friends' pads around Capitol Hill. No biggie. He hangs around the edges of the hardcore skin groups, but he's doesn't belong to any of them."

"Any arrests? History of violence? Threats against Kray or anyone in the Kray family?"

"Naw. A lot of these kids play at this shit outta sheer boredom. Hell, it's hip among teenagers these days to be racist."

The detective didn't know where David could find Marten, but he did add one more tidbit of information.

"The kid's into death music big time. He makes a few bucks organizing underground death dances around town. Illegal stuff, but we kinda ignore it. Keeps them off the street, anyway. You might find him that way. Just ask for The Undertaker."

The huge abandoned brick warehouse down near the South Platte River must have been well-constructed in its day. It wasn't until David passed muster at the guarded door and stepped inside that he could hear the deafening music.

He followed the noise—almost against his will—into a cavernous room whose ceiling shot forty feet up to blackened steel beams. In a mosh pit in the center of the room, two hundred people, most of them shirtless white teenage boys in long hair and punk makeup, slammed into each other in a sort of frenzied, jerky St. Vitus dance. On a makeshift stage a five-piece band played from inside a huge steel cage, pounding out its music through speakers the size of compact cars. Flanking the dance floor, vendors hawked keg beer, T-shirts, posters, and all sorts of death paraphernalia.

It had taken several phone calls and logging onto a computer bulletin board before David tracked down when and where the underground death dance was being secretly held. The bulletin board had provided directions to the location, which actually turned out to be a twelve-year-old boy with a fistful of maps—at fifteen bucks apiece—containing hand-printed directions to the real location.

A girl with a pierced eyebrow pointed out The Undertaker. Not that he needed pointing out. He was the only one who looked like a Nazi storm trooper: shaved head, creased khaki pants stuffed into the tops of heavy boots, a black T-shirt with a design he couldn't make out, and thin suspenders. Marten stood atop a large crate, overlooking the pit full of pulsating bodies. A familiar-looking girl dressed in black sat on the edge of the crate next to him, dangling her feet over the edge like a little kid on the end of a pier.

David battled his way through the sweaty, smelly bodies on the concrete dance floor, nearly getting hit at one point by a kid bodysurfing atop a swell of upraised hands. The music—the term suggested a more organized, coherent sound than they were actually producing—was the loudest here. The noise rumbled along the floor and up his legs and into every fiber of his body. The feverish, suffocating air vibrated and he struggled to breathe. By the time he reached the other side, gasping, his eardrums hurt and his head throbbed.

"You Jimmy Marten?" he shouted up at the young man on the crate. He could read the T-shirt now: "Hitler European Tour: 1939–1945."

The skinhead looked down, gave him the once over, and looked back out on the dance floor, rocking his body to the music. "I don't know a Jimmy Marten."

"All right. How about The Undertaker?"

Marten looked back down. A grin spread across his face, which had enough acne on it to keep a pharmaceutical company in profits for years. "Whattya want?"

The music quieted for a moment before it burst into what David could only think of as the sound of a gigantic trash compactor in its last seconds of life. The Undertaker ripped off an imaginary riff on an imaginary guitar, his fingers feverishly playing across his crotch as though he was masturbating at high speed.

"Their music just shreds, don't it," he yelled. What few snatches of lyrics David could make out sounded as though they'd been shredded, all right—out of the pages of a forensics textbook. "They're a local group. Called Rectal Exam."

David looked at the band. Five shirtless guys with long hair and muscular, tattooed bodies. "I'll be sure to watch for them at the Grammys," David shouted back.

Marten got the look of someone who suddenly realized he was being toyed with. "Who are you?"

"Somebody who wants to talk about the death of your girlfriend's father." David looked at the girl sitting on the crate. "You *are* Darcy Kray, aren't you?"

Outwardly, she didn't resemble a Kray. Not like Aspen. He wasn't sure what she resembled. Heavily mascared dark eyes glared at him. Her lipstick was the color of oxblood. Large earrings dangled from ears obscenely exposed below the spiked black hair and shaved sides of her head. A gold ring pierced her right nostril. She wore black pants, black combat boots with white laces, and a black T-shirt with a bloody skull and "Suicide Lives" in white letters—he wasn't sure if it was the name of a band or a philosophical statement. If he hadn't seen her enter the Kray house that night, he wouldn't have believed she belonged to the same family.

The Undertaker jumped down from the crate. Toe to toe, he topped David by three inches and looked muscular enough to be dangerous in a dark alley. Just because the detective had said he had no history of violence didn't mean shit. "You a cop?"

"No. Let's talk someplace where we can hear each other."

Marten jerked his head toward Darcy Kray. She slid off the crate and followed them around the pit and through a large sliding door into a huge adjoining room. Here, the music was mercifully muted and the air less stifling and rancid. The only light in the room was what little spilled in through the crack of the door, but David could make out large storage shelves, mostly empty now, and a massive overhead crane that ran along a track. The place felt deep in dust and mold.

Marten stopped in David's face, silent but demanding answers. Darcy closed in next to him, her right arm around his back, her hand slipped into his hip pocket. David told them he was tracking down Bayne Gibson.

"You must be the asshole who hassled my mother!" Darcy said angrily. "You and that woman. I don't want to talk to you."

"I didn't come to talk to you," David said. "I came to talk to your boyfriend."

"I don't know anything about where Gibson is," said Marten.

"Any of your skinhead buddies?"

"Why would they know anything about him?"

"Maybe they know more about her father. Any of them claiming to have killed him?"

"Gibson killed my father!" snapped the girl. Even in the shadows, and under the punk makeup and clothes, David began to notice a few resemblances to her sisters—the deep anger, the strong chin, the hips that were a little too wide.

"Another man's been murdered looking for Gibson," David said to her. "We don't think Gibson was the one who killed him. That raises the possibility that someone else may have killed your father. He angered a lot of people, Darcy—including the local skinheads."

This was still his aunt's tangent, not his. To him, Gibson remained Numero Uno. But he knew he had to ask the questions. Ruby would grill him on every detail, every nuance when he got back to the office.

The girl looked uneasy for a moment, then snapped, "Fuck, you're just another one of society's hired pigs. Protecting the rich bastards like Gibson . . . and my parents. It's embarrassing to be around them. They're the ones who've fucked up this country. But you people keep trying to blame shit on the people trying to make America right."

What the hell did she see in this pimple-faced punk? Was it just sheer rebellion against her father, as Deveraux had speculated? If so, why hadn't she dropped him after her father's death? Or was she really infatuated with this Nazi goon? He looked at Marten. "Any buddies to place in nomination?"

Marten stood silent.

"All right. What about you? Where were you the night Kray was murdered?"

"He was with me!" interjected Darcy.

David kept his eyes on Marten.

"I was with her," said Marten, grinning.

"Where?"

"A place called The Pit."

"Where's that?"

"A dance joint up in Westminster. The Corpse Grinders played that night."

"Ahhh, another Grammy nominee, I'm sure. Can anybody attest that you were there during the time frame Kray was killed?"

Marten pointed in the direction of the light and noise. "Go ask anyone. They all know me."

David laughed. "I doubt any of them are even going to remember *they* were here tonight, let alone where you were a month ago."

"Look, man, Darcy's father was a real asshole, but I didn't kill him."

"You're a prime candidate. He said he was going to drive every skinhead out of town if it was the last thing he ever did. He must have hated it every time he knew you were with his daughter. He threatened to kill you if he ever caught up with you. I'd say that's pretty good motive for murder. Beat him to the punch."

"Hell, he didn't give a shit about Darcy. He didn't give a shit about anyone in that family. You know, when he found out his old lady'd tried to snuff herself he didn't even bother to come home from the station. If that dyke sister of Darcy's hadn't found her in time, she woulda fucking croaked."

"Sarah?" interjected Darcy.

"Yeah, whatever that cold fish's name is."

"No, no, it was Aspen who found her," insisted Darcy.

"Whatever. All I know was, the prick was a mean motherfucker. The sonofabitch deserved to die." Marten tapped his finger on his chest. "But I didn't kill him."

"Jimmy . . ." Darcy pulled her hand out of Marten's hip pocket and put a hand pleadingly on his chest.

"He was an asshole, Darcy. You've said so yourself."

"I don't want to talk about my father with this guy, that's all."

But The Undertaker was on a roll. "He was like my parents. They all came outta the sixties. They always make a point about that, like the sixties was some kinda fucking holy era and they're its goddamn disciples. They talk about equality and justice and equal opportunity. That's what her old man preached on the radio. But they don't do shit about it. They put people like me down and pretend they're for the mud people and the Jew-dykes. But they're not. It's a sham—just another way to keep themselves in power and keep us out."

"Jimmy . . ." She tried to push him toward the door. "Let's go back. I wanna hear the music."

Marten shrugged her off. "Don't get all wigged out about it, baby. Your father was one fucked-up asshole. Admit it. Everybody in your family needs to admit it." He looked at David. "You wanna know how really fucked up her old man was? Did you hear what he did to her brother?''

''Jimmy! No!'' Even in the dim light David could see panic in her face.

''People gotta hear it, babe. That's what your old man was about.''

She started pounding on his chest. ''You promised you wouldn't tell anyone. You promised!'' He shoved her away.

''Get lost, bitch,'' he said. ''I don't need that shit from you.''

She staggered back into the darkness several feet.

Marten looked back at David. ''He was Darcy's fraternal twin. Did you know he killed himself a coupla years ago?''

David said he'd heard that, that he'd heard what Kray had said about his son not even killing himself like a man.

''That was sick, man. People call skinheads sick . . . shit, that was really fucking sick to say on the radio. You know why her father said that? You know why her brother killed himself?''

David shook his head.

'''Cause he was a fucking fag, that's why.''

David heard Darcy sobbing.

''Not a street cruiser, you know. He wasn't poking around or nothing. He was just a kid who knew he was queer and his old man picked up on it. Hounded him! Now I don't like fags myself. They belong with the Jews and muds. But her old man was supposed to be this fucking pious liberal, champion of homos and dykes and the niggers—all of 'em. 'Cept when he finds out his son's as queer as a three dollar bill. Then all that liberal shit turns out to be so much white-trash cocktail hour sociology.''

A low animal moan growled in the darkness and suddenly Darcy charged her boyfriend with a lead pipe. Marten deftly closed the distance between them before she could take a serious windup and swing, jerked the pipe out of her hand, and hurled it out into the darkness of the room. It bounced off a metal standpipe and skittered noisily across the concrete floor until it crashed into an old coil of wire.

''Jesus, bitch, what the fuck is your problem?''

She spit on the floor in Marten's direction and stomped out of the room into the light and noise.

Marten turned back toward David as if Darcy had been only a minor inconvenience. "Skinheads aren't hypocrites. We're straightforward. We don't want to kill muds or Jews or homos. We just want to send them back home where they belong. We just want to make America a white Christian nation again. We want to rebuild white pride, like the pride that founded this great country. I'm proud of being white. You should be proud of being white. We're imperiled, did you know that? Whites are imperiled. We're gonna disappear one of these days under all these wetbacks and niggers. We gotta fight that. We gotta stand up for the heritage that made this great nation great. We gotta . . ."

The skinhead ranted on. Yet for all the inflammatory language, David found the kid's voice curiously lacking in passion. Certainly not the passion he'd dug up moments ago for Royce Kray. The speech had a canned quality to it. He cut the teenager off.

"This is all a game to you, isn't it?"

"Whattya mean?"

"This Nazi getup you wear, this white supremacist, racist, macho shit. You just enjoy playing at hate."

"Don't fuck with me, man."

"What kind of ridiculous name is The Undertaker, anyway? I bet it sells tickets. The Undertaker drags in another death band. The Ed Sullivan of Suicide and Hate. Kids eat that crap up these days. The only problem is, Jimmy, hate's toxic even when you're just fooling around with it. It destroys anything it touches."

"You can't make skinheads scapegoats for what's corrupt in this society," said Marten.

"You know, Jimmy, when I first saw you I thought to myself, this guy looks like the kind of badass who'd catch Kray in a dark alley with six Aryan brothers and stomp him to death. No way did he plan a slick murder that framed Gibson. But I think you're smarter than you act. I think you're smart enough to know that boots in an alley would have pointed to you and your buddies. I think you're smart enough to have sneaked into Gibson's penthouse and shot Royce Kray."

23

Where his aunt had dug up Barry Greenfield, David didn't know. He was forever amazed by the people she could call on—not just officials in the judicial system and the attendant lowlifes one would expect in the bail bonding business, but politicians, athletes, the wealthy, executives, artists, journalists, and society grande dames. Barry Greenfield was a lawyer. Not just any old lawyer, but a lawyer who specialized in broadcast law.

"You're the second person to ask me recently what I knew about Crystal Age," said Greenfield from his wheelchair in his modest downtown office.

Ruby leaned forward in her chair. "Who else?"

He rested his interlaced fingers on the shelf of his stomach and looked at them through hornrimmed glasses. "I'm trying to remember. I got a call one day from someone at KPOL. It was a woman. A young woman judging by her voice. She said she worked on Kray's 'Back Talk' show."

"You don't remember her name?"

"I'm trying, I'm trying, Ruby. Uhh . . . Reynolds, that was it. Susan Reynolds."

"When was this?"

"Several weeks before Kray was murdered."

"What did she want to know?"

"She said some listener had called complaining that there was something suspicious about Crystal Age. She wanted me to tell her what I knew about it."

"What did you tell her?"

"All is not kosher with Crystal Age Radio Network. Rumors are the state securities division is investigating it."

"A scam?"

Greenfield shrugged. "I wouldn't charge that publicly, but I wouldn't recommend you put any nickels into it either, if that's what you've got in mind."

"No investment planned."

"Good. Religious scams are big business these days, Ruby. Guys quote God and scripture on the phone or in their offering documents. Hell, I saw a promoter claim he was going to make a fortune for his investors by drilling in Israel for oil and gas based on Old Testament prophecies. Fundamentalists are real suckers for this crap."

"Could you be a little more specific about Crystal Age, Barry?"

"Over the past three years, the Network has been assembling general partnerships to purchase or construct New Age FM radio stations across the country."

"To spread the voice of Chac," cut in David.

"And to line the pockets of Tanner," said the lawyer. He opened a drawer, pulled out two brochures, and tossed them across his desk to Ruby. "Here's their prospectus and sales brochure. The prospectus is pretty circumspect in its claims. The law wouldn't allow otherwise. But people don't read the fine print of a prospectus. They read the sales brochure. It does all the thinking for them. The brochure claims that investors will earn a fourteen-to-one return on their money."

Ruby whistled.

"Their illustration shows an investor putting up ten grand a share in the partnership and another thousand in equity toward actually building the station, and reaping a hundred fifty grand when the station is sold after four years on the air."

"That sounds preposterous," said David.

Greenfield shrugged again. "People buy the preposterous every day if they think they can make easy money."

"So how does this scam work, Barry?" Ruby asked.

"What do you know about owning a radio station?"

"I turn on my radio and sound comes out."

"That's about as much as most of these investors know.

The fact is, to own a radio station you have to apply for a license from the FCC. That application process takes expertise and money. What Crystal Age does is assemble partnerships for investors—probably five to thirty investors in each partnership."

"How much to buy in?"

"Five to ten thousand apiece."

"Whew!"

"Then each partnership coughs up seventy to ninety grand to the consulting firm—Crystal Age—to cover expenses, salespeople, consulting engineer fees, attorney fees, and the cost of filing the app with the FCC."

"How are they selling these partnerships?" asked Ruby.

"Boiler room telemarketing. It's easy, inexpensive, and very effective. All you do is assemble a computer list of targets and start calling."

Ruby and David exchanged glances.

"That would explain all those phone jacks," said David. "They weren't using that WATS line to sell real estate . . . they were hawking radio partnerships."

Greenfield looked from one to the other with questions on his face.

Ruby asked a question instead. "How many of these partnerships has Crystal Radio assembled?"

"At least a hundred twenty. Most likely more."

David performed a little quick math in his head. "Jesus! That's nearly ten million dollars!"

"This isn't a little quick suitcase operation. These guys are in it for big bucks."

"But doesn't most of that money have to go toward the application process?"

"In theory. But out of those one hundred twenty partnerships, only *five* have formally applied to the FCC for licenses. Plus, there are ways to scam the system even within the application process itself. It's as easy as dialing for dollars."

"Doesn't the FCC monitor this stuff?"

Greenfield laughed. "They're understaffed like every other government regulatory agency. During the eighties, the FCC deregulated the application process to make it easier for people to apply. The idea was to put new stations in the hands of minorities and women. It was a laudable goal. The problem was, the FCC couldn't handle the volume of apps.''

''So as usual, those who least need it skim off the cream,'' said Ruby.

''Exactly. The sweetener in this deal is that because the application process takes so long, the payoff to investors can be years down the road. Crystal Age doesn't have to produce an immediate return. But, just to prime the pump, Crystal has kicked back early returns to a few investors. High returns. Word gets around, and more investors sign on.''

''A Ponzi scam?'' said Ruby.

''That's what it smells like.''

''I've heard of Ponzi scams, but I'm not sure exactly what they are,'' said David.

Greenfield explained. ''You get money from the initial investors—the Pauls of the scheme. Then you get money from the next round of investors—the Peters. You use some of the money from the Peters to pay off a few of the Pauls. The return is impressive, so the Pauls spread the word. More Peters invest. You pay back a few more Pauls, and they keep recruiting more Peters. Eventually you get a helluva lot of Peters who never get a dime back.''

''But don't the Peters eventually catch on?'' said David.

''Sure. Ponzi scams always collapse eventually. But a good scam is designed to run for a certain period of time. Then the guys with all the dough disappear. Rumor is, Tanner and a few of his Chosen ones are diverting most of the money into a phony suitcase bank in the Grand Caymans.''

That's where Gibson has his $2 million account, thought David, glancing at his aunt.

She looked at Greenfield. ''Any evidence that Bayne Gibson's mixed up in this Crystal Age scam?''

''*Bayne Gibson?* No. I've never heard his name linked to anything with Crystal Age. I've always had the impression he's a Sunday painter when it comes to radio. Certainly not like his father. Other people run KPOL for his son. But that does remind me. Guess who's the principal lawyer handling the five FCC applications?''

The answer was written all over Ruby's face: ''Lamprey!''

* * *

"The whole charge is preposterous," said E. Ezzard Lamprey. "And if you breath so much as a word about this, I'll sue you for libel, *Mzzzz* Dark."

"You're denying any involvement with Crystal Age Radio Network?" asked Ruby.

"Of course not. It's a matter of public record that I'm assisting legitimate partnerships negotiate the FCC's application process. It's a very complicated process. Crystal Age pays me for my services and my expertise. But I categorically deny that I've done anything illegal, that I or Crystal Age or the partnerships I've represented have in any way abused the FCC applications process, or that I in any way have done anything to mislead or misrepresent Crystal Age to either investors or the FCC."

By big city standards, Lamprey's law offices were small—a handful of rooms compared with multiple floors occupied by the large firms. But the furnishings were plush and the suite was high up in the office tower, a cut well above Barry Greenfield's office.

"Is Gibson involved in Crystal Age?" Ruby asked

"He has no involvement."

"Does he know you do work for Crystal Age?"

"Crystal Age is one of many clients this firm represents. I make it a policy to keep each client's interests distinctly separate from the others."

"Even if there's an obvious conflict of interest?"

"I wouldn't interpret my services for Crystal Age as a conflict of interest with Gibson Media."

"Maybe you wouldn't, but I think Gibson would. Unless he already knows about it. Does he know Tanner?"

"Personally?"

"Personally."

"Not that I'm aware of. Why would he?"

"Don't play stupid, honey. Crystal Age was running its little scam out of the Evergreen home where my friend was murdered—at a home owned by Gibson. Which, by the way, you neglected to mention in your financial documentation to us."

The lawyer's eyes furrowed. "You continue to make accusations that have no foundation or basis in fact! That home was managed by a real estate division of Gibson Media. Bayne did not personally own it nor did he use it for business or personal purposes. Hence it was unnecessary to include it in the financial documents we provided to you. The real estate division runs its own telemarketing operation from there. The WATS line is in their name. Crystal Age had no involvement with that home or with Gibson Media.''

''Oh, come on, Lamprey, we found a Crystal Age poster on the wall in that room. Besides, why would the realty company set up a telemarketing operation in a hidden room in an expensive home in Evergreen when they could rent cheap office space in Denver? And if it was a legitimate operation, why *hide* the office?'' Lamprey made an attempt to answer but Ruby kept going. ''But it would be a perfect place for the Brotherhood to operate a Ponzi scam. I figure their ranch and the house are less than thirty minutes apart.''

''Lots of places are thirty minutes apart. That proves nothing.''

''I also find it curious that you spent half an hour in Gibson's penthouse the day he failed to show for his prelim. His place is big, but it doesn't take thirty minutes to go through it looking for a grown man. My hunch is you were making a hurried sweep for evidence that might link the Brotherhood and Gibson.''

''That's a very serious charge, *Mzzzz* Dark. I trust you're not planning to carry it outside of this office.''

''I'll carry it to wherever it helps me find Gibson. Did Royce Kray know about your work for Crystal Age?''

''I have no idea. I told you before, I seldom dealt with the man.''

''A woman, apparently from his staff, was asking around about Crystal Age a few weeks before he was murdered. Kray crucified Transcendental Light on the air and Tanner threatened him on his show. What do you think Kray would have done if he'd found out that you—and maybe your boss—were mixed up with Tanner and Crystal Age?''

''Are you implying that I was somehow involved in the murder of Royce Kray?''

''I'm implying a lot of things, honey.''

* * *

Jack Deveraux stared morosely into his Scotch on the rocks and said he knew nothing about any radio partnership scam involving Crystal Age, Lamprey, or Bayne Gibson.

''Why would Bayne risk his media empire and his fortune and his good name for some scam that a crazy like Tanner might be running?'' he asked Ruby.''

''Greed . . . power . . . there are a dozen possibilities. Why do any men do the stupid things they do?''

The program director took a sip of Scotch. ''I shouldn't even be talking to you!''

He'd reluctantly agreed to talk to Ruby and David, but only in the dark recesses of a dark bar several miles from the radio station. He said an order had come down earlier in the day that all station personnel—all employees in Gibson Media for that matter—would not have contact with one Ruby Dark, or any associates of Ruby's Bail Bonds.

''Did you get any hints that Kray might have known about the scam and Lamprey's connections to Crystal Age?''

Deveraux ground out a cigarette in a stamped metal ashtray and said, ''Royce was not a man who confided in others. When he wanted to talk about something on his mind he was apt to talk about it on the air. The booth was his confessional. We never knew what he was going to blurt out next. He enjoyed keeping us on edge.'' Deveraux grew silent for a moment, then said quietly, ''For all of Royce's bravado, he was really a very depressed, insecure man. He didn't like feeling vulnerable. That's why he was so nasty on the air. It was his way of protecting himself.''

''He ever talk about Crystal Age on the air?''

''He mentioned it when he and Tanner went at it, but he never said anything about it being a scam.''

''A woman named Susan Reynolds, who apparently worked on Kray's show, called a lawyer friend of mine who knows quite a bit about Crystal Age. He told her he thought it was a scam. She may have passed that on to Kray.''

Deveraux looked puzzled. ''No one named Susan Reynolds worked on the Kray show.''

Ruby was momentarily taken aback. ''Anyone by that name at the station?''

"No."

"My friend said this caller was a young woman."

"The only young woman who worked with Royce was his daughter."

"His *daughter*? Which one?"

"Sarah. She worked part time as a researcher for the show."

"She gave me the impression she hated her father."

Deveraux smiled gloomily. "Nobody *liked* Royce. That never stopped people from working for him. She's majoring in journalism at CU. Getting the chance to be researcher on the city's most popular radio talk show is not something to pass up lightly—even if it is with your father. She's very capable. A very very bright researcher. Royce's program producer—a guy named Mershon—usually did most of the lead tracking for stories. But Sarah may have come across something about Crystal Age."

"But she never mentioned anything to you about it?"

"Absolutely not."

"And Kray never said anything about Crystal Age being a scam?"

"If he knew, he never said anything to me."

Ruby scooped out a stringy strand of refried beans, cheese, and hot sauce from the plate of nachos. When she finished chewing she said, "While we're on the subject of Kray's daughters, was Aspen Kray having an affair with Gibson?"

Deveraux shook his head. "No. I know that's what people are saying, but no. Bayne liked his women, but he wouldn't have gone for the daughter of his number one talk show host."

"Why not? He went for Kray's wife."

The program director shot a hard look at Ruby. "Where did you hear that?"

"It doesn't matter. Did Kray know about his wife's affair?"

Deveraux chuckled and took another shot of his drink. "Sure he knew. He was the one who set them up."

"Kray hooked up his wife with Gibson?"

"They didn't realize it—at least not at first. He was very

crafty. But he arranged their affair as smoothly as a Jewish matchmaker.''

''Why on earth would he do that?'' asked David.

Deveraux leaned across the table, clenching an upraised fist. ''Because he wanted a hold on them. Royce liked having a hold on everybody around him, from top management down to the secretaries. He'd find their weaknesses, he'd find something he could get his grubby hands on and twist around until they'd do his bidding. He drove his wife and Bayne into each other's arms and then he tyrannized them by not-too-subtly letting them know that he knew. For all the money he has, Bayne is an easily manipulated man.''

''Is that why Kray's wife attempted suicide?'' asked Ruby. ''Because her husband knew of the affair?''

''I don't think the woman's been stable since her son killed himself. But I'm sure Royce's little games didn't help.''

''Was he blackmailing Gibson?''

''Not for money. At least not money stuffed in an envelope and left in a phone booth. Royce wanted to go national with his radio show. Syndicate it. Bayne wasn't that hot for the idea. There's a lot of work and a lot of money and a lot of risk going national, and Bayne didn't think it was worth it. There's lots of popular local talk show hosts all over the country, but not many Larry Kings or Rush Limbaughs. Bayne didn't think Royce's style would fly outside of Colorado.''

''Did you?''

''No.''

''Is that what they were arguing about at the party the night before Kray was murdered?'' Ruby asked.

''I don't know. I didn't hear what their beef was about. I'm not sure anyone did.''

''Weren't people around?''

''The two of them had been off alone for a while somewhere in the penthouse. They'd returned pretty heated. It was a few minutes later when Royce started threatening to piss on the fish. He was drunk as hell and in a foul mood that was bad even by his standards.''

"How do you know Kray arranged this affair between his wife and Gibson?"

"Royce told me."

"He *told* you?"

"He boasted about it."

Ruby shook her head in disbelief. "You said he never confided in anyone. Why would he tell you?"

Deveraux looked sourly into his drink. "He wasn't confiding. Not his feelings. Just the facts. It was his twisted way of letting me know he had control of me."

"I don't understand."

"You see, he had Bayne's nuts in a vice—if you'll pardon the expression. And because I was Bayne's wonder boy, that was Royce's way of letting me know he had me by the balls too."

"A nice man," commented David.

Deveraux looked his way, his eyes bleary with drink and weariness. "You know what really pisses me off? I was the guy who discovered Royce Kray—who made him what he became. I found him on a ten watt radio station in Waterloo, Iowa, five years ago, while I was traveling through to see relatives. The station wasn't using him right. The format straitjacketed him. But I could tell he had potential. I snapped him up, brought him out here, and made his show. Then the ungrateful sonofabitch wants out!"

"Almost makes a guy want to kill him, doesn't it?" said Ruby.

24

"Go away! You can't talk to my mother."

"We didn't come to talk to your mother, Sarah," said Ruby.

"Go away or I'll call the police."

"We came to talk to you," said Ruby.

"I don't want to talk to you. I don't have to talk to you. I looked up the state statutes. There's nothing in the law that says I have to talk to you. You have no authority to harass our family. I can have you arrested."

Sarah started to shut the front door.

"What did you tell your father about Crystal Age?"

The door stopped. The young woman canted her head slightly. She was breathing hard.

"I don't know anything about any Crystal Age."

"Yes, you do. It's a big Ponzi scam. You talked to a lawyer named Greenfield about it. You used a false name, but I know it was you. Then you told your father."

Sarah Kray exhaled a large breath, backed up, and slowly opened the door. They followed her into the sitting room.

The heroin addict was gone.

"I called the museum," said Sarah. "They were very excited to get it."

"What did your mother say? She had to release it."

Sarah shrugged. "I told her she could take a tax write off for it. Actually, I think she was relieved to get rid of it. We all were."

Ruby and David sat in the same chairs they'd sat in before.

Sarah sat on the edge of the sofa in shorts and starched pink blouse. Most of what Sarah proceeded to tell them they'd heard from Greenfield. But Deveraux's words in the bar came to David as she spoke in her matter-of-fact tone: she was a very very bright woman.

"What tipped you about Crystal Age?" asked Ruby. "The program producer ask you to investigate it?"

"No. Actually, it was just dumb luck. Which is how a lot of investigative stories are broken. A man called the station one day—a local chiropractor who'd dumped all his life savings into one of these partnerships. The producer was gone that day, so I took the call. This guy told me he was suspicious about the whole Crystal Age operation, and he thought we might know something about it since my father had criticized the Brotherhood many times on the air. We didn't. It was the first I'd heard that Crystal Age might be a scam, though I think my father had always been suspicious of it. Of course, he was suspicious of everything."

"Did you tell him about the call?"

"Not right away. I followed up this guy's lead on my own. I was taking an investigative journalism class at school at the time—I kinda wanted to surprise them. There wasn't much to go on. The chiropractor had more hunch than credible hard information. He told me the vibrations didn't feel right. So I started digging around on my own."

"That's when you called Greenfield?"

"Among others."

"Why did you use a false name?"

"I was scared that my nosing around might get back to the Brotherhood."

"But you eventually told your father?"

"When I felt I had enough credible facts, yes."

"What was his reaction?"

"He was furious. Especially when I told him that Lamprey was the applications lawyer for the partnerships."

"Did you ever mention any of this to the program producer or the station director?"

"No. Just my father."

"Was this before or after Tanner appeared on the show?"

"A couple of weeks before."

"But during that show your father never accused Tanner of running a scam, did he?" said Ruby.

Sarah Kray's face clenched in controlled anger. "No."

"Why not?"

"I don't know."

"Did you dig up any evidence that Gibson was involved in the scam?"

"Not directly. But I'm sure he was."

"Why are you so sure?"

Sarah studied her hands before she spoke. "Because I found out that he was secretly funding the Brotherhood of the Transcendental Light."

David whistled.

"Funding it? How?" Ruby asked.

"He was washing it through one of his companies," said Sarah. "Real estate. I don't know how, exactly. Stuff's too complicated for me. But I'm sure he was involved in some way. And I'm sure he knew about the scam. He had to."

"How deeply was he involved? Did he go up to Tanner's ranch? Chat with this dead Mayan?"

"From what a couple of sources told me, yes, he went there often."

"Any idea how much money he funneled to them?"

"I don't know for certain. Maybe a million dollars."

"Jesus!" said David. "He just gave it away to them?"

Sarah looked at him. "He didn't take a tax deduction on it, if that's what you mean."

"How did you find all this out?" asked Ruby.

"I can't tell you."

"Why not?"

"It's a confidential source. Two of them, actually. I promised I wouldn't divulge their names."

"Don't give me this journalistic shit, honey! We're talking about the murder of your own father. This could be invaluable evidence about why he and our bounty hunter were killed, and who did it."

"Look, it doesn't take a rocket scientist to see that Gibson killed my father to hide his connection to the Brotherhood and the scam. But I won't tell you or anyone how I found out. It doesn't make any difference, anyway. The police have the right man . . . they just have him for the wrong reason.''

''You told your father about Gibson bankrolling the Brotherhood?''

''Yes.''

''When?''

Sarah bent over and cupped her face in her large hands. She mumbled something and Ruby asked her to repeat it. She looked up. Her eyes were clear. ''A few days before he was murdered.''

''Do you think your father didn't say anything about the scam when Tanner came on his show because he was using the information to blackmail Gibson?''

''Why would he blackmail Gibson?''

''He wanted to syndicate his show. He needed Gibson's help, and Gibson didn't want to do it.''

The anger still burned her face. ''I don't know.''

''Were you at Gibson's party the night before your father was murdered?''

''Of course. My father insisted we all go.''

''Darcy too?''

A tiny laugh escaped Sarah. ''He tried.''

''But the rest of your family went?''

Sarah nodded.

''Did you overhear the argument between your father and Gibson by the fish pond?''

''No. I'd left the party early. I wasn't feeling well. I heard about it later.''

''Who from?''

''Aspen.''

''She stayed at the party? She didn't leave with you?''

''No. She stayed with mom. I wasn't that bad that night. A touch of the stomach flu. I felt worse the next day.''

''Aspen tell you what the source of the argument was about?''

''No. I don't think she knew.''

''Why didn't you tell the police about all of this? You're convinced Gibson shot your father. This only makes the case against him stronger.''

Sarah looked agitated. ''Because . . . because I was scared.''

"You don't strike me as someone who scares easily."

Sarah jumped to her feet and walked around the back of the sofa. "My father was murdered by the very man I told him about. Believe me, I was scared."

"But you have evidence that could help convict him."

"*Had*. I burned it! I burned all my notes, every scrap of evidence I had about Crystal Age."

"I don't believe you. I think you were trying to protect your mother."

Sarah glared at her. "I *was* scared. I'm not lying about that. But yes, I was afraid that my mother would get mixed up in it."

"Because she was having an affair with Gibson?"

Sarah's eyes looked down. "I was afraid if I said anything to the police it might drag her into it. She's into this New Age shit. Gibson got her into it, the bastard. I didn't know what the police might find out so I just burned everything I had about Crystal Age and said nothing. I figured they had him dead to rights, anyway, so why involve my mother."

"Is that why Aspen went to the house in Evergreen? To protect your mother in some way? Maybe to remove evidence? Or was she having an affair with Gibson and she went there to warn him?"

"I don't think my sister was having affair with that man. But I wasn't here when she left that night, so I don't know why she went. I didn't know a thing about it until mom called later."

"None of this was very smart," said Ruby.

Sarah's eyes burned with rage. "I don't care what's smart. You tell the police any of this I'll simply deny it. There's no evidence and no proof, so any testimony against Gibson by me would be useless in court, anyway."

"Proof isn't on my mind, right now, honey. I want Gibson and I want the killer—the real killer. I'll worry about proof later."

25

The waitress leaned over the table to make herself heard above the bar music.

"I ain't seen him, Angel, and I don't wanna see him."

"Street talk says Spider Jack hasn't left town, honey," Ruby yelled into the waitress's ear. "He's still pimping."

"I ain't into that shit no more!"

Sure, thought David. The young black woman, whose face looked much older than her twenty-three years, was squeezed into a black leather miniskirt, white blouse, sheer stockings, and black spiked heels. She looked like a hooker out of a bad movie.

"Please leave . . . please stop coming here," she said. "I got a good job and I wanna keep it. The manager don't want no bondsmen hanging around. Makes the customers nervous."

Ruby looked around. Faces stared back. "I can see why. It smells like jump city in here."

The waitress pushed a soggy rag around the table, sweeping popcorn onto the floor. She was trying to make it appear normal that she was chatting with the only two white folks in the bar, one of whom was dressed in a white straw hat and an expensive suit and whose red Lamborghini with the license plate BONDED was parked out front.

"Just tell us where Spider Jack is, Clara, and we'll be out of your hair," Ruby said.

The waitress glanced nervously at the dozen black faces in the smoky bar. "He's got friends. He finds out I'm ratting, he'll come git me. He's got a mean streak wider 'n a road."

"You won't be safe until he's in jail, honey. That's why we want to find him."

That and the small matter of a failure to appear on a $10,000 bond on pimping charges, David said to himself.

"I'll never be safe from his friends. I won't be safe talkin' to you."

Ruby settled back in the booth and ordered a cup of coffee. She was going to wait it out. The waitress looked pleadingly at David. She was on the edge of tears. "Nothing for me," he said, his small way of telling her he wasn't with his aunt on this one. Why were they wasting their time chasing penny-ante skips who had nothing to do with Gibson, anyway? If they didn't find Gibson what the hell difference would a $10,000 forfeiture make?

As the waitress walked away like a prisoner on her way to execution, David leaned across the damp table so his aunt could hear him above the music. "Why do we keep coming in here and hassling her, Aunt Ruby? She's not going to tell you anything. She's too scared to talk."

"We keep coming in here and one of these days she'll have to decide between turning in his ass or waiting for him to beat her up."

"What if she really doesn't know where he is?"

"Then she'll find out."

David shook his head. "I hate this part of the job."

"It's better we scare her than let Spider Jack roam free and beat up more of his girls."

"Fine," he said, waving the discussion to a close. "What about Gibson? Shouldn't we be checking out the Brotherhood again instead of spending our time screwing around with people like Spider Jack?"

"I don't think he's there. I don't think Tanner would risk hiding him on the ranch."

"But you're convinced Tanner persuaded Gibson to skip?"

"Even a prelim goes into enough detail that Tanner must be worried Gibson will crack and spill everything about the scam. The whole thing would topple early."

David shook his head. "I still can't believe that Gibson—

especially if he didn't shoot Kray—would voluntarily give up a fifteen million dollar empire just because Tanner tells him to."

"We know Gibson's a weak man. Deveraux said he's easily manipulated. Tanner could have used this Mayan dude to have persuaded him to do anything."

"If you're right, I bet Gibson's dead. I bet Tanner engineered his skip and once he got him to the ranch he killed him and buried him God knows where up there."

"You could be right."

Ruby suddenly pulled her beeper out of her purse and looked at it. He hadn't heard it above the music. She went to the bar's pay phone. While she was gone, the waitress, looking frightened, angrily plunked down Ruby's coffee, spilling a few drops.

Ruby returned a couple of minutes later, visibly excited.

"That was Johnny Archuleta," she said, sliding into the booth. He's coming by in a few minutes."

"*Blood?* What the hell does he want?" David made no effort to keep the contempt out of his voice. Anybody who had nicknamed himself Blood—short for Bloodhound—deserved his contempt.

"He claims he knows where Gibson's hiding."

"You actually *believe* that asshole?"

"I never believe anything unless I can taste it or touch it or feel it. But I'm willing to listen to what he has to say."

"The man's a loaded gun, Aunt Ruby! Cocked and ready to go off. I still don't understand why this state allows ex-cons to be bounty hunters and bondsmen."

Archuleta had served time in Texas for assault and battery. Stir time in the toughest penal system in the nation hadn't reformed him, from what David had heard. Blood was notorious for roughing up his skips and ripping them off. Still, a lot of bondsmen in town used him, actually swore by him, despite his unsavory reputation. Ruby's husband had even used him occasionally, when Brodie wasn't available, though once Ruby had taken over the business she'd dropped Archuleta in favor of less notorious bounty hunters.

"I don't understand why Archuleta's even looking for Gibson," said David. "Why does he care?"

"Because I hired him," said Ruby.

"You *hired* Blood!"

"He called with a tip," she said. "I'm paying standard percentage and expenses if he can find him. Just like everyone else."

David looked away in disgust. "Why can't you just let the others handle it?"

After Brodie's murder, several local bounty hunters and even a couple of bondsmen offered to help Ruby track down Gibson. They were angered and saddened by the death of one of their own and one of their best, and they didn't want to see Ruby go under. Some of them even volunteered to bring Gibson in free.

Ruby leaned across the table. "We need somebody good, David. Real good. Or we could be out of business. I know Blood isn't the kind of guy who brings a lot of good PR to this industry. But he gets results, and frankly, I'm damn desperate for results. After Big Jim, Blood's the best bounty hunter in the business."

"Sure, by breaking heads."

"I'll keep him on a tight leash."

Johnny "Bloodhound" Archuleta showed up ten minutes later, dressed in black. He was always dressed in black. He said it made him look professional. He was a small, wiry man, with a pullover too tight for his muscular upper body. A mass of wild curly black hair framed a face that had a coarse, unfinished quality to it. A small diamond earring winked from his left ear even in the dim bar light.

Ruby introduced David as Archuleta slid into the booth next to her. He extended a hand across the table. A tattoo of a hawk was carved into the inside of his wrist. His grip was harder than it needed to be.

"So where's Gibson?" pressed Ruby as the two men sized each other up.

"Hiding out at the home of a guy named Saunders," said Archuleta, his eyes still on David. "Barry Saunders."

"That name sounds familiar," David said to his aunt.

"Yeah, it does."

"He's a big shot at Gibson's headquarters," said Archuleta, looking at Ruby. "A vice president or some fuckin' title."

"Where's this Saunders' home?" she asked.

"It's one of them fancy sprawls down in Cherry Hills Village. Half the fuckin' city jail could hide in the place."

The waitress showed up, took Archuleta's order for a beer, and disappeared, looking edgier than ever.

"How do you know he's there? You see him?"

"Naw. You know you never see these pricks until you're ready to cuff 'em. But he's there. I know he's there."

It had begun with a tip, as do so many skip traces. Blood had learned that Gibson had lent Saunders a bundle of money to cover extensive gambling debts from betting on sports teams. "Guy was up to his fuckin' eyeballs in debt," said Archuleta. "Owed Fat Alice thirty-five grand on last year's Super Bowl and a couple of college games. Fat Alice leaned on him and suddenly the guy coughs up the money—thanks to his buddy Gibson. You know Fat Alice, don't you?"

She did. In David's first week as a bondsman, Ruby'd taken him with her to see Fat Alice in his swank Italian restaurant in Denver's north side. Fat Alice was the kind of guy people went to see, not the other way around. He needed a cousin bailed out, part of Fat Alice's crime family, which David learned was a pale, almost comical imitation of the big boys in Chicago and New York and Vegas.

Ruby looked dubious. "Saunders may owe Gibson plenty, but that doesn't prove he's willing to hide a murder fugitive."

"I'm getting there, Ruby. Be patient."

The waitress arrived with the beer. Archuleta snatched the bottle by its long neck, drained half of it, wiped foam off a wispy moustache, and grinned. It was actually more of a smirk from David's view. "You want proof? Come on. I'll give you proof."

Ruby dropped enough money on the table to cover drinks and they trooped out to the parking lot behind the bar. Archuleta lead them to a scuzzy panel truck that advertised a furnace cleaning service on the side. He looked around, then opened the van's rear doors, whose windows were blacked out.

Inside squatted a young heavyset Hispanic-looking woman. One of her wrists was handcuffed to the interior frame.

"Meet Dolores," Blood said.

The woman shifted so she faced them, her body tensed at their presence. David could hear her frightened breathing echo in the van.

"Who's she, a skip?" asked Ruby.

"Nope. She's Saunders' nanny."

Ruby scowled at Archuleta. "Why's she handcuffed?"

"'Cause she's an *illegal* nanny. From Peru. I didn't trust her to stay here while we talked inside. She's seen Gibson—in Saunders' house."

Ruby climbed into the van and the woman tried to melt into the metal walls.

"It's okay, honey, it's okay," Ruby said softly. "I'm not going to harm you." She scowled at Blood. "Get the damn handcuffs off!"

"Okay, okay, hold your horses, Angel."

Archuleta climbed into the truck, handed his beer to Ruby to hold, and unfastened the cuffs. He let them dangle from the frame. The woman rubbed her thick wrist with thick fingers and looked at Ruby with wide eyes.

"Your name's Dolores?" Ruby asked her.

She nodded.

"Do you speak English?"

"A little."

"You work for Barry Saunders? At his house?"

She looked down at the hard grooved metal floor. "Yes."

"Is a man named Bayne Gibson staying at the house?"

"A man is there. They said his name is Mr. Williams. From Atlanta. They said he was visiting for a few days."

"She doesn't know a fuckin' thing about the murder," interjected Archuleta. "She don't read newspapers or watch TV."

"How long's he been there?" Ruby asked her slowly.

The woman thought about it. "Three or four days."

Just about the time they found Brodie.

"Turn on the interior light, Blood," directed Ruby.

Archuleta did as instructed. Ruby took half a dozen photographs from her purse and spread them on the floor of the van. David knew them as pictures of skips she usually carried with her.

"Is the man staying at the Saunders' home one of these men?"

The woman studied the pictures in the weak light and then pointed unhesitantly at Gibson.

"Where's he staying in the house?"

"Uh, how you say—" She pointed a finger downward.

"In the basement?" Ruby said.

"Yes."

"Who else lives in the house?"

"Mr. Saunders . . . Mrs. Saunders . . . and Chad."

"Chad? Is he a son?"

She nodded. "Four years old. He is a very nice boy. I take care of him a lot."

Back outside of the van, with the doors shut on the woman inside, Ruby asked Archuleta how he came up with her.

"I don't give away trade secrets, Angel."

"You do if you want to work for me."

"Okay, okay. I find out about this Saunders guy and I start nosing around his neighborhood. Neighborhood like that, just about every other house has a nanny, and most of 'em are illegals. I got contacts. It didn't take me long to come up with her name and where she hangs out when she's off work. Picked her up after some language class. Told her I was with Immigration. Told her she was in fuckin' big trouble for aiding and abetting a fugitive. Said if she didn't cooperate I'd ship her ass back home. She got real cooperative after that."

"Isn't it kind of risky for Saunders to have her and Gibson in the same house?" asked David. "Why didn't they send her away?"

"Hell, I don't know," said Archuleta, irritated. "Probably raise questions if they did. It's not like she even knows the guy's a fuckin' fugitive. Besides, she's in this country illegally. She goes to the cops, she gets kicked outta here like a fourth down punt."

Archuleta leaned toward Ruby. "Whattya think, Angel? He's in there. I can smell him."

What Blood could smell was money, thought David. Standard fee for a successful skip trace was ten percent of the face value of the bond. That meant a hundred grand—two thirds of their entire premium. Still, maybe Blood was on to something. Better to pay an asshole like him $100,000 than the courts $1 million.

"I'll check it out," said Ruby.

"Jesus, Angel, what's to check out! The guy's in there. I can get two buddies here in ten minutes and we can nail this guy's ass tonight."

"We'll check the home out tomorrow. I'm not charging in there blind tonight."

"Gibson could be gone tomorrow! What if this broad squeals, Angel? She sure as shit isn't gonna look at Gibson the same way. They'll get suspicious."

Ruby thought for a minute. "Tell you what. You and a coupla your pals watch the place tonight. Just *watch* it, got that? You don't go in, you don't do a thing unless you're damn sure Gibson's making a break. Nobody's busting into a fancy home in Cherry Hills Village unless I'm dead certain he's in there. I'll call you tomorrow morning."

Archuleta turned back toward his van but Ruby snagged his arm with her hand. "One other thing, honey."

"What?"

"This checks out, and I think Gibson's in there, I go in with you. No freelance stuff. I'm in charge. Got it?"

Archuleta shrugged. "Sure, Angel. I figured you wouldn't want it any other way."

26

Saunders' home was a low, sprawling place almost completely obscured by shrubbery, pine trees, and small stands of aspen. Two roan horses stood lethargically in a corral behind the house. Beyond the horses, in crystal clear morning light, stretched a picture postcard backdrop of the Rocky Mountains. And like a picture postcard, there was no movement, no sign of life, either around the Saunders' home or on the adjoining streets.

''Toldya it was easy meat,'' said Archuleta from the back seat of Ruby's big dark Buick, which was idling half a block from Saunders' home.

''That's the kind of stupid arrogance that gets people hurt, Blood,'' said Ruby, putting down her binoculars. She sat in the passenger side. David sat behind the wheel.

Archuleta draped his head and arms over the front seat between the two of them and pointed out Ruby's side of the car with a bony finger. ''We can park on that side road and go in from the back. There ain't many houses around, and with all them trees and shit, nobody'll see us.''

''At least the place is accessible. A lotta homes down here are stashed behind walls and security gates.''

''I tell ya, Angel, it's gonna be easy.

Saunders' home sat on a corner acre lot. The street fronting the house, Dartmouth Lane, was paved, but the side street was gravel. The two nearest houses on the gravel street sat a third of a block away and were hidden behind thick shrubbery and trees. At night, their residents wouldn't be able to see a tank corps go by.

"What about security patrols?" Ruby asked.

"The guys I left here last night said rent-a-cops went by twice and city cops once, but that was about it. Shitsure the house is alarmed, but we can cuff his jumpin' ass and have him on the way to city jail before the cops show up."

"You *are* going to tell the city cops, aren't you?" said David, unease in his voice. As a courtesy, and sometimes to protect themselves, bondsmen alerted the local police when they were going to break into a place. Cops had been known to park outside a building while the bondsman or the bounty hunter went in.

"No way, José," snapped Archuleta. "They'd fuck it up for us."

David looked over to his aunt but she was nodding in agreement with Archuleta. "He's right. I know the cops down here. They wouldn't let us raid one of these homes."

"You can't be serious, Aunt Ruby," he said.

"Gibson's no different than any other skip. He's wanted for a crime and I intend to bring him in. I don't care where he's hiding."

But Gibson was different. David had once busted into an apartment with Big Jim Brodie looking for a skip, and that had been scary enough. You never knew what lay on the other side of the door. But it had been a low rent place on the west side of town, and it had been a small-time skip wanted for a small-time crime. Nothing as big as murder, in this kind of neighborhood, with this much money at stake.

Not that they didn't have a right to bust into Barry Saunders' home. Too much right, as David saw it. He'd never been comfortable with the wide latitude given bounty hunters and bondsmen when it came to apprehending bail jumpers. An 1873 U.S. Supreme Court ruling gave them extraordinary powers, more powers than law enforcement officers. Bounty hunters didn't need search warrants, extradition papers, or legal notices. They could legally kick in a front door and enter anyone's home—as long as the defendant was there. They didn't have to call the cops before they did it and they didn't have to read the defendant any Miranda rights. When he'd debated this point with his aunt before, she'd conceded that some bounty hunters exceeded their constitutional authority, but she staunchly defended the extraordinary powers as the only effective way the private bail bonding system could work.

David looked out the driver's window at the other houses. He shook his head. "It's too dangerous."

"That's what makes this such a great job, kid," cut in Archuleta, his voice rising. "You got a plan, Angel?"

"I'll think of something."

"I say we hit 'em at 3:00 A.M. You snooze, you lose."

"Move on, David," commanded Ruby with a wave of her hand. "I don't want us to attract attention."

David put the Buick in gear. His hands trembled. He cruised by the front of the house. A crescent-shaped driveway swung in front of a low-slung roof that was stretched over a stone veranda flanked by evergreens.

"The place ain't the projects, is it?" said the bounty hunter. "We can't kick in the front door. I figure we bust in through a window or crowbar open a rear door."

Ruby spun around in her seat. "We're not busting in anything, unless absolutely necessary, Blood. You hear me?"

"They ain't gonna let us walk in the front door, Angel."

"That's exactly how we're going in. Right after dark we set up people around the house. Then I go to the front door and knock."

"You gotta be kiddin', Angel! We're talking a guy with cleaver fever. You think he and this Saunders dude are just gonna let you waltz right in and cuff him?"

"I don't think Gibson killed anybody. I don't think he's gonna resist."

"Well, I sure as shit ain't taking that chance, Angel. I say we hit hard and fast. You can get killed otherwise. Just ask Jim."

"There's a family in there, a young boy. Bustin' in creates panic. Innocent people could get hurt. We knock first. It's easier that way and less risk to everyone. If Gibson knows we've got the place sealed off, he'll give up. If that doesn't work, then we go in."

"That's as crazy as cat shit, Angel."

"That's my decision, Blood. Live with it or I find somebody else to do it."

Back at the office, Ruby ran a quick background check on Saunders. David was still amazed, and not a little appalled, at how easy it was for her to run checks on people. After half a dozen phone calls and the use of the computer, his aunt confirmed that one Barry G. Saunders lived at 3812 E. Dartmouth Lane. She also dug up his Social Security number, his credit rating, a description of his $348,000 house, and the fact that he was vice-president of finance at Gibson Media and raking in $270,000 a year. At age thirty-nine, he'd been divorced and had remarried five years ago to a woman named Karen. Nothing turned up an illegal nanny, but they did have a son, Chad, age four. Saunders owned three cars (none of them over three years old), and two horses that his wife rode in horse shows. Saunders, like his boss, belonged to the Denver Athletic Club and was a marathoner. He served on the Colorado Opera board and he had no known police record, in Colorado or anywhere else.

Most of the information was easily accessible through public records. What wasn't available through public records was Saunders' addiction to gambling. A call to Fat Alice corroborated Archuleta's story, though the bounty hunter had been wrong about the details. Saunders' gambling debts had run closer to fifty grand than thirty-five. No, Fat Alice didn't know where Saunders had suddenly come up with the money to pay off his debt. And he didn't care.

The clincher came from Ruby's source in the telephone company.

"Three calls came into Saunders' home the night Gibson disappeared," Ruby said, late afternoon shadows spreading across police headquarters behind her. David had just returned from an errand. "One at nine fifty-nine, one at eleven fourteen, and one at—" she referred to the notebook in front of her "—twelve-twenty-seven."

"Where from?"

"The first call came from a pay phone two blocks from Gibson's penthouse. The next two came from the house in Evergreen."

David whistled. "So he's there."

"Yes, I think he's there."

"And you're going to hit the house?"

"I've already set it up with Blood. We meet at nine tonight. Here. He's bringing three bounty hunters and his panel truck."

David shook his head. "I don't like this, Aunt Ruby. Just call the police and let them bring Gibson in."

"They wouldn't do it."

"Why, because they wouldn't believe Archuleta?" he said sarcastically.

"David, please, I need your help on this."

"You don't trust Blood any more than I do."

"Gibson's in that house. I want him."

He didn't say anything for a moment. "I can't help you. I won't go with you, Aunt Ruby."

She didn't look surprised, but she asked why.

"It's wrong."

"It's legal."

"That doesn't make it right."

"Since when did that ever stop a lawyer?"

"It just doesn't feel right."

"Now you're talking like me."

"This isn't a joke, Aunt Ruby."

"It bothers you because it's a rich man's home, doesn't it?"

"No. That has nothing to do with it."

"If it was Capitol Hill or Five Points you wouldn't think twice about it."

"At least tell the police what you're doing. I'd feel better if they gave their approval."

"I can't risk it. They'll either screw it up or try to stop me."

"Then I won't go along with you."

He expected more words, more argument from her, but she merely nodded her head in acknowledgement of his decision.

He glanced uncomfortably at his watch. "I have to go to class."

"I'll see you later."

He hesitated. "Are you going to be okay, Aunt Ruby?"

"I'll be fine."

"I don't trust Archuleta. Or the goons he's bringing along."

"I'll be fine. I rejected the first two guys he wanted to bring along. These guys are okay."

David stood still, saying nothing.

Ruby pointed to the door. "Go to class, David."

"I feel responsible for Gibson."

"Don't be. We'll bring his ass in tonight. It'll be over with soon."

"Yeah. I hope so. Good luck."

27

Professor Gideon A. Rothschild bore only a slight resemblance to Professor Kingsfield, that pedantic tyrant of first-year contracts from *The Paper Chase*. No, Rothschild was no mere tyrant. He was a reincarnated Nazi, given to gleefully torturing defenseless first-year law students at night when he wasn't otherwise handing down misery by day to defendants who appeared before him in federal court.

Since David's aunt rarely bonded defendants out of federal court—the day a defendant failed to show up for an appearance you paid up, no ifs, buts, and ands about it—neither one of them had ever dealt with Rothschild in court. But Ruby had heard of him and of his reputation as one tough sonofabitch who'd graduated fourth in his Yale law class, clerked for a U.S. Supreme Court justice, and served as an assistant secretary of Labor in the Nixon administration. What he was doing teaching night school in Denver was the basis of much speculation.

Rothschild, dressed in a black three-piece suit even though the air conditioner wasn't working and the lecture hall would have kept pizza hot, stood six two with massive shoulders and a menacing voice. Despite his presence, there was a deceptive awkwardness to his movements as he patrolled the front of the lecture hall. The unwary would be momentarily lulled into relaxation by this awkwardness, until he would turn and suddenly pounce on the inattentive student.

Rothschild scanned the lecture hall, fixing all ninety-four students like deer frozen in headlights. At the start of each class, he selected someone to brief that evening's assigned case. Like death, there was no escaping Rothschild's baleful eye. Sooner or later during the semester he would call on you. But once your name was picked, however well or poorly you did, he checked it off the seating chart on his lectern with a flourish, never to call on you to brief a case again. Under the right circumstances you could pass for the night, but that was only postponing the inevitable. Those who felt exceptionally prepared and wanted to get it over with, raised their hands, but Rothschild rarely picked them. He preferred to snare the most apprehensive, the most ill-prepared students. What was the fun in torturing those who could take it?

Rothschild looked down at the seating chart and matched his selected victim with a name on the chart. "Mr. Piszek, would you please brief tonight's case for us."

David jerked at the sound of his name. His eyes had been on Rothschild but his mind had been on his aunt. She was crazy going off alone with Blood and his three goons. He'd tried to figure out what he could do to prevent the raid. He'd thought about returning to try again to talk some sense into her, but she was too stubborn for that. He'd thought about calling Blood to say his aunt had suddenly taken ill and couldn't come—if he could reach the man. He'd even considered calling the Cherry Hills Village police to tip them off, but he knew he couldn't betray his aunt like that.

"Mr. Piszek?" Rothschild repeated.

David's heart sank. He could hear sighs of relief among the other students.

"I wish to pass, sir," he said, trying to work his frozen mouth.

"Pardon me?" Rothschild was going to make it as painful as possible.

"I wish to pass, sir."

"Pass?"

"Yes, sir."

"Perhaps you think we're playing bridge here instead of studying the law?"

"No, sir . . . of course not. I just wish to pass."

David spoke with a mentholated cough drop in his mouth.

The long hours of tracking down Gibson and Brodie, worrying about the future of his aunt's business, and worrying his own future had become so exhausting he'd gone to sucking the drops in his classes in an effort, usually in vain, to stay awake.

"What you're telling us, Mr. Piszek, is that you're not *prepared* for today's session."

"Yes, sir, I guess that's what I'm saying."

Damn, he should have stayed with her! He shouldn't let her go alone! It was his fault that Gibson . . .

"You guess? Either you are or you aren't prepared. Don't you know?"

"I'm not prepared, sir."

He wasn't prepared for any of his classes these days, but he especially wasn't prepared for tonight's class. He'd skimmed the twenty-five-page case shortly before class started, but there was no way he could brief it. He had hoped—in vain, he now knew—that Rothschild wouldn't pick him.

"At least we have settled on a fact, Mr. Piszek. That's progress. However, the rule is that to pass you must turn in a written request *before* the start of class."

"I meant to do that, sir."

"You *meant* to do that?"

"Yes, sir."

"Meaning to do something but not doing it is how court cases are lost."

Rothschild stepped from his lectern to the first row of seats and stared at David, who was seated toward the back of the steeply pitched lecture hall. Rothschild could have simply moved on and called on someone else. Three students had their hands eagerly raised, as though fighting for the right to pick the pockets of the dying. Or the professor could have gone on to other names unchecked on his seating chart. He had done that before when students had asked to pass. He would get the student another day. But the look in the professor's eyes made it clear that tonight, even after David's humbling admission, he wasn't going to let go. The pit bull had clamped his teeth on bone and nothing was going to shake him loose.

"You're developing a disturbing history of not being prepared, Mr. Piszek," continued Rothschild. "You've missed classes and you've done poorly on exams lately."

Christ, tell the whole damn class while you're at it! Didn't the ass have something better to do with his time, like drown kittens or sentence drug dealers to forty years?

"I've been extremely busy at work, sir."

"Busy?"

David could tell immediately that this excuse garnered as much sympathy as if he'd said, "I was born with a silver spoon in my mouth, sir, and I don't feel obligated to do the work."

"Most of your fellow students are busy, Mr. Piszek. Many of them have full-time jobs. *I* have a full-time job. That's why most of us are here at night school. But *we* come to class prepared."

David struggled not to scowl at his fellow students, as if they were somehow responsible for this humiliating predicament. Hand them a million dollar skip and a dead bounty hunter and an aunt who was putting her business and God knows what else in the hands of a sociopathic ex-con, and see how goddamned focused they'd stay! Hell, on her best days the dull-eyed woman seated next to him was no more prepared than he was tonight. Why the hell didn't Rothschild call on her?

"What kind of work do you do, Mr. Piszek, that makes it so difficult to put sufficient effort into your studies?" Rothschild asked.

To admit in front of a room full of law students and one fascist judge that he was a bail bondsman would be to admit that he was the lowest form of life, a scumbag, a leech on the judicial system. It was the difference between being a bank executive and bank robber. Both might be in the same line of work, but they were worlds apart on the social scale. Expediency told him to take the same tack he took with his father. He lied.

"I drive a cab, sir."

"A lot of people need rides these days?"

"Uh, we've been shorthanded. I've had to put in a lot of overtime."

''A change of working schedule would be in your best interest, Mr. Piszek.''

''Yes, sir. I understand. I'm trying to get it changed.''

David glanced at his watch. 8:17. His aunt and the four men would leave in less than forty-five minutes. Class wouldn't be over until . . .

''Are we keeping you from something?'' asked Rothschild. ''Perhaps someone is in need of a cab.''

''No, sir. Sorry, sir. I am listening.''

''Good. Because we are here to study law,'' the professor said, suddenly addressing the entire class. ''Some of these cases may appear unimportant or mundane to you, but let me assure you that they form the foundation of legal theory. Contracts is the most important course any of you will take your first year. Your other law courses will constantly refer to and build on the material you learn in this room. Contracts, may, in fact, be the most important course you will ever take in your entire student career. Contracts are what constitute the fabric of our legal system, our cultural and social systems, our very lives. Your every contact with other human beings, with the world around you, is a form of contract. Everything you do is determined by how scrupulously—or *unscrupulously*—you treat that contract. As students, you have a binding contract with me. It is a contract that says that each and every one of you come to class *fully* prepared to discuss that evening's material . . . or don't bother to come to class at all.'' Rothschild's eyes riveted again on David. ''Is that understood, Mr. Piszek?''

''Clearly, sir.''

''Then you may pass for the night, Mr. Piszek. But be forewarned that you won't get a chance to pass again.''

David sneaked out of class ten minutes later, in the midst of Rothschild skewering one of the eager handraisers who thought she was prepared but wasn't. If he raced, and made all the lights, he'd get there in time. Ruby would be surprised, and Blood probably pissed. But the hell with them. He wasn't going to let her take the risk alone. She was his aunt and he'd come to like her too much to let her go off with a psycho like Blood.

Alone with four thugs in a van. Jesus, how stupid could she be!

He felt his own stomach knot at the thought of going off to raid Saunders' house. Jesus, how stupid could *he* be!

Johnny Archuleta's panel truck bounced over what felt like a speed bump. David's stomach turned another cartwheel.

David tried to read his watch but couldn't. The interior of the van was black, the rear windows darkened so no one outside could see in. Everyone but Archuleta, who drove, was crammed into the back. It was hot and stuffy and claustrophobic.

The plan had all the trappings of a commando raid on a group of terrorists holding hostages. Everyone was dressed in dark colors. Even Ruby wore black slacks, a black blouse, black cowboy hat, and jogging shoes, though she was in makeup. They were to approach Saunders' home under the cover of darkness, quickly surround the house, and strike with the precision of a well-oiled special forces team. That was the game plan, anyway . . . the way Archuleta had laid it out.

But the original plan had not been without modifications by Ruby. No one was to be armed. This had not gone down well with Archuleta or the other men. What with "make my day" laws and nine year olds sporting automatic weapons these days, anybody could be armed, especially a guy wanted by the cops for two homicides. Ruby dug in. Blood and the others nearly quit on the spot, but Ruby had prevailed. They left their guns locked in the office.

Maybe that explained the incessant chatter and edgy laughter of the bounty hunters in the back of the truck. They traded war stories with each other and with Ruby, each trying to top the other about skips they'd tracked down. David had seen one of them before—the one wearing a blue baseball cap with a Denver Police emblem on it. Frank, he thought his name was. He seemed to have the best stories. The other two he didn't know, but they had the same quality he'd seen in many bounty hunters: big, burly, and not to be messed with.

The van turned off the paved road onto gravel. Everyone

fell silent. David's stomach tightened again. This really wasn't what he wanted to be—

The truck stopped.

"It's kick ass time!" bellowed Archuleta.

They burst out the rear doors. David stumbled behind the others, disoriented in the darkness. With Archuleta in the lead, they crossed a small drainage ditch by the road, slithered between strands of barbed wire, and cut across the corral, scattering the two horses at their approach.

There was nothing to lead the way, except for the muffled lights coming from Saunders' house. A quarter moon dodged behind clouds. Suddenly the ragged line of people in front of him stopped. They huddled thirty feet off a back corner of the house. They were still in the corral. A wooden jump stood nearby. One of the horses, a paint, wandered close to them. His breathing sounded like that of a creature from another planet. There was the strong smell of manure and horse piss.

Archuleta handed Ruby one of two walkie-talkies. "Give us a coupla minutes to set up around the house. I'll call with the go-ahead when we're ready."

"No one goes in unless I give the say-so! Got that?"

The bounty hunters murmured in agreement. They broke up. Ruby and David skirted the house from a dirt footpath that wove through trees, shrubbery, and Colorado field stone. Twice Ruby peered in windows or listened for hints of who was inside and where. The laugh track of a TV show droned on somewhere, but David couldn't pinpoint the room. They slipped between a stand of aspen and a corner of the house and found themselves on the darkened veranda, which was full of hanging pots and the cloying smell of flowers he couldn't identify. He banged his head against one of the pots and stopped its swinging with his hands.

"You okay?" whispered Ruby.

"Yeah. Fine . . . fine." His hands shook. He clamped them to his sides, hoping she wouldn't see how scared he was. He fought not to throw up.

Ruby's walkie-talkie crackled to life. "We're in place, Angel," came Archuleta's whispered voice.

"So are we. I'm ringing the doorbell now."

David stood to one side so that whoever came to the door would only see a pretty fifty-year-old woman dressed in black yet respectable clothes.

Ruby rang the bell again. Finally, footsteps approached. Light steps. A woman's?

A porch light flicked on. The blinding yellow light made David blink.

"Who is it?" came a woman's voice.

"My name is Ruby Dark. Of Ruby's Bail Bonds. I've come for Mr. Gibson."

"There's no one by that name here. You must have the wrong house. Please go away."

"We know he's in there, Mrs. Saunders. Just tell him to come out peacefully. We don't want anyone hurt."

"What do you mean, hurt? I'm not Mrs. Saunders. I don't know anyone named Saunders. You have the wrong house. Go away or I'll call the police!"

The woman sounded frightened.

"He can't escape. We have the house surrounded."

"Oh, my God! I'm calling the police!"

"We have a legal right to enter your home and arrest him," Ruby yelled through the door.

Footsteps hurried from the door. "Girls!" she screamed. "Girls!"

Suddenly, from the back of the house, came the sound of shattering glass. Then came the sound of screams.

28

"Blood?" Ruby barked into the walkie-talkie.

No answer.

"What the hell's going on back there, Blood?"

The sounds of more broken glass and more screams came from the interior of the house.

"Oh, my God!" shrieked a woman's voice inside. "Valerie? Laura? Are you all right?"

David cupped his hands over his eyes and peered through the window that faced the veranda. Directly inside was an unlit formal parlor with piano and flower-print chairs. Through the open doorway of the parlor he could make out a hallway faintly lit by the spill of lights from a distant room. But he could see no one, and had no clue as to what was happening.

"Answer me, Blood!"

Nothing on the walkie-talkie. More screams from inside, one of them loud and piercing, like that of a young girl.

"Go round back," Ruby commanded. "I'll stay here by the front door in case he comes out this way. Watch yourself."

Shaking, David retraced their steps along the dirt path, racing faster than his eyes could see, unseen branches slashing at his face, shins striking rock.

"Watch yourself," his aunt had warned. What the hell was he going to do if he suddenly came face to face with Gibson? He wasn't armed. None of them were armed. Images of Brodie's body in the cabin flashed in his mind.

More screaming and yelling from inside. He looked in a window but he couldn't see anyone.

At the back of the house, where they'd left Archuleta and the other three bounty hunters, he found the back door smashed open, the frame splintered. He stepped into the kitchen, glass crunching under his jogging shoes. He froze. He started to yell for Blood, then thought better of it. If Gibson was still loose . . .

He followed the voices, the yelling, and the screaming, through a formal dining room and into a family room with a huge sunken pit and a fireplace. The television was on. Two of the bounty hunters were in the room. One of them dangled a small kicking, screaming girl under one arm, like a student holding his books. His other hand held an automatic. The second bounty hunter was wrestling a woman to the floor. Mrs. Saunders, he guessed. She fought and cursed at him, but he was too big and too strong. He snapped handcuffs on her, and when she was calmer, she looked through tears in the direction of her other daughter, a teenager, sitting on the floor propped against a brown leather couch in a night shirt. She called her name but the girl only moaned groggily.

David had barely taken in this incomprehensible scene when Ruby and the third bounty hunter, Frank, rushed into the room.

"What the hell's going on?" Ruby demanded.

"They resisted," said the man who'd handcuffed the woman. He nodded in the direction of the teenager propped against the couch. "I had to stun the bitch. She was tryin' to claw my fuckin' eyes out." He rubbed at three long scratches on his cheek and examined the blood on his fingertips.

David knew bounty hunters used electric stun guns to subdue skips—Big Jim had shown him his once—but he'd never seen the effects of one before.

Ruby looked around the room. "Where's Gibson?"

"We haven't found him yet," said Frank. "I checked the basement first thing. There's nothing down there but storage."

"Probably hidin' under a bed or sumpthin' said the man still dangling the little girl under his arm. "Shit, I once found a skip hiding up a fireplace chimney."

"Put the girl down, Pete."

The big man let her go and she cowered next to her half-conscious sister, her eyes huge.

"Where'd you get that gun? Is it theirs?"

The big man shook his head.

"It's yours?"

He nodded sheepishly.

"Dammit, I said no guns! We locked the guns away."

"We brought extras. Blood told us to bring 'em. He figured you'd take ours. He didn't want us up against a killer like Gibson without firepower."

Ruby stepped toward the bounty hunter. "I specifically told you *no guns!* I didn't want anyone hurt." She swept her arm around the room. "This is exactly the kind of mess I wanted to avoid. You coulda killed one of these girls!"

"We didn't wanna get killed, too, Angel. Gibson already took out Big Jim. And what the fuck do we know about this Saunders guy? Guy does business with a hood like Fat Alice, who the hell knows what he might do."

Where's the little boy? David suddenly wondered. Chad, the nanny had called him. And who were these girls? The nanny hadn't said anything about any girls.

"By the way, where the hell is Blood?" Ruby asked.

The men shrugged their shoulders.

"Didn't he come in with you?"

"We all came in different routes," said Frank.

"Why did you guys bust in? I didn't give you the go-ahead."

Frank answered. "Blood said you was in trouble. Said you wanted us to go in."

"Shit!" said Ruby. She went over to the woman. "Who are these girls, honey?"

"They're my daughters. Who are you? Who are these men? Why have you broken into our home?"

Ruby motioned to the bounty hunter to uncuff Mrs. Saunders. She crawled over to the two girls and huddled over them, crying. Ruby sent the bounty hunters off to finish searching the house. "But *don't* do any more damage."

She knelt by the groggy teenager. "She'll be all right, hon.

The effects wear off pretty quickly.'' The girl looked at Ruby and David, pulled her knees up under her, and stretched her night shirt down as far as it would go.

''Are you going to kill us?'' the woman said, her voice full of terror.

''Nobody's gonna hurt you.''

The woman didn't look reassured. ''Please leave, then!'' she said through sobs.

''Where's your son?''

''I don't have a son.''

''A four-year-old boy named Chad, Mrs. Saunders.''

''I told you, I don't have a son. I have my two daughters and that's all. I know my own children. And I'm not Mrs. Saunders! My name is Julie Brooks.''

''Do you have a nanny named Dolores?''

''I don't have a nanny. Why are you asking these stupid questions? Why have you broken into my house and hurt my children?''

''I'm Ruby Dark. I run a bail bonding company. I'm looking for a fugitive named Bayne Gibson. I have reliable information that he's hiding in this house.''

''I told you, nobody by that name lives here.'' An expression of comprehension suddenly broke across the woman's face. ''You mean the man who killed that talk show host?''

''Yes. Where's your husband?''

The woman glared at Ruby. ''My husband died two years ago in a car accident. There's just my two daughters and me. We're the only people in this house.''

''This thirty-eight twelve East Dartmouth Lane, right?''

''No. It's thirty-six sixty Princeton. Dartmouth is blocks from here. You have the wrong street! You have the wrong house! You have the wrong family!'' The woman's shock and fear was turning to outrage.

''Can't be,'' said Ruby. ''I checked the house number myself when I was standing at the front door.''

''Well, you're wrong!''

Ruby looked at David. ''Double check the number and the street sign.''

He hurried outside and found the house number half hidden behind a hanging plant. Raised black metal numbers that said 3812. Jesus, didn't the woman know her own house number?

He went out to the street. The light by the corner street sign was busted and he had to walk up close to read the sign.

Princeton and Ivanhoe.

Not Dartmouth Lane . . . *Princeton.*

He ran across the street. The house number on the house directly across from the home they'd entered was 3645.

"Damn!" He hurried back to the house, and on the way he realized two things. This house had no curved driveway cutting through the front yard like the one they'd seen with Archuleta, and now that he thought about it, he didn't remember seeing hanging plants on that porch either. He stopped again at the house number and looked closer. He could make out the faint outline of old numbers where the paint had weathered around them.

3660.

The woman was on the telephone calling the police when he broke the news to his aunt. "Somebody switched house numbers."

"Shit!"

The bounty hunters reappeared. No signs of Gibson, Saunders . . . or Johnny Archuleta.

"Wait here," she told the bounty hunters. She and David went out the back door and stared into the blackness in the direction where Blood's panel truck was parked.

It was gone.

"The bastard's skipped on us!" snapped David.

"No, he didn't skip," said Ruby, her voice as cold as David had ever heard it. "We've been set up."

"Set up? Why? Blood?"

"I think I know who. But right now I want you to get outta here."

"What do you—"

"There's no reason for you to get caught up in this. You didn't even want to come along."

"But I did. I want to stay here with—"

"Go! Scram! Haul ass! Go on up the dirt road until you catch the bike path. Take the path as far as you can from here and stay outta sight. Don't call any cabs near here. Catch a bus if you see one."

"Aunt Ruby, the family's already seen me."

"They're too frightened to remember anything straight. They'll just remember me and the big guys."

"What about the bounty hunters?"

"I'll take care of them. Now get the hell out of here."

In the distance came the wail of a police siren.

Ruby pushed him away with her hand. David started toward the corral, then suddenly stopped and yelled back to Ruby. "The horses!"

"What about 'em?"

"I should have noticed when we came in. See the paint. There wasn't a paint this morning when we checked the place out with Blood. Two roans. Who set us up, Aunt Ruby?"

"Go!"

29

"Cadillac Johnson?" repeated Cyndee Valone.

"There's nobody else," said Ruby.

Valone laughed. "There can always be somebody else in your business. Besides, I still think it was a mistake. It's not the first time bondsmen have raided the wrong place."

"That was no mistake, Cyndee, and you know it."

"Why are you so positive it was Johnson?"

"I know."

Exasperation laced Valone's voice. "Another Ruby Dark hunch, is that it?"

"This was done by somebody who knows the bail bonding business . . . and how I work."

"What about this *Blood* character?" She shivered. "Creepy name if I ever heard one. Maybe it was his idea."

"He's not that devious. Cadillac is. And Blood doesn't have a reason to stick it to me unless somebody else is paying him to. But Cadillac—he'd love to see me go under."

"So would a lot of other bondsmen."

David sat in a chair and watched the two women circling and sparring like boxers. Valone was one of the few people he'd met who wasn't intimidated by his aunt.

"Trust me, honey, he's the only one who could have pulled it off."

"Well, your trust and hunches aren't going to help us a lot here, Ruby. We need something a little more substantial—like evidence." Valone looked at David. "What about you? Can you provide any concrete insight into this matter?"

David glanced at Ruby then back at Valone. ''I—I wasn't there, so . . .''

''Did you know about it?''

''Forget about Cadillac for the moment, Cyndee,'' Ruby cut in. ''I'll get him in my own way in my own good time. What kind of trouble am I in with the Cherry Hills Village cops?''

''You mean besides breaking and entering, criminal trespass, felony conspiracy to commit first-degree trespass, and felony menacing?'' Valone ticked the charges off on her fingers as if she were counting the dead. ''Oh, and they were working on more when I left the DA's office at two o'clock.''

''Didn't they find it a little odd that somebody changed the house numbers?'' questioned Ruby.

''The police think it was you.''

''Why the hell would I swap house numbers so I could break into the wrong house?''

Valone shrugged. ''Reasoning doesn't have anything to do with it. They don't like bondsmen. God, Ruby, did you take leave of your senses going down there? You might as well have raided the governor's mansion.''

David refrained from saying, ''I told you so.''

''What about Blood's panel truck?'' said Ruby. ''Any tire tracks they could match?''

''There's no truck registered to a Johnny Archuleta.''

''Probably collateral from one of Cadillac's clients. That, or he stole it.''

''They've talked to Archuleta. He denies ever being there. Swears he was off chasing some skip on the north side of town.''

''Ruby and the bounty hunters identified him!'' said David.

Valone smiled a tight hard smile. ''No, just Ruby. The three goons have refused to say anything about this Blood character.''

Or about me, David thought with some relief. Aloud he said, ''Why would they lie about Blood? They're in as much trouble as we—as Aunt Ruby is.''

''They aren't going to say anything against Blood,'' Ruby

said. She took an album out of a well-worn jacket. David recognized it as one of her favorites: Charlie Parker's *Yardbird in Lotus Land.* She put the record on the turntable and gently set down the needle. "They don't want to piss him off."

"What about pissing off you?"

"They know I won't kill 'em."

The hauntingly slow yet complex sound of an alto sax filled the room.

David grew angrier. "What about the nanny?" he asked Valone. "Anybody talked to the Saunders family about her?"

"They claim they don't have a nanny. Mrs. Saunders stays home with her kid."

David humphed his disbelief.

"Wouldn't make any difference, anyway," said Ruby. "The woman in that van wasn't a nanny. She was an actress. A good one, too. Just somebody else Cadillac used to set me up."

For the umpteenth time, David glanced at the front page of the *Denver Post* lying on the desk in front of him. It was like driving by a gory car accident. He didn't want to look but he couldn't help himself. The headline in the lower right hand corner screamed "Bounty Hunters Raid Wrong Home." The subhead read "Terrorize Woman and Two Daughters Looking for Kray-Killer Suspect."

If it had been a small-time skip instead of a big-time murderer like Gibson, and if the home had been in the projects instead of one of the wealthiest suburbs in America, the incident probably wouldn't have made the paper, let alone the front page. But "if it had been" didn't mean much now.

Ruby's name and the names of the three bounty hunters were in the article. His own wasn't mentioned, but the article said a fourth man, as yet unidentified, had escaped. He had followed his aunt's instructions. He'd walked the bike path and small streets until he reached Hampden Avenue where he caught a bus out to Aurora. From there, he'd taken a cab to downtown Denver, then walked to the office. It took him three hours to get back. Ruby didn't show up for another hour.

Valone shook her head. ''You really got yourself in a fine mess this time, Ruby. The woman's threatening to file a lawsuit. Probably at least as large as Gibson's bail. Emotional distress . . . all that stuff. Considering the ludicrous reasons people sue for these days—and win!—I'd say she's got a helluva case.''

Ruby had said she'd apologized to the woman and her daughters that night as they waited for the police to arrive. It was too late, of course. As the headlines accurately portrayed, the family had been terrorized. Breaking glass and hulking men and guns and handcuffs will do that to the average family. No amount of apology could ever erase that nightmare.

Valone went on. ''The State Insurance Commission will come after you. You could lose your license over this—even with your reputation. There's going to be a lot of political pressure to have your head.''

''Thanks for the cheery note of support, Cyndee.''

Valone sighed. ''I've got good relations with the DA's office down there. I'll see what I can do to delay or mitigate any criminal charges. Maybe you can pin it on Johnson by then.''

''I plan to pin it on his ass.''

''I can't do much about any civil lawsuit until she picks a lawyer. There'll be plenty of them banging on her door.''

Valone headed out, stopped when she passed David, and pointed to the scratches on his cheek. ''What happened to you?''

His hand went to his face. ''Uh, the cat.''

''I'm surprised the little shit let you get that close.''

''Hey, Piszek the Pole.''

Aspen Kray stood in the office entrance. Her deep blue eyes, set against her pale face and blond hair like shimmering alpine lakes, instantly mesmerized him again. The bright blue silk blouse made her eyes even bluer, made them almost snap.

''Yes?'' David said warily, setting down his law book.

''I read about your aunt in the paper. You guys really fucked up.''

"I'm glad you stopped by to remind us."

"Actually, I stopped by to ask you to go shopping with me."

"Shopping?"

"Yeah . . . you know, browsing through stores, trying on clothes, making purchases . . . shopping."

"Why on earth do you want to go shopping with me?"

She had not responded to their repeated phone calls and personal visits since the night they'd followed her to the Evergreen home and Big Jim's body. Not that he was surprised. They only had a zillion questions to ask her. Like why was she there? How did she know about the secret room? Was she trying to protect her mother? Or was she herself having an affair with Bayne Gibson? Did her father know?

"My mother doesn't feel like shopping and my sisters aren't around. I hate to shop alone. You're the only one left."

"Don't you have friends?"

"Ever the anal-retentive lawyer, David. Got to know every detail, got to have all the answers before you can even take a crap. Can't you do something just because you want to?"

"You're assuming I want to go."

"I know you do."

Why was he being so coy? Granted, he hated to shop. But he'd follow Aspen Kray through the aisles of Wal-Mart if that's where she wanted to go.

"I have a lot of studying to do. Plus, I've got to watch the place and take calls. I can't just up and leave."

"You need your aunt's permission?"

"She just left and I don't know when she'll be back."

"I know. I watched her go."

30

No Wal-Mart for Aspen Kray. She drove them—in the same white Honda he'd followed to Evergreen—to the upscale Cherry Creek Mall. It was the first time he'd been in the place, and he felt like an imposter sneaking in with someone who had a pass. They wouldn't have let him in on his own. Security would have stopped him at the entrance, their money detectors set off loudly by the paucity of his wallet.

They parked in the attached garage, and from there David was in a foot race with Aspen, who went like a homing pigeon to a women's clothing shop called Gantos. Within minutes she'd grabbed two dresses off the rack and an $85 hat, and tossed her Visa card to the saleswoman, who seemed to know her.

"Aren't you going to try them on?" David asked as the saleswoman rang up the purchases.

"No. What for?"

"To see if they fit."

She shrugged. "I don't even know if I'll wear them."

"Then why are you buying them?"

"It's a hobby," she said as she signed the charge slip. "Everybody should have a hobby, don't you think?"

"What, like collecting stamps or gardening?"

She stepped up close to him, her face inches from his. "To tell the truth, David, just between you and me, I get sexually aroused at the sound of the credit card machine going back and forth across my Visa card."

He trailed her into Lord & Taylor, Saks Fifth Avenue,

Neiman Marcus, and half a dozen small shops whose names he didn't recognize but whose appreciative clerks recognized her on sight. She bought something in nearly every store—colored soaps, belts, perfumes, a diamond pendant, four swimsuits, a back scratcher, eleven CDs, a pair of hiking boots, vitamins, a garlic crusher—though she didn't seem to pay much attention to what she bought. If shopping was a hobby or a form of sex, she didn't seem to have much fun at it.

Despite her constant proddings, he didn't buy anything, though he did donate twenty-five cents in the Nature Company to save ninety square feet of rain forest.

Within an hour, they had so many sacks they had to return to her car to unload. No wonder she needed someone to go shopping with her. He was her jungle porter, her skycap, her water boy, her Sherpa.

"Pardon my anal-retentiveness but who's paying for all this?" he asked as she transferred the sacks from his arms to the trunk. As a student, he knew she wasn't making much money, especially after her talk about McJobs. Yet by his rough calculation, she'd blown several hundred dollars in a single hour.

"My father."

The initial puzzlement on his face turned to comprehension.

"No, it's not what you think," she said. "He didn't leave us a big insurance check. Not like what the radio station had on him or what the media's implied. Hell, he didn't leave us much of anything. He thought money would spoil us. But what he did leave I'm damn sure going to spend."

"I'm sure he'd understand."

Aspen Kray slammed the trunk hood and looked him straight in his eyes. "You're either very naive, David, or you're trying to kiss ass."

"I was only—"

"My father hated it when I shopped. He'd take away my credit cards and call my favorite stores to warn them that he wouldn't pay for anything I bought. I found ways around it, of course. The Kray women are nothing if not resourceful. My mother would try to disguise the bills, but Father usually found out eventually.'' She smiled at this, as if she had enjoyed getting caught by him.

''So why did you bring me along? You need an audience? Someone to document your revenge? Or just an errand boy to carry sacks?''

''I told you, I hate to shop alone.''

He didn't believe her. He knew she wanted to talk to him about something. He didn't know what it was or when she would talk about it, but she would talk. Yet he knew such talk would only ruin the afternoon. He really didn't want to know why she'd brought him along. He didn't want to ask her the zillion questions about her and Gibson and Evergreen. He didn't want to think about Big Jim anymore or the raid on the house in Cherry Hills Village or the fact that his law studies were going into the toilet. He just wanted to tag along and smell her perfume and listen to her bitch about the bitches who went to Wellesley College.

When she did finally talk, it came unexpectedly. And it had nothing to do with her and Gibson and the house in Evergreen.

They were in the Disney store. Turned out she loved Mickey Mouse knickknacks. Her family had gone to Disneyland years ago, one of the few times they'd taken a real vacation together. She'd fallen in love with everything Mickey Mouse, she confessed with surprising sheepishness, though she couldn't explain what exactly it was about the little bugger she found so fascinating. David would have dismissed it as a line of bull, but he couldn't help notice that it was the one store she seemed to genuinely enjoy shopping in.

She was turning a Mickey Mouse telephone over in her hands when she suddenly looked him and said, ''Darcy wasn't with her boyfriend the night my father was murdered.''

''You mean the skinhead? The Undertaker?''

Aspen shuddered. ''Whatever ridiculous name he calls himself.''

''They claimed they were together that night. At some death dance at a club up in Westminster . . . called The Pit.''

''They lied. Darcy was with Sarah that night. She's trying

to protect her boyfriend. She's trying to give him an alibi."

"An alibi for what? You seemed certain Gibson killed your father. Are you saying Darcy's boyfriend may have killed him?"

"I . . . I don't know. My father hated the guy . . . hated skinheads. Everyone knew he hated them. A bunch of them could have killed him. They all ought to be in jail anyway, just on general principle."

"Do you have proof that he or any of his skinhead buddies murdered your father?"

"No. But why would Darcy lie for him if he didn't have something to hide?"

"Could be a lot of reasons. He'd be a prime suspect, obviously. Maybe she was just trying to protect him from being hassled by the cops."

"She's got the hots for this guy. God knows why."

"Did she and your father argue about him?"

"Constantly. Big battles. That's why she was gone much of the time this past year."

"But think about this. Do you really believe she would protect him if she knew he killed your father?"

Aspen put down the phone and looked at David with sad eyes. "My father wasn't a very likeable man. I'm sure that's not news to you. It's not a nice thing for a daughter to say, and my family has tried very hard not to say it. But it's the truth."

"Being an unlikable man doesn't justify murder."

She smiled sarcastically. "You'll make a swell lawyer. But the reality is I think Darcy would lie to protect her boyfriend—even if she knew he killed our father."

"I don't understand why you're telling me all of this. I thought I and my aunt would be the last people you'd talk to."

"You two keep butting in, that's for sure. You don't seem satisfied with just catching Gibson, you have to play detective, get us involved. I know you've talked to Darcy and Sarah. But we're not involved, that's what I'm telling you. I think who you need to be harassing is this skinhead."

"Have you told the police about Darcy and her boyfriend?"

"Absolutely not! If this skinhead really did murder my father I'm worried that Darcy could get mixed up in it. She told the police she was with him that night. If they find out she lied . . . well, I just don't want her to get into trouble."

They left the Disney store and sat down on carpeted steps in a large circular pit in the center of the mall. Nearby, clear glass elevators trimmed in lights rose and fell silently between the two levels of the mall, like rocketship rides at a fairground. But the mall didn't have the chaotic appeal of a fairground. It was clean and polished, with the homeyness of an aircraft hanger and the inviting sterility of a hospital ward. He saw few kids and fewer men. Mostly well-dressed women, alone or in pairs, high heels clicking smartly on the floor.

Aspen slipped a contact lens out of her right eye and rolled it around in her mouth to clean it. David leaned over for a better look at her watery eye. "Your eye's green," he said, astonished.

"Both of them are."

"Oh," he said, disappointment in his voice.

"Something wrong?"

"No . . . no. I just thought they were blue."

"My contacts are blue. I'm always losing one of them. They're easier to find if they're tinted."

When she finished slipping the contact into place—watching people put in contacts always made his skin crawl—he asked her, "How do you know she was with Sarah that night?"

"She told me."

"Where were they?"

"Sarah's apartment. She lives over on Pearl. Sarah was sick. Flu or something like that. She'd gotten sick the night before at Gibson's party. Left early, in fact. She was the lucky one—Mom and I had to stay. Though I guess she was home sick all the next day."

"Darcy was at Sarah's without The Undertaker?"

Aspen laughed. "Darcy knew never to bring him around any of us."

"Sarah can confirm Darcy's visit?"

Aspen lit a cigarette. "Sure. But I don't know if she will."

"Why not?"

"To help Darcy protect her boyfriend."

"I thought all of you hated him."

"Sarah would lie for Darcy if Darcy asked her to."

"I had the impression none of you sisters got along."

"There you go again with your impressions, David. Yeah, Darcy can be a real shit, but she's still our baby sister and we'd do anything to protect her."

David looked evenly at her. "Including lie?"

"You don't believe me."

"I find it pretty difficult to believe that out of sisterly love, Sarah would lie for Darcy to give a false alibi for a skinhead who may have killed Sarah's own father."

"Well, maybe Sarah won't lie for her. The fact remains, Darcy wasn't with her boyfriend."

"Where were you that night?"

"With my mother."

"I think who you're really worried about isn't Darcy but your mother."

She took a hard drag on the cigarette. "I'm always worried about my mother. She's not a strong woman. This hasn't been easy for her."

"I think you're worried about her because she may have had something to do with your father's death."

Aspen glared at him. "You and your aunt just aren't going to let go of that bone, are you?"

"Sarah claims she had evidence that Bayne Gibson was secretly funding the Brotherhood of the Transcendental Light—a group that threatened your father's life. There's also evidence that the Brotherhood is running a big-time scam. Gibson almost certainly knew about it, and may well have been involved. Your father found out about that scam from Sarah and about Gibson's connection to the Brotherhood. That's what they were arguing about the night of the party. Your father's knowledge of that scam may well be what got him killed. If the police find out your mother and Gibson were having an affair, that doesn't put her in a very good situation, does it?"

"She wasn't having an affair with Gibson."

"Then why did you go to Evergreen? Either you went

there to warn Gibson for your mother . . . or you went there for another reason."

"What would that be?"

"How did you know where the house was? You had to have been there before. You found it too easily."

She didn't respond.

"Why were your fingerprints all over the place? How did you get into the house? How did you know where the trapdoor was?"

Still no response.

"Were you and Gibson lovers?"

Aspen jumped to her feet and flung her handbag over her shoulder. "You're hopeless, Piszek."

He stood up with her. "Look, I understand your protectiveness toward your mother. Finding her like that must have been rough on you."

Aspen looked at him, puzzled. "Finding her how?"

"When she tried to kill herself. You saved her life."

"I didn't find her. Sarah did. Sarah saved her life."

"Oh. I thought Darcy said it was you who found her."

Aspen got a queer expression on her face. She bent over and hurriedly began to fumble for the sacks at her feet. "I have to go. Find your own damn way back to your office."

She dropped a sack, leaned over to pick it up, and spilled two silk blouses out of another sack.

"Let me help you," he said, leaning over to pick up the blouses.

She swatted him away. "Leave me the hell alone!" She crushed her cigarette out on the carpeted step and shoveled the blouses into a sack. She stood up and tried to juggle her armload again, but another sack fell, spilling two bottles of perfume this time.

David reached for the bottles.

"To hell with them!" she said, tears filling her eyes. She spun on her heels and left the mall.

David picked up the perfume, found a pay phone, and paged his aunt for a ride back to the office.

31

Alabaster meowed from the narrow ledge outside one of the office windows.

"How did you get out there, Alabaster?" scolded Ruby.

"She must have sneaked out when I went to my car," David said as Ruby opened the window. Alabaster leapt in and disappeared again. "I didn't see her go out."

Ruby started to shut the window, then suddenly stopped. "What did you say?"

"Say about what?"

"About seeing Alabaster."

"I said I didn't see her leave."

A queer expression clouded Ruby's face.

"What's the matter?" he asked.

"I think Alabaster and Kray's killer have something in common."

"What do you mean?"

She shook her head. "Nothing." She shut the window and snatched a hat off the hat rack. "I've got a bond to write at the Arapahoe County Jail. Kidnapping. Thirty-five grand. While I'm gone, keep trying to reach Sarah Kray."

"We've tried," David said, exasperated. They'd tried to reach her at her apartment, the Kray home, and the radio station where she'd gone back to work part-time, but she'd returned none of their phone calls.

"Be inventive," Ruby said on her way out the door. "We need to make or break the skinhead's alibi."

Be inventive. Swell. Not one of his strong suits.

He tried all three places again, and this time the switchboard at the radio station put him through without asking his name. Nothing inventive. Just dumb luck.

"This is Sarah Kray," came a cool voice.

"Was Darcy with you the night your father was murdered?"

Until the last moment, David wasn't sure what he would say first if he did get through to her. He decided to go for maximum impact, before she had a chance to hang up.

"Who the hell is this?"

"David Piszek."

She said nothing. Sensing she was about to hang up, he yelled, "What about Darcy?"

The line remained open but silent. Finally, she said "What about her?"

"Was she with you the night your father was murdered?"

Another eternal pause. "Why do you want to know?"

"She claims she was with her boyfriend that night . . . the skinhead. But Aspen says Darcy was with you, not him."

"Aspen said that?"

"She said you were sick and that Darcy was with you at your apartment the night your father was murdered."

Another long pause, and this time David was certain she was going to hang up.

"No, Darcy was not with me that night," she finally said. "As I told the police, I was home alone."

"Sick?"

"Stomach flu. I told you that before, remember? I think it was something I ate at Gibson's party."

"Then why would Aspen say Darcy was with you?"

"I wouldn't know. Maybe she was misinformed. That happens. Especially with Darcy. What difference does it make, anyway?"

"If Darcy was with you, and not her boyfriend, that would leave him without an alibi."

"Why does he need an alibi? Gibson's the killer."

"Maybe not."

"You think Darcy's boyfriend killed my father?"

"If Darcy wasn't with you that night, do you know where she was?"

A little sarcastic laugh escaped her. "I don't keep track of her comings and goings."

Someone was badly mistaken . . . or lying. Perhaps, as Aspen had predicted, Sarah was lying to protect her sister. Yet Sarah's obvious contempt of Darcy and her boyfriend did not make it seem likely she would lie for them. Why do Darcy the favor? Was blood really thicker than love? Maybe Aspen had lied in a desperate attempt to protect Darcy. If The Undertaker really had murdered Royce Kray, and Darcy was with him . . .

That was the problem. Darcy was always with him. And the rare times she wasn't with him, she was at the Kray home, where they knew no one was going to let them get within shouting distance.

Early one afternoon, David followed the black and silver hearse from the Kray home to downtown. The skinhead dropped Darcy off at one of the intersections of the 16th Street Mall, the mile-long outdoor pedestrian strip that ran through the heart of downtown Denver. Moments later, she disappeared into a three-story upscale mall known as the Tabor Center. David followed The Undertaker another three or four blocks, figuring the skinhead was looking for a place to park his trashy car, but when he realized Marten was headed back out of downtown, he quickly turned around and parked in the lot under the Tabor Center.

It didn't take him long to spot Darcy. She was milling around The Sharper Image with several other punker kids under the watchful eyes of two sales clerks. He'd been in the mall once before and had noticed punkers. He wasn't sure what attracted them to it—they couldn't afford the boutique shops anymore than he could. Maybe they'd just come to five-finger discount.

He called his aunt from a pay phone.

"We got lucky . . . maybe," he said. "She's hanging around with five, six kids. Mostly girls. But she's not with The Undertaker."

"I'll be right over."

Ten minutes later they met outside one of the Tabor Center entrances. Ruby had no plan, as usual. It was improv time.

Since Darcy didn't know what Ruby looked like, Ruby did the close tailing while David kept himself well back. Darcy and her friends didn't spend much time in the stores. Mostly they walked the floors and rode the escalators and sat around the indoor fountain. The group grew and shrank as other punkers joined them or split off. Twice they went out to the 16th Street Mall to smoke, and once Ruby rode with them on one of the shuttle buses that plied the granite mall. Each time they returned to the Tabor Center.

After an hour, David began to worry that The Undertaker would show up before they had an opportunity to talk to Darcy, but finally they got their break. She and her friends were up in the third-floor food court, drinking pop and eating giant cookies, when Darcy headed off alone past the string of fast-food outlets in the direction of the rest rooms in the back, just around the corner of a pizza by the slice outlet. Lucky again, thought David. Didn't women always go to rest rooms in pairs? Ruby got up from her table, where she was nibbling at a plate of Japanese food, motioned subtly to David, who was standing in front of a Greek outlet, and headed after Darcy. David wandered casually to the back, keeping an eye on the rest of the punkers, but none of them appeared to be paying any attention or making any moves toward the rest rooms.

He bent over a drinking fountain near the door to the women's bathroom as two women came out, talking. The moment they turned the corner, he slipped in through the door.

Only Ruby and Darcy appeared to be in the rest room. Both stood silently by sinks several feet apart. Darcy leaned close to a dirty cracked mirror, touching up her purple lipstick, paying no attention to Ruby. She whirled when she saw David's reflection.

"What the fuck are you doing in here?"

"We need to talk, Darcy. Away from your friends."

Her initial shock had vanished, replaced by an almost expectant look on her face.

"I'll fucking scream if you don't get outta here."

"That wouldn't be helpful, honey," Ruby said mildly.

Darcy jerked her head toward the woman next to her.

"Who the hell are you?" Ruby started to reply but the girl cut her off. "Never mind, I know. You're the bond lady, ain't you?"

"We want to talk about your boyfriend," Ruby said.

Darcy's eyes flicked between Ruby and David like those of a trapped animal.

"There's nothing to talk about. We already told bozo here everything we have to say."

"You lied about being with him the night your father was murdered."

"I was with Jimmy. At The Pit—just like I told him."

"You were with Sarah that night, at her apartment."

"That's a lie."

"Your boyfriend doesn't have a good alibi if you were at Sarah's. And if you were with him that night, and not with Sarah, then you don't have a good alibi."

"I don't need an alibi. I didn't kill my father, and neither did Jimmy."

Darcy headed for the door. David blocked it.

"Out of my way, fascist."

"Sarah was sick and you went to see her that night," Ruby said.

"Who's telling you this bullshit? My mother? She hates Jimmy just like my father did. Everyone in my family does. They all hate it that I love somebody with balls."

"Sarah said you were at her place that night."

Darcy turned. "She told you that?"

"Yes." Ruby's voice sounded so sincere David almost believed it himself.

Darcy stared at the floor. "Damn her! She promised me she wouldn't say anything."

The swinging entrance door banged into David's back. He peeked outside. A young woman with a small crying boy in tow was trying to get in. She backed up a step, glanced at the stylized woman on the door, then back at David.

"It's temporarily closed, ma'am," he said. "A water leak. You'll have to use the one on the first floor."

The woman rolled her eyes in exasperation, scooped up her son, and hurried off.

"When were you at Sarah's that night?" Ruby asked.

Darcy looked up. "What?"

"When were you at Sarah's that night? From when to when?"

"I don't know. I don't wear a watch."

"Was it during the time your father was killed?"

She shrugged. "I suppose it was."

"And Jimmy wasn't with you, was he?"

Darcy had a trapped, desperate look on her face. "Oh, God, he's going to be pissed."

32

Catching Jimmy Marten without Darcy was an easier proposition. Ruby tracked down where he lived and sent David over to talk to him early one afternoon. She would have gone with him except she and Cyndee Valone had an appointment at the Arapahoe County DA's office concerning the Saunders' fiasco.

The address she'd given him belonged to a rundown brick bungalow on Sherman, a mere five-minute drive from the Kray home but a world apart. David parked half a block away and walked to the house. A motorcycle sat in front of a weedy, unmowed yard. Woody, overgrown bushes barricaded a concrete porch. Beer and pop cans lined a railing like targets on a backcountry rifle range. Several faded green metal chairs with swastikas spray painted on the backs sat empty on the sagging porch floor. A pizza box lay half open on one of them.

No one was home. Or at least no one answered the door.

He sat in his car and tried to study, looking up every few moments to see if anyone had arrived. Finally, around four, Marten, accompanied by a tall man and a teenage girl, suddenly appeared on the porch. They'd apparently come in through the back. He'd neglected to check if there was an alley.

The three of them hung a huge red, white, and black Nazi battle flag from the porch ceiling in plain view of passing cars and sat down in the chairs.

David watched them for a few minutes. It was broad daylight on a busy street, and he didn't think Marten would be foolish enough to become violent. Still, he wasn't sure what the kid was capable of, especially a kid who was now a prime suspect in Kray's death. Finally he got out of his car and walked toward the house.

The three of them were drinking beer. Heavy rock music, not unlike the indecipherable mess he'd heard at the death dance, blared out open windows and the screen door. Marten's heavy boots were propped up on the porch railing. The late afternoon sun gave the porch and its occupants a warm glow, sort of a Norman-Rockwell-goes-fascist look.

They watched David approach. The tall man and the girl eyed him suspiciously, but Marten didn't look particularly surprised or disturbed by David's appearance. As David walked up the cracked sidewalk that led to the porch, Marten bellowed out over the music and traffic noise, "I was beginning to think you weren't going to do anything but sit and watch us."

David stopped at the foot of the porch steps. "I didn't realize I was so obvious." They didn't teach surveillance in law school.

"Believe me, buddy, I know when I'm being watched. I have shadows all the time. Look up the street there."

Marten pointed in the direction David had parked. All he could see were parked cars and passing traffic.

"The white Dodge," said Marten.

David finally spotted the Dodge and realized someone was sitting in it. He'd walked right past it and not noticed.

"That's a plainclothes detective, probably from DIU," said Marten. He waved in the Dodge's direction. "Probably got a call in right now trying to figure out who the hell you are."

David snapped his head back in the direction of the car.

"It's too late," Marten said with a touch of malicious enjoyment in his voice. "Nothing you can do now. They had you made the moment you walked up here. You're on their permanent watch list now. Suspicion of dealing with local skinheads. You'll never get your name off their shit list, you know. There for life. Get yourself elected pope and you'll stay on that list. Course, from what I've been reading about that bonding company you work for, you probably are already on their shit list, and you probably won't be elected pope."

David looked back at Marten. "Why are they watching you?"

"'Cause they think we're dangerous shit." He grinned at the other two, and they broke into grins.

"Are you?" The Intelligence Unit detective had told him that Marten was a fringe skinhead, a hanger-on, in it more for youthful rebellion than to crack nigger heads. Why waste manpower on him? Or was it the tall man sitting next to him? Maybe he was a skinhead VP? He looked in his early twenties, with a shaved head under a cap with the number 88 on the front. He wore fatigue pants like Marten, storm trooper boots with red laces, thin suspenders, no shirt, and tattoos on his right arm. A cigarette was tucked behind his left ear. He had heavy-lidded eyes and a dyspeptic look to him.

"Some guys are into boot parties, but we don't want to hurt nobody," said Marten. "We just want a white sovereign homeland, that's all. North of the Rio Grande. Shit, you hear people say 'black power' or 'Chicano power' and nobody raises an eyebrow. But you say 'white power,' and everybody comes down on you."

"Ain't that the fuckin' truth," piped in the girl. She was probably fourteen or fifteen, and dressed in shorts and sandals. She had a mouth full of braces that some parent had mortgaged the house to pay for. A swastika was tattooed on her right big toe. She looked bored.

"Sit down," said Marten. He pointed to the chair next to him with the pizza box on it. He tipped the chair forward and the box slid to the dirty porch floor, spilling dry, curled pizza.

"That's okay, I'll be brief," said David, staying put. He struggled to be heard above the music. The band, which sounded British, was singing something about a "prisoner of peace." "I came to check again where you were the night Royce Kray was murdered."

"The same place I was when you asked before. At The Pit in Westminster."

"Your alibi says no."

Marten cocked his head. "What do you mean?"

"Darcy says she wasn't with you that night."

"So that's why you've been tailing me and Darcy. You wanted to talk to her. I thought it was me you were following."

"She says she was with one of her sisters that night."

"Which one?"

"Sarah."

Marten nodded his head slowly. "So it's finally come down to that, has it?" he said, more to himself than David.

"Hey, he was at The Pit that night," said the girl. "I was there. I saw him and Darcy."

"Are you willing to testify to that?" said David.

She looked nervous. "You mean in court?"

"Before a judge and jury. Under oath."

"Why would I have to do that?"

"If The Undertaker here goes on trial for murder, he's going to need a new alibi."

The girl looked at Marten. Her eyes were big and brown and full of uncertainty.

"Don't shit green, Jennifer," said Marten. "You're not gonna testify. Nobody's going to put me on trial for Kray's murder."

"You just lost your best alibi," David reminded him.

David had expected denial and anger from Marten, yet now the skinhead looked at him strangely resigned, almost sad.

"On your way back to your car, buddy, why don't you stop at that Dodge and tell the guy we'll be here for another coupla hours, just in case he wants to go get something to eat."

Morgan Reed was firmly ensconced in his usual chair in front of Ruby's desk. Collateral had moseyed over to the detective and sprawled at his feet, draping his head over a shoe. Reed scratched the dog behind his ears.

"I did a little checking on Tanner like you asked, Ruby," said Reed. "You're aware he was arrested on possession of illegal firearms a couple of months ago?"

Ruby nodded. ''They've already dropped two of the charges. Think the rest will stick?''

Reed shrugged. ''Who knows. We just arrest 'em. But I did turn up a tidbit of info you might be interested in. Guess who handled bond for Tanner?''

''Cadillac Johnson?'' said Ruby.

''Bingo.''

David whistled. ''You think *Tanner* engineered Blood's setup?''

Ruby shook her head. ''Not the details. Cadillac did that. But it sounds like Tanner may have been behind it.''

''You must have struck one raw nerve when you visited the Brotherhood,'' said Reed.

''That, or when we cornered Lamprey about the Crystal Age scam. I'm sure he called Tanner right after we left.'' Ruby was on her feet, pacing the office floor, snacking on Cajun-Creole Hot Nuts. David could see the sudden glint in his aunt's eyes, the fevered look she always got when a storm was brewing inside her head.

She stopped. ''No, I'm wrong. They set us up from the beginning.''

''What do you mean?'' David asked.

''Remember the day Cadillac ran into us at the courthouse?''

''When we brought in Alvarez?''

''Right. That was no accident. Cadillac was pushing my buttons. He baited me through you—and I bit. He knew I'd figure he was after Gibson's bond, and that I'd do my damnest to make sure he wouldn't get it.''

''You mean from the beginning Gibson was going to skip?'' said Reed.

''From the get-go. My God, their entire scam was at stake if Gibson started singing. The last thing Tanner and Lamprey would want is a big trial with Gibson sitting on the stand spilling his guts about Crystal Age and his secret financing of the Brotherhood. They knew he'd crack.''

Reed shook his head skeptically. ''Sounds like another hunch, Ruby.''

Ruby stopped in front of the detective. ''Look, Morgan, why didn't they just use Cadillac as the bondsman, instead of me or someone else? Tanner had already used him on the weapons charge.''

''Maybe Cadillac had scammed him. Probably couldn't resist all that Brotherhood money.''

''Even Cadillac wouldn't have been stupid enough to try to scam a scammer.''

''Fine. That still doesn't explain why they picked you.''

''Look, Tanner and Lamprey must have known they were going to persuade Gibson to disappear if it looked like the case was headed for trial.''

''Persuade? . . . Or kill him?''

''Either way, he was going to disappear. They weren't going to leave Cadillac stuck with a million dollar bond. Probably figured they'd need him again some day. Too risky, too. He was still holding Tanner's bond on the weapons charge. So they ask him for names of other bondsmen, and he sees a chance to stick it to his old rival.''

''But when we linked Tanner and Gibson, they panicked,'' added David.

''Cadillac forgot to tell them that I won't quit on a skip. Once they found out I knew about their scam, they set me up on the Saunders deal, to keep my nose out of their business.''

''Then you think Tanner or one of his goons killed Kray?'' said Reed.

''No.''

''But if Kray found out about this connection between Gibson and the Brotherhood, and he was going to broadcast it on the air . . .''

''Assuming Gibson and Tanner are linked,'' interjected David, ''then the last thing Tanner would have done was gun down Kray in Gibson's fish pond and then hide the murder weapon in Gibson's penthouse. Why frame his chief money supplier?''

Reed looked at Ruby. ''David's right,'' she said. ''Somebody else framed Gibson. But when they did, they put Tanner and the Brotherhood in a bad spot.''

''Who?'' asked the detective. ''This skinhead?''

''I have my suspicions,'' she said.

Reed looked exasperated. ''Which are?''

"Unconfirmed."

"So where does that leave Gibson?" asked David.

"Dead," said Reed.

"Not necessarily," said Ruby.

"Didn't you say the scam may have already brought in ten million bucks? People kill for a helluva lot less money than that. Framed or not, Gibson would be useless to them after his arrest. You said yourself they couldn't afford to have him testify. And Tanner's got a history of violence."

David cut in. "They could have buried Gibson anywhere out on that ranch and it'd be *years* before we'd find him. And with no body, we can't get the judge to release the bond. Without the release, we're stuck with a million dollar—"

Ruby raised her hands for silence. "Gentlemen, gentlemen, let's show a little more optimism. I agree, Tanner had cause to kill Gibson. But his connection to Cadillac puts a new twist on it."

"How's that?" Reed asked.

"If Tanner had murdered Gibson, why have Blood set us up?"

"Because they knew you were onto the scam. Now they've got you preoccupied with the Arapahoe DA's office and a possible lawsuit and a lot of nosy reporters. And if you accuse Tanner of anything, who's gonna believe you."

"Perhaps. But that scam was a lot of trouble and a lot of risk. I think the reason they did it is because Gibson's alive and they're worried I'm going to find him."

"But why keep him alive, Ruby?" said Reed. "Tanner's not going to leave him alive out of some kind of loyalty or do-goodism."

"There's two million in a secret account in Grand Caymans, for starters. And who knows what else we don't know about."

"Okay, for the moment let's assume he is alive. Where?"

"Mexico," said David. "I still think he's in Mexico."

Ruby shook her head. "No, it's too far away. Tanner needs to keep his finger on Gibson. If he didn't kill him, he's got to keep him where he can control him through Chac."

"You think he's hiding at the Brotherhood?" asked David.

"It's a much stronger possibility than it was a few minutes ago."

"Tanner wouldn't hide him there," David argued. "Too much risk. One of those Keepers of the Light would eventually expose him—as brainwashed as the lot of them are. Or some visitor would stumble across him. I still think he's in Mexico guzzling margaritas."

"There's only one way to find out," Ruby said.

33

The loud monotonous chanting made the hair on the back of David's neck bristle. The chanting rose from the other side of the ridge, at least a mile away, yet was so powerful the very air around him vibrated like a million angry bees. He'd never heard anything like it in his life. Judging from the intense level of noise and the eerie coppery glow painting the night sky beyond the ridge, there must be thousands of them chanting around a huge bonfire.

"Can't take you no closer," said the rancher, leaning heavily on a cane in front of his battered pickup truck. "The road's too dangerous to drive without lights. Fenced off quarter of a mile up, anyway. But you can walk in from here easily enough, if you stick to the road and keep your eyes sharp for the guards." He jabbed his cane in the direction where the narrow road—more ruts than road—vanished quickly into the blackness of the thick trees. The three of them—Ruby, David, and the rancher, Vernon Waters—had driven the last mile without headlights so as not to attract the attention of any Brotherhood guards.

"Thanks for bringing us this far, honey," said Ruby. "We'd have never found our way here on our own."

"Owned most of this land once," Waters said sadly. "If I'd known who I was selling to I'da *given* it away to the Feds for taxes."

"What the hell are they chanting?" asked David.

"Can't rightly tell you. Shit goes on for hours . . . two, three times a week. Keeps neighbor folks awake. Hard to believe they're educated, intelligent people. I've talked to 'em myself."

"God, it's awful!" said David, cupping his hands over his ears, to no effect. The chanting penetrated right through his hands, right into the nerves of his brain. "No wonder you and your friends want them gone."

"We'da left 'em to themselves," said Waters. "Don't bother us what fool shit a guy's about up here, long's he keeps it to himself. But when the streams running through there started getting polluted and we hear stories about stockpiles of guns and that Tanner fella gets himself arrested — folks gotta look out for themselves."

"We should be back in two or three hours," Ruby said.

"Still think you're crazy, lady, just the two of you going in like this," the old rancher said. "You oughta go in with the sheriff."

"Got no legal grounds to take the sheriff in. Take him in, they'd have Gibson hidden before we reached the Visitors Center. This way, we got at least a slim chance of catching them by surprise."

"Still think you're crazy," Waters mumbled.

You're sure as shit right there, David said to himself.

"If things go wrong, and you smell trouble, honey, you get outta here. I don't want you hurt. There's been enough people hurt. We'll find our own way out."

Swell, thought David. Burn our bridges and march off deep into enemy territory. For this he skipped his tort class?

"Things go wrong, lady, I'll make sure we'll get you out. I got friends."

The barbed wire gate was where the rancher had told them it would be. The wire was new and taut, but they clamored over it easily enough. From there, the road switched back and forth up the ridge. It quickly grew steeper and rockier, and their waffled boots fought for a toehold in the darkness. Both of them were soon breathing heavily. The chanting, louder and fiercer as they grew closer to the top of the ridge, made it all the more difficult to concentrate on the road.

Under normal circumstances, David would have welcomed the physical relief of cresting the ridge and getting his wind back. But the intensity of the chanting doubled to an almost deafening hum that filled the entire earth and stole what remaining breath he had. There below them, in a huge meadow surrounded by trees, blazed a three alarm bonfire that must have been alarmingly visible to jetliners passing overhead. Ruby sank against a rock and scoured the meadow through a pair of binoculars. After a minute she passed them to David. He could make out hundreds of people, though not the thousands they sounded like, circling the bonfire, swaying rhythmically to the chanting.

He handed the binoculars back to her. "What exactly is your plan?"

"Don't have one. I figured we'd improvise as we went along."

"Aunt Ruby, there are several hundred people down there—none of them our friends and probably a fair number of them armed. Just how do you propose to find Gibson? He could be anywhere down there—*if* he's down there. Even if we do find him, how the hell are we going to get him out of there?"

She pushed herself off the rock and started down the ridge road in the direction of the meadow.

"We'll ask Chac."

"Great! Waters is right, Aunt Ruby. We're crazy to be trying this. Let's go back and see if there isn't another way."

"I'm not going to let a twerp like Gibson skip on me! I'm not going to let down Marian, either. I promised her I'd find Jim's killer!"

He caught up with her, his feet sliding on treacherous rock. "We could get killed finding Jim's killer."

"I told you not to come."

"I wasn't going to let you come alone." She'd refused to bring along any armed bounty hunters—she didn't trust any of them after the Blood incident.

Ruby stopped. In the light of the distant fire, David could see her smile. "I don't have much family left, David. But I'm glad I've got a nephew."

"Yeah . . . well, if this doesn't work out, you aren't going to have one for long."

They moved down the ridge road another thirty yards before the chanting suddenly stopped. David and Ruby froze.

The abrupt silence left a dizzying echo in his ears, and he struggled to keep his balance.

"They can't see us, can they?" he whispered.

The chanters had stopped in nearly perfect unison, like a well-rehearsed chorus under the control of the baton, as if every chanter had simultaneously spotted them on the side of the ridge. But that was impossible. They were still too far away—maybe half a mile—and there was no way the chanters could see them in the darkness. Was there?

Then a lone voice echoed up from the meadow, strong and commanding, carried over a PA system. He couldn't understand the words at this distance, but it was clear that the voice was not directed at them. The circle of people around the huge bonfire wasn't breaking up, no one appeared to be moving toward them.

Ruby signaled to move on.

The road wound down the side of the ridge to the valley floor, skirting the meadow and shooting off in the direction of the main compound of the Brotherhood. They could see the white dome of the Visitors Center amid the trees. A thick band of pine trees separated the road from the incandescent meadow and it was into these trees that David and his aunt hurried, using the reflected light of the mammoth bonfire to pick their way through the brush and jabbing branches. But the flickering light also created strange shadows, phantom images. Everything in the forest looked alive. Armed guards seemed everywhere. Every few feet David or Ruby jerked to a stop, certain they'd been spotted or heard, only to realize moments later that it was only a playful trick of the light. David's heart pounded in his throat. Tanner and his men weren't going to kill him, he realized. He would save them the trouble by simply dropping dead from a heart attack.

They reached the edge of meadow and ducked behind a large dead log. They were close enough to hear the crackle of the dead wood and smell the acrid smoke of the bonfire. Most of the chanters—Seekers? Light Keepers?—had congregated toward one side of the bonfire, their backs to David and Ruby. In the middle of the chanters, on a permanent wooden platform ten feet off the ground, stood a lone man in glasses, chinos, and an open white shirt. He clutched a microphone in his right hand, and his whole body was aglow from the firelight. David couldn't see the speaker's face clearly at this distance, but he estimated that the man reached all of five five. He stood stiffly, as if someone had run poles through his body. He looked about as commanding as the owner of a dry cleaning establishment.

Yet the audience stood rapt, fastened on his every word. David could hear him plainly now over the loudspeaker.

". . . Listen to your spirit, not your body. Your five senses will mislead you into believing in limitations that don't exist."

The voice was low, forced, trance-like. The voice of Chac, the Mayan warrior-king?

"Tanner?" he whispered to his aunt, who was watching through her binoculars.

"Looks just like his pictures."

People in the crowd besieged Chac with eager questions, like an audience participation show on cosmic television wired into time itself.

A man asked about a troubled relationship.

"Love yourself unconditionally," answered the warrior-king. "Self-love is the purest of all loves."

A woman asked what lay ahead in her future.

"Whatever you choose it to be."

Before each response, Tanner's body went into spasms and twitches, as if each new question required the cosmic connection to be redialed. Despite the fact that Tanner wasn't home, that he had sublet his body to a dead man, the puppet on the platform had the presence of mind to lift the microphone to his lips whenever he spoke. For a Mayan warrior-king dead for 1,100 years, Chac was amazingly with it technologically.

"Any sign of Gibson?" David whispered.

Ruby was searching among the chanters with her binoculars. "Nothing yet."

"I still don't think they'd risk letting him show his face, even among the true believers."

"He could be disguised, or standing along the edge."

"Outsiders say you are a lie, Chac," asked another man. "They say you don't exist, that you're a fraud."

Spasms, followed by the low, trance-like voice. "Liars and nonbelievers corrupted my time, too. It is so through all the ages. People don't believe because they are not honest with themselves, because they don't love themselves."

"But how can we be sure you are true?" the man went on.

David began to suspect the questioner was a shill. Who among this crowd would have the nerve to question the very being of Chac?

"Truth is what you believe," came the Mayan's reply. "What do you feel inside . . . in your spirit-being where no one can touch you but yourself? Do you believe in me?"

"Yes. Yes, I believe in you, Chac."

"Then for you I am truth."

"Well, well, well," Ruby suddenly said.

David jumped. "What?" He scanned everywhere at once, looking for onrushing armed guards.

His aunt handed the binoculars to him and pointed toward the back of the crowd. "See the woman off by herself, the one in the red shorts and white blouse? With the long blond ponytail."

David adjusted the focus of the binoculars. The glasses were powerful and he swung them wildly a few moments before he found his bearings. Then he spotted her, dressed as Ruby had described, standing along the edge of the crowd. A tight ponytail of blond hair snaked down to the middle of her back. A muscular back. A muscular body evident even under the blouse. A beautiful muscular body he had once seen working out on an exercise machine.

"Christina Nilsson!" he said.

"Chac works in mysterious ways," said Ruby.

"What the hell's she doing here?"

"That's what I'd like to find out."

David focused the glasses on Tanner. Chac was speaking to a woman who'd asked why she had constant back pains. "You were a knight in the Crusades," he told her. "You were speared in the back and died. In time, after many lives, your karma will heal you."

"I can't believe these people fall for this crap," said David. "Chac sounds like a bad New Age therapist. This shit's no more believable than pro wrestling."

"A lot of people watch wrestling."

Suddenly the highbeams of a four-wheel drive bounced along the road behind them, in the direction of where they'd walked down from the ridge top. They hunched lower behind the dead tree trunk and scanned the forest for signs of armed guards. The vehicle passed them and headed up the road, its motor laboring up the steep grade.

"Shit!" whispered David huskily.

"Give me the binoculars," commanded Ruby.

But instead of peering through the trees at the passing vehicle, she focused on Tanner. "Remember the guy who kicked us out when we were up here before—Stahl?" she whispered. "He's standing by the platform talking to Tanner."

Chac spoke again, this time in a more hurried, tense voice. "I must leave now. My enemies are close at hand. They pursue me through the ages, relentlessly . . . dark spirits who know no rest, who allow me no comfort. Enemies are here too, nearby. It is a dangerous time. Be watchful. Be faithful. Our enemies can hide the truth from others, but they cannot destroy it."

Suddenly Tanner was gone, and a wave of anxiety rippled through the crowd. They began to break up and move edgily back toward the compound, voices buzzing nervously, heads scanning the surrounding darkness. David sensed movement along the perimeter of the meadow, men melting into the trees. Or was it his mind and the light playing tricks again? Headlights from another vehicle appeared along the road, moving more slowly. A searchlight mounted on its door swung menacingly through the trees, missing them by only a few yards. The vehicle moved on up the road in the direction of the other vehicle.

It was quiet for a moment. Then, off in the direction of the ridge, back where they'd left the rancher and his pickup, came the sound of gunfire. Two quick shots, then a single shot.

34

"Shit, they know we're here!" said David. "They must've spotted Waters! Or shot him!"

"Come on," whispered Ruby, getting up from behind the safety of the fallen tree and heading off in the direction of the Brotherhood's main compound.

David grabbed her arm. "Where are you going? We came in the other way!"

"It's not safe to go that way now."

"What are you planning to do? Walk into the Visitors Center and call a cab?"

"Shhh!" she whispered. "I want to talk to Christina Nilsson."

The chanters had panicked at the sound of the gunfire and were fleeing into the safety of the surrounding trees, some dangerously close to where Ruby and David had been hidden.

"Are you crazy? We need to get out of here!"

"We need to talk to her. She may know where Gibson is."

"How are we going to find her in this mess? We'll be spotted sure as hell."

"We'll melt into the crowd. They'll just think we're visiting Seekers running like everyone else."

Common sense told David he should have forcibly dragged his aunt out of this insanity. Armed guards or not, the only escape lay back over the ridge and Waters' pickup—if the old coot's pickup was still there, if the headlights and the gunfire hadn't already scared him off, if he wasn't already . . . David stifled the thought.

But common sense lost out. Ruby bolted toward the center of the compound, and David went after her. They stayed in the trees and skirted the edge of the meadow, past the platform where Tanner had put on his cosmic vaudeville show and the huge bonfire whose heat David could feel even through the trees. Ahead, disembodied voices, curses, and the sound of trampling feet filled the darkness.

"Who's there?"

The unfamiliar voice, only a few feet away, seized David's heart like a cold hand.

"What?" said Ruby.

"Who are you?"

A woman's voice.

David still couldn't see who was talking, but he could hear as much fear in the bodiless voice as he felt in his own heart.

"We heard gunfire," said Ruby, looking around, trying to locate the source. "Did you?"

"Yes. From up on Sutter's Ridge."

The silhouette of a woman emerged from behind a tree. Then another woman. The first woman came up closer to them. A small woman with dark hair.

"Who are you?" she demanded. "I don't recognize you."

"Alice. Alice Hobson," Ruby said. "This is my son, Peter. We're Seekers. From California. We just got here today. We came to hear Chac. Do—do you know who fired the shots?"

"No."

"We saw somebody . . . farther back in the trees. It looked like three men—it was hard to tell in the darkness. They were running toward the road, toward that ridge. Maybe they were people from here—I wouldn't know. But maybe they weren't. Maybe we better tell somebody about them."

The woman looked back in the direction where David and his aunt had come, then back at Ruby. "Come with us."

They followed the two women through the trees until they joined a hard dirt path that led from the meadow toward the lights of the compound. The path was crowded with other shadowy figures stumbling in darkness broken only by the rapidly fading light of the bonfire and the occasional flashlight. People talked in hushed voices.

"It's the damn feds. Chac's warned us about them."

"I heard that vigilante group in Pine Junction was planning some kinda attack."

A child cried.

The path spilled onto the roadway that came down from Sutter's Ridge and the shadows hurried along it toward the center of the compound. Few lights were visible, as if they'd been blacked out for an air raid, but David could make out the ghostly domed shape of the Visitors Center. The crowd thickened as people flowed in from all directions, edgy talk in the air. David felt like he was being helplessly swept into the center of hell. All they had to do was stumble into Stahl or the woman from the Fulfillment Center, or Christina Nilsson for that matter, and it would be all over.

Ruby stopped the woman who was guiding them.

"We were with Christina Nilsson when we heard the shots. We got separated. Do you know her?"

The woman and her companion looked impressed. "Of course. She's a Chosen one. You're friends?"

"She and I have done a few computer deals together. Would you go tell security about those three men we saw? I really would like to find her. I'm sure she's worried about us. Where do you think she is?"

The woman looked hesitant, then said, "Try Father's house."

"Oh, yes, of course. I'd forgotten. Where is that from here exactly? I'm all turned around in this darkness."

The woman gave directions, described the house, and then disappeared in the crowd with her companion.

"Tanner's house!" David exclaimed, trying to keep his voice down, as they headed off in the direction the woman had given. "We're going to Tanner's house? Why don't we just surrender now and make it easier on everyone!"

"Hush!"

Tanner's house was a rambling, impressive two-story stone and log structure south of the Visitors Center, away from the major flow of people. Two smaller homes flanked it. During their earlier visit, David had noticed several private homes scattered throughout the ranch, reserved, no doubt, for the Chosen ones. Everyone else made due in dormitories or other communal shelters.

They slipped off the road into a stand of Ponderosa pine with a direct view of the house. The crowd had thinned out on the road, but Tanner's house was a virtual command center: lights blazed and a seemingly endless stream of people came and went past an armed guard standing on the front porch. Periodically, two-way radios cackled.

They waited.

Twenty minutes later Nilsson came out of the house, flung her purse over her arm, yelled something angrily back through the open door, and stomped off along the road back in the direction from where Ruby and David had come. Nilsson passed them in full stride, muttering to herself. Ruby let her pass before slipping out of the trees onto the path and heading after her.

Nilsson didn't notice Ruby until she was nearly up with her.

"You!" Nilsson's mouth opened to scream but Ruby raised a hand.

"Not a peep, honey. I'm armed and I'm scared and my electroshock treatments didn't take."

Nilsson closed her mouth. David caught up with them. Nilsson looked sharply at him, then back at Ruby. "So you're who they're looking for!"

"Didn't Chac confide in you?"

"No. He doesn't know who—" She stopped at the implications of Ruby's remarks. "What are you doing here?"

"I came to ask you the same question."

"It's a long story. Not one you want to hear at the moment considering the tenuousness of your situation."

"Then let's work on finding Gibson," said Ruby.

"Gibbie? I don't know where he is. You think he's hiding *here*?"

"It's very possible."

"Why?"

"I know about his bankrolling this place, honey. And about the Crystal Age scam. And about setting me up. You do know all about that, don't you? About Tanner's scams?''

There was a long pause in the darkness. ''Gibbie isn't here, that's all I can tell you. Nobody knows where he—''

A shadow hurried by them, suspiciously glancing their way. Nilsson said hello.

''You can't stay here,'' Nilsson whispered when the shadow was out of earshot. ''They're going to find you sooner or later, and I don't want to be around you when they do.''

''You think they'd kill us?'' David squeaked out.

''I don't know what they'll do. Father's pretty pissed off right now. You two and Gibson have caused him a lot of sleepless nights.''

''Then let's find a safe place to talk,'' Ruby commanded, taking Nilsson by the arm.

Nilsson led them to an unlocked corrugated steel shed three hundred yards from Tanner's house and off the pathway. The shed was filled with small gas engines, tools, and sacks of what smelled like organic fertilizer. A small window afforded them the only hint of dim light from the compound.

Nilsson barely closed the door behind them when Ruby said, ''Those shots weren't fired at us. Who were they shooting at?''

''I don't know. We got a tip that the vigilantes were up to something tonight, but we're always getting tips. Father's got everybody so paranoid about outsiders these idiots'll shoot at anything that moves in the dark.''

''You sound less than a loyal follower of Chac,'' Ruby said. ''Is that why you left Tanner's so angrily?''

''Let's just say I could do without some of his buddies.''

''Like Gibson?''

''Damn, you're a stubborn-ass woman!'' snapped Nilsson.

''You're sure he's not hiding around here someplace?''

''I told you, nobody knows where Gibbie is. Nobody's seen him since he disappeared.''

''Didn't Tanner help him skip? He couldn't afford to have him go to trial.''

''He tried.''

''What does that mean?''

There was a long pause, then Nilsson said, ''You're right,

a public trial threatened to expose everything. The problem was, Gibbie didn't want to leave. Not that I could blame him much. He swore he had nothing to do with Kray's murder and he wanted to fight the charges. He promised Father he'd say nothing about the Brotherhood. But nobody trusted him. Gibbie's a pretty weak man, I've come to realize. He wouldn't have held up under prosecution examination. He would have talked sooner or later. It took a while, but Father finally persuaded him that Chac wanted him to temporarily disappear for the good of the Brotherhood."

"Tanner could talk him into becoming a fugitive and leaving behind a fortune?" said David.

In the dimness David sensed Nilsson turn toward him. He could hear her nervous breathing. Even over the stench of the fertilizer he could smell her perfume. "Father can be very . . . persuasive, and Gibbie is an easily persuadable man. He wanted to break free . . . but he couldn't."

"So what about the skip?" Ruby asked.

"I don't know the exact details, but I know that two of Father's men were supposed to pick Gibbie up a couple of blocks from his penthouse the night before the preliminary hearing. They were going to hide him here first and then smuggle him into Mexico after things eased off."

"What happened?"

"According to Father, Gibbie never showed up for the rendezvous. They called but he didn't answer. They figured he'd gotten cold feet. They couldn't risk going to his penthouse that night, but Ezzard went over early the next morning to try to talk Gibbie out of showing up at the hearing. But Gibbie was gone."

"Maybe he went to his villa in Mexico," suggested David.

"No. We've already checked."

"And no one's seen him since then—or heard anything?" Ruby asked.

"No."

"Maybe Tanner lied to you. Maybe he had him killed."

David could sense Nilsson shudder. "No," she said, more of a plea than an answer.

"He had good reason to kill him. It would be less risky than leaving him alive. Kill him and bury him some place."

''Father . . . Father wouldn't do that.''

''Guns are going off, honey. And you weren't real assuring about our personal safety.''

''I'm not a fool, Ms. Dark! Things were *tense* of late between Gibbie and Father. When Gibbie started seeing Anna Lee Kray—Father was furious. It jeopardized the entire Brotherhood. When Gibbie disappeared . . . I . . . I wondered. But Father's had people looking for him since the day he disappeared. Especially after your bounty hunter turned up dead. He doesn't know where he is . . . and he's worried.''

''Why was he so worried about Gibson and Mrs. Kray? I understood she was into this New Age stuff. Didn't she come up here?''

''Anna Lee Kray? Up here? You gotta be kidding! She turned fundamentalist after her son died. She didn't want Gibbie to have anything to do with the Brotherhood. She thinks we're a bunch of weirdos.''

Maybe Anna Lee Kray was smarter than he'd given her credit for, thought David.

''What about Big Jim—the bounty hunter?'' Ruby said. ''Tanner have him killed?''

Nilsson gave a vehement no.

''We found his body in the room you people ran your scam out of,'' said Ruby. ''Everything was stripped.''

''Some of the people working the phones found his body in the living room one morning. They figured out who he was and they tried to hide it. Clumsily, I might add. Jesus, somebody was bound to find him there eventually. Then they stripped the place of anything that might have tied us to the body or the house. But he was already dead. Nobody in the Brotherhood killed him.''

''Tanner know who did?''

''No.''

Loud voices and flickering beams of light passed close by the shed. The three of them crouched and held their breath. The voices moved on.

''You have to get out of here!'' said Nilsson.

''How did you get up here?'' asked Ruby.

''I drove up . . . last night.''

''Where's your car?''

"In a parking lot a quarter of a mile from here."

"Good! You can drive us outta here."

"That's impossible. Father ordered the roads sealed off."

"You'll figure out something."

"What happens to me if Father finds out I drove you out of here?"

"Why are you so afraid of him?"

"He blames me for Gibbie wanting to leave the Brotherhood. I don't think he trusts me anymore."

"Why don't you just leave?"

"I'm weaker than I look."

"If he finds out about you, tell him I forced you at gunpoint. Let's go. And let's not attract any attention."

Nilsson cursed under her breath.

35

They followed a hard dirt path that cut behind the Visitors Center. It was too dark to see their feet in front of them, but Nilsson seemed to know the way by memory. David, trailing both women, walked with an arm up in front of his face, afraid of getting an eye poked out by a passing branch.

"What was Gibson's mood after his arrest?" Ruby asked Nilsson as they walked.

"I told you, I wasn't around him then. But Ezzard told us he was pretty depressed. Who wouldn't be? But even before that, when he found out about Crystal Age, he—"

"He wasn't in on the scam?"

"No. That was Ezzard and Father's creation. But Gibbie found out about it somehow. Not too long before Kray was murdered. He got real angry and real depressed. Gibbie could be pretty moody. He felt used by Father . . . betrayed. Frankly, I don't blame him. Gibbie's self-centered, but deep down he's an honorable man. He wanted to cut his ties with the Brotherhood—especially after he started seeing Kray's wife. But he could never quite break free."

Two people passed them in the darkness. David could hear their breathing and their footsteps before he could see them. Nilsson said "hi" but kept walking.

She had a two-year-old white Lincoln parked in a graveled lot of two dozen cars a stone's throw from the Visitors Center. They drove out past the Center where stragglers were still going into the domed building and out the main entrance road. A hundred yards down the road a pickup and a four-wheel drive were parked nose to nose across the road. Two men stood guard with automatic weapons.

"Shit!" said David.

"Duck behind the seat," Ruby told him.

Moments later David felt the car slow to a stop. The power window on Nilsson's side rolled down.

"Oh, it's you, Miss Nilsson," came a male voice.

"Hi, Ed. This is . . . uhhh . . ."

"Alice Hobson," Ruby said. "A Seeker from California. An old friend of Christina's."

"I'm taking her back to Denver," Nilsson said. "I don't think it's safe for her here."

"I can't let anyone out right now, Miss Nilsson. Strict orders from Father. It's for everyone's safety. We have reports that some of them damn vigilantes are headed this way. We're trying to get people down to the Meditation Center."

"It's important I get her out of here, Ed," Nilsson said sternly. "She's extremely upset about the gunshots. It's not good for her health."

"My doctor's warned me about undue excitement," Ruby added. "Weaker ticker, if you can believe that at my age."

"I'm sorry, ma'am, but no one's to leave. It'll be safer at the Meditation Center, anyway. There's medical people down there that can take care of you."

Nilsson backed the car up, turned it around, and headed back toward the compound.

"I have an idea," Nilsson said after they were away from the guards.

"It better be a damn good one," said Ruby.

"There's a back way out, an old logging road. I can't drive it, but you can walk it. It'll bring you out to the main road half a mile below the guards. Then it's another three miles to the highway."

Nilsson veered left when they reached the Visitors Center and drove past a series of long, dorm-like buildings. The high, narrow headlights of a four-wheel drive suddenly appeared ahead. Nilsson slowed. David ducked behind the seat again. The oncoming lights grew brighter, filling the Lincoln's interior, then faded as the car passed. Nilsson audibly sighed in relief.

"That was one of Father's personal guards," she said.

Suddenly lights again filled the interior, this time from the rear.

"Shit, he's turned around."

"Look, up ahead!" yelled Ruby.

The Lincoln slowed.

"What's the matter?" David whispered to the women.

"We're boxed in!" Ruby said.

The Lincoln stopped. Lights filled the car.

"Dammit, she tricked us!" he said.

"No, I didn't!" Nilsson yelled, her voice full of fear. "Those guards must have alerted them."

David peered out the back window. The car had pulled to within twenty feet of them, its high-beam lights pinning them like stalked deer. Ahead, through the glare on the Lincoln's windshield, he could make out the vague shape of two vehicles blocking the road, their headlights aimed at them.

For a moment, nothing happened. Nobody said anything. The stillness was terrifying.

Then came a man's voice, strong and not unlike the voice they'd heard over the PA system in the meadow. "Christina! Are you okay?"

"Tanner?" Ruby asked Nilsson.

"Yes."

"Tell him you're okay."

Nilsson rolled down her window and yelled out that she was fine.

"Who's in there with you, Christina?"

She looked over at Ruby.

"Go ahead."

"It's Ruby Dark, Father, the bondswoman."

"Anyone else?"

"Her assistant."

A long pause. "Get out of the car, Christina, and come over here. Then Miss Dark and I can talk a little."

Christina looked at Ruby, fear etched into her face. Ruby motioned to her to stay put. Ruby rolled down her window.

"Miss Nilsson was going to drive us back to our car, down

in Pine Junction, but it seems you've got the place shut down 'cause of some kind of crisis."

Tanner's disembodied voice came out of the lights again. "It's for everyone's safety, Miss Dark. Your safety as well."

"Is that you talking Tanner—or Chac?"

"How exactly did you get up from Pine Junction?"

"We hitched a ride."

"Are you driving them voluntarily, Christina?"

Nilsson started to speak but Ruby answered for her. "Let's just say I've *persuaded* her to take us outta here."

"That sounds like kidnapping, Miss Dark."

"Call it what you like."

"I'll be happy to take you on in to town personally, Miss Dark. You and your assistant. Christina will remain here. That way we can talk on the way."

"That's a kind offer, honey, but we already have a ride and I have nothing to talk to you about."

"You were very eager to speak with me a few days ago."

"I have my answers now."

"Answers to what?"

"To where Bayne Gibson has been all this time."

David and Christina look at her, shocked.

"Are you trying to get us killed?" David snapped. "That's the last thing to tell him."

There was a long pause before Tanner spoke. "That's encouraging news, Miss Dark. We've all been deeply concerned about Bayne's welfare. Would you care to enlighten us as to his whereabouts?"

"Can't tell you. That's our ticket outta here."

"If you know where he's hiding, why did you come here? He's not here, Miss Dark."

"That was my mistake. I thought he was. Now I realize he isn't."

"Somehow I don't believe you, Miss Dark."

"You don't have to. You just have to have reasonable doubt that I'm lying."

"You understand that I have a problem here, Miss Dark."

"The problem you've got, honey, is that you want to find Gibson real bad but you don't know where he is. I do. So that's my trade. Miss Nilsson here drives us out safely and I produce your missing boy."

"How are you going to guarantee that? You're on the hook for a million dollar bond. As soon as you find Bayne you're going to turn him over to the police."

"Life's a gamble, isn't it?"

"I'd say I'm holding all the cards at the moment, Miss Dark."

"People know we're here, honey—including friends in the Denver Police Department. If we don't show up soon, you're going to have Royce Kray's homicide investigators swarming over this place like flies on shit, making connections they haven't made before."

"So what exactly is your offer?"

"You tell Lamprey to meet me at my office at—" She looked back at David. "What time is it?"

He held his shaking wrist up to the light. "11:20." Was that all? It felt like it was four in the morning.

"—at 6:00 A.M. tomorrow morning. Six and a half hours from now. I'll take him directly to Gibson and turn Gibson over to him, not to the police. You have my word on that. In return, we drive out of here safely with Miss Nilsson."

"I don't know you well enough to take you at your word, Miss Dark."

"Then put in a goddamn call to Chac and tell him to do a little divining. Otherwise we could have a mess right here on this road that nobody is going to be happy about."

What the hell kind of bluff was his aunt trying to pull? Tanner's men could open fire and they'd be dead in seconds.

Tanner didn't say anything. David laid on the floor of the car and braced himself for the opening salvo of gunfire.

Suddenly, the car behind them began to back up.

"6:00 A.M., Miss Dark," yelled Tanner. "Your word."

Nilsson turned the car around, drove slowly by the four-wheeler, and headed back toward the entrance road. The two vehicles that had stopped them earlier were separated by a car width now, the two armed guards standing to the side of the road. Nilsson slowly drove between them and on down the road.

* * *

David collapsed in the back seat and rubbed his trembling hands over his face. His entire body was shaking.

"Shit, I've never been so scared in my entire life!"

"Would he have killed us?" Ruby asked Nilsson.

Nilsson hesitated longer than David liked. "I don't know."

David leaned over the front seat. "I do. The man was ready to shoot us all on the spot. What bullshit was that about knowing where Gibson is, Aunt Ruby? Couldn't you have come up with a better line?"

"I wasn't bluffing, David. I know where he is. At least, I think I do."

"You *think* you do? You just risked our lives on a goddamn hunch!"

"We're out, aren't we?"

"Okay, okay. So how are you going to uphold your end of this Faustian bargain? Where exactly do you *think* he is?"

"In his refuge Lamprey told us about," she said softly, and, if David was right, a little sadly.

"His refuge? What refuge? Where?"

Suddenly high-beam headlights raked the treetops ahead of them on the road. Nilsson slowed the Lincoln.

"Shit, they've tricked us!" said David. "They just wanted us away from the ranch. Gun us down out here where—"

Ruby ordered the Lincoln stopped, and everyone scattered into the trees. They listened as the sound of engines grew louder, and they could see the headlights of several vehicles climbing the hill.

"It's Waters!" Ruby suddenly exclaimed as the vehicles grew close. She stepped out into the lights of the first vehicle, a pickup truck, waving her arms. The truck ground to a sudden halt.

"Christ, don't do that, lady!" yelled Waters, flinging open his door. "We coulda shot you."

"You okay?" she asked, walking toward him. "We heard gunfire in your direction earlier. That's why we couldn't get back over the ridge to you."

"I'm okay. Truck's got a hole in the side of her. Luckily those assholes shoot worse than they chant. Brought along some friends to get you outta there."

A dozen men had piled out of the vehicles behind the pickup. Most of them were armed, but with rifles and shotguns and handguns. They would have been no match for the Brotherhood's firepower. David and Nilsson stepped out of the trees to join Ruby.

"Did you find Gibson?" Waters asked, suspiciously eying Nilsson and the Lincoln.

"No. He's not there."

"Let's go pay Tanner a call anyway," the old rancher said with a certain kick-ass glee in his voice.

"There's a barricade up ahead a mile or so," said Ruby, "with a coupla armed guards. And there's a lotta people running around the damn place with guns. And a lotta people without guns. I don't want to see anyone get hurt, honey. We're out, and we're okay. We got a ride back to our car."

Waters looked disappointed. "Maybe another time, lady."

"I think your troubles are going to end sooner than you think. But right now we need to get back to Denver."

36

"I don't know what kind of game you're playing, *Mzzzz* Dark," said E. Ezzard Lamprey as he unlocked the heavy front door to Bayne Gibson's penthouse. "What precisely do you expect to find here?"

"Our client."

"I told you before, I came here to take Bayne to his preliminary hearing that morning, but he was already gone. I went through every room of this place looking for him."

"You didn't look hard enough, honey."

They stepped into the dim penthouse, danker and more airless than the first time they'd visited. The curtains were drawn, but David could see slits of light along the edges where dawn was slithering in. He shook his head to clear an exhausted, disoriented feeling. He'd dozed fitfully on the way down the mountain after Nilsson had driven them back to Ruby's car, and they'd grabbed three hours sleep at the office before Lamprey showed up promptly at 6:00 A.M.

"Anyone been up here since Gibson skipped?" Ruby asked.

"I haven't," Lamprey said. "I can't speak for the cleaning staff or building security."

"What about the cops?"

"I'm not aware that they have."

"What about the fish?" asked David.

The lawyer cocked a haggard and edgy face at him. "What about them?"

"Who's been feeding them?"

The lawyer frowned and made no comment.

David opened the French doors out onto the patio and went over to the pond. The waters were smooth. The waterfall had stopped running. Four koi were already floating belly up on the surface. The rest, moving sluggishly at the bottom of the pond, would soon join their dead brethren.

''So much for our collateral,'' he said.

They followed Ruby into the bowels of the penthouse. The deeper they went, the more David noticed that the staleness he'd smelled upon first entering the penthouse was turning stronger and more pungent. He thought of the house in Evergreen, of Big Jim, and started to feel queasy.

Ruby stopped in front of Gibson's mind gym. The door was shut, but the pungent odor, which now had turned rancid, seemed to be seeping through the very pores of the door.

''I wouldn't open that,'' David warned her, trying to hold his breath as he spoke.

Ruby pulled a tissue out of her purse.

''Aunt Ruby, please—''

The door was unlocked and she swung it open.

''Oh, God!'' said Lamprey, staggering back and gagging at the stench that assaulted them, like heat rushing out of an open oven. His skin turned as pale as celery stalk and his eyes watered profusely. His hand smothered his nose and mouth.

Ruby groped for the light switch. A red glow flooded the room. David swallowed hard and glanced hesitantly into the room, afraid of what horror would greet his eyes. Yet nothing appeared out of the ordinary. Nothing looked in disarray or disturbed. The furniture and the electronic equipment was still intact. No apparent signs of a fight—or a body. Still, the overpowering smell left no doubt something terrible had happened here.

Suddenly David knew where Gibson had been hiding all these days.

Ruby was already headed for the flotation tank, the black, coffin-shaped, salt-water box where Gibson went for refuge from the world, from Tanner and Chac and the rest of the Mad Hatters. David, hanging back by the doorway, felt his stomach roil. The lid was closed. Ruby opened it a few inches.

And quickly closed it.

But not quickly enough. Not before an indescribable foulness from hell, a foulness so overpowering and so wretched it buckled David's legs, spewed out and overwhelmed them as if the Devil himself had breathed on them. David turned his head away and gagged.

"Tell Tanner I've upheld my end of the bargain," Ruby said to Lamprey as the lawyer bolted down the hallway.

David was dimly aware of Lamprey vomiting before he himself took off in the opposite direction, down a hallway he thought led back to the fresh cool air of the deck or the front door and the elevator. He wanted to escape to anywhere far away from that coffin of death. Sweat chilled his face and he stifled another urge to puke.

The hallway twisted in a direction he didn't remember. He passed bedrooms and bathrooms and a kitchen and a game room. The place was so goddamn big! Where the hell was the fucking front door?

He felt clammy and he gagged again. Then he could no longer hold back the horror.

He sagged on one arm against a wall and threw up in gut-wrenching, belly-emptying heaves all the terror and anger and self-doubt and death he'd felt since Bayne Gibson and Big Jim had disappeared.

37

Two dozen uniforms, homicide investigators, crime technicians, and EMTs milled around the lobby of The Polo Club. They didn't all need to be there, but from what David had heard, cops hung out at crime scenes like groupies at a rock concert. Det. Reed said he'd once found twenty-five uniforms crammed into a tiny motel room where a hooker had been beaten to death, and only three of them belonged. Apparently, she'd made a lot of friends on the force.

But only a handful of cops were upstairs in Gibson's penthouse. The groupies didn't want to get *too* close to this one.

David didn't either, but one of the detectives who'd initially interviewed them had instructed them to remain in the lobby until he could take them to police headquarters to make formal written statements. Lamprey sat in a lobby chair, his head between his knees. David wanted to join him, but Ruby had dragged him off to talk to the white-haired doorman.

Gérard Damonte didn't look any better than Lamprey. Twice death had visited his fiefdom, had burrowed into the very soul of the building. The stench would remain as long as the building stood, and even after it was gone, to be recounted down through the years in street tours and history books about the seamy side of Denver. The glazed look in the old man's eyes said this would be his last day on the job.

"How'd Kray get into the penthouse the night he was murdered?" Ruby asked.

He'd barreled into the lobby, obviously drunk and agitated, replied the doorman, jangled what he claimed was Gibson's penthouse key, said Gibson would be arriving shortly, and went on up the private elevator.

"Kray'd been to the penthouse before?"

Several times—though Gibson had always been there.

"You sure he had Gibson's key? You see it up close?"

The doorman bowed his head slightly, as if in penance for a momentary lapse in the execution of his official duties. No, he hadn't seen it up close. But Kray couldn't have gone up the elevator without an authorized key.

David recalled from the copy of the police report Det. Reed had smuggled to Ruby that Gibson had denied giving Kray a key that night or at any other time. The cops found an elevator key on Gibson but they didn't find a second key in Kray's clothes or anywhere else in the penthouse.

It seemed improbable, Ruby had once theorized to David, in light of the argument between the two men the night before, that Gibson would have given a key to Kray. She believed Kray had intentionally gone to the penthouse while Gibson was away at a dinner, perhaps to poke around for evidence of Gibson's links to the Brotherhood of the Transcendental Light and the Crystal Age Radio Network. He'd found what he was looking for and had angrily called Gibson away from the dinner.

But where had Kray gotten a key?

Ruby dragged the dispirited doorman over to the penthouse elevator. A technician dusting for fingerprints warned them not to touch anything.

Like the two main lobby elevators, the penthouse elevator was trimmed in brass and mahogany, but had a slightly smaller door. There was only one button, internally lighted, with the letters PH and a keyhole next to it. David remembered seeing no other floor numbers on the inside panel. The elevator went only to the top.

"Who has keys to this elevator?" she asked the doorman.

Building security had one and the concierge kept a key at the loge, well hidden, according to Damonte. Even the cleaning staff had to borrow the key from the doorman. Lamprey was the only other person Damonte knew of who had a key.

"What about Gibson's ex-girlfriend, Christina Nilsson? She have a key?"

Damonte hesitated. Yes.

"They broke up not long ago. She return it?"

He didn't know. Gibson would have taken care of that.

A tall, distinguished-looking man arrived at the elevator carrying a gas mask under his arm.

"Well, if they didn't send the Top Chop," said the technician.

"Heard it's a stinker, Ed."

"I'm starting to smell the fucker down here. Give us your five-day forecast and get the damn body outa here."

"What can I touch?"

"You can hit the button. I've dusted everything inside, too."

The tall man pushed the PH button. Damonte stepped forward, said the elevator had to be unlocked first, put his key into the hole, and punched the button again. The elevator came down and opened.

The smell of death rode down with it.

The man with the gas mask—the medical examiner, David assumed—disappeared behind the closing doors.

"You *have* to have a key to operate the elevator?" Ruby asked the doorman.

No. In fact, usually when Gibson had visitors the doorman would call up to the penthouse and Gibson would send down the elevator.

"How did people go up the night of the party?"

The doorman had checked them off a typed guest list and unlocked the elevator himself. No, he no longer had the list. The police were holding it.

Ruby walked over to a gray metal door a few feet from the private elevator. "This been dusted?" she asked the technician.

"Yep."

She rattled the doorknob. It was locked. "Where's this go?"

The doorman said it opened to an emergency stairway that wound all the way to the penthouse. But the heavy metal door at the top could be opened only from the inside.

The three of them went back to the loge. ''How soon did Gibson show up after Kray got here?'' Ruby asked.

The doorman thought for a moment. Twenty to thirty minutes.

''What was his mood when he arrived?''

The doorman rocked on his feet. Gibson had been furious! He wanted to know how Kray had gotten into his penthouse. Threatened to have the doorman fired. Then he'd stomped off to the elevator.

The police had confirmed that a man had phoned Gibson at a Chamber of Commerce dinner, that Gibson had left immediately after the call, and that Kray's fingerprints were found on a telephone located on the penthouse deck.

In the police report, Gibson claimed that Kray called from the penthouse demanding that he leave the dinner and come over immediately. Gibson said Kray wouldn't tell him how he'd gotten into the penthouse or why he wanted him to come over, but that Kray's illegal entry was enough reason to warrant leaving the dinner immediately. When he arrived fifteen minutes later he couldn't find Kray, and he spent several minutes searching for him. He assumed Kray had chickened out and left, but about that time the police and building security showed up. They'd received a report that a man had been shot on the penthouse deck. They'd quickly discovered Kray's naked body floating in the koi pond.

The shooting tip had come from a call to 911. A woman working late and alone in an office building that flanked The Polo Club sheepishly confessed that she'd been watching—through a pair of binoculars—a naked man wading in the pond. A second man had suddenly appeared and shot him. She'd also admitted spying on the big party the night before, but she wouldn't admit her name. The police had never been able to trace her through either of the two office buildings that flanked The Polo Club.

''When Gibson got here, did you call upstairs for Kray to send the elevator down?'' Ruby asked.

No, said Damonte. Gibson used his own key.

''But Kray claimed he was using Gibson's key.''

The doorman looked perplexed.

''Did Mrs. Kray have a key to the penthouse?''

The doorman hesitated.

"Don't play dumb, honey. I know they were having an affair. Did she have her own key to the penthouse?"

The old man shrugged.

"She see Gibson alone in his penthouse?"

The doorman nodded almost imperceptibly.

"She ever go there herself, before Gibson arrived?"

Another tiny glum nod. David could see in the doorman's eyes the guilt of a once-principled concierge who'd forever sold out the trust and confidence of his tenants.

"What about Kray's daughter . . . Aspen? Spitting image of her mother. She ever come here alone to see Gibson?"

The doorman adamantly shook his head.

Ruby thanked him for his time, and headed toward Lamprey. David stopped her and whispered in the crowded room, "If Mrs. Kray had a key, then her husband could have taken hers."

"Maybe. But if that's the case, what happened to it?"

"Gibson hid it after he shot Kray. He probably realized it was the key he'd given her."

Ruby held up a single finger. "But the police found only one key on Gibson—the one he used to get up there. There was no other key in the penthouse. The only way he could have gotten rid of it was to pitch it off the side of the building. Besides, why hide it? He could have easily explained that it was just an extra key he kept around."

"Then how did Kray get up to the penthouse without a key?"

"He didn't."

"But—"

"The killer sent the elevator *down* to him. Just like Gibson did with his guests."

"What?"

"Kray knew his killer. He knew his killer was already up in the penthouse waiting for him. When he arrived, the killer sent the elevator down. The doorman couldn't have seen that from the loge. He assumed Kray used the key he'd waved in front of him. The killer didn't need a key to get out of the building. All the killer had to do was go down the emergency stairway and slip out one of the back doors when the doorman wasn't looking.''

''But if that's true, that means Kray's killer was someone he trusted—or at least someone he didn't fear.''

''That's right.''

David shook his head. ''No. No, it couldn't have happened the way you're saying it did, Aunt Ruby.'' He motioned with his hand around the small lobby, still filled with policemen. ''How'd the killer get up there in the first place? It's impossible to sneak through this lobby without being seen by the doorman, much less get up to the penthouse.''

Ruby nodded in agreement. ''The killer didn't sneak in, David. The doorman saw the killer go up. He just didn't realize it at the time.''

''But Gibson and Kray were the only two people he saw that night. It had to have been Gibson.''

''Give it some thought, David. I don't want to prejudice you. See if you can come up with my same line of thinking on your own.''

''Thanks a lot.''

''How'd you guess Gibson was in his penthouse?'' Morgan Reed asked Ruby in her office.

She sipped at a cup of coffee. In the light of the banker's light she looked haggard. ''I didn't guess. Lamprey'd said it was Gibson's refuge, where he got away from everything. The more I learned about Gibson—especially after I talked to Nilsson at the ranch—the more I became convinced he was a weak, suicidal man who'd decided to get away for good.''

''You don't suspect Tanner killed him?''

''Naw.''

Reed nodded. ''Autopsy's not in, but you're probably right. Gibson started taking prescription sleeping pills after his arrest. They found an empty bottle in his bathroom. It'd been refilled the day before he disappeared.''

''Kray woulda been disappointed in him,'' said Ruby.

''I thought men used guns or jumped off buildings,'' said David

''He woulda had a pretty tough time getting hold of a gun

after his arrest unless a friend gave him one," said Reed. "Jumping woulda worked. Especially from the thirty-first floor. Maybe he just didn't like heights. Too bad. It would have been a lot easier on everyone if he had. Jumpers you just scrape up and put in a bag. But this shit—tenants three floors down checked into hotel rooms for the night 'cause of the smell. You still look a little pale, kid."

David smiled weakly. "I'm okay."

"At least you didn't puke your breakfast on any evidence."

"Thanks," he said sarcastically.

"Hey, it's okay. I caught my first stinker when I was in uniform—a yo-yo we found hanging in his garage in the middle of July. Been there for two weeks. Something you won't forget in a lifetime."

"You puke too?"

"No. But I came close. Tell you a little secret, though, that'll impress your friends. If you can stand the first three minutes, you're home free. The nose goes numb after that. It's running in and out for fresh air that does you in."

"I'll be sure to remember that next time."

Reed turned toward Ruby. "That wasn't very bright, going in there without calling the police."

"You think they would have followed up on one of my hunches? After the Saunders business?"

Reed conceded she had a point. "You know, if the ME confirms it's suicide it won't help your theory that Gibson didn't kill Kray. Homicide figures he shot Kray, then Brodie, and in a fit of remorse, killed himself."

Ruby shook her head. "He woulda been spotted trying to sneak back into his penthouse."

"You still suspect somebody else?"

She nodded, but offered nothing more.

"Well, you can scratch one suspect off your list," Reed went on. "I checked with Intelligence like you asked. One of my old homicide buddies works there now. Jimmy Marten—aka The Undertaker—*was* under surveillance the night Kray was murdered. No way was he anywhere near the penthouse. He can't be your man."

"I had my doubts he was."

"So he *wasn't* kidding when he told me he was being watched," said David.

Reed said: "Intelligence says he's high up in the Denver Skins. May be their liaison to the Aryan Nation group in Idaho and some white supremacist group in Houston. They also think he may be behind some local violence. You know that skinhead who was badly beaten a coupla weeks ago because they thought he was singing to the police? Intelligence thinks Marten ordered it."

"But the IU detective told me he was just a fringe skinhead."

Reed rolled his eyes. "David, you don't really think the Intelligence Unit is going to tell a low-life bondsman who it's keeping tabs on?"

"Sometimes I lose my head and like to think we're on the same side."

"So where was Marten that night?" Ruby asked.

"At a Denver Skins meeting."

"Was Darcy Kray with him?"

"The daughter? No. Intelligence knows who she is. She hangs around with Marten The Undertaker, not Marten the skinhead. She wouldn't be at a Skins meeting."

Ruby eyed a half-open bag of blue tortilla chips on her desk but didn't touch them. David thought she looked unusually sad considering they were now off the hook for a $1 million bond.

Reed wagged his forefinger at her. "I've done a lot of digging for you on this case, Ruby. I've had to cash in some IOUs."

Ruby smiled. "I suppose I owe you a dinner?"

"At least."

"You're a public servant, Morgan. That would be bribery."

"I'm not above that, Ruby. Especially at this point in my career . . . and especially if you're doing the bribing."

She laughed. "Okay, dinner then. At Ciappino's."

Reed beamed.

"If Darcy wasn't with her boyfriend that night, where was she?" interjected David. "Sarah said she wasn't with her."

"Sarah's telling the truth," Ruby said.

"So why did Darcy lie to Aspen about being at Sarah's that night?"

"She didn't. Aspen lied to us."

David felt his mouth go dry. "I don't understand. Where was Darcy then?"

Ruby was silent for a few moments. "The truth lies in the truth, not the lies."

"That helps a helluva lot, Aunt Ruby. What am I supposed to figure out from that?"

"Let's take out an ad in the newspaper and find out."

38

A wooden step on the stairway—the fourth from the bottom, David knew by heart—creaked sharply under the weight of a foot.

Ruby and David exchanged silent glances. For a moment they heard nothing more from the stairway. Then the sound of footsteps, steadier this time, with no effort by the climber to conceal his—*her?*—approach. Ruby waved David into the darkened back room of the office.

Alabaster bolted to places unknown. Collateral, true to his genetic disposition, continued to sleep the sleep of the dead in a corner.

David threw the deadbolt on the door that opened onto the iron stairway that led down to the small parking lot. He glanced out into the darkness. Street lights spilled shadowy light over a handful of cars scattered in a public lot across the street, but he saw no signs of human movement in the hot, dry night.

He hurried back to the edge of the doorway. Ruby had settled down behind her desk. The footsteps stopped outside the closed door. There was a long pause, then a knock that was weak and uncertain.

''Come in,'' said Ruby.

Anna Lee Kray entered the room.

She was ashen-faced. She was dressed in designer jeans and starched white blouse and unbroken jogging shoes. A black handbag hung from her right shoulder. She glanced at

Collateral, then nervously searched the room. David jerked his head back.

"I—I saw the article in the newspaper," he heard Mrs. Kray say.

Since the Saunders debacle, Ruby had refused all requests for media interviews. But with the finding of Bayne Gibson's body, reporters had besieged her anew, and she'd finally granted one to a reporter on the *Post* she trusted.

Mrs. Kray went on. "You said . . . you said Bayne didn't kill Royce."

"That's right."

David peered around the edge of the door. Mrs. Kray had moved a few feet toward the desk where Ruby sat.

"Well, you're wrong, Mrs. Dark. He did kill my husband . . . and that other man."

"You can prove that?"

"He told me."

Ruby motioned toward the red leather chair across from her. Mrs. Kray sat down, put her handbag in her lap, and crossed her hands over the top of it.

"What exactly did he tell you?"

"That he shot Royce."

"Did he say why?"

"Because we . . . you were right. Bayne and I were . . . were lovers. Royce found out and got very angry. He went to the penthouse that night and argued with Bayne—threatened him, actually—and Bayne shot him. It wasn't Bayne's fault. Royce could become very angry, very violent. I know Bayne shot him in self defense."

"Is that why he shot my bounty hunter? In self defense?"

Mrs. Kray's head dropped. "He found out about us. Bayne felt he was a threat."

"Did you tell him Gibson was hiding in the chalet Evergreen?"

"I told him I knew where Bayne was and I'd take him there so Bayne could turn himself in."

"What happened?"

"We drove up and he went inside the house. I stayed in the car. He insisted I stay in the car."

"Whose car?"

"His."

"What kind of car was it?"

"I—I don't remember. I don't know cars."

"Then what happened? After he went inside?"

"I heard shots. I—I was terrified. Then Bayne came out and told me the man was dead and—" She stopped to compose herself.

"Did you go inside?"

"No."

"What next?"

"Bayne said he'd take care of things in the house and that I was to take the man's car and drive it back to Denver and leave it someplace inconspicuous. I parked it on top of that parking garage where the police found it."

"You realize this makes you an accessory to murder."

"Yes, I know."

"Have you told this to the police?

"No. But I'm going there from here. I've already called an attorney. He's arranged to meet me there in a few minutes. Bayne's attorney."

"Randall Taylor?"

"Yes." She looked out the window. "That's the police station, isn't it?"

"Yes."

"I probably should be going."

"I'd walk you over there, honey—if I believed you."

Mrs. Kray snapped her head back. "You . . . don't?"

"I don't think Gibson shot your husband. And I know he didn't kill Jim. Jim woulda never let him. Not like the way it happened."

"I—"

"Gibson was never in Evergreen. He never left his penthouse after the evening before the prelim. He couldn't handle the pressure from Tanner and the murder charge and the whole shebang. He OD'd on sleeping pills and climbed into his little coffin. And you weren't sitting in Jim's car when he was killed."

Mrs. Kray grew agitated. "The newspaper article . . . you said you had evidence about the real killer."

"Yes, I do."

From where David stood, he could see Mrs. Kray's entire body shaking.

"Have you told the police who?"

"No. Still a few stray facts I'm trying to pin down. The cops don't like outsiders intruding on their turf, so I'll have to be very convincing when I turn the evidence over to them."

The *Post* reporter had quoted the chief of detectives saying the Department remained convinced that Bayne Gibson had murdered Royce Kray. However, if Mrs. Dark had information relevant to the case, he'd told the reporter, then she had a citizen's duty to come forward with the information.

"What evidence?" Mrs. Kray asked.

"You haven't asked me who."

"What?"

"You haven't asked me *who* killed your husband, Mrs. Kray. You just asked what evidence I had."

Mrs. Kray look confused.

"The natural question first would be 'who,' " said Ruby. "I'd sure as hell would want to know who. I wouldn't care about the evidence."

"Well, I—"

"You didn't ask me who because you know who killed him, don't you?"

Mrs. Kray blinked her pale blue eyes. "I told you, Bayne did."

"Oh, come on. It's too easy to pick on the dead. Why did you come here first instead of going to the police station? I can't help you in any way unless you want me to bail you out."

"I—I just wanted to convince you, that's all. About Bayne."

"I'm not convinced."

"I—I brought something that might change your mind." Mrs. Kray dug into her purse, fumbling around for a few moments. Ruby sat forward in the chair, alert.

Suddenly a small black revolver appeared in Mrs. Kray's thin hand. David sucked in his breath.

"Is that the gun that killed Jim?" Ruby asked, staring at the weapon pointed unsteadily at her.

Mrs. Kray glanced at the gun, as though it were a foreign object and she had no idea how it had gotten into her own hand. "Yes." Her voice was small.

David tensed, calculating whether he could dash across the room fast enough before Mrs. Kray could turn and shoot him. His aunt had strongly warned him to stay in the back room, to watch and listen but to not interfere—even if it appeared she was in danger. This constituted more than appearance. But she'd been adamant that his presence would compromise the killer's boldness, that the only way this would work was for her to act as bait. She'd tried to reassure him that she was armed and well-protected, but now that seemed mere bravado.

"That's your husband's gun, isn't it?" said Ruby.

"Yes."

David had no idea what kind the gun was, but it looked deadly enough.

"Jack Deveraux told me your husband started carrying the gun with him after Tanner threatened him. But the police didn't find his gun at the penthouse. Whoever killed him took the gun with them."

Mrs. Kray stood up. "Yes. I took it that night."

"You killed your husband? And Jim?"

"Yes." Her voice was barely audible, and she was shaking so uncontrollably David feared the damn gun would discharge accidently. "I hated my husband and I loved Bayne. I killed Royce . . . and I killed your . . ."

"How'd you get into the penthouse that night?"

"I . . . I had a key."

"But how'd you get into The Polo Club and up to the penthouse? No one saw you enter."

"I . . . I sneaked in one of the back doors."

"They're locked to the outside."

"I don't remember now. I just got in, that's all I know. It was all so . . . horrible."

Ruby shook her head. "You don't remember much about that night, honey, because you weren't there. You didn't go to his penthouse, you didn't shoot your husband, and you didn't shoot Big Jim."

"Yes, I did! I killed both of them."

"Under the right circumstances, many people are capable of murder. Maybe even you. But those are usually murders of passion. This was a murder of cold calculation, and it was designed to frame Gibson. You're not capable of calculation, honey, and you wouldn't have framed your own lover."

"Royce found me at Bayne's and we argued. I grabbed Bayne's gun—he'd shown me once where he kept it—and I shot him. I panicked. I called Bayne for help. That's when he came over. He sent me away and said he'd take care of things. But they caught him before he could do anything."

"So he took the rap for you?"

"Yes."

"You're faster on your feet than I give you credit for, Mrs. Kray. But I don't think you and your husband would have argued much over your love affair. He already knew about you two. He may well have arranged it, in fact."

"He didn't know. He—"

"You couldn't have shot Jim, either. Maybe you could shoot your own husband in a fit of rage, but not a man you didn't know."

"He knew about me and Bayne. I had to shoot him to protect us."

"Oh, a woman shot him, all right, honey. Jim would never have let a man get that close to him—especially somebody he was trying to track down. But women were his weakness. He trusted 'em. Maybe he was too damn big for his own good. Felt he had to be a teddy bear to women. Whatever it was, it killed him."

Ruby stood up and came around the desk. Mrs. Kray backed up two steps and pointed the gun more directly at Ruby.

"Stay away from me! I'll shoot you too!"

David tensed to lunge at Mrs. Kray. He knew he couldn't sprint there fast enough to reach the gun before she shot at him, but if he rushed her, feigned in one direction and leaped in another, may he could avoid being hit by the first shot. Maybe, just maybe, it would distract her enough to give his aunt a chance to grab her own gun.

"You aren't going to shoot me, honey," said Ruby.

"Yes, I am. Yes, I am. I have to! I have to protect myself!"

Ruby was only three feet away now. Close enough to grab the gun.

"You didn't come here to protect yourself, Mrs. Kray. You came to sacrifice yourself, to protect someone else."

The gun in Mrs. Kray's hand shook. Ruby reached out and firmly took the gun away.

"I'm really sorry," Ruby said.

Anna Lee Kray began to cry.

Suddenly David heard movement behind him. For an instant, he thought it was Alabaster leaping from the top of the refrigerator, one of his favorite perches. But he realized it was the shadow of a person coming at him. Someone had been hiding in a dark corner of the back room, hiding since *before* he'd bolted the rear door.

The shadow swung something heavy at him. He ducked, and the object struck a glancing blow off the back of his skull and shoulder. His head rocked and he felt his left arm go numb.

Falling, he lashed out with his good arm and snagged clothing. He yanked as he fell, and he and the shadow sprawled into the office.

39

"Sarah!"

The cry sounded murky and far away, as though it was coming from behind a closed door at the other end of a long hallway.

"Sarah, are you okay?"

A little clearer this time. He thought the voice belonged to Mrs. Kray. Why was she talking to Sarah? Sarah wasn't here. He was here. He was sitting in the middle of the office floor. Cross-legged. Hunched over, trying to clear his throbbing head. He noticed that the heel of his right shoe was badly worn. He really needed a new pair of shoes. Big Jim had needed a new pair of shoes too. He didn't have the money and he didn't have the time, but he really needed new shoes.

"David, you okay?"

This voice was closer. And different. It was his aunt's voice. No mistaking that scorched sound. A hand touched his right shoulder.

"Yeah, I'm okay . . . I guess." He rubbed his left shoulder and tried to raise him arm. It was still half-numb, but he could feel sensation in his fingers now.

"Sarah . . . why did you come? Why are you here?"

The whimpery voice definitely belonged to Anna Lee Kray.

And she was talking to Sarah.

Sarah was getting to her feet. Her mother was helping her. A few feet beyond her, on the floor, lay a large silver-handled flashlight. The one they kept in the back room. The one he'd been struck with.

"I saw you sneak out of the house, mom, so I followed," Sarah said. "I was worried about you. Why did *you* come here?"

"I . . . I . . ."

"To protect you," said Ruby.

The young woman seemed clear-headed enough to turn toward Ruby. "Protect me from *what*?"

"From people discovering that you murdered your father . . . and my friend."

A cry escaped Anna Lee Kray.

"What's with you, lady!" snapped Sarah. "You've done nothing but harass our family since Gibson disappeared. He's dead and you still won't stop."

"I didn't ask your mother to come here tonight. I didn't ask her to threaten me with a gun."

"You goaded her. She's not well. You know that. That's why I followed her here, because I was worried about her. That's why I hit him, because I thought she was in danger."

"You're the one in danger, honey. Your mother came here because she knew you shot your father. Like your sisters know."

"You're mad!"

"Your father had driven your brother to suicide. You were worried your mother was next. She'd already made one suicide attempt. You figured if your father was out of the way, she wouldn't try to kill herself again."

Sarah blinked at Ruby with cold eyes but said nothing.

"She couldn't have shot Royce!" protested Mrs. Kray, wrapping her arms around her daughter. "She was in her apartment that night . . . sick. Darcy was with her."

"Darcy wasn't with her. Darcy initially claimed she was with her boyfriend. She couldn't have been, because he was at a skinhead meeting, under police surveillance. But she didn't know that. She probably figured *he* needed an alibi. Then suddenly she changes her tune and says she was with Sarah. That's odd. Darcy didn't strike me as the type who'd visit a sister sick with the flu. And Sarah didn't seem the type who would ask her over."

"That doesn't prove—"

"But Sarah didn't lie, Mrs. Kray. She said Darcy wasn't with her that night. That was the truth. What she didn't realize was that Aspen and Darcy were lying to protect her. If she'd gone along with it, she would have had an alibi."

David struggled to his knees and then his feet, Ruby pulling him up.

"How you feeling?" she asked.

"Like my head was run over by a car."

"We'll get it looked at. You could have a concussion."

"I'll be okay."

"We'll get it checked," she repeated firmly.

He stayed on his feet but leaned against her desk for support. The planet was moving.

Suddenly Mrs. Kray released her daughter and stepped toward Ruby. Her pale eyes look bright. "Sarah couldn't have killed Royce," she said in a voice full of conviction. "Even if Darcy wasn't with her."

"Why's that?"

"She couldn't have gotten into the penthouse without someone seeing her. You told me that's why *I* couldn't have killed him."

"She didn't sneak *into* his penthouse, Mrs. Kray. She was already there. She'd been there since the night of the party."

The conviction drained from her face. "That's a lie! She left early. She was sick. I saw her go."

"But you or Aspen didn't go with her. She left alone. It would be a simple matter to head for the door but then slip into one of the rooms. Most of the people were out on the deck. They wouldn't have noticed. After everybody leaves, all she has to do is stay out of Gibson's way. That's easy. The damn place is big enough. He's at the station all the next day. She calls in sick from one of his phones."

"Wait a minute," cut in Sarah. "How would I know Gibson would be gone all day?"

"A guy like him usually is. Besides, you work at the station. Couldn't have been too difficult to find out his daily schedule—including his going to a Chamber of Commerce dinner the night after the party. You saw an opportunity and you took it."

"So what did I do next?" challenged Sarah.

"You hung around all day in the penthouse. Found Gibson's gun your father had mentioned at the party. That evening you called your father. My guess is you claimed you had new evidence on Gibson and the Brotherhood. You'd had all day to search the place. Maybe you really did find something new, maybe you just made it up. It doesn't matter. Your father shows up and tells the doorman he has Gibson's key. In reality, you send the elevator down to him. Once he's there, you talk him into calling Gibson. Probably threatened Gibson with the new information. After your father hangs up, you force him to strip and then you shoot him with Gibson's own gun."

"Why on earth would I force him to strip?" said Sarah.

"That puzzled me for a long time. The police figured your father was wading around naked in the fish pond just to piss off Gibson. But that seemed farfetched even for your father. When I started to suspect you, it made sense. That's how you found your mother when she attempted suicide, wasn't it? Naked in a bathtub. And your brother died in the tub, too, didn't he? So you made your father undress, stand in the pond, and die like your brother."

"That's just psychobabble."

"You hid the gun, knowing the police would easily find it. Then you went down the penthouse elevator and slipped out a rear door. You watch Gibson arrive and then call the police to tell them you just saw a man shot. They catch him with a dead body. Mission accomplished."

Sarah shook her head. "This all sounds preposterously complicated and dangerous."

"Oh, it was. It was very bold. But not impossible. You're a smart girl, Sarah. Very smart. And a very angry, determined girl. It woulda been simpler to shoot him in some alley or parking lot. Make it look like one of his wacko listeners killed him. But you wanted to frame Gibson because he was messing around with your mother."

"You can't prove any of this," said Sarah.

"I can't, that's true. But once I point the police in the right direction, they can. They're very good once they know what they're looking for. They've just been looking in the wrong places. We all have. Besides, there's the little matter of the gun your mother brought.''

Sarah looked steadily at Ruby. ''What about it?''

''It's the gun that killed Jim Brodie. The same one you took off your father the night you shot him. My guess is your mother found it after she began to suspect you. Probably in your purse. It must have been quite a shock when you discovered the gun was gone.''

Mrs. Kray said, ''I told you, the gun was at our home, in our bedroom. Right where Royce kept it.''

''He wouldn't have left it there, Mrs. Kray. He was too scared after his run-in with Tanner. Besides, I'm sure the police found out he carried a registered gun. They woulda asked you about it right after the murder. If he'd left it in your bedroom that day, you would have given it to them.''

''I'm going to tell them I hid it because I used it to kill Royce.''

Ruby shook her head. ''It won't work, Mrs. Kray. A good confession has to match the physical evidence the police find at the scene of the crime—two crimes in this case. You won't be able to do it.''

''I'll try anyway.''

''No, you won't. Your daughter won't let you confess. She won't let the police arrest you for murders she committed. She loves you too much to do that. She killed her own father to protect you. She'll confess, and she'll make a good confession.''

''Oh, God,'' cried Mrs. Kray. She hugged her daughter.

Ruby said to Sarah, ''Why Jim? I can understand your father. But why did you have to kill Jim? He was a good man. He didn't suspect you, did he?''

Sarah stepped out of her mother's arms. Her voice was resigned yet steady. ''He'd found out from that Nilsson woman that mom was seeing Gibson. I didn't want her mixed up in it. I didn't want the police to find out about them. I was afraid they'd suspect her too.''

''Sarah!'' pleaded her mother.

''How did you get him to the chalet in Evergreen?''

''I told him I had a good idea where Gibson was hiding, but that I hadn't told the police because they didn't know about Gibson and my mom. Since he knew, I was willing to lead him there, but on the condition he not tell anyone who tipped him off."

"He promised you?"

"Yes. Of course, I couldn't be sure he wouldn't say something to you, but I had to take that chance."

"Weren't you worried Gibson might actually be hiding there?"

"No. I assumed you and the police knew about the place and had already checked it out."

"So what happened?"

"We met that night. I had the gun in my purse. I'd started carrying it after I took it from my father. Don't know why. It was stupid of me to have taken it now that I look back. We went to Evergreen in his car. He used the key I'd found in mom's purse. He never . . . suspected anything."

David saw his aunt wince.

"How did you know about the chalet?" Ruby asked.

"Aspen told me. She'd found out about mom and Gibson—I'm not sure how. She was pretty upset. When she was home on spring break, we even sneaked out there together to spy on them."

"Sarah!" Mrs. Kray said sharply.

Sarah turned toward her mother. "He wasn't any good for you, mom. He was a shallow rich bastard who loved his marathons—and that New Age quack of his."

"That's why Aspen went that night to the chalet, isn't it, Mrs. Kray?" said Ruby. "She didn't go there to warn Gibson for you, she went to make sure the police wouldn't find any incriminating evidence against Sarah."

"Why would she do that?"

"Because you and Aspen must have suspected by then that Sarah had killed your husband. Then my bounty hunter turns up missing right after visiting you. Maybe Sarah had something to do with that, too. You're not sure. So the night the police tell you they're closing in on a place in Evergreen, you find out from Aspen that Sarah knows about the chalet. You panic. You send Aspen out there. I suspect Aspen wasn't all that surprised to find Jim's body there. What really that the state securities division was investigating the Crystal Age Radio Network?''

''Yeah.''

''A grand jury just handed down indictment charges for Tanner and several of his pals, including Lamprey.''

''What charges?''

''Fraud, conspiracy to commit fraud, forgery, selling unregistered securities, using unregistered brokers, and a load of other charges. The securities division has issued a cease and desist order. Feds may be getting involved too. Taylor wants us to bail out Lamprey. A hundred grand.''

''Did you tell him to call Cadillac Johnson?''

Ruby didn't say anything.

David looked at her suspiciously. ''You *did* turn him down, didn't you, Aunt Ruby?''

Ruby snacked on a chile pepper. ''David, you know how much I hate to turn away work.''

and they would say she wasn't? It would have been in her best interest to go along with it. It would have given her an alibi.''

''Maybe she thought it was some kind of trap, that we were trying to trick her.''

Ruby nodded. ''Smart liars hone as close to the truth as they can. It's too easy to get your lies screwed up. But when she said Darcy wasn't with her, it got me to wondering why Aspen and Darcy would lie.''

''So you deduced they were trying to give her an alibi?''

''The alibi could have been for Darcy. But if it had, I think Sarah would have corroborated the story. You see, at some point, the rest of the family came to realize that Sarah had committed the murder. And when they did, each began to protect her in whatever way they could. Darcy was willing to roll over her own boyfriend. Aspen risked going to Evergreen. And Mrs. Kray was willing to go to jail for Sarah.''

The wail of a siren suddenly cut through the noise and activity of the emergency room.

David shook his head, which was a mistake since it still hurt like hell. The bitch swung a mean flashlight. ''It's tough to believe the family would conspire to do that. None of them seemed to get along with each other.''

Ruby's voice was distant. ''Families are like that, David. As much as they may hate each other, they'll do anything to keep the world from learning their dirty little secrets.''

''To the point of protecting a killer?''

''Sarah was blood. Besides, all of them had hated and feared Kray. My hunch is each of them secretly wished they'd had the nerve to do what she'd done.''

An emergency vehicle pulled up outside. Lights flashed through the doors. White coats scurried for the entrance. Moments later someone was wheeled in on a stretcher. David couldn't see much. The patient was covered with a blanket and surrounded by emergency personnel. But he caught a glimpse of an arm dangling out to the side. Dark streaks ran down it.

''The problem with family secrets,'' said Ruby after the stretcher was gone, ''is that no one ever wants to talk about them. So none of them told Sarah what they were doing. If the four of them had sat down at the kitchen table and hashed out an alibi for her, we probably wouldn't have caught her. But each tried to help her on their own. In the end, they betrayed her."

"You were still crazy to face down Mrs. Kray like that, Aunt Ruby. You couldn't be positive she hadn't killed her husband and Jim. And even if she hadn't, she might have shot you to protect her own daughter."

Ruby tapped her chest with her knuckles. He could hear something hard.

He leaned toward her. "You're wearing a bulletproof vest?"

"It was Al's. He'd gotten some threats before he died."

David nodded. A lot of good it did him, he thought. The man was shot in the head.

David sat in the office, hunched over one of his law books. He was still on the outs with half his professors, particularly Rothschild, and he'd thought seriously about giving up his studies, at least for a while. But the courts had dismissed Gibson's $1 million bond. Hell, he and Ruby had even made the $150,000 bond premium on the deal, though she'd twisted his arm to turn over most of his share along with her share to Big Jim Brodie's widow and daughter. Threats of a civil lawsuit and criminal charges over their breaking into the wrong home still hung over them, though Cyndee Valone was working hard to get the whole thing dropped. And the hospital said he didn't have a concussion. Hell, maybe he could focus on his studies again, and get back to becoming what he really wanted to become.

The phone rang.

"Ruby's Bail Bonds."

It was Randall Taylor. He wanted to talk to Ruby.

David handed the phone to his aunt.

While she paced the floor and talked, he tried to return to his studies. But he couldn't help overhearing snippets of conversation. He caught E. Ezzard Lamprey's name.

When she hung up, he asked her what Taylor wanted.

"Remember Barry Greenfield telling us he'd heard rumors

shook her up was the final realization that the killer was her own sister."

Mrs. Kray began to cry again.

"You know what the strangest part of it all was?" said Sarah, as if her attention had drifted elsewhere. "Even when I shot him I loved him. I *still* love him." She looked at Ruby. "Can you believe that?"

Ruby said nothing.

"I mean—he *was* my father."

40

Later, after the police had taken Sarah away, while David and his aunt sat in a crowded emergency room at Denver General, he said he still didn't understand how she'd been so certain it was Sarah and not one of the other daughters or even Anna Lee. They all had hated Royce Kray. They all had lied.

"Mrs. Kray's too weak and Aspen's too self-absorbed. Of all the daughters, Sarah was the closest to her mother, the most protective. She *was* the one who saved her mother's life. She's strong, bull-headed, and the most tightly wound of any of them."

"But what about Darcy? I watched her get pretty violent with her boyfriend."

"But the way you described it to me, she exploded. She wouldn't have meticulously planned a cold-blooded murder, she would have done it in a sudden rage. Sarah was the only one who could have engineered it—especially staying in the penthouse. That took planning and a lot of nerve."

A man sitting across from them stared at them with one eye. A slimy patch of gauze and masking tape covered the other eye. A voice over the PA system called a Dr. Hill.

"But how could you be sure it was Sarah?"

"Because she told the truth."

"The truth? About what?"

"About being alone the night of the murder. Aspen and Darcy both claimed that Darcy was with Sarah that night. Yet Sarah denied it. Now why would she say she was alone